Praise for Tell A T...

"Like most Wester... ... to
non-existent – limite ...ilionaire
and *White Tiger. Tel.* ...n eye-opener.
Rasana paints a vivic ...ects of village life
that no tourist will eve... ...e acquainted with. She
is a gifted story-teller who brings her characters to life
and takes us into a world we would not otherwise have
the chance to visit. I highly recommend this book."
Yael Politis, author The Lonely Tree

"The author's ability to set the scene is so strong you
feel like you are standing beside the characters as they
live their daily lives. The descriptions of the land and
the people pull you into the charm and the dichotomy
that is India. The story is both life affirming and heart-
breaking with a realism that leaves you wondering if these
people are characters in a novel or are they real."
*Karen Bryant Doering, book blogger – http://www.parentslbb.
com/books/2012/03/19/tell-a-thousand-lies-by-rasana-atreya*

"*Tell A Thousand Lies* is an emotional rollercoaster ride that
makes you keep rooting for Pullamma as Atreya delightfully
and hilariously infuses issues of class, religion, work,
education, sexual roles, and the ties between women."
Holly J Michael, book blogger – http://writingstraight.com

TELL
A
THOUSAND
LIES

by

RASANA ATREYA

rasanaatreya.com

Acknowledgements

A lot of people encouraged, cajoled, critiqued, proofread and handheld me through the writing of this book. They are (in no particular order): Vrinda Baliga, Carol Kean, Francene Stanley, Holly Michael, Jackie/Jonjo, Frank Chan Loh, Regina Zeller Wingate, Silvia Villalobos, Neil Lambert, Heather Jane O'Connell, Judith Quaempts, Dr. Parang Mehta, Ruth Zavitz, Bob White, Bill Backstrom, John Hutt, Deb O' Neille, Harimohan Paruvu, Yael Politis, Dr. V Haraprasad, Drupad Parsa and my sister, Vandana Atreya.

For helping me whip the book into shape, the credit goes to my editor, Patricia B. Smith, and also my husband, Aditya Gurajada.

For helping me fill in details about the various rituals and traditions in rural Andhra Pradesh, I owe my mother-in-law, Mrs. G. Satyakumari, a debt of gratitude.

Ben Shipley - thank you for helping with the formatting.

Hugh Ashton, thank you for your patience in formatting the book for print, as we went through endless rounds of typo fixing.

The Internet Writing Workshop - you guys are the best!

For my grade school children, Sunaad and Aamani, who really, really wanted to design the cover of this book. Maybe next time, kids.

For my parents.

TELL

A

THOUSAND

LIES

by

RASANA ATREYA

rasanaatreya.com

PROLOGUE

Mallepalli Village, June 1995

I am not my husband's wife, nor my child's mother. Who, then, am I?

ONE

Mallepalli Village, Dec 1986

"**G**ood thing you aren't pretty, Pullamma," Lakshmi *garu* said with a laugh. "Can you imagine the headache if we had to hide you, too?"

I bit the inside of my cheek. Lakshmi *garu* was here to lend moral support for my older sister's bride-viewing, and I mustn't forget it.

"Towering like a palm tree, you are," she said, "and skin dark like anything."

I wondered if *'garu,'* as a term of respect, was wasted on this friend of my grandmother's. Still. I was sixteen now. Couldn't let words escape my mouth without proper consideration.

Lakshmi *garu* studied me for a long moment, the wide slash of her mouth disappearing into the flat rectangle of her face. Shaking her head, she turned back to my grandmother.

It couldn't be easy for our Ammamma, saddled as she was with three orphaned granddaughters and no male support, to marry us off. If today's alliance for Malli fell through, where would we find another family willing to accept the limited dowry we had to offer?

Of the three of us, Malli was the most beautiful. But my fraternal twin, Lata, was pretty, too; it was for this reason she'd been packed off to a relative's house, out of sight of the groom's family. For, if they got it into their heads to take Lata home as their daughter-in-law, it would be hard for us to refuse them. Given that Malli was the best-looking, it was unlikely, but why take the risk? If they chose Lata over Malli, forever people would think there was some defect in Malli that had caused the groom's family to reject her. Who would marry her then?

Now, as Ammamma, Lakshmi *garu* and I waited for the prospective bridegroom's family to grace us with their presence and decide if our Malli was good enough for them, I surveyed our walled-off rectangular courtyard. Our house was a series of rooms lining the back of our courtyard, one opening into the next, like the compartments of a train. A veranda separated the rooms from the courtyard. Perpendicular to it was our cowshed. On either side of the cowshed were a tamarind tree and a *sampangi* tree. A coconut tree drooped against the far end.

Lakshmi *garu* was settled next to the *sampangi* tree, on a straw mat laid out on the mud floor. It was against this tree I sat, as I made my promise to Goddess Durga – if this alliance went through, I'd break coconuts at her altar.

That got me thinking. How many coconuts would it take to appease the Goddess? Two? Five? Twenty? Two seemed a little... miserly. This was bride-viewing, not some silly plea to have a cute boy smile at me. But, if I promised too much and couldn't deliver, the wrath of the Goddess would surely befall me. Even more important, if Ammamma were forced to pay for twenty coconuts out of our meagre household income, *she* would strike me dead. Five seemed safer all around.

"Pullamma," Ammamma said, interrupting my internal debate. "They should have been here twenty minutes ago. Go over to the post office and keep a watch for them."

The only way into the village was past the post office, so I sprang to my feet.

"Let the girl be," Lakshmi *garu* said. "How can they come here so soon? That, too, after travelling all night? They need time to freshen up, don't they?"

I flopped back on the ground.

"Pullamma!" Ammamma said reprovingly.

I sighed, carefully arranging my half-sari over my feet. Remembering to be ladylike wasn't as easy as it sounded.

Lakshmi *garu*'s sons were to pick the groom's family up at the railway station and take them to their relatives' house. There the visitors would take their baths, have breakfast, and don their finery before coming over to view the bride.

Ammamma face's reflected the tensions of the past few days. She stood, hands on hips, eyes locked on the narrow courtyard gate built into our compound wall.

"Oh, for goodness' sake, sit down." Lakshmi *garu* patted the straw mat. "It is hurting my neck to look up at you."

Ammamma sighed. She sank onto the mat, taking care not to wrinkle her orange silk sari. She fanned herself with a palm-leaf, despite the chill of the winter morning. Her eyes remained on the gate.

"At least the walls appear new," I said, proud that I'd helped make the house so festive.

Ammamma gave me a distracted smile. She had done her part by getting the vegetable seller to whitewash the walls of our house in return for a whole year's worth of homemade mango pickle. But I'd been the one to make the intricate *muggu* pattern on the court-yard floor, blending white rice flour with coloured chalk. I'd also been the one to apply a fresh coat of cow dung to the courtyard walls in an effort to gloss over the cracks. Now the walls looked almost new. But what I was most proud of were the flowers strung across our doorways – bright orange marigolds and pure white jasmines.

I'd risen before dawn to visit the wholesale flower market with Murty *garu*, husband of Lakshmi *garu*. Women were already streaming into the tight lanes, huge wicker baskets balanced on their heads and hips, the overflowing flowers a stunning contrast to the dusty by-lanes.

After the women settled alongside the road, squatting next to their baskets, Murty *garu* and I walked past, picking a small basket of flowers here, a length of woven flowers – measured from finger-tip to elbow – there.

If my efforts helped Ammamma get a granddaughter married off, I'd be forever grateful to Goddess Durga. I felt a pang at the thought of sweet Malli getting married and going off to her in-laws' home. Then it would be Lata's turn. Soon, I'd be the only one left. Oh well, at least I'd have Ammamma.

A fragrant yellow-green flower floated down in the gentle breeze. Ammamma reached for it and shredded its rubbery petals, her eyes fixed on the gate. The cow mooed, startling her. "Where are these people?" she asked again.

This event was all we had talked about, planned for and worked around for two whole weeks; actually all our lives. Ammamma had high hopes for this alliance. The marriage broker had assured her the groom's family was more concerned about the colour of Malli's skin than the size of her dowry.

This lack of interest in dowry was of particular worry to

Ammamma. "My Malli is a gem, no doubt, but why are they set-tling for less?"

For Lakshmi *garu*, the most suspicious part was the marriage broker's assurance that the dowry demands would be quite rea-sonable. "I just hope the boy doesn't have some disease they're hiding," she said.

Lakshmi *garu* was a great one at being supportive.

"If he limps or something, I'm okay," Ammamma said. "But any-thing more serious..."

Impatient at the delay, I jumped to my feet.

"Pullamma," Ammamma said sharply, "don't forget to be ladylike."

Nodding, I hurried through the gate to the post office on the other side of the village square.

The post office was a tiny, airless room which the postmaster rarely used; most days, he was to be found at his desk under the tamarind tree. Today, Murty *garu* was seated on a metal folding chair next to the postmaster, facing a line of squatting villagers. Letter reading was, of course, the job of the postmaster, but Murty *garu* pitched in whenever he could.

While Murty *garu* read a letter out loud to an elderly man, the postmaster was busy writing a letter on behalf of Lakshmi *garu*'s neighbour, a young woman whose husband had migrated to the city in search of work. He leaned forward, his ink-stained fingers tapping on the sun-dappled desk. "Do you want to tell your hus-band that your Chitti lost her first tooth?"

The woman nodded.

The postmaster bent forward and scribbled.

"About your mother-in-law's fainting spell?"

She nodded again.

"What about the child that is coming? You haven't given him the news, have you?"

The woman covered the lower half of her face with her sari and giggled.

"They're coming, they're coming," a hoarse voice shouted.

I flushed with excitement.

A couple of labourers, cotton towels wound around their heads to prevent sweat from dripping into their eyes, ran up the dusty road, heralding the arrival of the groom's family.

Murty *garu* looked up from the letter he was reading out loud and smiled apologetically at the old man squatting across from him. "I'm an elder at the bride-viewing for Pullamma's sister."

"Please, do go," the old man said, reaching for his letter. "This can wait." He went over to squat in the line awaiting the postmaster's attention.

I ran back to the house, trying not to trip over my half-sari. "They're coming, they're coming!"

Ammamma didn't even scold me for my unladylike haste. She hurried to the gate with Lakshmi *garu,* just as Lakshmi *garu's* two sons drove up in their shiny new tractor. An older man, most likely the groom's father, sat in the front, a child in his arms. A couple of men stood on the sideboards, clinging wherever they could get a hold. The rest of the groom's party was squashed up on the rug laid on the floor of the trailer. The tractor belched fumes of diesel and shuddered to a halt.

Across the road, all activity stopped. People turned to inspect the commotion. I puffed with pride.

Murty *garu* greeted our honoured guests, palms of his hands joined together. "*Namaskaram!* I hope your travel was comfortable."

"The train was late," the groom's mother said, as Murty *garu* helped her down. Being the mother of the groom, this was her chance to complain, and she did. "On top of it, we couldn't get seats in Second Class. So we had to travel like some low class people, no reservation, no nothing. Had to sit up all night on a suitcase. Now my back is paining me and my leg is swollen." Her voice quavered. "My head is pounding so hard, I might have to cancel today's bride-viewing."

Ammamma clapped her mouth in dismay. "Please, I beg you, don't even say such a thing. What will people *think* if the bride-viewing party turns back? They'll blame my Malli's bad fate, is what they will do. Who will marry her, then?"

"I'm at your command," Murty *garu* said. "Anything to help."

"Can you arrange for medicine?" the groom's father said.

"Right away." Murty *garu* flicked a finger at his younger son, who took off at a run in the direction of the xerox-cum-medical shop.

"These trains," the groom's father said, "they should have a lot more compartments. So many people travelling, no? The Railway

Minister should do more for the interior villages. We travelled all night, no rest, no place to sit. General Compartment. Just imagine!" He nodded at the child in his arms. "And with my grandson, too."

"So much headache merely to view the bride?" Murty *garu* shook his head in tandem with his raised hand, a what-is-this-world-coming-to look on his face.

The next to alight had to be the groom. In his early twenties, he seemed an agreeable fellow, of medium height and complexion, though on the skinny side. He bent at the waist to touch Ammamma's feet, then touched his fingers to his eyes in respect.

Well brought up, too. I hoped things worked out today. Malli and he would make a cute couple.

Kondal Rao *garu*, husband of Ammamma's friend Suseela *garu*, and honoured guest, was due anytime now, so our party of twenty waited by the courtyard gate. Murty *garu*'s son, back from the medical shop, handed the medicine and a glass of water to the groom's mother. She drank the water, and dropped the medicine in her purse.

Since the groom's family was from Kondal Rao *garu's* village, my grandmother had sought him out to make inquiries about the family. Before we could allow our Malli to be married into their family, we had to ensure that the groom was of good character, and his clan respectable, hadn't we? We were lucky that Kondal Rao *garu* had personally vouched for the groom's family.

Weren't we?

I felt a frisson of fear. What if Jhampaiah, the day labourer, were right? What then?

That day, from two months ago, was still clear in my mind.

When the marriage broker brought news about this alliance, Jhampaiah was perched high up on the coconut tree in our courtyard.

"Welcome," Ammamma said, smiling. The marriage broker was a most favoured visitor. "Please freshen up. So hot, isn't it?"

To me, Ammamma said, "Pullamma, pour out some buttermilk."

The marriage broker, a skinny woman with bulging eyes and sloped chin, slipped out of her footwear and walked over to the three-foot cemented square in one corner of the courtyard. Pumping the hand-pump till water gushed out, she washed her face first, then her feet. Wiping her face with the free end of her sari, she settled on the straw mat. "I have just the alliance for you," she said.

I handed her a glass of buttermilk.

"Who is the family?"

"You won't believe it." The broker's tone held reverence.

"Who?"

"The father of the groom is the right hand man of Kondal Rao *garu* himself."

"My Malli is favoured, indeed!" Ammamma raised her joined palms above her head, eyes shining. "Kondal Rao *garu*'s wife is my childhood friend. We couldn't get a better alliance if we tried."

Crash! A semi-circular knife buried itself at the base of the coconut tree.

Ammamma jerked her head up at Jhampaiah, balanced high up our tree, legs wrapped around the skinny trunk.

He looked down at the fallen knife in dismay.

Ammamma shook a fist at him. "What if someone had been standing below?"

Jhampiah shimmied down the tree and shuffled up to Ammamma, head hanging.

"What is done, is done," Ammamma said. "Just be more careful the next time."

He nodded vigorously.

"Did you pluck the coconuts?"

Jhampiah nodded again and started to shove the coconuts into a gunny bag. He had been hired to strip the tree of the coconuts. He'd sell them for Ammamma and take a commission for himself. After the coconuts were put away, he squatted next to the gunny bag, focussing his unblinking gaze on Ammamma.

"What?" Ammamma said.

Jhampiah shook his head.

The marriage broker laughed. "Must be waiting for me to leave so he can discuss his petty little issues with you." She pointed her sloped chin at Jhampaiah, the hairs on it glistening. "*Peetha kashtalu peethavi,*" she quoted in our native Telugu, reducing his concerns to those of a mere crab.

The broker drained her glass, walked to the cemented square which also served as a wash area, and put the buttermilk glass down. "I will set up the bride-viewing, then."

Ammamma joined her palms together in farewell. "That would be good."

The marriage broker let herself out of the courtyard.

As soon as the woman closed the gate behind her, Jhampaiah joined the palms of his hands in entreaty. "Please don't take offence. I am talking out of turn." Sweat beaded his upper lip.

"Speak freely."

"Don't go with the alliance."

I was startled. "But why?"

Ignoring me, he leaned forward, the cords in his neck straining. "There is lot of talk about Kondal Rao *garu*. Bad talk."

"*Bah!*" Ammamma reached for a coconut frond broom. "For this you made so much drama? Go to the market and sell your coconuts. Leave the thinking to me."

He got to his feet and slung the gunny bag over his shoulder. At the gate, he turned. "Amma *garu*, I beg you, don't dismiss this so casually."

Ammamma waved him away.

He scurried out, a frightened look on his face.

"These people," Ammamma said, sweeping the debris from the coconuts. "They have no education, no understanding. With my fifth class education, I'll need him to tell me right from wrong? I'll be scared of my own friend's husband, or what?"

Two

Almost everything in my past foretold my ordinariness in a family of extraordinary beauties – my unspectacular horoscope, the positioning of the stars at the time of my birth, even the inauspicious start to my life.

"How could a child so... ordinary-looking possibly be mine?" my father is said to have exclaimed moments after my birth, a frown marring his extraordinarily handsome face.

"Donkey's egg," Ammamma said with uncharacteristic rudeness towards a son-in-law of the family. "Whoever heard of a newborn being beautiful?"

But this was exactly the excuse he was looking for. Our mother had died in childbirth minutes after delivering us twin girls. This, after she'd already burdened our father with an older daughter. Had any of us been born the right gender, with the consequent ability to take care of our father in his old age, this question of paternity would have never come up. With no son and no wife, he felt justified in discarding us and taking on a new life.

Ammamma stepped in after the abandonment, not that she had much of a choice; my father had no family. Who else would take on the headache of raising, and marrying off, three girls? Other than a grandmother, that is.

My twin and I remained nameless for almost a year after our birth, a period of intense agonizing for my grandmother. She finally settled on Pullamma – twig girl – for me, the older twin. To bestow a fancier name would be to risk the wrath of the Gods, the current misfortunes being more than she could bear. She debated on Pichamma – mad girl – for my twin; the Gods must have been smiling on my sister because they intervened in the form of Ammamma's mother-in-law. The old lady decreed that it was only proper that such a fair and pretty child be named after her. So my twin ended up being named Lata.

Fair-skinned Lata was as delicate as the creeper she was named for, while our older sister Malli, with her pinkish-white complexion, couldn't be more flower-like if she tried.

All through childhood, I was teased mercilessly for my name. I was more a branch than a twig; a stump really, and the other children never let me forget it. They called me *Nalla Pulla* – black twig – for the colour of my skin. I swore when I had children of my own, I would give them the most beautiful names possible.

Many years later, when I did have my child, that choice would not be mine to make.

My grandmother was an elegant lady. Not very tall, but of fair skin. In her youth, she'd been as slender as Lata, though over the years gravity had caused her body to settle mainly around her hips. So renowned were her dowry, and her beauty, that her hand in marriage was sought far and wide. After great consideration, Ammamma's father settled on an alliance with my grandfather.

"The only bad decision my father ever made in his life," Ammamma said with a shake of the head. "Such a good man my father was, with complexion like fresh fruit, and on top of it – honourable like anything."

Everything my grandfather wasn't. Post-wedding, he gave up his prestigious *tahsildar* job; none of that tax collection business for him. Instead, he efficiently worked his way through Ammamma's not insubstantial dowry, along with most of his own inheritance before he passed on from drinking country liquor. Ammamma was forced to sell off much of her jewellery to marry off her four daughters, and would have been living on some Brahmin's charity, but for the fact my grandfather hadn't been able to sell his ancestral home from under her before he joined his ancestors in the heavens above. Then our mother died, and our father departed to find God in the Himalayas.

Losing her daughter to childbirth, and her son-in-law to irresponsibility, Ammamma had tough decisions to make.

A few years after she inherited us, the village elders stepped in to counsel. "Your oldest and youngest granddaughters are pleasing to the eye," they told Ammamma. "It will be easy enough to find good matches for them, even considering your limited dowry giving ability."

"What about my Pullamma?" Ammamma asked, distressed.

"You need to be practical, Seetamma," the elders said. "She has neither the looks, nor the dowry. Keep her at home. After all, you will need someone to tend to you in your old age."

"But who will provide for her when I am gone? Who will help her in her old age, I ask you?"

But the village elders had done their duty by the poor widow. They had dispensed the best possible advice. Having no answers to Ammamma's questions, they joined the palms of their hands in farewell and took leave.

Ammamma was angry, but Lakshmi *garu* believed their advice to be sound. "Pullamma is like a palm tree, bending over with her height. Hurts my neck to look up at her. That mole below her nose. And dark like anything. Be realistic. Where will you get a groom tall enough for her? And more importantly, how will you find enough dowry to take her off your hands?"

After daily discourses by Lakshmi *garu* on the rightness of this course of action, this began to make perfect sense to all concerned – me included. There was no question that Lata and Malli stood better chances of making good matches than I. Lata had inherited our mother's delicate build and flashing cat eyes, while Malli was blessed with a combination of Ammamma's and our father's best features.

I got the leftovers.

I resigned myself to my fate.

Though the village elders and Lakshmi *garu* had given up on my marital prospects, Ammamma hadn't. Not until the day of Malli's bride-viewing, anyway.

Ammamma worried about what would happen to me after she passed away. What protection would I have in society without a husband? What respect? Without the sanctity of the wedding *pustela taadu* around my neck, I would be excluded from everything a married woman was entitled to – the festivals, the social functions, the right to hold my head high in society.

I shuddered to think I might end up like Shantamma, that old hag who squatted by her front door all day, shaking clenched fists at the children who giggled at her as they passed by.

The village elders had told Ammamma often enough that a girl was someone else's property, her father's home being a transitional place for her. Tradition decreed the role of a girl's birth family was to nurture her, get her married, and send her off to her husband's home. It would be many years before it occurred to me that if my birth home was not mine, and my married home was my in-laws', which was the house I could expect to claim?

"Malli, I don't worry about," Ammamma said to her friend, Lakshmi *garu*, as she oiled my hair under the warm winter sun. She sat behind me on a straw mat in the middle of our courtyard. "Lata is also pretty enough. It is only this one." She thumped the back of my head with the flat of her palm, causing my head to hit my upraised knee.

"Ammamma!" It made me weary, this endless marriage-prospects discussion in our women-only household.

Ammamma massaged my head so vigorously, my teeth rattled.

"Like the other problems in my cursed life weren't enough, I made the blunder of sending this one and Lata to school all the way to 12th class. Just because that fool of a headmaster was after my blood."

"And look where it got you," Lakshmi *garu* said.

"Fanciful notions," Ammamma said. "He isn't the one with overeducated, unmarried girls on his hands."

I tried to keep my sigh inaudible.

Lata looked up from her book.

Malli continued weaving the jasmines into a garland.

Lakshmi *garu* settled on another mat, straw tray in hand. She peered intently at the rice, picking out stones. "These ration shop fellows, such cheats they are, Seetamma. Must be adding at least a quarter kilo of stones to each bag of rice."

I leaned back against Ammamma's knee and slowly closed my eyes, breathing in the odour of Parachute coconut hair oil. I must have lurched forward because it caused Ammamma to pull hard on my hair.

"Ow," I yelped.

Ammamma was too steamed to notice my distress. "Lata passed her 12th class in distinction," she said, stressing the word 'distinction' like it was deserving of particular disgust. "Can you believe it?"

Lata made a face.

I felt a tug of satisfaction. I might have passed 12th class, too, but at least I had the good sense not to do well.

Ammamma continued, "With such good marks, how am I to find her a suitable groom, I ask you?"

"At least Malli was smart enough not to study too much," Lakshmi *garu* said.

A smile hovered on Malli's perfectly shaped lips.

Ammamma nodded with grim satisfaction. Malli had failed her 6th class, then refused to return to school. That suited Ammamma just fine.

"Maybe I can hide Lata's education," Ammamma said. From the family of the prospective groom, she meant.

"But you can't hide Pullamma's appearance."

Ammamma dropped her head in her hands. "True enough."

I considered Lakshmi *garu*'s boxy face and protruding eyes, trying to ignore the hurt. Would marriage make my lack of looks irrelevant, too?

"A little dowry will get the other two good enough grooms," Lakshmi *garu* said. "They are pretty enough. But this one..." She inspected my face, one feature at a time, face devoid of hope.

In spite of myself, I laughed. Lakshmi *garu* could be such a drama queen.

Ammamma set aside the bottle of hair oil and nudged me to a sitting position. She started to braid, each pull on the hair jerking my head backward.

Lakshmi *garu* went back to her rice picking. "If you had a husband or a son, even a grandson to support you..."

"Such is my fate, Lakshmi," Ammamma said, slapping her forehead with the palm of her hand. "People are already asking me to give Lata in marriage. If I can't get this one married off" – thump on my back for emphasis – "how long will I be able to keep a younger granddaughter at home?"

My sister, Lata, was a whole minute younger than me.

"Who will accept her then, *hanh*?" Ammamma continued in agitation. "Headmaster *garu* keeps reminding me gov'ment has set eighteen years as legal marriage age for girls. Already past puberty, my granddaughters are. Is gov'ment going to pay the larger dowries if I delay their marriages, I ask you?"

The women shared a look of commiseration.

Shaking my head, I turned my face to the sun.

Ammamma whacked the side of my head. "The winter sun will make you darker." She bent down and kissed my forehead in remorse, her pale cheeks pink from the warming rays of the sun.

Lakshmi *garu* cocked her head and considered me for a moment, winter sun glinting off the powered smoothness of her mud brown face. Pursing her lips she said, "Nothing will make this one pretty. But at least use one of those fairness creams. I saw on TV if you use it regularly, the girl will become fair and marriage proposals will start pouring in like anything."

Ammamma snorted as she put a rubber band at the end of my braid. "Looting people is what they are doing. I tried and tried with that cream, but did it make her fair? On the Lord of the Seven Hills, I tell you, we've had to watch every *paisa* because of that cursed cream. Not to mention the money wasted on all those concoctions that quack in the village palmed off on me." For having taken the Lord's name in vain, Ammamma turned eastward and raised the joined palms of her hands in supplication. Not wanting to take chances, she also crossed her hands at her wrists and gave her cheeks gentle slaps. Then she held my face in her hands and sighed. "Oh Child! Why were you cursed with the colour of your wretched grandfather?"

Our grandfather, the wretched one, had been as dark as the underside of my best friend's sooty kerosene stove. For him, skin colour wasn't an issue; he had been able to marry the fair-skinned Ammamma, hadn't he?

Ammamma continued, "Why couldn't you have been fair like me, or pretty like your sisters? By now you would have been married off into a family with one tractor and two motorcycles, and lording over ten cows."

"And heavy with your first child, too," Lakshmi *garu* added.

Wearying of this dog-chase-tail discussion, I threaded my fingers through the looped string in my hands and pushed it up for my grandmother to see. "Look Ammamma! I made a bridge."

Ammamma bent down and kissed my cheek. "How I shudder to think of this foolish child's future."

THREE

I might have shared parents with Malli and Lata, but Chinni was the sister of my heart.

The twinkly-eyed Chinni, short, plump and pretty, her skin the colour of rice husk – and I dark, and tall like a bent-over palm tree – were fondly referred to as milk and coffee, both for the fact that we were always together, as well for the contrasting colours of our skin.

Chinni, Lata and I were in the same class, but it was my best friend I walked to school with, in our matching uniforms of blue pinafores, almost-white shirts and red-ribbons braided into our pigtails. Chinni and I sat cross-legged on the cemented floor of our classroom, sharing a slate, alternating the use of a slim piece of chalk and dreaming up ways to distract our Master.

"I am convinced you have a usable brain tucked away somewhere, Pullamma," our Master said on a daily basis, clutching at his head in despair, causing Chinni and me to burst into giggles. "Always dreaming up some mischief or the other. If only you would dust it out, and put it to good use."

But who cared? Of what use was education to girls? Would it help with cooking, or getting up to fill municipal water in the middle of the night, or dealing with mothers-in-law? We giggled and gossiped in the back row, while Lata settled up front and worked her way to the top of the class.

Our classroom was poorly lit by an overhead bulb hanging off a long, frayed electrical cord. Garden lizards darted between the cracks in the mud walls, flicking tongues, swallowing insects and providing entertainment to the class. Occasionally, after the boys had chased some poor lizard all over class, the frightened creature would make its escape, leaving behind its tail. Chinni and I stood with the boys, examining the detached tail as it writhed on the ground, while the rest of the girls squealed. Privately we thought they were a pretty silly bunch.

Chinni and I lived for such disruptions to our class. If our elders hadn't made us go to school, mainly to get us out of the way of their daily chores, we might have spent our time in more such pleasurable pursuits.

　　　　　　　　　　　　　RASANA ATREYA

Another thing we looked forward to were the power cuts which inevitably followed rising temperatures. When the fan in our classroom shuddered to a halt, our headmaster ordered us out under the cool of the large *raavi* tree. Classes resumed, with our teacher writing on a small, portable blackboard. Many times, Chinni and I would slowly lean against the tree and wink at each other. The other children clapped their mouths at the sight of us winking, horrified at our boldness. When they started to giggle, our Master would turn around, the glare in his rheumy eyes prompting us to sit up straight. The children would laugh. Too babyish for words; but it was the best we could come up with, given what we had to play with.

To pray for frequent power cuts, Chinni and I stopped at the Durga temple before heading off to school each morning, placing a flower at the altar to bribe the Goddess. The rest of the day was spent waiting for that escape to the *raavi* tree.

This was more than Lata could bear. "Pullamma," she said, "pray for something good. Brains, perhaps. No more mischief in class, I'm warning you. I want to do well in the exams."

Chinni made faces behind Lata's back. "I'm going to be a lady doctor," she mimicked my sister in a sing song voice. "I am going to be a lady Prime Minister."

Then she and I ran giggling, fleeing to escape Lata's wrath.

As we got to higher classes, our headmaster began to nurture high hopes for Lata. We didn't have any doctor in the village, let alone a lady one, so he thought it would be wonderful if she were the first. Lata had no problem with that. All she talked about was how she would walk around the village, stethoscope around her neck, tending to the sick and the powerful, the rich and the needy. When we giggled at her pomposity, Lata tossed her long braid over her shoulder, and stalked off.

School over for the day, I settled on the tyre swing in our courtyard, watching Malli, Ammamma and Lakshmi *garu* prepare the tomato for pickling.

Using a long wooden spoon, Malli turned over the sun dried tomato marinating in sesame seed oil. "Does this need more mustard powder? A little more asafoetida and turmeric, perhaps?"

Lakshmi *garu* put some in her mouth and pursed her lips. "I think too much salt is the problem. Add some more chilli powder to balance it."

Ammamma made the addition and mixed it well. "Needs another day in the sun."

Lakshmi *garu* nodded.

Dusk was approaching, so I helped Malli lug the fragile ceramic jars of pickle inside. We'd bring out the jars next morning, and open them to the sun again.

The courtyard gate rattled. The knock, this late in the evening, was as unexpected as road repairs in a non-election year.

Ammamma jerked her head up, startled.

Lata hurried forward, an expectant look on her face.

Lakshmi *garu* and Ammamma wiped their hands on their saris and got to their feet.

Malli started to sweep the courtyard.

It was the school Headmaster. When he'd been greeted and seated, Headmaster *garu* said, "Your Lata is extremely bright. I think she should study to be a doctor."

There was stunned silence.

Lakshmi *garu* erupted into a cackle so maniacal, the birds lined up on the top of the cowshed almost tripped over themselves in their anxiety to get away.

I gave a startled laugh, never having thought Lata's obsession more than a joke.

Malli clapped a hand over her mouth.

Headmaster *garu*'s eyes darted from Lakshmi *garu* to Ammamma, but my grandmother was of no help; she was quivering like a woman in direct contact with an exposed electrical wire. Soon the two women were clutching at their sides, gasping from laughing. "This is the best laugh I've had in years," Ammamma said, when she'd regained some control.

Headmaster *garu*'s lips tightened.

Ammamma wiped away her tears with the edge of her sari. Sniffing, she said, "What is a girl to do with all that education – a doctor, no less?"

"Use it to wash her children's backsides?" Lakshmi *garu* suggested, slapping her thigh like Duryodhana from the *Mahabharata*, laughter rumbling up her chest.

That set Ammamma off again.

Headmaster *garu* looked at the women, both of them rocking with laughter. He turned to Lata, sorrow on his face. He stalked out.

"But Ammamma –" Lata protested.

"Hush, Child," Ammamma said. "You think that pompous fool knows better than me what's good for you? Look at Pullamma, is she complaining?"

I shook my head vigorously. Not me. No reason to complain.

"And Malli, is she aching for education?"

Malli started to sweep energetically.

Ammamma sniffed, wiping away tears of mirth. "Him and his stupid notions. If girls study too much, they will get funny ideas in their heads. They won't do as they are told in their in-laws' home. Then what will become of our family honour, I ask you? How will we hold our heads high?"

No one but me noted the distress on Lata's face.

The news of Headmaster *garu*'s visit spread. The villagers shook their heads over Ammamma's foolishness. Letting a girl study all the way up to 12th. What was she thinking? What girl ever needed to read more than an occasional letter from her husband? And if that weren't bad enough, the foolish woman had sent Chinni and me to keep Lata company, and let me write – and pass – the exams, too. At least Chinni's mother, though a widow herself, had the good sense not to permit any exam-taking nonsense after 7th class.

Were the villagers fools to stop this school-going foolishness for their girls before it was too late? Were they brainless to marry their daughters off before the girls got grandiose ideas fixed in their heads, and brought dishonour to their birth homes by refusing to do as told by their in-laws? The villagers tut-tutted. Leave a woman in charge and look what happened. What else could you expect when there was no firm male hand to guide the family, no husband, no son, not even a grandson?

"*Aiyyo*," Ammamma lamented, "what have I done?"

"What is the point in regretting now," Lakshmi *garu* said, "after the girls have slid out of your hands, and the time for reining them in is past? Going behind your back, they are, sending Headmaster *garu* to demand more education. Like you need the headache. And that Lata, not even like a normal girl. Always getting out of housework, troubling her head with a book."

Ammamma hung her head in remorse.

For Chinni and me, things continued as usual. We passed time telling each other ancient sayings, within Lata's hearing, of course.

"Don't tell lies," Chinni said, her eyes twinkling in her plump face, "otherwise girls will be born to you."

"How about this one," I countered. "Help arrange a marriage, even if takes a thousand lies to do so."

"So you're racking up lies?" Lata asked.

"We want to get married," Chinni said, her face angelic. "Don't you?"

"How can you think so little of yourself?" Lata demanded, head inclined in that imperious way of hers, making us giggle even more.

"Don't you have anything better to do in life than giggle?"

"We tell lies, too," Chinni said.

Lata shook her head and walked away.

Lata had more use for books than friends. For her, marriage was yet another milestone; for Chinni and me, it was The Goal, The Ultimate Truth, The Purpose of Life. We spent all our free time discussing our future husbands – plump-yet-pleasing-to-the-eye Chinni kindly overlooking the fact that I had virtually no prospects – and how we would live out our lives.

When Chinni and I weren't together, it was because we had housework to do. One of our daily chores – mine and Malli's – was sweeping and washing the courtyard. Over the years patches of flooring had broken off at awkward angles, making the navigation of our walled-off courtyard an adventure for my friends and me. Ammamma had part of it cleaned up, exposing the earth below, before she ran out of money. Because of the uneven flooring, cleaning was a challenge. The walls of our courtyard weren't much better; the straw and mud were plainly visible. Patching them with cow dung was another chore I didn't care for.

Then there was the washing and milking of our cow. I complained about it endlessly, but Ammamma was quite unsympathetic; we should be grateful we even had a cow, she said.

Ammamma's tailoring supplemented the family income we got from selling milk and cow dung; Malli and I helped out by sewing buttons and hemming edges, but this was a bearable chore.

What I truly detested was the water duty. The well water was good enough for daily use, but we depended on the municipal supply for drinking water. The municipality, in their wisdom, chose to turn on the drinking water only at three in the morning. We arose, I – complaining that Lata wasn't doing her bit, Malli – calmly doing what she had to do. We filled all available utensils and drums with drinking water, because the days the municipal water man overslept, we had no water. Then we put utensils on the stove, one at a time, waited for them to boil over and left them to cool, so water would be ready for drinking in the morning.

Chinni and I swore that when we married, it would only be into rich families where we could expect a municipal water connection that worked during the daylight hours, but more importantly, where the servants took care of such menial chores, leaving us to do important things – like shopping and gossiping.

The one good thing my grandfather did – the only thing, if you asked Ammamma – in the short time he was part of my grandmother's life, was to get his name on the rolls of freedom fighters. He hadn't been one himself – too much of a coward, Ammamma said. How he got his name there was a mystery, but after he died, the pension from the Government of India was what kept us from lining the road to the temple, tin plate in hand, dependent on the generosity of worshippers.

Once the day's chores were finished, and Ammamma's head had hit the pillow for the afternoon, Chinni and I went in search of fun.

A favourite pastime of ours was to sneak past the house of our local oracle, Ranga Nayakamma, daring each other to go inside her house for a 'session.'

Four days a week Ranga Nayakamma was an ordinary woman.

For the other three, she transformed from a meek housewife tending three children and a goat, into a whiskey-guzzling, chicken-leg chomping, cigarette puffing oracle. She started her day by going into trance, out of which she erupted with frenzied dancing – lips curling, diamond-studded nostrils flaring, kohl-lined eyes flashing, bejewelled arms slashing – sort of like Goddess Kali after she had killed a demon, except I didn't think Goddess Kali drank, smoked or ate meat. This trance-and-dance routine continued for a good three or four hours before the oracle collapsed on the floor, ready to bless people with whatever it was they wanted – in return for gifts of whiskey, chicken (never any other meat – for, on her days off, Ranga Nayakamma was a staunch vegetarian) or *beedis* – the coarse, *tendu*-leaf cigarettes the villagers favoured. Her mostly-male followers were many.

Chinni and I couldn't imagine what would make a housewife give up a respectable life with a husband and children, for this kind of spectacle.

We were expected to spend our free time in the courtyard of my house, or in the village square, where the elders could keep us in check while Ammamma took her nap.

A huge banyan occupied the place of pride in the centre of the village square, with a cemented ledge running around it for people to sit on. In the heat of midday, when the chores were done, the men lay down to gossip, making themselves comfortable on creaky wooden cots made of coir. It being unseemly for women to lie down in public, they settled on the ledge, watching the children play, taking a breather from the labours of the day. The boys, for the most part, spent their time swinging from the hanging roots of the banyan tree, or chasing discarded cycle tires with a stick, while young girls played endless rounds of hopscotch. Older girls like us sat demurely on the ledge, pretending to be immersed in embroidering and sewing, but in actuality waiting out the elders. Inevitably, sleep overcame them and eyelids drooped. With the elders no longer awake to keep us in check, Chinni and I felt free to sneak looks at the boys and giggle.

Life was good.

FOUR

N ow, as we waited by the gate of our compound for Kondal Rao *garu* to arrive and bless Malli's bride-viewing, I tried to ignore Jhampaiah's words. Bad talk, indeed! Such a respectable politician like Kondal Rao *garu*!

The marriage broker hurried up to us, rubber slippers slapping against the dusty road. "Got late. Is Kondal Rao *garu* here?" She looked worried.

I shook my head.

She sagged with relief, and joined the anxious crowd.

A spicy smell wafted in the air. *Pulusu?* My stomach growled. Hopefully no one had heard. Where was Kondal Rao *garu* anyway?

Thirty-five minutes later two jeeps, each loaded with rough-looking men armed with bamboo sticks and scary-looking sickles, screeched to a halt behind Lakshmi *garu's* tractor. A fat little man, with a droopy moustache, and oily hair knotted at the nape of his short stubby neck, descended from the first jeep. Kondal Rao *garu* scared me now, as he had when Ammamma, my sisters and I visited his house two years ago.

He was dressed in the standard politician uniform of dazzling white *kurta* – which strained at his generous belly – and a white cotton *pancha* that barely skimmed the tops of his black patent leather shoes.

Ammamma and Murty *garu* hurried up to greet him.

Lakshmi *garu* took a few steps, then stopped. Turning to the villagers gathered by the gate, she said, "Such an important personage Kondal Rao *garu* is. A politician with so much power visiting this house!" She puffed up as if she'd herself conveyed the politician to our house.

They nodded, appropriately awed.

Ammamma joined the palms of her hands together in greeting. "I am honoured you have personally come to grace the occasion."

Kondal Rao *garu* shook his head and got back into the jeep, making me wonder why he had bothered to get down in the first place. "Too many things for me to do. Too little time. I am such a busy man, you see."

"Yes, yes, of course," Ammamma stammered, her face a bright red. She slapped her cheeks in remorse. "How could we even *think* that an important personage such as you would have the time to sit through a trifling event such as this?"

He inclined his head.

"Pullamma, Child," she said to me. "Seek blessings from Kondal Rao *garu*."

To Kondal Rao *garu*, she said, "With your blessings everything will go well today. My Pullamma's next in line."

I touched his feet.

This seemed to mollify Kondal Rao *garu*. "I came merely to reassure you that you couldn't be marrying your girl into a better family. My man," he said, pointing an imperious finger at the groom's father, "has often performed important jobs for me."

The groom's father preened.

Ammamma and Lakshmi *garu* exchanged a quick glance – had the market price for the groom just gone up?

As the engines rumbled, the groom's father hurried forward, palms of his hands joined together. Kondal Rao *garu* raised a hand and the drivers of both vehicles killed their engines. He cocked his head, waiting.

"Please," the groom's father said. "I humbly beg of you to consider staying on to preside over this occasion."

Kondal Rao *garu* tapped a stubby finger on his chin. "I drove seven hours to get here. I can't fritter away my time sitting through the whole bride-viewing, you know."

"*Aw-wa!*" The other man slapped his mouth. "How could I be so foolish as to expect you to waste your time over such trivial issues?"

"I suppose I could relax at the Party guest house till you finish with your function. Send word if the outcome is positive. I shall arrive and give my blessings."

"I'm deeply honoured." The groom's father bowed.

Tyres screeched. The jeeps were off. The atmosphere lightened, like the aftermath of a violent thunderstorm.

Murty *garu* gestured at Ammamma. "The girl's grandmother. Name is Seetamma *garu*. The mother passed away, such a tragedy. As for the father – well, the less said, the better. Poor lady, the grandmother, to be stuck with such responsibility. I am G. V. K. S. S. R. Satyanarayana Murty. I live next door, so it is my duty to help with the marriages of the granddaughters, you see."

Murty *garu*, named for a good number of Gods in the Hindu

pantheon, thereby accounting for most of the initials in his name, lived for the respect bride-viewings accorded to elders like him. In his daily life Murty *garu* was showed none – not by his sons, certainly not by his wife.

Tradition decreed that married women perform a myriad of rituals and prayers for the well-being of their husbands. Talk in the village was Lakshmi *garu* did these with barely concealed resentment. Since no respect was forthcoming from her, Murty *garu* spent a lot of time attending bride-viewings as an elder, trying to leverage his stately appearance to gain the respect he so desired.

"Please come." He led the party past the open shed. Our only cow, freshly scrubbed and decorated with a long slash of vermilion on its forehead, sat chewing cud. It watched our procession incuriously.

"Pullamma," Ammamma said.

I hurried forward and settled the parents of the groom, the young child and the groom himself on folding chairs borrowed from the priest's house for just this occasion; our two rickety metal chairs, with their curling edges, simply wouldn't do.

An assortment of relatives – the women in bright silk saris, the men in pristine white *panchas* and *kurtas* – sat on either side of them, while Lakshmi *garu*'s two sons arranged themselves on the straw mat. Lakshmi *garu* and I hovered by the door.

I wiped damp palms on the sides of my half-sari and took a jerky breath. *If they accept Malli into their family, I will circle the shrine of Goddess Durga one hundred and eight times, I will milk the cow for a whole month without complaining, I –*

"Time for refreshments," Murty *garu* said, pointing his chin at Lakshmi *garu*. He sat across from the groom's family in a straight-backed chair, his hand resting on a walking stick, the latter more for effect than anything.

"No, no, please don't bother," the groom's father protested, bouncing the toddler on his knee.

It wouldn't be proper for a guest to accept an offer of drinks or snacks without being cajoled, so Murty *garu* tried again. "What sir! You have come from so far to see our girl. What will you think? We don't know how to offer proper hospitality, or what?" Turning to his wife he said, "Tea."

"Coffee," said the father of the groom.

"Coffee," said Murty *garu* to Lakshmi *garu*. He turned to one of his sons. "And some *mirchi bajjis* from the shop. Pronto."

The groom's father frowned. "Why are you getting food from the shop? The bride doesn't know to cook, or what?"

Ammamma shot Murty *garu* a look. "My granddaughter made the *bajjis* with her own hands. She has been properly trained in cooking."

"Of course, of course," Murty *garu* said, dabbing his forehead with a handkerchief.

"Can't eat anything made with green chillies," the groom's father said, patting his expansive belly. "Too spicy. Some mixture, perhaps?"

"Mixture?" Murty *garu* said.

Ammamma nodded.

"*Laddu, laddu*," the child shouted from his grandfather's lap.

"*Laddus* for the little one," Murty *garu* said to his son. He leaned forward and put a finger under the child's chin. "Like sweets, do you?"

The child bit the finger.

Murty *garu* snatched it back.

"Cute, isn't he?" said the beaming grandfather.

"Of course, of course." Murty *garu* massaged the finger discreetly, his smile wobbling just a little. "Can I be of further service?"

"Some *kaajas*, perhaps?"

"Ah! *Kaajas*!" Murty *garu*'s face cleared, pain forgotten. He thumped his cane in approval. "Good choice. Our shop-man... uh... our Malli has magic in her hands when it comes to *kaajas*. Makes them in perfect shapes, she does. Fries them just right – a warm, honey brown." He leaned back in his chair. "And when you sink your teeth into their delicious sweetness..." He gave a dramatic shudder.

The groom's family exchanged looks.

Lakshmi *garu* cleared her throat, but Murty *garu*'s eyes were closed in bliss. "*Psst*!" she hissed, sounding desperate. Mortification at her husband's behaviour caused her face to appear even more angular than usual.

Murty *garu* jerked out of his trance and sat up, a beatific smile on his face.

The groom's father squinted at Murty *garu*, a suspicious look on his face, but Murty *garu* showed not a hint of embarrassment.

The two men resumed their chitchat. The child tried to put his finger up his grandfather's nostril. The groom's father waved it away, and accepted the glass of water I offered.

"Pullamma." Murty *garu* raised a bushy white eyebrow at me.

I nodded, heart kicking against my ribs. It was time to bring out the bride.

FIVE

Malli was hovering behind the curtained door. I escorted her out. No previous instructions on comportment were necessary for my sister. We had seen enough Telugu movies to know that the bride was supposed to walk demurely, head down. No need to peek at the boy or anyone else – what else were the elders for?

She stood still, a large tray balanced in hand, staring at her big toe, newly painted a shiny red. I stood by her, willing the day to go well for my sister.

A round of introductions ensued. "The bride-to-be is the eldest granddaughter of Seetamma *garu*," Murty *garu* said.

"And the grandfather?"

"Passed away."

"So sorry. The father?"

"Has found a nubile maiden in the Himalayas." Murty *garu* tittered. "She is helping him find God, you see."

Ammamma's jaw slackened.

At the glare from his wife, Murty *garu* hastily turned his snicker into a cough. Poor Murty *garu*. Always getting into trouble with someone or the other.

The groom's father chose not to probe further – about our father, or anything else; he would have made inquiries about the suitability of our family, too.

"The poor lady has two more granddaughters to marry off," Murty *garu* said.

"Two?" the groom's father asked, a frown marring the oily smoothness of his forehead. "Who is the number two granddaughter?"

Murty *garu* pointed at me. "That's Pullamma."

There I stood in my lime-green-and-yellow half-sari, which was splashed with big purple splotches, which I supposed were flowers. I was miserably aware that this hand-me-down from the fair-skinned Malli – the nicest I owned – was an unfortunate choice of clothing because it clashed violently with the colour of my skin.

The groom's father leaned forward. Using his hairy caterpillar fingers, he adjusted the angle of his thick-rimmed oversized spectacles. He shook his head as if to say he couldn't believe Malli and I came from the same stock.

I tugged at my half-sari, conscious it was five inches too short. Would he compliment me, as people often did after realizing I was sister to the fair-skinned Malli and Lata – on the clearness of my skin and the lustre of my long hair, as if in consolation for my coffee coloured skin and abnormal height of 5′ 9″? Or would he pity me?

He moved his head to inspect Malli. As he scrunched his nose, the hairs within quivered.

My sister stood queen-like, elegantly draped in a red-and-gold Kanchi-silk sari. Basket-shaped earrings dangled from her ears. A strand of delicate *malli*-flowers, woven through her long braid, adorned her hair. She had taken special care with the henna on her hands and feet. The *bottu* on her forehead, chosen to accentuate the beauty of her large eyes, shimmered red and gold.

She stood with the tray in hand, tea cups clattering just a little.

"So where is number three?"

"Umm. Well." Murty *garu* put a fist under his chin in contemplation. "Actually she has gone to help out a relative. Such a sad story, you see. Seetamma *garu*'s second daughter's third son broke his leg." He tapped a slim finger on his lips. "Or was it her third daughter's second son?"

Ammamma cleared her throat.

"Anyway," Murty *garu* said, "They needed help at home, so the girl was sent over."

"*Hanh!*" the groom's father said.

The groom's parents exchanged suspicious glances. They knew about the hiding of prettier, younger daughters, of course; they would have done the exact same thing. The question was – did what was being hidden concern them in any way?

The groom's father concluded his prolonged inspection of Malli. "We shall proceed."

I released my breath.

"Come," the groom's mother said, patting the stool next to her. Luckily, her headache seemed to have gone away. "Put the tray down."

Barely in time. Malli's tea-laden tray was beginning to tilt.

Malli was trained in household chores, of course, but balancing fully loaded trays for long periods of time hadn't been one of them. As she walked across the room, the groom's mother stared intently at Malli's feet. Couldn't blame her; Lakshmi *garu*'s own sister's brother-in-law had been tricked into marrying a girl with diseased legs – with the sari tied low enough to cover her feet, there had been no way to tell she had elephantitis.

Taking Malli's hand in hers, the groom's mother said, "Come, sit here. What is your name?"

"Malli."

Putting a finger under Malli's chin, she said, "What a pretty name. Almost as pretty as you are. My son's name is Ram."

Murty *garu* chuckled. "This is what happens when we name our children after Gods and Goddesses. Because, if this alliance goes through, the Gods Ram and Seeta will no longer be a couple."

Ammamma, who was named for the Goddess Seeta, turned red in the face.

Lakshmi *garu* frowned at Murty *garu*.

"Anyway," Murty *garu* said, "why don't you question the girl?"

"What have you studied?" the groom's mother asked.

"6th class fail," Malli said in a whisper.

"Good, good. Our son almost passed his 7th. Missed by a mere two marks, he did," she said, holding up two fingers. "Two marks, can you believe that?"

Murty *garu* clucked in sympathy.

"T...o...o educated girls," the groom's father said, sinking his teeth into a luscious *kaaja,* "won't comfort us in our old age." He flicked his tongue to lick the syrup from the corner of his lip. "Worried about themselves, they will be."

"Shouldn't allow these girls to think," Lakshmi *garu* said, jumping in. "Then they won't listen to us." Lakshmi *garu* should know. She had daily battles with her 9th class passed younger daughter-in-law.

"We want a girl who has been trained well," the groom's father said. "We are getting old. She will be needed to take care of us, no tantrums, no nothing."

"My Malli will be the perfect daughter-in-law for you," Ammamma said. "No mind of her own. Just does what she is told."

The groom's mother nodded approvingly.

"We won't let our daughter-in-law leave the family home for

work, or gossip, or any such nonsense," the groom's father said. "We have our honour to think of."

"Our girl is a homebody," Ammamma said. "You needn't have any fears on that account. Our Malli will maintain the honour of your family – only time she'll go out is to the temple. Otherwise always home."

The groom's father nodded. He raised an eyebrow at his son. At the groom's nod, the older man said to the room in general, "We like the girl. She may be taken inside now. We elders need to talk."

"Pullamma." Murty *garu* tossed his head at me.

I hurried to take Malli's arm.

Six

"Shall we proceed with the alliance?" the groom's father said, as I returned from escorting Malli the nine steps back into our house.

Murty *garu* looked at Ammamma. She nodded.

Thank you, Durga Devi! I held my arms out for the little boy, not wanting the grandfather distracted during the negotiations. The child came to me grinning, two front teeth sticking out. Hopefully, he wouldn't bite. He grabbed my long braid with sticky fingers and shoved it in his mouth.

"We want the wedding to take place in our village," the groom's father said. "Can't expect all our relatives and friends to come all this way now, can we?"

Ammamma blanched. Tradition demanded that the groom come to the bride's house for the wedding. But what could the girl's side do if the groom's family tried to weasel out of their share of the expense?

In our village we could perform the wedding in our courtyard and be done with it. But in the groom's village... I shuddered, thinking of the additional cost.

"We'll want twenty silk saris for our relatives," the man continued. "This is in addition to the saris you will be giving to the bride, and to my immediate family, you understand." He ticked off on his fingers. "One scooter for the groom. One gas connection. One Godrej Almirah for the newlyweds to put their clothes in. Five *tolas* of gold."

"I'm just a poor widow," Ammamma said, raising the joined palms of her hands in entreaty. "I, myself, cook in a coal-fed earthen stove; I can't even afford a kerosene one – it would be great hardship to acquire a gas connection. On top of it, the gold, the Almirah..." Her hands trembled.

The face of the groom's father remained impassive.

"I have two more granddaughters after this one. No male support in sight. No husband, no son, not even a grandson. Where will I get that much money from?"

"Oh!" The groom's father seemed taken aback. He turned to the marriage broker, but the woman was busy examining the strand of flowers strung across the doorway.

To Ammamma, he said, "Remember, our boy has a good job as a flour mill operator. He'll keep your granddaughter in comfort."

Ammamma looked uncertain.

"I'm Kondal Rao *garu's* right hand man," the groom's father said.

"Unlikely to forget it, am I?" Ammamma muttered under her breath.

Murty *garu* looked enquiringly at Ammamma. Her lips tightened, then sagged. She nodded slowly.

"It is settled, then," Murty *garu* said rather heartily.

I managed to pry my braid away from the child's mouth.

He stared unblinkingly, then smiled, his plump cheeks dimpling.

I smiled back. Now that the negotiations were concluded, I handed him to his grandfather.

The groom's mother leaned to whisper something in her husband's ear.

"Oh, that's right," the groom's father said. "I forgot. After all, we are taking home a fatherless girl."

No father meant no one to bend backwards for the *maryadalu*, the to-the-point-of-servitude catering of the family of the groom, during the wedding and after; who else would bear the endless indignities associated with being the father of the bride?

The anxious expression was back on Ammamma's face.

"But we are willing to overlook it," the groom's mother added, face radiating sympathy.

"For –" the groom's father said.

Ammamma's back stiffened.

"Five hundred rupees. Cash."

SEVEN

Lakshmi garu's sons were dispatched to inform Kondal Rao *garu*, the politician, of the success of the bride-viewing. For almost an hour we mingled with the guests, talking to them, making plans for the wedding.

Ammamma's lips were a thin white line, betraying her tension. She probably wanted to finalize the details before the groom's family thought up more demands. Not that finalizing the details now would stop them later.

Finally Kondal Rao *garu* showed up, entourage in tow.

The gathering arose.

The groom's father hurried forward with the best chair and placed it near Kondal Rao *garu*. Then he removed the ceremonial white cotton *khanduva* draped over his shoulder and dusted off the chair, though there was not a speck of dirt on it. "Please." He bade Kondal Rao *garu* to sit.

Once Kondal Rao *garu* was settled, sweets and Malli were brought out to conclude the deal. Lakshmi *garu* had instructed Malli to say she'd been up all night making the round *rava laddus*, but no one asked.

The groom's father set the child on the ground.

"Whee!" the child called out as he ran around, arms spread like a plane, weaving through chatting elders. He crashed into a chair. Tears threatened.

"Come, come," the groom's mother said, pulling the child onto her lap. She offered him a *rava laddu*. The child opened his mouth wide.

The woman laughed. "Such a greedy little fellow, my grandson is." The boy grabbed the whole sweet and stuffed it in his mouth.

Murty *garu* smiled indulgently.

I grinned, thinking how much fun it would be to tease Malli; she had no idea what her husband to-be looked like. I would have sneaked a peek, but sadly for Malli, she wasn't quite that brazen. He was a decent-looking fellow, my brother-in-law to-be, but I planned to terrorize my sister with stories of his defects.

A man hurtled into the courtyard, a bundle clutched close to his chest.

Startled, I looked at Ammamma. She frowned in puzzlement.

The man looked around wildly. Spotting Kondal Rao *garu*, he rushed to the politician and threw himself at his feet, shuddering sobs wracking his body. "*Aiyya*, after twelve years we were blessed with a male child. Now he is dead."

Kondal Rao *garu* jumped to his feet. "Why are you at my feet, you stupid man? Go to the doctor or something."

"No, no, no." The man breathed in jerks of air. "Ranga Nayakamma sent me here."

"What is he babbling about?" Kondal Rao *garu* looked at a henchman in irritation.

"Ranga Nayakamma is the local oracle," the henchman said. "She often foretells events of great significance."

Ammamma snorted. "Rush the child to a hospital, you foolish man." She jerked her head at Lakshmi *garu*'s younger son. "The tractor. Right now."

Lakshmi *garu*'s son jumped to his feet. "Let's go."

The infant's father continued to look up at Kondal Rao *garu*, face blotchy, palms of his hands joined together. "I placed my child at the feet of Ranga Nayakamma, and she went into a trance." Tears dripped down. He struggled to his feet, the bundle clutched to his chest. "Ranga Nayakamma said the only way to bring the child back to life was to place him at the feet of the Goddess."

"Go to the temple, then," Kondal Rao *garu* snapped. "I look like Goddess Durga, or what?"

"Goddess Durga is of no use to me," the man said.

Kondal Rao *garu* looked at the man questioningly.

"Goddess Pullamma."

The birds stilled. The breeze stilled. Even the leaves on the trees stilled. The only sound in our courtyard was the harsh breathing of the man.

Murty *garu* broke everyone out of trance by raising his stick at the man. "Is this some kind of joke? Look at Pullamma. She's no Goddess. She's just a young girl."

I turned to Ammamma in desperation. She seemed frozen, her eyes wide with horror.

"Here," Lakshmi *garu* said, pointing at my feet.

The man rushed to me. "Save my son, oh Pullamma *Devi*," he begged. "Let him live."

"Are you mad?" I squeaked.

"What is the harm, I say," Kondal Rao *garu* said. "Let him put the baby at the girl's feet. When that fails, he can admit the child in the children's ward, himself in a mental ward."

"No!" I pleaded. "Please. I'm no Goddess." I stumbled backward.

"Wait," Lakshmi *garu* said. Her nails dug into my arms.

My lungs began to squeeze. Breaths came out in short bursts.

The man fell to his knees, and began to unwrap the bundle. A pale child emerged. The man placed the unmoving child at my feet.

I began to shiver. *God, don't let the child be cured at my feet. Please, please, please.*

Its eyes remained tightly closed.

"Live, Child, live," the man urged the infant, fanning it with a piece of cloth. "Goddess Pullamma blesses you."

No change in the infant.

He then balled the cloth, and thrust it under the baby's nose.

I swallowed.

The infant wailed!

"My baby lives." Crying and sniffling, the man pulled the infant close to his chest, raining kisses on its forehead. Then he touched his own head to the ground. "A thousand thanks to Goddess Pullamma! My baby lives!"

I turned to Ammamma in confusion. Her jaw dropped.

Suddenly Kondal Rao *garu* shoved the man aside. He fell heavily at my feet, his back forming a hump over the belly that squished on the ground.

What was he doing? I tried to move back, but he hung tight to my ankles. He, an elder, touching my feet!

"Pullamma *Devi*," he said, angling his head upward. Tears started to make their way down. "Oh *Devi*! Oh Goddess incarnate! Thank you for arriving on the earth to bestow your blessings on this innocent life."

Everyone eyed each other in bewilderment. The groom's father considered the prone Kondal Rao *garu*, a frown on his face.

"A miracle! We're witnessing a miracle!" Kondal Rao *garu* tilted to a side, like a prone buffalo raising itself in the mud pond, put a hand on the floor for support and settled on his knees with effort.

Then, astonishingly, he began to sway. "We're witnessing the birth of the Goddess herself!"

The groom's father lurched in the direction of my feet. I stared down at their heads, not trusting my eyes. This couldn't be happening. Not to me. I giggled in disbelief as the groom's party tumbled at my feet like broken-stringed puppets.

EIGHT

Early next morning, I set off for Chinni's house at the very edge of the village. I was dying to tell her about yesterday's happenings. Though she was bound to have heard – hard to miss gossip this juicy – only I could give her the details.

Who would have thought Malli's bride-viewing would turn into such a drama? Imagine a powerful politician like Kondal Rao *garu* falling at my feet! *My feet,* like I was a holy person or something. As for saying I was a Goddess, that joker oracle – I quickly took God's name for this disrespectful reference to an elder – was completely mad. Anyone with two functioning eyes in their head could see I was just a normal girl who had to milk that stupid cow twice a day.

Ammamma and Murty *garu* were going on like something unfortunate had happened. I couldn't understand why they didn't see the funny side of it; an elder – a really fat elder – tumbling at my feet. Life in the village could be incredibly boring. Chinni would be so upset she'd missed out on something this exciting. Served her right for not being at the bride-viewing. Even as the thought occurred, I knew I was being unfair. Chinni was getting married in five days. As the wedding date drew nearer, her mother grew strict. No loafing about in the village, no getting into mischief, no going out – not even to my house. Her virtue and reputation had to be safeguarded until she was handed over to her in-laws. *Bah!* Aunty was taking all the fun out of life.

"*Tataiyya!*" I called out to a classmate's elderly grandfather, as I hurried past their house.

He peered up into the tree.

Did he think I was perched up there? This *Tataiyya* was getting to be too much. Growing ancient, but still refusing to wear the hearing aid his grandson had sent all the way from 'foreign.'

I crept towards old Devamma's house and aimed a stone at a particularly luscious guava. *Crack!* I looked at the shattered window in disbelief. I was known throughout the village for my deadly aim; I was better than the boys, even.

I waited fearfully for Devamma to storm out and twist my ear, but all she did was poke her head out, give me a startled look and hurriedly close her doors.

RASANA ATREYA

"Vanita." I waved to an old friend walking towards me.

Vanita suddenly veered towards the temple.

Had everyone lost their hearing today?

I walked towards Chinni's, feeling sad. Summer on its way and Chinni wouldn't be around for it. Life was just not fair.

We'd spent our entire school life waiting for summer, and with it, the freedom from the tyranny of school – no lectures from the Master, no homework.

By the time March rolled around, we were quite beside ourselves in anticipation. Shimmering waves of heat rose from the parched earth. Even the cows couldn't be bothered to moo. This was when Chinni and I were at our best, or some might say, our worst.

Our families never had the money for frivolous things, but neither did most of the villagers. Cinema was our great escape. Sunday evenings, films were screened under the banyan tree in the village square. The films were projected on the flat wall of our village *sarpanch's* double-storied house. Come time for re-election, no one forgot whose wall it was the movies were screened on.

Most popular were the movies starring the Telugu superstar Chiranjeevi. Each time he made an appearance on the screen, the village boys screamed themselves hoarse. We pretended to be above such immature behaviour but, of course, we were waiting for the raunchy, high energy songs that were his trademark. For the suggestive kissing behind big flowers, for the lewd, heroine's-bottom-smacking dances Chiranjeevi's movies were so famous for.

For movie watching all of us sat on the ground, men on the right, women on the left, a pathway in between. Village elders, along with the rich and the powerful, sat on chairs positioned for the best viewing. The projector was placed way in the back, behind the audience. Each time someone got up to move about, their shadow blocked the hero's knee or the heroine's backside onscreen, causing the audience to boo out its displeasure. If the cinema was particularly serious or boring, or if an especially embarrassing scene came on and the audience began to fidget – an intimate scene between the hero and the heroine, for example – we pretended to get up for the bathroom, giggling as the indignant booing started.

Our antics made Lata mad. "Can't you immature creatures control yourself for two-and-a-half hours?" she hissed.

After a while, this became a game for the two of us – the more engrossed the audience, the greater the challenge to position our heads so the obstruction was the funniest.

I sighed. No more fun at the movies; my best friend was getting married and moving away.

I sidled past the whiskey-chicken oracle's house, not particularly wanting to encounter the crackpot. Not after what she'd done at my sister's bride-viewing.

I walked past the Durga temple, where I could hear chanting. A couple went by, doubles on a bicycle, the woman sitting demurely on the crossbar, both legs to one side. Neither looked at me. A child ran past, raising dust on the un-tarred road. I sneezed.

I finally reached Chinni's street. Their lane was narrow, as were most in the village. Open gutters lined either side of the lane, with narrow footbridges leading up to each of the houses. I stopped in front of Chinni's and took a deep breath. Her house was sure to be filled with people busy with the wedding preparations, but I couldn't wait for everyone to leave. The best I could do was to go through the back door. I circled behind, eyes half-closed, trying not to look at the ancient Kali temple perched on the rocky cliff above. It was rumoured that human sacrifices had been performed on the temple premises in the days kings did such things. Children whispered of spirits of those unfortunate souls still haunting the area. A few boys assured us that grinning, half-buried skulls littered the back of the temple. Chinni and I often talked about checking this out for ourselves, but we were too scared to even let our glance graze the temple (though I'd die before I admitted this to anyone).

I knocked at the door. Chinni's mother opened it. I gave her a distracted smile, and tried to walk past.

"Wait, Pullamma," she said.

"*Hanh*? Oh. What is it, Aunty?"

"Chinni is getting married in five days."

"I know." I gave her an uncertain smile. Was something wrong with her, too?

"I am a poor widow," Aunty said. "If Chinni's wedding gets cancelled, I won't be able to fix it again."

I looked at her, puzzled. "Why should it get cancelled? Is the boy's party demanding more money?"

"Bad things are happening."

I cocked my head, checking Aunty out carefully. Was Chinni's upcoming wedding making her mad? "I don't understand all this," I said impatiently. "I have something important to tell Chinni. Can I go in?"

"No!"

I froze.

"There is talk about you in the village."

"What kind of talk?" I was getting a sinking feeling in the pit of my stomach.

"I can't afford to let any scandal touch my Chinni. Not this close to the wedding." She averted her eyes.

That silly incident at Malli's bride-viewing, where Kondal Rao *garu* had actually believed I was a Goddess!

Now the behaviour of the villagers began to make sense. "Aunty," I said. "You know I'm no Goddess. And even if I were, Goddesses are revered. They are not like oracles, who make such a spectacle of themselves."

"Who knows what you are – an oracle, or a Goddess, or even the devil? I can't afford to give the groom's side any reason to withdraw their proposal."

Shocked at her words, I peered past the door.

Chinni stood in the back, a stricken look on her face.

"Aunty," I begged, "you have known me all my life. How could you— "

"Pullamma." Aunty's face was hard. "Please."

"Will you at least let me say something to Chinni?"

"Say it from here." Aunty pulled the door closer, leaving enough space that I could see Chinni, but not so much that I could step inside their house.

"Chinni, do you believe what they are saying about me?"

Chinni wouldn't meet my eyes, though I could see her shoulders shake.

My chest got so tight, it hurt to breathe.

Chinni and I had been friends since we were babies, since the time her newly widowed mother came to my house to learn tailoring from Ammamma, five month-old Chinni in tow. She and I had learned to crawl together. We'd shared our first meal ever on the same plate and had been fast friends since. We had spent long, hot summers in each others' houses, eating raw mangoes with salt and chilli powder, squealing when the sourness spiked its way to the backs of our jaws. We'd planned important roles for ourselves in each others' weddings. Our children were going to be close as cousins; closer even.

"Well, then," I said, the back of my throat tight with unshed tears. "May that *Yedukondalavada* shower his benevolence upon you."

Chinni didn't look up.

I turned away from a lifetime of shared confidences. I had thought it bad enough that Chinni was leaving the village. How much worse that she was leaving my life.

Outside, I looked up defiantly at the Kali temple. The ascent was steep, the stone walls a stark black. A sharp contrast to the green and brown earth below.

Do your best, I sneered at the Goddess above.

In the blindingly bright sky, puffy white clouds sailed by. I thought of the days Chinni and I had lain on our backs in my courtyard, looking at the fat clouds, making up improbable stories about the shapes and giggling ourselves silly, while Lata sat in a distant corner, shaking her head at our foolishness.

I rubbed a hand over my chest, forcing myself to take shallow breaths.

How could everything on the outside remain so normal, when everything on the inside had died?

NINE

I have no memory of how I got home. Lurching onto the veranda edging the train-compartment rooms that comprised our house, I curled up into a tight ball.

"What happened, Child?" Ammamma asked, feeling my forehead.

Unable to get any words out, I tried to drag the free end of my half-sari over my head, but shook so hard I gave up. In desperation, I turned on my stomach and tried to burrow my head in the cold cemented floor.

"Pullamma?" Ammamma sounded scared.

"Chinni," I choked out. "Doesn't want me at her wedding." My teeth started to chatter.

"Proper Krishna-Kucheludu the two of you were, weren't you?" Lata clapped her hands together in emphasis. "Great friends who get stories written about them. The slightest puff of gossip, and your bosom buddy washes her hands of an epic friendship."

"Lata!" Ammamma said.

"Where's your precious friend now, *hanh*? So scared for her reputation that she kept her best friend away from her own wedding?"

I sat up, dismayed. I'd always assumed Lata had no use for friends. It shook me to realize she might be jealous of my friendship with Chinni. Where was Malli when I needed her? I wished Ammamma had not sent her off to a relative's house to protect her from the gossip arising from The Incident. I wished she hadn't told Lata to return home, instead.

"What's wrong with you?" Ammamma said to Lata.

"Good thing your skin is black," Lata said.

I breathed in sharply.

"Whoever heard of a brown-skinned Goddess?" Goddesses were all really fair – like Durga Devi, or really dark – like Kali.

Ammamma put a hand on Lata, but Lata shook it off. "You might as well throw away your fairness creams, Pullamma. They will serve no purpose now."

"Why are you saying such things?" Ammamma looked bewildered.

But Lata would not be stopped. "You have no hope of marriage anyway. Be grateful the oracle declared you a Goddess. One sensible thing she did in her miserable life. Now you'll have respect and money, which are the most important things anyway."

Not to me, God! I just wanted to be an ordinary girl, married to a man who would provide me with a municipal tap, and three meals a day, while I cooked and cleaned for him. I lay down, stuffed my ears with my fingers and shut my eyes tight, trying to drown out Lata's voice. I must have fallen asleep. When I opened my eyes, it was late afternoon. There was a pillow under my head and a bed sheet protecting me from the chill.

"Want some milk?" Ammamma asked.

I shook my head, but she forced a glass of it down my throat anyway. I huddled in one corner of the courtyard, watching Lakshmi *garu* and Ammamma.

"My Pullamma is cursed," Ammamma said, as she settled on a straw mat to chop vegetables for the following day.

Lakshmi *garu* sat on her haunches, putting away pieces of salted tomato that had dried under the morning sun. The tomato was piled in ceramic pickle jars that had once belonged to Ammamma's mother.

I wondered at the sense in making pickle when everything around was falling apart.

Was I really cursed?

I shivered. Who would dare to be friends with me on the off-chance I might be a Goddess? Who would want to marry me? Who would have the nerve to treat me like a normal girl? How could I expect the rest of the villagers to give me a chance, when my best friend hadn't?

Ammamma pulled the wooden base of the floor knife forward and wedged a firm foot over it. Picking up a long ridge gourd, she held the vegetable over the vertical semi-circular blade with both hands. Practiced motions guided the vegetable over the sharp cutting edge. She suddenly thrust aside the floor knife, its upright blade gleaming menacingly in the fading sun. She dropped her head into her hands. "What am I to do?" Her voice cracked. "I am scared for this foolish child."

Lakshmi *garu* leaned over and patted Ammamma. "You will have to leave Pullamma to the mercy of The Lord of the Seven Hills."

"What are you saying, Lakshmi?" Ammamma's lips quivered.

I listened to the two women discuss my life as if they were talking about someone else.

"Take care of one responsibility at a time," Lakshmi *garu* said. "Malli's alliance is already fixed. Grab this chance and get Lata a good match, too. After all, who in their right minds would refuse a match with the family of a Goddess?"

No one. They would only refuse a match with the Goddess herself.

"I can't do that to Pullamma."

"What other choice do you have?"

Lakshmi *garu* liked to think she was a practical person, but this was too much, even for her.

"Why don't you blame that baby's stupid father," I burst out. "The baby was probably alive all along. Only, the man was too stupid to see it."

Someone knocked.

I couldn't summon the energy to open the gate.

Since Lata was out delivering an order of homemade pickle, Ammamma got to her feet. She wiped away her tears and tucked in the end of her sari at her waist. Before she could get to the gate, it was pushed open.

"Anyone home?" the village headmaster asked, stepping into the courtyard.

"You!" Ammamma shouted shrilly.

The cow mooed its displeasure.

"You ruined my Pullamma's life," Ammamma exclaimed, veins popping out in her forehead. "How dare you show your face around here?"

Headmaster *garu* looked startled. "What did I do?"

"You filled Pullamma's head with a lot of rubbish, is what you did," she said, voice rising. "Education will make her life better, you said."

That was unfair. Headmaster *garu* had never claimed I'd amount to anything – it was Lata he'd pinned his hopes on. Besides, what did this have to do with The Incident?

But Ammamma was too angry for such nuances. "Now people are saying she is a Goddess."

"I just came to see how Pullamma was coping."

"Somehow that baby came alive at Pullamma's feet. Your

education," she shouted, unstoppable now, like the waters from the spillway of an overflowing dam. "Did it help my Pullamma? *Hanh*? It ruined her life, did it not, you pompous fool? You stay away from me, you bringer-of-bad-fate! Thinking you can use your fancy education to change centuries of tradition. *I* didn't want to send my girls to school. *You* said it would change their lives." Ammamma wiped away an angry tear. "It certainly changed Pullamma's life, didn't it?"

"But this is all superstition," Headmaster *garu* said, hands fluttering like aimless butterflies. "You and I know she is no Goddess. Ignorance breeds superstition. If we educated more girls, we wouldn't be in such a situation."

"Education," Ammamma screamed. "He says education."

I clutched my chest. Ammamma never shouted like this. Never.

"Get out of my house, you... you..." She grabbed the floor knife and waved it threateningly. "If you show your black face around here again, I will personally separate your head from the rest of your body. I will make your wife a widow. Then we will see how lives get changed."

TEN

Ten minutes after Headmaster *garu* hustled out, the courtyard gate rattled again. Ammamma was still upset, Lakshmi *garu* not inclined, so I forced myself up.

I opened the gate, and Malli's mother-in-law to-be fell at my feet. "Oh Goddess, please do me the honour of giving your sister, Malli, in marriage to my son."

Stumbling in my haste to get away, I darted behind Ammamma and burrowed my face in her shoulder. My heart galloped in panic.

"Please, Savitri *garu*," Ammamma said. Her voice sounded scratchy. "Please get up, and have a seat." She pointed at the cot.

Savitri *garu* got to her feet. "How can I sit in the presence of the Goddess?"

Her husband, Nagabhushan *garu*, seemed to have no such compunctions. He wiggled on the itchy coir cot till he found a comfortable position, then tucked his feet under him.

"I don't know what happened," I burst out. "But I did not give that child life. I'm not a Goddess."

The father-in-law to-be stuffed tobacco in the side of his mouth and started to chew. His wife said to Ammamma, "Please do our family the honour of giving your oldest granddaughter in marriage to our second son."

"I am honoured to accept the proposal."

"I would like to request that Goddess Pullamma bless the wedding."

What was she saying?! "No, no, no!" I clapped my hands over my ears.

"Hush, Child," Lakshmi *garu* said, pulling my hands away.

Ammamma's face turned grey. "My Pullamma is an innocent young girl." Her voice wobbled. "Please don't ruin her life with such demands. If people begin to think of her as a Goddess, who will marry her?"

When the woman didn't respond, Ammamma turned to the husband, voice breaking. "I'll give you our only cow in dowry. Have pity on a widow. Let my Pullamma be."

"Ammamma!" How would we survive without the money the cow brought in?

"Our son will marry your granddaughter on the 24th," Nagab-hushan *garu* said. "With Goddess Pullamma in attendance."

"I'm no Goddess," I screamed. "I'm just a normal girl. I am no Goddess." Ammamma put an arm around me, hugging me tightly to her side. Lakshmi *garu* tried to put a hand over my mouth.

My breath started to come in short bursts. "I'm no Goddess." I pushed Lakshmi *garu's* hand away.

She tried to hold my arm down.

I shoved her aside.

She gave me a resounding slap.

I sank to the floor, and dropped my head to my knees.

Lakshmi *garu* said, "When do we hand the dowry over?"

With some effort I moved my head to look up at Ammamma, willing her to distance herself from this alliance. But Ammamma said nothing. She didn't meet my eyes, either.

"Taking money from the house of a Goddess?" Savitri *garu* hit her open mouth with a palm. "*Siva! Siva!* How could we commit such a sacrilege?" In contrition, she slapped her cheeks with both hands.

I was stunned. This woman genuinely believed I was a Goddess!

"But –" Ammamma began.

"We will pay for the wedding."

Ammamma opened her mouth, then closed it.

Lakshmi *garu's* eyes almost popped out.

Nagabhushan *garu* got up, grabbed his wife's arm and pulled her to the cowshed. I couldn't hear what was being said, but could tell it was a heated discussion.

Savitri *garu* turned to us and said, "We'll have the wedding in our village, as previously discussed. In addition, we will bear all the wedding expenses."

Ammamma's eyes glazed over.

Lakshmi *garu* gave Ammamma a triumphant glance.

Nagabhushan *garu* sat on the cot heavily, expression unhappy.

"If you really believe I'm a Goddess," I said to Savitri *garu*, "why is your husband sitting in my presence? Why isn't he falling at my feet, *hanh*?"

"Pullamma," Lakshmi *garu* said in warning.

Nagabhushan *garu* looked up, face devoid of expression.

"Pullamma *Devi* will preside over the wedding," he intoned. "And Kondal Rao *garu* will be our honoured guest."

I sank to the floor, watching in a daze as Malli's in-laws to-be finalized all the details. Then it was time for them to leave. Savitri *garu* fell at my feet. "Bless this union, Oh Goddess!"

"Come, come," Nagabhushan *garu* said from the courtyard gate. I watched the back of the woman's head. She got up and said something to me, the palms of her hands joined together. Her lips moved, but I heard no sound. She touched my feet once more and left.

Ammamma tried to get me to move, but my limbs were frozen. She hadn't committed to having me preside over the wedding, but I was devastated by her betrayal all the same. This Goddess thing wasn't as funny as I'd thought. People were either afraid of me, or in awe. My best friend wouldn't talk to me. How would I ever get a husband now?

Visions of oracle Ranga Nayakamma haunted me. Her children were alternately tormented and ostracized in school. Who wanted to be friends with someone so scandalous? The villagers were split between Ranga Nayakamma being a joke, or Goddess-incarnate. I didn't want to end up the village joke. Or its Goddess, for that matter.

Ammamma unrolled her sleeping mat and lay down across from me.

"How could you?" I said. "How could you finalize the wedding after they put me in such a position?"

"See it from my side." Ammamma's eyes begged forgiveness. "They aren't asking for dowry, they are even paying for the wedding. Think of the money we'll save. We'll be able to use all of that for your wedding, and Lata's."

"And how will you marry me off? By finding me a God?"

Ammamma had no answer.

"So you're going to sacrifice the life of one granddaughter for the benefit of the other two?"

Ammamma covered my mouth with her hand. "Say good things,

Child," she begged. "The Goddess issue is out of the hands of even Malli's in-laws. People are beginning to think of you as a Goddess. Nothing I do, or say, will change this."

"So you might as well take advantage of it, and get two grand-daughters married off. If the life of the third one is ruined, well... too bad."

Ammamma broke down. *"Yedukondalavada!* Oh, Lord of the Seven Hills! The sins of my previous births must have been of immense magnitude that such great misfortune has befallen my grandchild! I don't know whether to be happy at my Malli's good fortune, or be terrified at my Pullamma's horrifying one."

I started to cry, too. Ammamma stopped her crying and looked at me. Her helplessness scared me as nothing else could have.

ELEVEN

Two more days went by. Each time I stepped out of the house – to the village shop, to the temple, or for some other errand – people fell at my feet. I waved my hand over their heads, not sure what I was supposed to be doing. A few thrust money in my hands. Parents of my friends no longer welcomed me in their homes. They sought my blessings, or looked at me fearfully. Elders no longer scolded me. They gave me gifts, instead.

Lata continued with her nasty comments.

All Ammamma did was weep. I wish she'd let Malli come home from our relatives' house so I'd have someone sensible to talk to. But Ammamma didn't want the scandal touching my older sister, didn't want to give her prospective in-laws any reason to back out of the alliance.

Unable to take any more of this, I stormed out of the house.

I saw my schoolteacher out for his stroll. "Master *garu*." I waved desperately, trying to catch his attention.

His eyes darted from side to side, like a trapped squirrel's, before he acknowledged me. "Yes?" But he wouldn't meet my eyes.

"Please, Master *garu*. Everyone is behaving so strangely with me. You've always said we shouldn't be superstitious. You, of all people, should know I am just an ordinary girl, no special powers, no nothing. The very people who caught me by the ear and dragged me home to Ammamma, complaining about a stolen guava, or a plucked flower, are now avoiding me." My voice broke. "They don't know if I am really a Goddess-incarnate, or possessed by the devil."

"I have to go," my teacher said.

I watched him hurry away. Could it be true? Was I really a Goddess? I shook my head at the stupidity. I walked around the village. Everywhere, people rushed at me, fell at my feet. So many people, so many of them strangers.

"Seetamma!" Lakshmi *garu* called out from the courtyard.

"I'm in the kitchen." Ammamma squatted by the earthen stove on the floor.

I sat by her, waiting for the pot of rice to bubble over. I wasn't particularly hungry, but eating lunch would give me something to do.

Lakshmi *garu* burst into the kitchen. "People are gathered outside your compound wall." Her voice sounded odd.

"Whatever for?" Ammamma swiped a hand across her forehead, leaving behind a swathe of coal-soot.

"For Pullamma's *darsanam*." Lakshmi *garu*'s eyes feverish were with excitement. "They want an audience with the Goddess."

Ammamma fell back against the steel bin of water.

Lakshmi *garu*'s husband, Murty *garu*, followed his wife in. "I have to be honest, it isn't looking good out there," he said.

Later that afternoon Lata and I climbed the staircase that ran the length of the courtyard, trying to get a count of how many people waited for an audience with me, their 'Goddess.'

The line of devotees went through the village square, snaked past the post office, and disappeared in the direction of the Durga temple. I walked down the stairs on rubbery legs, across the courtyard, to the veranda. I sank onto the mat next to my grandmother.

Lakshmi *garu* and Murty *garu* sat on another mat. Murty *garu* leaned against the wall behind, eyes scanning the courtyard. Thank God, the walls were too high for people to see inside.

"How many people?" Ammamma said.

"I don't know," Lata said. "The line is going back past the temple, maybe beyond the school." For once, she had a frightened look on her face.

The voices outside grew louder.

Ammamma joined her palms together and raised them above her head to the pantheon of Gods on the wall of the front room, visible through the window. "*Yedukondalavada, Venkata Ramana, Govinda!* What did we do to incur your wrath? Why are you testing us like this?"

Chanting of some kind had started up beyond the walls of the courtyard. We strained to hear what was being said. "Open up. Open up," the devotees chanted in rhythm from the other side of the gate, their combined voices drifting up over the courtyard walls. "Give us *darsanam* of the Goddess."

Ammamma looked at Lakshmi *garu*. "What do we do?"

"Let them in," Lakshmi *garu* said. Her eyes shone.

"What are you saying, Lakshmi?" her husband said. "Think of that the poor child."

I slumped against the wall across from Ammamma, struggling to blank out my thoughts. The chants increased in volume.

"Think about it. They've been queuing up all day," Lakshmi *garu* said. "Patiently waiting their turn. You think they'll go away without receiving an audience?"

"What do we do? What do we do?" Ammamma twisted the free end of her sari between her hands.

Another roar went up. "Pullamma Devi!"

I broke down. "Ammamma, please don't make me do this. I promise to be good. I'll milk the cow and wash her, cook and clean. I'll get up in the middle of the night to fill water, no need for help. I'll practice to be more ladylike. I don't care if I never get married, I will take care of you in your old age. Just don't make me do this."

Ammamma closed her eyes, but the tears leaked through.

"Pullamma Devi!" The roar was louder now, scarier than the time the dam up the river had breached, hurtling a wall of water towards the village, ravaging everything in its path. *God, I'd rather be in the path of raging waters, than in front of raging devotees.*

"Give us your *darsanam*! Pullamma Devi! Pullamma Devi!"

The gate to the courtyard began to rattle.

Ammamma jerked her head to the gate, her mouth a wrinkly 'O'.

The five of us watched in horror as the gate was pushed more and more. It gave way. Hordes of frenzied devotees ploughed across the fifty feet to the veranda – the village sweeper, the parents of my classmate Vanita, the flower seller. "Where are you, Pullamma Devi?" they cried. "Bestow your mercy upon us. Give us your *darsanam*."

I cowered on the mat, cheek pressed against the wall, trying to make myself smaller.

Lakshmi *garu* grabbed me by the shoulders and swung me sideways. "Gods should sit facing the East." She settled next to me and raised an arm. "Seek relief from your deepest pain here. Come with a clean heart. Be blessed by the Goddess."

Dozens of hands reached for me – the temple priest, the village shop keeper, and the one that shocked me the most – my former teacher.

I rested my chin on upraised knees, trying to hide my face in my half-sari.

They came at me from all sides, heads bent, touching my feet, while the others continued the chant, "Bless us, bless us." The rich, and not-so-rich. Young men, and elderly women. All manner of people. They jostled each other as they brought out their incenses and their bells, their sweets and their money. As each person passed by me, Lakshmi *garu* guided my hand to the tops of their heads in blessing. She accepted the offerings on my behalf, placing the money and the jewellery in neat piles. The rest, she shoved aside.

I watched from the corner of my eye as the piles at my feet – coconuts, and saris, and flowers, and everything else – grew. A few, frenzied worshippers produced scissors, snipping off their hair to place the locks directly on my feet. My toes twitched from the itchy hair. The scent of burning incense, crushed flowers and overripe bananas mingled with sweat from the people to make me feel sick.

News of my 'miracle' seemed to have spread, because strangers, perhaps from neighbouring villages, poured into our courtyard. I had always thought of our courtyard as huge. Now I felt suffocated.

They thronged for my audience.

"Cure my daughter's cancer," the doctor from three villages over sobbed at my feet. I stared down at him in shock. He was the doctor. Why was he asking me for help?

"Curse my wife. She ran away with her lover," my teacher said, face hard. For the first time in my life I felt intense distaste for gossip.

The postman shoved the teacher aside, and fell at my feet. "Find a good groom for my daughter, Oh Pullamma Devi!"

If I had those kinds of powers, I'd have got one for myself, wouldn't I?

Devamma pushed through to making an offering of guavas. The very fruit my friends and I had routinely stolen from her tree, and had our ears twisted for.

Murty *garu* watched for a while, then took charge. "Form two lines, one for the ladies and the little ones, one for the men. No need to trample each other. Don't fall on Pullamma, stay back, stay back."

A few men separated from the crowds, and started herding people in lines. The line moved in a 'U' – people came from one side, made their offerings, and exited from the other. Finally, I felt as if I weren't suffocating.

The day lengthened. I sat in a daze, feeling removed from it all. This wasn't happening to me. That didn't seem to dampen the ardour of my devotees. They came, and they came, and they came. Lakshmi *garu* must have guided my hands in blessing to a few hundred heads that day. She didn't seem to tire, because she had a constant smile on her face.

I didn't say a word. After a while the faces began to blur.

I blanked my mind, trying to visualize myself walking by the river, stick in hand, chasing Chinni and her goats. The sounds outside my head swirled around, not touching me, leaving me in a curious vacuum.

I felt myself being shaken. I blinked.

"Look," Ammamma hissed.

I found Kondal Rao *garu* at my feet. He lay prone for quite a few minutes before being helped up by his swarthy henchmen. He raised a hand at the clamorous crowd. The noise died away. Turning partially toward me, still facing the gathering of devotees, he began to sob noisily. "Oh Pullamma Devi," he cried. "You have showered me with such blessings. By making an appearance in your earthly form in my constituency, you have shown the world my chosen path is the right one."

"Jai Kondal Rao *garu*," a henchman roared. Long live Kondal Rao *garu*.

"Jai Kondal Rao *garu*," the crowd roared back.

A man hobbled up on crutches.

Kondal Rao *garu* stepped back.

The cripple touched my feet. "My legs have failed me. Cure me, Oh Devi."

Lakshmi *garu* guided my hand to the top of his head.

The cripple closed his eyes for a long moment. When he opened them, he bowed to me, and rested a foot on the ground. An expression of wonder swept over his face. He shoved one crutch aside, then the other.

The crowd watched with bated breath.

He took a step, then another, then another. He walked ten steps, circling back to me. He fell at my feet. "Pullamma Devi has cured me. For the first time, I can walk." He was overcome.

"Jai Pullamma Devi," Kondal Rao *garu* said.

"Jai Pullamma Devi," the crowd roared back.

I had cured him? I had those kinds of powers? I looked at Ammamma.

She stood to a side with Lata and Murty *garu*, face ashen.

First the baby, then this cripple. When the first miracle occurred, I'd been too innocent to recognise it. One miracle, I could overlook. But two? A sense of awe at my own power enveloped me. Kondal Rao *garu* was right. I was a Goddess. I sat up straight, filled with sense of purpose. *Maybe I should stand up to give my devotees darsanam.* Everyone deserved an audience with me. I struggled to my feet. Hours of sitting in the same position had caused my legs to go numb.

Ammamma rushed forward and grabbed my arm. "Pullamma Devi needs to meditate now," she announced to my devotees. She started to drag me into the house.

I tried to pull free. "Ammamma, I need to cure the suffering of these poor people. They need me. I can't just walk away –"

Ammamma held my arm so tightly, it hurt. "She will give audience again at seven a.m. tomorrow."

Kondal Rao *garu's* nostrils flared, but he stepped aside.

"This way," Murty *garu* said, pointing a hand at the gate. Obediently the devotees bowed before me, and began to file out of the courtyard.

Kondal Rao *garu* joined the exodus.

I watched the leaving devotees with a sense of panic. What was my grandmother doing? "Ammamma! Everyone's leaving."

"Not now, Pullamma."

Why was Ammamma doing this? What would happen to my devotees? How could I let them down? All of a sudden I felt deflated, unable to move, unable to respond. Thoughts seemed to have been sucked from my head. Ammamma walked me past the huge piles of offerings – sweets, coconuts, money, gold and silver ornaments, hair.

I could hear soft sounds of weeping. It occurred to me much later that the person weeping was me.

Over the next few days, news of my miracles trickled in. A woman whose jaw I'd touched was cured of cancer. A man, on whose documents I'd hovered a finger, won his case after a twenty year fight in the courts. Four miracles that I knew of. How many others that I knew nothing about?

Ammamma wasn't letting me do anymore audiences. She had told the devotees that I was in meditation, and was not to be disturbed. What could I do? My poor devotees were desperate for an audience with me, and here I sat, trapped by an unreasonable grandmother.

Ammamma had no cancer I could cure, no court cases I could help win. How was I going to convince her that the powers I possessed were very real?

TWELVE

lang! Clang!

The wall clock clamoured twelve, shattering the stillness of the night.

Ammamma sat in one corner of the veranda breathing through her mouth, head thrown back, tracking the motion of the fan with her eyes.

Lakshmi *garu,* and her husband, Murty *garu,* sat next to each other, staring bleary-eyed in different directions.

I watched Lata's head bob when sleep got the better of her, followed by jerky wakefulness – till her head fell to a side again. I huddled next to Lata, head on my knees, feverishly trying to come up with ways out of my predicament. The devotees outside were desperate for an audience with me. I had so much wisdom to impart to them, it was only natural they would repay me with gold, jewellery, silk saris, and money – so much money!

The Vedas, the Upanishads – all the ancient texts that had answers to life's deeper questions – did they have nothing on dealing with unyielding, unreasonable, stubborn grandmothers? Did Ammamma not realise she was keeping me from the fame and fortune due to me?

To think I'd have been satisfied with a good husband, and a municipal water connection that supplied water during daylight hours.

The gate rattled. I looked up, exhaustion mingling with hope.

"Pullamma, go inside," Ammamma ordered.

What, she was going to order me, a Goddess, around? At the look on her face, I scrambled to my feet. Lakshmi *garu* and Murty *garu* exchanged a quick glance.

"Let me see who it is," Murty *garu* said in a fake hearty voice. "If it is the devotees, I'll send them on their way." Taking a deep breath, he headed to the gate, opening it cautiously.

It was just Headmaster *garu.* I sat down, heart settling.

"You!" Ammamma jumped up, blood rushing to her face, tiredness forgotten for the moment. "Didn't I tell you not to blacken my doorstep with your face again?"

Headmaster *garu* was dishevelled, unusual for a man who took pride in his appearance. He was never seen in anything but a pristine white *kurta* and a stiffly starched *pancha;* now, both these articles of clothing looked like they'd lost a bout with the frisky goat by the tea shack.

A tallish young man, dressed in citified clothes of pants and shirt, followed him in.

Lata bobbed her head from Headmaster *garu* to Ammamma, and back again.

"Please," Headmaster *garu* said, palms of his hands joined together. "I feel terrible for the trouble Pullamma is in. I am only trying to help."

"What trouble?" I said.

No one paid attention to me.

"God save me from the likes of you." I could tell Ammamma's heart wasn't in the scolding. She raised her joined palms above her head. "Leave us alone to our misery. I don't know why the *Yedukondalavadu* is testing us so."

For Ammamma, every setback in life was a test set by the *Yedukondalavadu*, that God residing on the Seven Hills of Tirupati.

"Give me five minutes," Headmaster *garu* begged. Pushing aside the rickety chair, he sank onto the straw mat on the floor. "Five minutes. That's all I ask." He leaned against the leg of the chair, and rubbed his eyes with the heel of his palms.

"Why should I?"

"Remember Renuka?"

"I remember my husband and son-in-law, too, those non-men. What of it?"

I shuddered and closed my eyes, trying not to think of Renuka *pinni*, not succeeding. Three or four years ago I'd watched Renuka *pinni*, childhood friend of my mother's, run through the streets of our village – clothes torn, body full of welts – sobbing in terror as a frenzied mob pursued her. She fell at our doorstep, bleeding profusely, begging for shelter.

Ammamma closed the gate on her, and leaned against it, tears rolling down her cheeks.

"Why didn't you help her?" Malli cried, as Lata and I cowered behind our older sister.

Years later, Ammamma's reply still had the power to haunt.

"She went beyond our help when she became a witch," she said of the loving woman who'd helped keep our mother's memory alive.

An hour later Renuka *pinni* was dead – stoned by the hysterical mob. Ammamma's intervention might not have made any difference, but at least *Pinni* would have known we cared.

Now Headmaster *garu* said, "Kondal Rao was behind that incident."

What was wrong with Headmaster *garu*?

Ammamma snorted.

"It is true," he insisted. "He planted the dead chicken, and the heap of *kumkum* at Renuka's doorstep."

I was shocked. In my mind the red *kumkum* powder belonged on the foreheads of married women. To think this, combined with dead chicken, was a sign of witches...

"But Shankar said his wife was behaving abnormally due to Renuka's sorcery."

"And I'll say the angle of your nose is causing my granddaughter to come only second in class, instead of her normal first."

Ammamma made a face.

"Easy to blame Shankar's wife's running away on Renuka. But the fact is she ran away because of brutal beatings by her husband."

"But the villagers proved Renuka was a witch, didn't they? When they demanded that she put her hand over fire as a test of purity?"

"Which person do you know whose hand won't burn when put on fire, *hanh*?" He shook his head in despair. "That girl grew up with your daughters. How could you not believe in her innocence?"

"What can I do if the devil possesses someone's soul?"

"Like it has possessed Pullamma's?" he said softly.

Oh no! I was possessed by the devil? I wasn't a Goddess, after all? My heart started to thump. Ammamma had a scared look on her face for the briefest instant. Then she squared her shoulders, as if gearing for battle.

Headmaster *garu* paused for a second before adding, "That's what the villagers are beginning to say, you know. The ones who're not convinced she's a Goddess, that is."

"They don't know what they're talking about." Ammamma dismissed an entire village with the toss of her head. "You haven't said what this has got to do with my granddaughter's predicament."

"Kondal Rao is behind the escalating frenzy of Pullamma's Goddess-hood."

"I'll doubt my friend's husband, or what?" Ammamma gave a caustic smile. "The past few days have been overwhelming for my granddaughter, I grant you, but the curiosity will die soon enough."

I looked at Ammamma in amazement. Wasn't this the same lady who'd been crying over my fate?

"He has been bringing in people by the truckloads."

Ammamma harrumphed. "A few people from the village don't make a truckload."

"It does." Headmaster *garu*'s voice rose in frustration. "If you're trucking people in from the surrounding districts."

"Pray, what will these truckloads of people do?"

"Consecrate the birth of their Goddess, of course."

Thirteen

A mmamma's face drained of colour.

"Kondal Rao is searching for land to build Pullamma a temple, as we speak," Headmaster *garu* said. "The head-counts pouring into the village are mostly daily wage earners, quite happy to do their leader's bidding, and wave at the television cameras in return for a day's pay, and free country liquor."

So I was a Goddess, after all?

Ammamma didn't seem convinced, however, because she blindly felt for the cot behind her, and collapsed on it. Why didn't Ammamma realize if I had my own temple, it would be so much easier on all of us? My devotees would be able to seek me out, I would be able to do what I had arrived on the earth for.

"You better believe the seriousness of it," Headmaster *garu* said. "In Renuka's case, Kondal Rao planned the whole thing after her husband's death. After all, who is an easier prey than a widow? Witch-hunting in the olden days might have been due to fear and ignorance, but in these times, greed plays the bigger part."

"But Kondal Rao *garu* is my friend's husband!"

"And that makes him a good man?"

Headmaster *garu* leaned forward, tone urgent. "Kondal Rao is diabolically ambitious – he makes Shakuni look like a thumb-sucking innocent. He will stop at nothing to get what he wants. He is desperate to become a Minister in the State Government. Has for years."

Headmaster *garu* wasn't saying anything that Jhampaiah, the labourer, hadn't already told us. But Kondal Rao *garu* couldn't be bad. He *knew* I was a Goddess.

"What does this have to do with my Pullamma?"

"Goddess by his side. Elections around the corner. What do you think?"

"What do my powers have to do with elections?" I was confused.

"Pullamma, Child, you have no powers." Headmaster *garu*'s voice was gentle.

"But I saw it with my own eyes, I saw that man throw his crutches away, and walk again."

"He's Kondal Rao's man. Never had a problem with his legs."

"But... but... doctors did the test. That woman didn't have cancer."

"That's right, and she didn't have cancer when she sought your blessings, either. Kondal Rao has been sending his people with made-up ailments to trick people into believing you have miraculous powers."

"What about Ranga Nayakamma? She said I was a Goddess."

"She'll say anything for a crate of whiskey."

"Oh!"

"He's also behind the miracle rumours."

Ammamma began to moan.

"This young man came in search of me late last night," Headmaster *garu* said, indicating the younger man leaning against a veranda column. "He has horrifying tales to tell about Kondal Rao's various attempts to grab power."

What am I going to do, God?

"Where does he get the authority to pass judgment on someone like Kondal Rao *garu, hanh*?" Lakshmi *garu* said.

"Srikar is Kondal Rao's only grandson."

Lakshmi *garu* closed her mouth abruptly.

My heart thumped. Kondal Rao *garu's* grandson. That couldn't be good.

"You've grown up," Ammamma said. "I didn't recognize you."

Srikar was already working in the city when we visited his grandparents in the village, so I'd never seen him. He looked too nice to be related to someone like Kondal Rao, no more respectful *garu* for him. How could I have been foolish enough to have been taken in by that vile man?

The younger man bent and touched Ammamma's feet.

Ammamma put her hand on his head in an automatic gesture of blessing.

"If his grandfather is as wicked as you say, should the boy be here at all?" Lakshmi *garu* said.

"First of all," Headmaster *garu* said, "you need to believe Kondal Rao is a dangerous man."

"But he is helping my Malli get married!" Ammamma said.

I gritted my teeth. Hadn't Headmaster *garu* just gone over how Kondal Rao had tricked me?

Headmaster *garu* took a deep breath. "He is here to marry Pullamma, if you are willing. No dowry."

"Who is?" Ammamma asked.

Headmaster *garu* clicked his tongue. "Srikar, of course."

I raised my head, not trusting I'd heard right.

"What is the need?" Lakshmi *garu* said. "Kondal Rao *garu* gave Pullamma the power, and the money. This, when she had no other options in life. He helped her. What's wrong with that?"

"My grandfather is manipulating Pullamma through that oracle," Srikar said. "That's what is wrong."

"If people really believe Pullamma is a Goddess, why would she need someone else to interpret her actions?" Ammamma said.

"Because it is convenient for Kondal Rao," Headmaster *garu* said. "It also helps that Pullamma hasn't spoken out loud during her audience."

All because I hadn't opened my mouth? But what could I have done? Nothing wise had come to my tongue.

"Seetamma *garu,* what's your answer?" Headmaster *garu* prompted Ammamma.

"To what?"

"Will you give Pullamma in marriage to Srikar?"

My stomach lurched. He was really willing to marry me? Could he not see how black I was?

"But why?" Ammamma asked.

"I prefer not to sit back and watch as he ruins yet another life," Srikar said.

I studied him. Could he really mean it?

"That man is your grandfather," Lakshmi *garu* said.

"Don't I know?" Srikar's jaw tightened. "We're talking about the man who seized all of Renuka *garu*'s lands and emptied out her bank accounts. When I close my eyes each night, it is her blood I see on my conscience."

"You'd believe that of your own grandfather?" Ammamma clapped her mouth in horror.

"I wish I could say 'no.' But I've been hearing rumours for years. When I finally set out in search of the truth, I found out more than I'd ever wanted to." His eyes looked bleak. "Much as I'd like to, I can't deny his involvement anymore."

"What about your parents?" Lakshmi *garu* demanded. "Do you

think it would make them happy if you ran off with a dowry-less girl? They must have spent hundreds of rupees raising you, educating you. The girl you marry will enjoy the fruits of their labour. Don't they deserve to get some of that money back?"

Lakshmi *garu* never forgot to talk like the mother of sons.

"And... Pullamma is so... black. Don't you deserve better?"

"Lakshmi!" Murty *garu* gave me an apologetic look.

Lakshmi *garu* shrugged.

"Srikar's father died a few years ago," Headmaster *garu* said to Lakshmi *garu*. "His mother disappeared when he was two. No one knows where."

I considered Srikar. Something we had in common. I didn't have parents, either.

Headmaster *garu* turned to Ammamma. "Please don't argue just for the sake of arguing, Seetamma *garu*. Time is of essence now. Accept this offer of marriage."

"But he isn't tall enough for her," Ammamma wailed.

Headmaster *garu* worked his mouth, but nothing came out.

Despite the thick tension, I giggled. The look of incredulity on Headmaster *garu's* face was comical. He shook his head before finally finding his voice. "We're trying to prevent Pullamma's life from being ruined, and you are comparing heights? Forgive me for saying this, Seetamma *garu*, but have you lost your mind?"

"No... no... of course not," Ammamma stammered.

"We can't afford to waste time," Srikar said, his voice sounding more strained than ever. "Don't underestimate my grandfather. Come morning, he'll be here with a new plan, which could even place Pullamma's life in danger."

I suddenly realized this wasn't easy for him.

"My grandfather thinks he can manipulate people's lives to suit his own. Our family won't be able to wash away the sins of Renuka *garu's* murder for a hundred generations."

"Have you thought about what will happen when he finds out his grandson has married his Goddess?" Ammamma asked.

"If I do end up marrying Pullamma, I'll have to cut off contact with my grandparents."

"And that is all right with you?"

"I'm perfectly fine if I never again set eyes on my grandfather. But my grandmother... I'm all she has." He cleared his throat.

"Still, I wouldn't be able to live with myself if inaction on my part caused something to happen to Pullamma."

"Your grandfather will find out eventually."

"I don't doubt it. But, by then, Pullamma will be my wife. As member of his family, I hope she'll come under his protection."

"You can't be sure," Lakshmi *garu* said, "and yet, you want us to place our girl in your hands?"

I was astounded. When had I been *her* girl?

"Who can be sure of anything?" Srikar said. "But what is the alternative?"

"The risk is too big," Ammamma said.

"It is one we'll have to take," Srikar said. "I'm not so naïve as to think he will be happy about the disappearance of his Goddess. But realistically, I'm the best chance your granddaughter has."

"How can you be so sure?" Ammamma asked, wiping sweat from her face, despite the chill of the night.

"Do you see any other way?"

Ammamma's shoulders slumped in defeat.

"Then give us your blessings."

"Kondal Rao *garu* can go from MLA to Cabinet Minister," Lakshmi *garu* said. "Even Chief Minister. Who knows?" She wagged a finger at Ammamma. "Seetamma, don't bring misfortune upon your head by taking on such powerful people. Let Pullamma be a Goddess. Where is the harm, I say? It will set Malli and Lata up for life. You, yourself, will be able to lead a life of comfort. And it's not like Pullamma will be left destitute or anything. She'll have all the clothes she desires, all the jewellery, all the comforts she could ever think of. Which fool would walk away from something like this?"

Please, God, if you do just one thing for me, shut this woman up.

"What about a life free from manipulation?" Srikar cut in. "What about a husband, children, a house of her own?" He turned to Ammamma. "Don't you want all these for your granddaughter?"

"Ranga Nayakamma is as good as a Goddess," Lakshmi *garu* said. "She is married. She has children."

Headmaster *garu* snorted. "Ranga Nayakamma is a joke. Besides, her so-called visions started after she was married. Which young man will have the guts to come forward and marry Pullamma, the

Goddess, *hanh*?" He looked earnestly at Ammamma. "Srikar is the only young man you will find willing, given what is going on now."

"No dowry, the girl black like anything." Lakshmi *garu* darted a quick glance at Murty *garu*.

Murty *garu*'s lips tightened. "Seetamma *garu*," he said. "Pullamma can't possibly spend the rest of her life giving *darsanams*."

At this moment I could have forgiven Murty *garu* anything, even being married to Lakshmi *garu*. A deep tremble started up my legs, then spread to my upper body. Ammamma hurried to me and pulled me into her arms. I hid my face in her shoulder.

"Srikar works in Hyderabad," Headmaster *garu* said. "He has a respectable job as a construction supervisor." Headmaster *garu* looked at his watch. "It is just past 1:00 o'clock. If we leave immediately, we will be in Hyderabad by morning. We must get them married right away."

Ammamma looked at me.

Not knowing how to react, I turned to Lakshmi *garu* and Murty *garu*, who wore identical expressions of disbelief.

"I don't know what to think," Ammamma said.

"This isn't the time to think, this is the time to act." Headmaster *garu* struggled up. "A car and driver are waiting outside. Let's go."

"Wait," Srikar said, raising a palm.

My heart missed a beat. Had the colour of my skin affected his nobleness?

"We're all making decisions on Pullamma's behalf," he said. "This is her life we're talking about. I want to hear from her that she is ready to come away with me to Hyderabad, to marry me."

I looked at Srikar, shyness forgotten in my shock. Whoever asked a girl what she wanted?

Ammamma appeared as shell-shocked as I felt.

Everyone waited expectantly.

I sneaked another glance at Srikar. My heart skipped another beat. He was slim and nice looking, almost as tall as me. A lock of hair fell endearingly on his brow. He was as different from his grandfather as an auto-rickshaw's horn was from a cow's. He gave me a small, encouraging smile.

Warmth flooded my chest. I could do worse.

I gave a small nod in the direction of my grandmother, a smile quivering on my lips. Unable to address my husband to-be directly,

I said to Ammamma, "I will never be able to come back?" The finality of it hit me. I started to cry.

"No, Child," Headmaster *garu* said gently. "Not for a while, anyway. Maybe, in a few years, who knows? But I can assure you, you won't find a better boy. Twenty-one years old, and already very responsible. He will take good care of you."

"Ammamma," I said. "If I leave...?"

"Yes, Child?"

"What will happen to Malli's alliance? And the devotees?"

Ammamma's shoulders slumped.

"Let us worry about this, Child," Murty *garu* said. "You worry about getting away."

To Ammamma he said, "Seetamma *garu*, we must move fast." He gave me a gentle push. "Get ready." To Lata he said, "Gather up a few clothes for your sister, a toothbrush, some essentials. Quick, Child."

In the bedroom, I grabbed my best half-sari with sweaty palms, then thrust it aside. As a married woman, I wouldn't be needing them. Instead I pulled out the four saris I shared with Lata, packed one away and wore the other one. The other two I left for Lata.

Lata rushed about the room gathering things.

In a few minutes, I was ready.

Ammamma took my hand and hurried me out.

Lata thrust the bag in my hand and gave me a tearful hug. Today – in our shared terror – would be the closest I'd feel to my twin.

"There's no time," Headmaster *garu* said. "The devotees will start to queue up soon."

"Can I come, too?" Lata asked Headmaster *garu*.

"No, Child, you need to stay back with your grandmother. But Hyderabad isn't that far. You can visit when things settle down."

Ammamma handed me some money. "It's not much, I know." She looked apologetic.

"What about the Goddess money?" Lakshmi *garu* said. "The jewellery, the saris..."

At Ammamma's look, her voice trailed away.

"Take this," Murty *garu* said, giving me a figurine of Lord Vinayaka – the destroyer of obstacles, creator of new beginnings. From their altar at home.

I looked at Murty *garu*'s bushy white eyebrows, his kindly eyes brimming with emotion. I bent to touch his feet. He was taken aback, but I could tell he was pleased. "Please take care of Ammamma," I whispered to him.

Murty *garu* nodded.

Ammamma gave me a fierce hug and kissed me on the forehead. "Be happy," she said, voice breaking. She unclenched my fist and put something in, covering my hand with hers.

I opened it to see her diamond earrings – the only jewellery she had left of her mother's. I clung to Ammamma, unable to let go, trying to absorb her warmth, and her love.

"Come, Child," Headmaster *garu* said. "Time to leave."

I gave Lata another quick hug. Heart thumping, I ran to the car and slid into the back seat. I curled up in a foetal ball on the floor of the car as it tore out of the village.

FOURTEEN

Headmaster *garu* sat in the back with me while Srikar sat up front with the driver. After what seemed like hours, Headmaster *garu* leaned over and tapped me on the shoulder. My heart almost stopped. "You can get up, Child," he said. "We are safe now."

My muscles burned as I struggled to the seat. I saw we were on the two-lane State Highway.

"Are you okay?" he asked. "We have a few more hours to go."

I nodded, not trusting my voice. Soon Kondal Rao would be mobilizing his men to track us down.

"Here," Srikar said from the front seat, handing me a bottle of water. A lock of hair fell over his forehead. He smiled lopsidedly, causing my heart to trip.

I smiled back, feeling a little shy. I took the bottle and gulped down half its contents. Returning the bottle, I leaned back and closed my eyes. The events of the last few days seemed to have a touch of unreality. Now that I knew I had no powers, that first day seemed scary, when all those devotees – some of whom I'd known all my life – had stormed into my grandmother's house. When I thought of that throng of people desperate for a glimpse of me, I felt a shudder rip through. After a while, my mind seemed to drift away.

The next thing I knew, we were stopped at a roadside tea-stall. I could see Srikar through the window of the car, sitting on a sagging cot, drinking tea, two flower garlands by his side.

Garlands! He does intend to go through with the wedding.

I made my way to the bathroom, washed my face, reapplied the red *bottu* on my forehead and re-braided my hair. At the tea stall, I stood hesitantly, not sure what to do.

"Breakfast?" Srikar asked.

I nodded, and started to reach into my purse.

"It's okay," he said, smiling.

I flushed and dropped my hand.

After some tea and a plate of steaming, mouth-watering *upma*, we were off again. We reached Hyderabad around 9:00 in the morning. People rushing to offices, children in uniforms rushing to schools, scooters and motorcycles rushing somewhere. Rush, rush, rush. I felt a sudden rush of loneliness. How would I manage without Ammamma and Chinni?

The driver navigated the lanes and by-lanes until we stopped at a small temple.

I got down and tried to walk the cramp out of my leg.

"Are you okay?" Srikar asked.

I nodded.

We went past the temple, to an official looking building in the back.

"What is this?"

"Registrar's office," Headmaster *garu* said. "You're getting married here."

The high arch of doorway led into a long dank corridor with rooms on either side. The doors had various nameplates nailed to them. Headmaster *garu* led us into the third room on the left.

I looked about in dismay. The small room was high ceilinged, with years' worth of cobwebs swaying from above. A scarred desk sat in the middle of the room, behind which was a man wearing thick framed spectacles.

Headmaster *garu* stood in front of the official, but the official continued to read his novel.

"Can you help us?" Headmaster *garu* asked.

"What do you want?" The man looked annoyed at the interruption.

"These youngsters are here to get married."

The man sighed, pushed his spectacles to the top of his head and dragged out a dusty register. "Girl is eighteen?"

I froze. I was only sixteen.

Headmaster *garu* nodded, flushing.

"Boy is twenty-one?"

Srikar handed him his driving licence.

The official pushed some paperwork at us. "Come back in a month's time." He went back to his book.

Headmaster *garu* cleared his throat. "Why don't the two of you wait outside?"

Fifteen minutes later, Srikar and I went back in.

The man pushed a register at us. "Sign here."

Srikar signed.

"Now you sign," he said to me.

"Then what?" My dismay made me bold enough to question an elder.

"Then you're married."

Getting married without Ammamma, Chinni or my sisters by my side was bad enough. But to have this bored official perform our marriage... "Headmaster *garu*?"

"Yes, Child?"

"Can't we get married in the temple outside?"

"Hanuman temple." The official grinned.

Just my luck the nearest temple was that of the bachelor god's. Defeated, I signed the register.

Srikar knotted the *pustela taadu* – a turmeric coated thread, two gold coins at the base – at the nape of my neck.

Headmaster *garu* gave us the garlands.

Srikar bent his head.

I placed the garland around his neck.

He did the same.

We were married.

Headmaster *garu* dropped us off at the auto-rickshaw stand. "May God watch over you." He got into the waiting car. I watched teary-eyed as this last link to the village was cut off.

After the car left, we got in an auto-rickshaw to take us to the flat of Headmaster *garu*'s friend, because we couldn't go to the flat Srikar shared with his friends; it was too dangerous. I looked at the passing traffic, heart heavy. This wasn't how I'd envisioned my wedding, the start to my new life. It hurt so much that I ordered myself to stop that sort of thinking. I tried to imagine the life I was heading to, instead of the one I'd left behind.

I reminded myself that now that I was his wife, I must address Srikar only as "*Yemandi*" – that oblique reference married women had used to address their husbands since the beginning of time.

FIFTEEN

January 1987, Hyderabad

M y new husband and I entered our new home together, right foot first for good luck. I felt a pang. Someone from Srikar's family should have been at the doorway, tray in hand, lighted lamp and sweets welcoming us. Someone from mine should have been a few steps behind, supporting me as I stepped into my new life.

I entered our tiny one-bedroom flat, not sure what to expect. A front room, a miniscule kitchen to the side, a tiny bedroom. No bathroom.

In the bedroom, cobwebs swayed gently in the breeze, in rhythm with the dust motes. I walked over to the window. Branches of a mango tree pushed against the rusted mosquito netting nailed to the window frame. Dust sat on the built-in shelves in the wall, a layer so thick it was a wonder the shelves hadn't crumbled under its weight. A piercing sound startled me. The building shuddered in its wake. I pushed my head against the mud-encrusted mosquito netting, which gave way, raising a wave of dust. I leaned out. Railway tracks ran parallel to the apartment building, on which a train was groaning past.

Then it hit me. Here I was in my own house, married, ready to start life with my husband, when I had never expected to marry. A frisson of pleasure fought its way through my apprehension. I promised myself I would be the very best wife possible. I would cook for Srikar, clean for him, make sure there was never a speck of dust anywhere. His clothes would be spotless, his lunch box filled with the tastiest food I could prepare. I would tightly shut my eyes, do my wifely duty. I would somehow make up to him for my dark skin.

"Pullamma," Srikar said. "I need to go down and talk to the landlord. After that I'll go buy milk, and a few other things. I will be back in an hour. Do you need anything from the market?"

I shook my head with a combination of embarrassment and

pleasure. From now on, even in the minutiae of daily living, our lives would be entwined.

After Srikar left, I pulled out a small hand towel from my bag and started to clean the cement shelves. Another wave of dust rose up, only to fall heavily to the floor.

Just like that, I collapsed.

What am I doing here?

I sank to the floor, struggling to contain my tears. How would I manage? What did I know about being married, anyway? Where were Ammamma and Chinni when I needed them? I dropped my head on my knees, breaking into sobs. Though every person I knew, other than Ammamma, had given up on my marital prospects, I'd harboured secret hopes of getting married. The wedding I'd imagined hadn't been anything like the rushed affair of this morning. In my dreams Ammamma and Chinni would be by my side, supporting me; they'd accompany me to my new marital home, helping to ease the transition. And here I was, in a new place, trying to start off life with a man I hadn't known twenty-four hours ago.

It took some time before I was able to drag myself off the floor. I didn't want Srikar to find me like this. I didn't want him to regret marrying me. Using the edge of my sari, I wiped the dampness from my face, then went back to dusting. A few sneezes later, I could almost tell the colour of the shelves. I dug into my handbag for the idol of Lord Vinayaka that Murty *garu* had given me. I bowed my head, closing my eyes in prayer.

"Hello!"

I turned.

A young woman stood at the door to the flat, a friendly smile on her face. Though she wasn't tall, she was shapely, with braided hair that came down to her waist.

I felt gawky next to her effortless grace. I forced myself to smile back.

"My name is Geeta. Are you going to be living here?"

When I nodded, the other woman clapped her hands childishly. "I'm so glad. It will be so nice to have another young woman in the building." She leaned forward. "You are not from the city?"

I shook my head.

"From the village?"

I nodded.

Geeta frowned. "You don't talk much, do you?"

I laughed. No one had ever said that of me. "Now that I have a new friend, I will have to, won't I?" I felt good, positive even. The stresses of the past few days drained away. I promised myself I would make a good life here with Srikar.

"Where is your husband?" Geeta asked.

I felt warmth flood me when Geeta said *husband.* "He's gone out on some work."

Geeta leaned forward, a curious look on her face. "When did you get married?" The sacred thread around my neck, freshly coated with auspicious turmeric, gave me away. If I had been married longer, the cotton thread would have dulled in colour, or been replaced by gold if we could afford it.

"This morning."

"*Aiyyo*!" Geeta squealed. "Newlyweds! I knew it. You *have* to come to dinner at my house."

"Are you sure?" I was hesitant. "You don't even know us."

"Oh nonsense," Geeta said with a flick of her hand. "We're going to be neighbours, aren't we? Good time to come. My in-laws are away, visiting their other son." She took my hand. "Come, I'll show you where I live."

We walked out into the narrow, grimy corridor overlooking the weed-choked front yard below. Our flat was one of eighteen in Madhuban Apartments – a fancy name for a building of three-room tenements. There were doors on either side of our apartment. "I live on your left," Geeta said. "So you'll come?"

"I will have to check with my husband," I said, trying hard not to grin foolishly.

Sixteen

O n the way to the city, Headmaster *garu* had decided it would be too dangerous for Srikar to return to his old job. Before he left to go back to the village, Headmaster *garu* cautioned us against retaining old ties. He said to Srikar, "Stay away from your old flat. I'll arrange for someone to pack your belongings and bring them to you."

Someone had already packed his belongings and left them outside our door by the time Srikar returned. As Srikar carried the suitcases over the threshold of our new home, he said, "I only bought what we'll need right away. Tomorrow we can buy the rest. Then I will have to start searching for a new job."

"*Yemandi*?" I said hesitantly, feeling a little strange to be joining the ranks of married women, and addressing my husband thus. "Uh... I made a new friend. She has invited us to dinner."

"It's good you're already making friends," he said, placing the suitcases by the wall. "But don't say anything about our circumstances. She's going to want to know why we're here on the day of our wedding, when we should have been with our families. Just smile and evade the question."

I nodded. "Can I ask you something?"

Srikar nodded.

I took a deep breath, trying to gather up the courage. "Why did you marry me? That, too, without a dowry?" The primary reason was to protect me from his grandfather; that much I understood. But I wanted to know if he felt pity for me – the dark, dowry-less girl.

"I found out my grandfather was up to something in your village," Srikar said. "I was scared this might be another Renuka *garu*-like situation, so I came to see for myself. I was part of your audience."

"I didn't know."

"How could you? There were hundreds of people clamouring for your attention. I didn't come up to you. I just watched from the side." He paused. "Despite your obvious terror – or perhaps it was only obvious to me because of what I knew – there was a quiet

dignity about you that drew me. Marrying you was no hardship."
Smiling gently, he put an arm around me.

I smiled back shyly, feeling warmth spread in my chest.

We knocked on Geeta's door at 9:00 that night. "Come in, come in," she said, smiling widely.

Her husband, the stocky Murali, wore a collared, button-down shirt with a lungi wrapped around his waist, in lieu of trousers. You make quite a pair," he said to Srikar. "Like day and night."

"Good, isn't it?" Srikar said with a smile. "Every household should have such a balance."

"Of course, of course," Murali said. "Please come in."

Murali wasn't being rude, I knew. More than a few people would have commented on the contrast in our complexions. Still, it rankled. With a determined smile, I walked in.

Geeta leaned over and whispered, "How did you manage to snag such a cute husband? Good dowry?"

I shook my head, smiling. It would be many years before I learned to be offended by such intrusive questions. For now, it was just the way things were.

Over a noisy dinner, with Geeta's two children shouting to make themselves heard, Geeta regaled Srikar and me with the happenings in our new locality – which milk-diluting milkman to avoid, where to get our clothes ironed without having holes burned in them, who sold the best rice, and so on. Murali seemed friendly, though not nearly as talkative as his wife. I sent up a silent prayer for both Srikar, and my new friends. I thought of my old friend, Chinni. I hoped she was happy, too.

I hope Kondal Rao isn't harassing Ammamma! Don't think about it, don't, don't.

Headmaster *garu*'s last piece of advice, before returning to the village, had been to not look back, so I forced my thoughts away from the village. God had been kind to me. I couldn't let my blessings go to waste.

Dinner was over, and we were back in our flat. I huddled by the window, watching as my new husband unrolled the mat and spread out a bed-sheet on top. My face felt hot and numb.

He smoothed out the creases, sat on it and held out a hand.

"What are you going to do to me?" I bit my inner cheek, trying not to show my terror.

Srikar smiled. "Nothing you don't want me to do."

"That isn't what Ammamma said. She said, if you beat me, I have to put up with it. If you ... you ... whatever you do, I have to close my eyes tight, grind down my teeth, and bear it."

Srikar laughed. "I won't beat you, I promise. And you won't have to do any teeth grinding, either."

I didn't move.

He held out an arm. "Come and sit next to me, at least."

"You won't beat me?"

He shook his head, his lips twitching.

I sat as far away from him as I could, my chin on upraised knees, hands clenched.

"Relax." He fluffed his pillow, and lay down. "Beating you isn't what I had in mind."

I pulled my pillow away from him, and lay down at the very edge of the mat, feeling terrible embarrassment.

"Can I hold your hand?"

"Do I have to?"

"No, you don't have to," he said. I could hear the smile in his voice.

'Be a dutiful wife,' Ammamma's voice in my head commanded. I took a deep breath. "Okay," I whispered.

He pulled me closer.

I let him. My face flushed.

He touched me slowly, looking into my face. His breath felt uncomfortably close.

I shut my eyes tightly, feeling funny. This wasn't anything like Ammamma had warned. This was a good funny.

I opened my eyes. Through the rusted mosquito netting I could see pink streaks across the sky. I scrambled up. Grabbing fresh clothes, I pulled the door to our flat closed and hurried to the bathroom at one end of the corridor. A quick bath and I was back. I pushed the door open. Srikar looked up. He'd freshened up, too. Probably in the bathroom at the other end of the corridor. Unable to meet his eyes, I closed the door. Wordlessly, he pulled me into his arms. I buried my face in his shoulder, feeling a smile tremble on my lips.

SEVENTEEN

Everything in my new life was different – exciting most of the time, overwhelming occasionally. The faster pace of the city. Living in quarters so close that we could hear raised voices from the flat next door. Movie songs fed through outdoor loudspeakers for major Hindu festivals. The amplified prayer call from the nearby mosque at dawn. Over Christmas and Easter, the Church joined in. Auto-rickshaws darting through traffic, unmindful of traffic rules. Cinemas in real theatres. How I wished I could have shared this with Chinni. This, and my newfound knowledge about the pleasures of marriage.

Back when I was still a giggly teen, when Chinni and I were still best friends, when the most vexing problem in our life was which of Chiranjeevi's many movies we liked best, my friend and I had giggled and speculated about what exactly happened between a married couple. I hoped Chinni hadn't had to do any teeth grinding.

In the village, getting up early was something I'd hated. Now I was eager to begin the day, make tasty food for Srikar, iron his clothes, do all those little things a wife did for her husband. I felt great pleasure in having the right to touch him on the shoulder to draw his attention, ask his opinion on a new recipe.

We shopped together, filled water together, laughed together. While I took care of the cooking, Srikar cut the vegetables for me. The first time he picked up a knife, I was shocked. "What are you doing? This is my work!"

"I'm just cutting vegetables, not putting flowers in my hair."

"How can you joke about such a thing? What if Geeta or Sandhya see you?" Sandhya was our neighbour on the other side.

"Pulla, you need to stop worrying about others, start living for yourself."

Bah! What did men know of such things? I made sure the front door was locked when we cooked. Didn't want anyone to think I was harassing my husband. I watched as he put the milk to boil, another thing he did in the kitchen.

"What?" he said.

"I can't believe you are... his grandson."

He gave a short laugh. "I grew up seeing his terrible treatment of my grandmother, as well his own daughter. Then I started to hear things about him that no child should hear – the beatings of people who got in his way, the breaking of bones of others who displeased him, and so on. My grandmother said I must always remember, what kind of a person I became was up to me. I've tried to be as unlike my grandfather as possible."

I was glad he was a good person, but it embarrassed me when he did things that were women's work – he folded the bedclothes and put them away. Once he even came shopping with me for utensils, helping me select a few. While he was paying for them, I slipped into the shop next door, a bangle store.

"What are you looking at?"

I turned at Srikar's voice.

"Oh, nothing." I stepped away.

"Madam was admiring the bangles," the shopkeeper said.

"I... just... I don't need any. Really." *Please, God, don't let him think I am greedy.*

"But you have such plain ones, no design, no nothing," the shopkeeper said. "Madam, take it from me. Nowhere in this whole city will you find such a good collection of bangles."

"Why don't you buy some?" Srikar asked.

I flushed.

"Which ones was my wife looking at?" Srikar asked the shopkeeper.

The man laid out a few.

"Wrap them up," Srikar said.

Feeling a flush of happiness, I took the package.

As I was putting it in my shoulder bag, a man exclaimed, "*Ammavaru!*" and dropped at my feet.

I froze.

The shopkeeper's eyes went round.

"Don't bother my wife!" Srikar grabbed my arm, and pulled me away. Turning to the shopkeeper he said, "All kinds of mental people you run into."

The shopkeeper nodded in sympathy.

The man on the ground looked up in confusion.

"Don't look back," Srikar said to me under his breath, as he marched me to the bus stop.

I was so shaken up by this incident that I shivered all the way home. For a week, I had nightmares.

I stopped going out, fearing I might run into people who'd known me as a Goddess. I spent time with Geeta, instead.

"Why do you patronize that vegetable fellow?" Geeta said. "He's robbing you."

I bought vegetables from the seller who came by each morning with his vegetable laden pushcart – a rolling wooden platform on four slender wheels. He was often accompanied by his wife, who sold leafy greens from the huge wicket basket she carried balanced on her head.

"Go the wholesale market," Geeta said. "Murali buys vegetables there. Much cheaper."

"But it is out of the way for Srikar." I couldn't go out. The risk was too great.

"Take a bus and go yourself. Just because your husband doesn't demand accounts from you, doesn't mean you spend his money recklessly."

"Why don't you come with me?"

Geeta leaned forward, took a quick look over her shoulder and hissed, "The devil who resides in my house won't let me go."

"I'm glad I don't have a mother-in-law sitting on my head." I shuddered. Chinni and I had discussed endless strategies for dealing with mean mothers-in-law. How lucky that I didn't need to bother.

I set off to the bus stop that afternoon, feeling very grown up. I was tired of hiding in the house. I'd surprise Srikar with the money I saved. How proud he would be of me.

At the market, I was overwhelmed, almost choking on the smell of vegetables ripening under the sun. And the shouting and haggling... I wanted to clap my hands over my ears.

We had a wholesale market in the village, too, and many times larger, but this place packed so much in such a tight space.

Mini mountains of vegetables on burlap sacks. Narrow lanes. Vendors shouting out prices, each trying to outdo the other in convincing me that their produce and price were the best.

For the first half hour all I did was wander, trying to get a sense of the place. "Amma, Amma," the vegetable sellers shouted, waving their arms. "Come here, I will give you the best price. Nowhere else will you find such fresh vegetables."

I looked around, eyes darting, not sure where to begin. An old man squatted by his vegetables, smoking a *beedi*, blowing smoke rings in the air. He wasn't demanding my attention, so I went across and picked up a snake gourd the size of Srikar's arm.

"How much?"

"For you, my best price."

We haggled back and forth till we reached a price both of us could live with. I broke the vegetable into three pieces and put it in the plastic basket slung from my forearm. I moved on. An hour later my basket was overflowing, and I had to buy an additional bag for the extra vegetables. But the prices were so good!

Not bad for a village girl. Smiling to myself I dragged the bags along to the bus stop. The street lamps had come on. The bus was pulling away as I reached the stop. With a sigh, I settled on the bench. The next bus lumbered up forty-five minutes later. It wound its way through the city before finally shuddering to a halt a ten minute walk from home. 8 o'clock! I hadn't realized it was so late.

"There you are." Srikar hurried forward and took the bags from me. "I'm glad you told Geeta where you were going. When you weren't on the previous bus, I got worried."

He'd waited forty-five minutes at the bus stop! Warmth flooded my chest. I'd happily give up my dreams of the municipal water connection just to be with Srikar.

Speaking of the municipal water connection, everything else might have changed, but the one constant in my life was the water situation. Municipal water was turned on between 10 p.m. and midnight in our not-so-well-to-do corner of the city. The owner of our building was too cheap to provide a motor to pump water up to each of our flats, so the women gathered by the municipal tap by 9:45 p.m.

"You are all young, can afford to go to bed late," old Rukkamma said, invariably pushing her way to the front of the queue.

"Gossipy old crone," Geeta whispered, not daring to say it to her face. Any gossip worth knowing in Madhuban Apartments filtered its way through old Rukkamma.

As we women awaited our turn at the tap, the men sat on a couple of discarded coir cots, smoking hand-rolled *beedis*, catching up on the day's gossip. A lot of business got transacted around the municipal tap despite the lateness of the hour. Enterprising vegetable sellers brought fresh vegetables in straw baskets balanced on their heads. Banana vendors came with pushcarts, buyers of used newspaper wobbled by on loaded bicycles, calling out – 'pay-paaaar-ye' for paper, women came with shiny steel utensils, ready to bargain them away in exchange for good quality used-clothing.

Every so often, a *bajji* vendor swung by with his rickety, wooden pushcart, frying us kerosene-scented spicy *mirchi bajjis* on the spot, in a shallow pan balanced on a grimy kerosene-fuelled stove. Sandhya, Geeta and I complained about his outrageous prices, but bought the savouries anyway, bouncing the hot *bajjis* between our hands till they cooled enough to eat.

Sometimes fights broke out if the municipal tap on the road, meant for the adjoining building, decided not to dispense water for the evening. People from that building tried to push their way into our courtyard to get to our tap; men from our building blocked their way, insisting their women be the first in line. On those days we finished up as late as 2 a.m.

Even without disruptions, it was close to 11:00 p.m. by the time our turn at the tap came. Then it was multiple trips up the stairs, pots resting on our hips, before we had enough water for washing and cooking. I had to climb two flights of stairs to get to our flat. It was hard work, but over shared hardships and endless cups of tea, a friendship developed between Geeta and me.

My relationship with Srikar also blossomed. He and I started to get more comfortable with each other. "*Yemandi*?" I said to him one day, my mind on the latest recipe I was practicing.

"Hyderabad is a big city, you know," he teased. "Not your little village in the interior. Here it is quite acceptable to call one's husband by name."

I smiled at his dear face, his irresistible one-sided smile, that stubborn lock of hair a constant over his brow. I wasn't so brazen as to call him by name. He gave me an affectionate hug, probably not expecting a response. We settled next to the window, waiting out the rattling train.

"Do you miss the village?"

"A little bit," I said, snuggling up to him. "I feel bad leaving Ammamma with all those devotees, and two granddaughters who might never get married because I ran away."

"Nothing you could have done." He put a finger under my chin and raised my face. "Miss being a Goddess? I can't give you all that money or jewellery, you know."

"I have everything I need right here." I burrowed my face in his shoulder.

Eighteen

Our three-storey building had six flats to each floor, a bathroom on either end of the corridor. Two bathrooms shared between six families. Each bathroom comprised a 4x4 square to wash clothes and bathe in, and a 3x3 square which housed the toilet. Each with its own door. A rusty sink was bolted to the wall between the two doors. Common bathrooms or not, water problems or not, I had no idea it was possible to be this happy.

In my contentment I'd think – if my looks and my name were the price I had to pay to attain Srikar, so be it. Then someone would comment on the colour or my skin, or ask how much dowry I'd brought, and suddenly I'd be wracked by doubts. Did Srikar look at other girls, fair-skinned, and with dowry, and feel cheated? Was I his sacrifice for the sins of his grandfather? He'd never behaved in a manner to cause this doubt, but we women were simple folk. What did we know of the pressures of men?

Srikar had been forced to leave his well-paying job as a site supervisor with a big construction company. The only work he could find in a hurry was as assistant to the supervisor for another site on the outskirts of town. The new job meant more work with less pay, but that didn't bother him. He had big plans for our future. We walked to the park near our house after dark, when the kids of the locality were long in bed. Srikar leaned against a metal slide, while I settled on a swing, and swung my way through grandiose plans.

"We'll form our own construction company," he said. "We won't have to be at the beck and call of others. Let us not rush into having children, Pullamma."

I blushed.

"You should go to college, get a degree. Then we will work together, and build the best company in India."

I was endeared by his silliness. I knew my station in life was to bear heirs; without a male child, I was nothing. That I had studied up to 12th class was unusual in itself. In the village the search for a groom began as soon as a girl hit puberty.

Back in the village, when Headmaster *garu* suggested a second time that Lata be allowed to go on to college, Ammamma had pulled the two of us out of school right in the middle of the school year. It took a solemn promise from him that he wouldn't be putting anymore silly notions into our heads before she would allow us appear for the final exams of 12th class. After that, she wasn't open to negotiation.

So, of course, I knew Srikar was teasing.

What I did do was practice my housekeeping skills. By the time Srikar got home from work, I was ready with hot food. Because he was so appreciative of anything I cooked, I started experimenting – nothing out of the ordinary, just tastier ways of making the same *pulusu, pulihora* and *payasam*. Soon I was cooking so much that the women in our building, and then the women in our locality, started ordering food from me. No one had ever expected anything of me before, so I bloomed from this unexpected attention. I pushed myself to cook better and better. It didn't hurt that Srikar was so encouraging. I was proud the money I earned was a welcome addition to our household budget.

Then it occurred to me to try my hand at pickle-making. At the municipal tap one night I made the suggestion. "We have eighteen flats here, at least eighteen women. Instead of making pickles in each house, why don't we get together and make pickle in the courtyard? The area is big enough to dry the mangoes, and do the pounding."

"Why?" old Rukkamma asked.

"Because the labour involved will seem lighter if all of us do it together."

"And it will be fun." Geeta clapped her hands in glee.

Old Rukkamma looked me up and down. "You're what – eighteen years old?"

"Sixteen," I said.

"Sixteen!" She snorted. "And you are going to teach us how to make pickles? Child, I'm four times your age. I've forgotten more about pickle-making than you'll ever learn."

"Well, I want to join in," Geeta said.

I gave her a smile of thanks.

There was a chorus of acceptances from the other women. After we finished with our water duties, we settled on the steps. There were ten of us, not including Old Rukkamma.

"I can't wait," old Rukkamma said, spitting out red *paan*. "This should be fun."

"Ignore her," Geeta whispered.

I said to the women, "We'll share the costs between the ten of us. If we allocate twenty mangoes per family, that should last us the year." The women nodded. We calculated the amount of ingredients we'd need. Early next morning, Sandhya and I set off for the market. We bought vast quantities of red chillies, rock salt, mustard powder, fenugreek, asafoetida, turmeric and sesame seed oil.

Over the next three days, we spread out thick sheets of plastic in the central courtyard. Two women were assigned to the mortar and pestle. After the women in charge of preparing the chillies cleaned them, pulled off the stems and sun dried them, the women in charge of pounding took over. Huge amounts of chillies were poured into the two-foot diameter mortar. One woman stood on either side. The first woman pounded once with the four foot long pestle, then passed it over to the other woman. Back and forth the pestle went, in rhythm with the singing women, till the red chillies were reduced to a fine powder. Same with the rock salt. Then the turmeric roots. We pounded and sieved, then pounded some more before sun-drying them. Finally, the ingredients were ready.

The next morning, Sandhya and I bought two hundred raw mangoes at the farmer's market after testing to make sure they were very sour. "Are you sure you can handle so many mangoes?" she whispered.

"Back in the village, we did as many as two thousand mangoes in a season." I might not know a lot of things, but thanks to Ammamma, I knew my pickle-making.

We paid a coolie to deliver the sacks home. Then we washed each mango and dried it with a cloth; any hint of moisture, and the whole batch of pickle would be ruined.

We'd planned the mango cutting for the following day, a Sunday, when we'd have our men around. We piled up the mangoes on plastic sheets in the courtyard.

"Let me try," Srikar said, as the men behind him flexed their muscles.

I showed him how to use the cutting board. One end of the long eighteen-inch knife was attached to a wooden platform which rested on the floor. The other end swung free. I sat on the floor, next to the platform, centred the mango on the platform beneath the knife, raised the blade, moved the hand holding the mango away, and brought the blade down with so much force that it sliced through the pit cleanly.

Srikar's first few tries didn't work.

"No, no. Let me show you again," I said. "If it doesn't slice through cleanly, the pickle will spoil."

"Enjoying bossing me, aren't you?" Srikar teased.

I blushed.

It took Srikar a few tries to get it right. Then a few more men volunteered. Each mango was sliced into eight pieces.

Sandhya dragged out big, aluminium utensils. I washed my hands up to my elbows, thoroughly dried them, then had Geeta pour in the dried ingredients. I dug in. When they were mixed well, I instructed one of the women to pour in enough oil to make the ingredients damp. Then we made sure each mango piece was coated with the mixture before we dropped them into huge ceramic jars. By the end of the day I was exhausted.

On the third day, we removed pickles from the forty-odd jars, adjusted seasonings to taste, hand mixed them again to make sure that everything was smoothly blended, then put them back into the jars.

By the end of the pickle-making session, I was firm friends with Geeta and Sandhya.

Between all that cooking and carrying water up the stairs, I failed to notice what else was happening. One day I was standing in front of our Godrej bureau, with its full length mirror, tying my sari when Srikar came up and put his arms around me.

"Did you see that?" he asked.

"See what?"

"You silly girl," he said, nuzzling my neck. "You've lost so much weight. Look."

I looked.

I turned sideways, then around, and finally had Srikar hold up a mirror so I could view myself from behind.

"What do you think?" Srikar asked.

"Hmm."

"What kind of response is hmm? You're pretty!"

"I wasn't before?"

He turned serious. "Your weight isn't what makes me happy, Pullamma. It's your goodness."

Did my colour not bother him? I wished I had the courage to ask. But I blushed with pleasure.

"Still," he said, faking a sniff, "I have lost one-third of my wife."

I discovered that I liked this concentrate version of me – I was like the *ghee* that remained after all the impurities in butter had burned away. This was like getting a wish without having prayed for it. Very unexpected, but still very welcome.

Soon enough, Geeta from next door was giving me tips on how to improve my appearance. "First," she said with the natural authority of the good looking, "get rid of that ghastly hairstyle."

Ammamma had taught me to oil my hair till the strands glistened, then braid my hair very tight.

"Stop using so much oil," Geeta ordered.

"But it makes hair grow," I wailed.

"Maybe so, but you need to apply a little bit, not dump half a bottle over your head."

Next, we experimented with a few different ways of doing my hair. Even Geeta wasn't so forward as to suggest I leave it unbound – the style that suited me best – but we finally settled on braiding it so it no longer stuck to my scalp.

"And for God's sake, keep using those fairness creams!"

That I did.

After Lata had pronounced, back in the village, that Goddesses were rarely of medium colour, I doggedly stuck to using the fairness creams. Twice daily I inspected my skin between applying a liberal helping of the cream, and dousing myself with Pond's Talcum powder. At the municipal tap, old Rukkamma recommended a mixture of turmeric and milk cream. She didn't know about my Goddess past, but felt sorry that I was forced to live with all that darkness on my skin. There had been no change in my skin tone as yet, but who knew? Like Geeta said, "All that blackness might get tired of being on your skin and finally take itself off."

Then Geeta took on my clothes. "You have such a good figure, why do you drape your sari like you are wrapping a pole?"

We practiced tying my sari till she was satisfied. When we finally got it right, Geeta said in surprise, "Why, you look almost as good as me! Too black, of course, and too tall, but still..."

Geeta made me give away one of the two saris I'd brought with me. I'd always known that particular shade didn't suit me, but since almost all the clothes I owned were hand-me-downs from Malli, or ones I shared with Lata, I hadn't had a choice.

"You don't need a cupboard full of saris," she instructed. "Just a few that enhance your appearance."

Not that I had a cupboard full. Srikar had bought me three brand-new saris, but that was it. I wasn't complaining, though. Now, when I went with Srikar to the city, I no longer worried about embarrassing him. We often took a bus to Tank Bund and walked along the lake. Our favourite corn-seller beckoned us to his cart and roasted us the most tender cobs of corn, coating them with just the right amounts of salt, chilli powder and lemon juice. When I had enough of the walking, we settled on the grass and stared out at the water, watching the lights come on. Talking, making plans, feeling grateful to be alive.

One day Srikar said, "I have a good offer, Pulla." He had taken to calling me 'Pulla' – twig – in honour of my new, slim appearance. Coming from him, this diminutive of my name made me feel cherished. "We should move closer to the city. I can get to my new job easily, and you can start college."

I was taken aback. "I thought you were joking. About the studies, I mean."

He looked at me, eyes serious. "It is true that girls in the village don't study too much. But we now live in the city. You're already at an advantage, being sixteen, and 12th class pass. In the city, students join college at seventeen, even eighteen. Don't you want to do something with your life?"

"I have everything I need right here," I said, resting my head on his shoulder. I tried not to think about how happy I was. I wasn't stupid enough to tempt fate.

"Think, Pulla," Srikar said, putting his arm around me. "Think. We are young, still. Let us make something of ourselves. There will be plenty of time for children. You want a better life for them, don't you?"

"Yes..."

"Why the hesitation?"

"It's nothing."

"It can't be nothing."

"I have no burning desire to study. That is my sister Lata's department. I'd rather settle down."

"Have children, you mean?"

I nodded, my cheeks warming.

"And?"

"I'd like to have two children. Hopefully they will be closer than my sisters and I were. I want them to grow up with a mother and a father. I want them never to doubt our love for them."

I'd name them the nicest possible names, I added silently, so they'd never face the kind of teasing I'd suffered.

Srikar smiled. "You don't have to do only one or the other. Why don't we go with both our plans? Get your college degree, then we can have as many children as you want."

I wasn't convinced, so he said, "Don't dismiss the college option completely. Keep an open mind. If you really don't want to do it, we'll reconsider."

I nodded reluctantly. I felt disloyal even thinking this, but Srikar's whole plan seemed to be against the natural order of things.

If God had meant for women to study, he wouldn't have made dowry, would he?

NINETEEN

S rikar and I spent our Sundays in the city. My favourite destination was the historic Charminar area, built some four hundred years ago by Quli Qutub Shah, and past it, the Laad Bazaar – known the country over as the Mecca for bangles and other artificial jewellery. The main bazaar consisted of one narrow lane lined with at least a hundred shops, each crammed with stone and "lac" bangles, stone-studded necklaces, elaborately designed sari-belts, earrings, bags, purses, mirror studded earthen jewellery boxes, adornments to put in the parting of hair, embroidered clothes, the list was endless. As we walked past the shops, the wares dazzled us with their brilliance. So many frivolous things. How Ammamma would shake her head.

Srikar would point to one set of jewellery or the other, saying, "When we have our own company, we'll drive down here in an Ambassador, and I will buy you that. Head-to-toe you'll be in shiny jewellery. Or, you know what? I'll buy you your own shop." I'd shake my head and walk on. We peered into each shop, smilingly ignoring the blandishments of the bangle sellers, enjoying the incredible beauty of their glittery creations.

Most things were beyond our budget, but Srikar did buy me a globe – a papier mâché sphere, the surface of which was decorated with small hexagons of mirrored glass. When I held it up by its thread, it spun around, catching sunlight on each individual piece of mirror, casting its brilliance as far as the rays reached.

"What is this for?" I asked.

"To remind you of me."

I giggled from embarrassment. The only person I knew who talked like this was the Telugu superstar Chiranjeevi, and that was onscreen.

When Srikar was at work I spent most of my time with Geeta. She hovered by her door till he left, then streaked in, shutting the door behind her. Geeta was a talker; she talked with her hands, her mouth, her eyes. Once she tucked the free end of her sari at her waist, and did an impromptu Goddess Durga dance. With the huge red *kumkum bottu* on her forehead, her eyes lined with kohl, and a dozen glass bangles encircling each perfectly rounded arm, she even looked the part. Sandhya, a skinny girl with protruding front teeth, applauded. She came over frequently, but not as often as Geeta. There were no in-laws she needed to get away from.

Most days Geeta grabbed a pillow, propped it on the floor against a wall and settled down for a few hours of gossip, till her mother-in-law came in search of her, screaming, "Oh, where did that useless girl go and die?"

"Anything to escape that house," Geeta said with a sigh and got up to go cook.

TWENTY

I t was almost three months of idyllic existence, with occasional bursts of loneliness because I missed Ammamma and Chinni, before I felt safe enough to telephone my grandmother.

Srikar cautioned me against revealing too much information, for both my grandmother's safety, and our own.

Hoping desperately that my grandmother hadn't had any visits from Srikar's squat-necked grandfather, I dialled Lakshmi *garu*'s number. At this time of the evening, Ammamma was almost always at Lakshmi *garu*'s house.

"'allo?"

"Are you well, Lakshmi *garu*? This is Pullamma." A sharp longing for the village, for Ammamma, for Chinni, for Malli, for Lata, even for Lakshmi *garu*, welled up. It didn't matter that Lakshmi *garu* had looked down on me due to the colour of my skin. It didn't matter she'd bossed over Ammamma. She'd stood by Ammamma's side in her time of need, and in the end that's what mattered.

What does that make Chinni? I had an unbidden memory of my best friend, five years old, sitting by our cow and tying a bright red ribbon to its tail.

"Pullamma!" Lakshmi *garu* said. "Oh my God! Wait, let me get your grandmother."

It was Lakshmi *garu*'s dowry of the telephone connection that was allowing me to talk with my beloved grandmother. Because of Lakshmi *garu*, Ammamma didn't have to line up at the village *kirana* shop like every other villager, waiting to use the phone. Talk in the village was that too much money in her mother's home had caused Lakshmi *garu*'s disrespect for Murty *garu*. I could only be grateful – for Lakshmi *garu*'s support of Ammamma; not her disrespect of Murty *garu* – never that.

"Child, is that you?" Ammamma's voice sounded choked.

I started to cry, too. "Ammamma, I miss you so much."

"I miss you, too, Child. How are you? Are you happy? Is my son-in-law treating you well?"

"Very well, Ammamma. I didn't know it was possible to be this happy," I said softly.

"I'm glad."

"How are you?"

"I have my work, and Lakshmi. Nothing has changed for me, Child. You don't need to worry on my account."

Despite what Ammamma said, it couldn't have been easy dealing with the devotees after I went into hiding.

"How's Chinni?"

"Married, and settled in Kurnool."

Her wedding had been delayed when the groom fell sick. I was grateful for this because the wedding took place only after I left for Hyderabad. I don't think I could have borne it otherwise. "Did you go to the wedding?"

"No."

I pictured Ammamma, sitting by the phone, tears pooling in her eyes. She had loved Chinni, too. "And Murty *garu*?"

"He's gone over to the neighbouring village for a bride-viewing."

"Hopefully, no Goddesses will emerge from there." I laughed nervously.

"Don't come back to the village," Ammamma said, voice serious. "That man's goons keep haunting our house to see if I have been in touch with you."

"Oh, Ammamma! Did he find out...?" That I had married his grandson? I found my throat closing.

Srikar put his ear closer to the phone. I held the phone slightly away so he could hear, too.

"Ammamma," Srikar said, "I am on the phone with Pullamma."

"God bless you, Child," Ammamma said without breaking her flow. "I don't think he knows. But his Goddess is on the run. As you can imagine, that isn't making him too happy."

"Oh."

"The day after you left, he came with a huge platoon of goons. He screamed and shouted, and threatened all kinds of vile things. He said we had no right to hide his Goddess."

Three months of wishing the infernal man away had made not one whit of a difference. I started to tremble. Srikar put his arm around me.

"Luckily," Ammamma was saying, "he still doesn't know of that other connection."

"I am very sorry, Ammamma," Srikar said into the phone.

"Son, you – of all people – shouldn't have to apologize. May

God always watch over you with benevolence for having given my granddaughter a married name." She started to cry. Srikar moved away from the phone.

"How are Malli and Lata?"

"Malli is with her in-laws –"

"She's married!"

"Well, yes. The in-laws didn't want to let go of a good alliance like ours. Even though you were no longer around, the mother-in-law insisted only our Malli would do as their daughter-in-law. She has settled so well in her new house."

"They... they didn't ask?"

"About you? No. Kondal Rao must have told them something."

"Ammamma, I hate to put you to more trouble..."

"What, Child?"

"Will you break five coconuts at Goddess Durga's altar for me? And circle her altar a hundred and eight times? I promised to do it if Malli's alliance went through." I couldn't afford more trouble with the Goddess.

"Of course!"

Much as I enjoyed the hustle and bustle, this was one wedding I was happy to have missed. Not because of my sister, but because of her in-laws. If I'd been forced to preside over the wedding... I shuddered. Still, my brush with Goddess-hood seemed to have done some good. "I missed Malli's wedding."

"And I missed yours. I wish I could see you as a married woman." Ammamma sighed. "And Lata is going to be married off to Malli's husband's cousin."

"But she always wanted to be a doctor!" I was genuinely shocked. Though Ammamma had forbidden us from studying further, a part of me believed she would relent when it finally came to Lata – hadn't my twin always gotten away with skipping household chores just because she had schoolwork? I couldn't see Lata in the role of a housewife, cooking and cleaning, getting up in the middle of the night to fill water.

Ammamma snorted. "I'm an old woman. Haven't I raised two generations of girls? Don't I deserve to finish up with my responsibilities? After that, if her husband permits, she can go be a doctor or train ticket collector or lorry driver."

"Did she agree to the marriage?"

"Do I have to ask for permission to settle my own granddaughter's wedding?" Ammamma harrumphed. "It is a good alliance. The boy has passed 12th class, too. He is a motorcycle mechanic. What more can one ask for?"

I felt deep sorrow for my twin. For as long as I could remember, being a doctor was all she had talked about. But there would be no changing Ammamma's mind. So I tried to be supportive. "I'm glad, Ammamma. All your granddaughters settled."

"All my earthly responsibilities are fulfilled," Ammamma said. "Now I can concentrate on spiritual matters, and hope to die in peace."

"Ammamma! No talk about dying. You are healthy. We need you around for many, many years." Finally I found the courage to ask what I had been avoiding. "What about those devotees?"

"Don't think badly of them, Child. They are honest people who sincerely believed you had divine powers."

"What about..."

"Kondal Rao? Oh, he tells the devotees you followed in the footsteps of your father and went off to the Himalayas to meditate."

"And they believe it?"

"He orchestrated another miracle, Child." Ammamma sighed. "He put chickpeas under the soil near a tree, and put a faceless idol on it. Because the idol was being prepared for prayers each morning, all that water caused the seeds to germinate and raise the idol slightly. He claimed that the Goddess had risen. He then installed that idol in the Durga temple. Now his only problem is exposure. If you stay away, both he and you should be safe."

"**S**omething smells good." Srikar hooked his cloth shoulder bag on the peg by the door. He stepped out of his slippers, and sniffed. "Vankay?"

I smiled. He could sniff out the curry from a thousand different delicacies.

He smiled back, but it was the sort of smile one gave under duress.

"What's wrong?"

"Grandfather called. At work."

"He found your workplace!"

"No, no. I meant, he had Headmaster *garu* call me."

My heart hitched. "Did he ask about me?"

"He did."

"And he wants me back." That familiar dread.

"No, no. I'm sorry for scaring you. That isn't what he wants, according to Headmaster *garu*."

"What, then?"

"He wants us to come home."

"He found out you married me!"

"That was bound to happen, Pulla. He says my grandmother wants to meet you."

"That can't be bad. You've been wanting to take me to your grandmother."

"He's up to something."

"If he is involving your grandmother, it can only be a good thing, right?"

He didn't answer.

"Right?"

"Right." But he didn't sound convinced.

"I am glad you accepted my peace offering," Kondal Rao said, greeting Srikar and me at his doorstep. He reached up and touched the top of my head in blessing.

I looked at his smile, unable to reconcile Kondal Rao, the grandfather, with Kondal Rao, the manipulative politician.

"Come in, Children."

"You men," an elderly voice scolded, smile in her voice. "Always in a hurry. No patience for tradition. My new daughter-in-law will walk directly into the house, or what?"

Srikar grabbed his grandmother in a bear hug.

"You crazy boy," she said, laughing, "let go of me."

The women standing behind her giggled.

From the side, Ammamma watched teary-eyed. I went to her and hugged hard. Then Srikar and I bent to touch her feet for blessings.

Srikar's grandmother took a tray from one of the women, lit the oil lamp, smeared a little *kumkum* on my forehead, and started to move the tray clockwise. The women burst into a song praising Lord Venkateswara. Then she ordered Srikar to offer me a sweet. Flavours bursting in my mouth, and Ammamma by my side, I put my hennaed foot over the threshold, right foot first, and entered my new home. Exactly how I'd envisioned it. But for the absence of Chinni, and my sisters, it was perfect. We bent down to touch Srikar's grandmother's feet. She pulled us into an emotional hug. Drawing back, she cupped my face. "Welcome home, Child."

I was a little emotional myself. I could see why Ammamma, and this beaming lady of comfortable proportions were such good friends. I could see her sitting on the floor, legs stretched out, massaging my babies under the warm winter sun.

She smoothed back my hair with a shaky hand. "Granddaughter of Seetamma, now daughter of my house." Her voice quavered. "What more could I ask for?"

A fair-skinned daughter-in-law?

For as long as I lived, I'd be grateful to this wonderful lady for not stating the obvious.

Srikar's grandmother shooed the men away before settling me down on a cot in the courtyard. She took my hands and slid a couple of gold bangles up each arm. Then she presented me with a platter displaying the jewellery she was gifting me.

"I have nothing to give to Pullamma," Ammamma said, not meeting her friend's eyes.

"Nonsense, Seetamma," Srikar's grandmother said. "We have been friends all our lives. You think I seek dowry from you? Isn't it enough you have given us such a sweet daughter for our house?"

She gave me a smile of great warmth. "God has showered so many blessings on us, I needn't put out my hand in front of anyone. Besides, I won't pack it and take it all with me, will I?"

I had come home.

Kondal Rao left after lunch.

"That wasn't too bad, was it?" I said. Since Srikar had refused Kondal Rao's offer of a car, we were taking the bus back to the city. "Your grandmother is a wonderful lady."

"She is, isn't she?" Srikar's eyes softened. "She never let me feel the lack of a mother. I am very lucky."

"Your grandfather was also trying hard."

"You noticed only my grandparents welcomed us?"

The two giggly women were the maids of Srikar's grandmother.

"They probably didn't want to share us because we were there for such a short visit."

He snorted.

"What?"

"Politics and power always have, and always will, come first with that man. He can't afford to expose his connection to the Goddess, Pulla. Otherwise, a morally deficient, self-important politician like him, don't you think he'd have commandeered the district machinery and thrown us a huge bash?"

Twenty-Two

A loud noise dragged me from sleep. I squinted at the clock across the room. "It's past midnight!"

The pounding on the door resumed. Srikar and I looked at each other. He got out of bed. "I'm coming, I'm coming," he called as he hurried to the door.

Straightening my sari, I followed.

Geeta's husband was at the door. "Sorry to disturb you. Phone call."

Geeta often preened theirs was one of the few houses in the whole area with a telephone. They'd been so excited when the landlord put the building phone in their flat. Murali wasn't looking too pleased now. In fact, he had an unmistakeably annoyed expression on his face.

"Who is it?" I asked, not sure I wanted to know; news this late could only be bad.

"Your sister is calling from the village. She is crying very hard."

Ammamma! Something had happened to her.

It was more than a month since I'd talked to my grandmother. I turned to Srikar, face tight from the tension. He touched my hand briefly. "Whatever it is, we will deal with it."

In Geeta's flat, I could see her six-year-old daughter through the open door of the bedroom, fast asleep. In the front room, where the phone was, the father-in-law slept in his corner. On the floor next to him, the mother-in-law was propped up on an elbow watching us, lips pursed.

Srikar apologized for Lata's middle-of-the-night phone call.

The two year old started to wail at the commotion.

Murali took the toddler out to the corridor.

Geeta sat on her own mattress inside the bedroom, hand resting protectively on her daughter's head.

"Pullamma, I can't believe it," Lata said between sobs. "I... Ammamma... it is terrible."

For a second, I wanted to hang up and pretend the phone call had never happened. "What is it, Lata?" I said, trying to keep panic from my voice. "What happened?"

From the bedroom, Geeta's eyes blazed with curiosity. Closer to me, the mother-in-law put her head back on the pillow and threw an arm across her eyes, emitting long-suffering groans.

On the phone, Lata was sobbing so hard, she was incoherent.

I tried taking a deep breath, but my chest hurt. "Is it Ammamma?"

"No!" Lata was shocked out of her crying.

"Chinni?" My voice got shrill. "Something's happened to her?"

"You think I'd waste my money on a phone call for her?"

"What, then?" I loosened my grip on the phone receiver.

Lata started to cry again.

"Lata, if you don't stop crying, how will I know what's wrong?"

"Pullamma," Lata said sniffling, "my wedding has been cancelled."

"My God! What happened?"

"Like you care."

"Lata, please," I said.

Srikar put a hand on mine.

"I'm a fool, Pullamma, a fool. I ruined my future with my own hands."

"Just tell me," I said, shouting.

The mother-in-law glared.

I lowered my voice. "Please."

"I had been pleading with Ammamma to let me study."

I nodded, before realizing she couldn't see me. "Yes."

"Like always, Ammamma had been insisting that she wanted to marry me, the last granddaughter, off and be done with her responsibilities."

"Yes."

"I begged and begged her not to do it. She said she would never be able to explain to the villagers why she hadn't done her duty by me. I told her I'd be happy to remain unmarried all my life, if only she'd let me study."

If Ammamma let Lata study, instead of getting her married off, she'd face the scorn of an entire village. Even if she did stand by Lata, how would she come up with a boy worthy enough to be the husband of a doctor? It wasn't like we were rich city dwellers or anything.

Lata continued between sniffs, "Finally Ammamma said 'we'll see.' She has never said that before, Pullamma." She gave a little sob. "I really thought she was thinking about letting me study. Instead she went behind my back and arranged a bride-viewing."

Lata started to cry noisily. I ached for the tough position each was in. Lata, because being doctor was the only thing she'd ever wanted, and Ammamma, because she couldn't easily defy social norms.

"Lata, don't cry," I begged, conscious of Geeta's family's impatience.

"I felt so betrayed by Ammamma, that the day the groom's family was to come, I ran away to Jikki's house."

What dishonour for Ammamma!

"I begged Jikki's parents to let me stay in their house till Ammamma's anger cooled down."

"And?" With Lata, there was always an 'and.'

"A boy called Venkatesh was also there. He's from the city, the son of Jikki's family friends."

Please, God, don't let it be what I think it is.

Lata drew in a shuddering breath. "He promised me all kinds of things, Pullamma. He promised to take me to the city, marry me, and help me become a doctor."

"What did you do?" I asked, voice rising despite my late night audience.

She said instead, "Kondal Rao is demanding you come back, Pullamma."

I breathed in sharply, conscious that Geeta was listening. Friend or not, gossip was her first loyalty. I was also conscious that Lata hadn't answered my question. But the mention of Kondal Rao had rattled me.

"That's right, Pullamma." Was that satisfaction I heard? "He came home and shouted at Ammamma."

"Why?" I said, trying to force my voice out. How could he do this to us? Hadn't our visit meant anything to him?

"He's going to get you back one way or the other. You'd better be prepared for it."

"He can want all he wants, but I am never going back," I said, putting my mouth to the receiver. "Ever." I breathed in shallow, soundless breaths and forced myself not to think of The Incident, with its attendant throngs of people. I instead focussed on my current life with Srikar. My voice softened. "I had no idea it was possible to be this happy, Lata. I just can't give this up."

Lata broke down again.

Murali leaned against the door, his fingers thrumming against the back of his sleeping son.

"What?" My palms were damp.

Lata sobbed harder.

"Lata?" I asked, voice rising again. "Stop crying and tell me what's wrong."

"I am with child."

Twenty-Three

L ata, pregnant!
       I gasped, though I knew this was coming. I felt my face go
numb from the shock.

Srikar, then Geeta gave me questioning looks.

I shook my head.

"Pullamma? Are you there?"

"Uh, how... how did this happen?"

"The usual way." She sounded belligerent.

"What about the... you know?"

"He ran away to the city." Sobs started to come in great heaves.
Struggling for control, she said, "If Ammamma hadn't arranged my
marriage behind my back, I wouldn't have been so angry. Then I
wouldn't have fallen for that boy's sweet talk."

When I didn't respond, her tone turned pleading. "Please, Pullamma. Help me get married to Venkatesh. Once I'm married, I'll
help you get away. Ammamma lost face in the village when I didn't
show up for the bride-viewing. If Venkatesh doesn't marry me either..." She drew a shuddering breath. "After all, didn't our elders
say – *help arrange a marriage, even if you have to tell a thousand
lies to do so*?"

I was incredulous. Was this the same Lata who hated the traditional sayings related to marriage and girls? *Tell a lie, beget a
daughter. Bringing up a daughter is like fertilizing and watering a
plant for someone else's courtyard.* "Didn't you say he ran away?" I
said, trying to keep my voice down.

"Jikki's parents will be able to track him down. After I'm married, I'll convince Venkatesh to let me study further."

With a newborn at home? "What does Venkatesh do?"

"He works in a tea stall on the outskirts of the city."

"Where will he get the money from?"

"Headmaster *garu* told me that fee-waivers are available from
the government for needy students. He said he would help me get
into a government sponsored hostel, so I wouldn't have to worry
about boarding and lodging."

Why would a boy, who worked by the roadside for spare change, allow his wife to study? "This was before, uh, you know. These places take only unmarried girls."

"If I get married, I'll have my own place, which is almost as good. I'll still be able to study."

Lata's naiveté overwhelmed me. "What do you want me to do?"

"Tell Ammamma about my situation," she said in a small voice. "She will kill me if I tell her myself."

A week went by, spent mostly in dodging Geeta's relentless questioning. The rest of it went in trying not to think about Lata's situation, about Kondal Rao's demands to have me return, about Ammamma's shock at Lata's indiscretion.

I opened the front door for the milkman early one morning, ready to dart in if I spotted Geeta. Instead I found Headmaster *garu*, hand poised to knock. So unexpected was his presence at my doorstep I just stared.

"You won't invite me in?"

"Yes, of course," I said, recovering. "Please forgive my manners, Headmaster *garu*. Please come in."

He stepped over the threshold and ducked his head to enter our house.

"Come in, come in," Srikar said, hurriedly buttoning his shirt.

Headmaster *garu* waited for me to unroll the mat before settling on it. "Please forgive me for coming at this early hour."

"No, no," I said, waiting for more. This was no courtesy visit.

Headmaster *garu* took a deep breath. "I don't come bearing good news."

I wiped my palms against my sides, tense.

"What happened?" Srikar asked, trying discretely to rub sleep from his eyes.

"Elections are in a few days," Headmaster *garu* said.

"We spent an entire day with him and Srikar's grandmother," I said. "In their own house. He would never put his grandson's wife in such a position." *Would he?*

"Word on the street is that Kondal Rao is poised to lose. Even the idol trick didn't help. He is a desperate man."

"No...!" My voice sounded guttural, even to my ears.

Srikar put a hand on me in silent support. "Why don't we let Headmaster *garu* finish?"

"It is what Pullamma suspects," Headmaster *garu* said to Srikar. He sighed. "Kondal Rao is convinced Pullamma can help him reverse the situation. He wants her to come back to the village as a Goddess."

That first time I'd been naïve, thrilled by the power, the money, the adulation. Now I had much more to lose. My husband, my life with him. If I were to go, how would I return to him? I started trembling violently.

Srikar hurried to get me a blanket.

Despite the thick material, I was chilled to the bone. "But we are on talking terms now," I said.

Srikar said nothing.

"Your grandmother," I said. "Can't we seek her help?"

"No, my grandfather will not listen to her. She tried to fight him when they were first married, but when she realized she had no influence on him at all, she gave up. She lives her life trying not to be tainted by his evil."

"I need to... uh... bring up something indelicate," Headmaster *garu* said, a flush crawling up his neck. "Lata's... uh..."

I almost died of the humiliation. How could Lata have done such a thing? How would Ammamma ever look Headmaster *garu* in the face?

"I'm so sorry, Child," he said. "I know this is very hard for you." He was apologetic. "But Kondal Rao found out."

The world seemed to stop. No sound. I saw Headmaster *garu*'s face, saw the motions his mouth made.

Srikar shook me gently.

I took quick, shallow breaths. Slowly, the sounds came back.

"He spread word about the... you know," Headmaster *garu* was saying. The tip of his nose reddened. "And then he let your grandmother and Lata stew in the resulting scandal."

Yedukondalavada! Neither of them deserved this, even if Lata had done the unthinkable. The villagers might forgive a girl a lot of things, but premarital pregnancy wasn't one of them.

"Then he went to your grandmother with a deal," Headmaster *garu* said. "He would track down the boy – Venkatesh – and arrange a marriage between him and Lata.

"Provided?"

"Provided you went back as his Goddess," Srikar said.

Headmaster *garu* nodded, eyes full of compassion.

My face felt numb.

"Is that why you are here?" Srikar asked.

"To take Pullamma back?" Headmaster *garu* said, shaking his head. "No, no. Pullamma's grandmother refused the offer outright. She said she could never barter the happiness of one granddaughter for another."

Oh, Ammamma!

"I wish that were the end of it," Headmaster *garu* said. He leaned forward and put his hand on my head briefly. "Kondal Rao, in preparation of your return, has sent out foot messengers with shoulder drums. They're walking the villages, beating their drums, announcing the return of their Goddess. They're converging in on your grandmother's house from all directions."

"But I am married to his grandson," I said, struggling for breath.

"Since when did that make a difference?" Srikar said.

"Your grandfather wants me to assure you that Pullamma will be free to return to her life after the elections," Headmaster *garu* said. "He said that after all, Pullamma is the daughter-in-law of the house."

Twenty-Four

"Run away," Ammamma said. She put her hand in blessing on my head, then on Srikar's. "Take my granddaughter, and leave." She stood by the door to our flat, the handle of her shoulder bag tightly clutched.

"Come in, please," Srikar said. "Freshen up. Have some coffee. Then we'll talk." He held out a hand for her shoulder bag.

Ammamma stood still, lips pinched tight.

"Please," Srikar said.

Ammamma shook her head, then released her grip on the bag before stepping into our house. Srikar helped Ammamma on to the mat. "Bless you, Child," Ammamma said as she sank down with a sigh. "First time in my granddaughter's house, and under such terrible circumstances."

I handed Ammamma a steel tumbler of coffee, and sat down next to her. "You think he'll really force me back?"

Ammamma turned to Srikar, tone urgent. "Don't waste time, Srikar. Take my Pullamma and run to some remote corner of the earth. Disappear." Her face showed lines that had not been there before.

"What would happen to Lata and you if we did that?" Srikar said.

"Leave us to our fate. We are already in the middle of a frightful scandal. It can't get any worse. Lata will never be able to get married, but that can't be helped. At least the two of you will be able to live your lives without interference."

"The elections are still a few days away," I said. "Maybe something will come up by then."

"Headmaster *garu* visited me in the village last night," Ammamma said.

"And?" Srikar said.

Ammamma seemed reluctant to continue.

"What is it, Ammamma?" Srikar said.

"I am so sorry, Child," she whispered.

"What?" I asked, my voice coming out shrill.

"Kondal Rao's threatening to anoint you *Graam devata* if you don't return to endorse him."

I stared at Ammamma in disbelief. "Don't you have to be an

idol? Or at least be dead a few hundred years?" *Graam devata.*
Graam devata. Graam devata. The chant pounded inside my
head. *Graam devata.* Resident Goddess of the village.

"It is true that *Graam devatas* are normally idols, not real people, but it's not hard to whip up a frenzy and convince people. You,
of all people, should know that, Pullamma."

"A bottle of whiskey down Ranga Nayakamma's throat, that's all
it takes," Srikar said.

"I am the wife of his only grandson! What kind of a man is he?"

"I know you pretend to be unintelligent to please me." Ammamma sighed. "Surely you can't be that naïve?"

"If my grandfather follows through on his threat, you're
doomed," Srikar said. Since Headmaster *garu*'s visit, deep grooves
had appeared on either side of his nose. "He might direct the villagers to search you out and bring you back."

So they could install me as their *Graam devata*! I shivered. If
that happened, my destiny would forever be tied to that of the village. Then I might as well give up on my husband, any children,
my municipal water connection.

I thought of Srikar's grandfather that day in their village – laughing, smiling, joking around. Kondal Rao, the loving grandfather.
Kondal Rao, the treacherous politician.

Ammamma took a long draw from the glass of water Srikar
handed her. Wiping her lips with the edge of her sari, she said,
"Kondal Rao has sent me to escort you back. He says if you come
back voluntarily, there will be no declaration of *Graam Devata*. He
is still claiming that you can disappear after endorsing him in the
elections."

"Till the next time," Srikar said.

"*Yedukondalavada*!" Ammamma raised joined palms of her
hands above the head in supplication to the Lord of the Seven Hills.

"But," I said, "if we don't do what he says, and he declares me the
Resident Goddess, all our lives will always be in danger." I closed
my eyes. The drumbeats from the shoulder drums of the barefoot
searchers reached a crescendo inside my head.

"What about Lata?" Srikar asked.

"They're holding her hostage to make sure I return with
Pullamma."

Such things didn't happen to dark, insignificant girls like me,

I thought a little desperately. I watched Srikar's mirrored globe. Back and forth, back and forth it swayed gently in the breeze, scattering its tiny mirrored reflections across the room.

"Your only option is to run away."

"Run away, where?" Srikar asked.

"Burma, Russia, London – somewhere they would never think of looking."

My chest hurt at the thought of living in some strange land, of never seeing Ammamma again.

"How can we leave you behind to deal with my grandfather?"

"Pullamma," Ammamma begged. "Make your husband listen."

"I agree with your son-in-law," I said.

She looked at me, love in her eyes. "Listen to me, Child. I am an old woman. My life is almost over. Yours is just beginning. I do not know what good deeds I did in my last birth, but it must have been something, to be blessed with such a wonderful son-in-law."

Srikar flushed.

"Your place is with your husband." Her voice quavered. "Make a good home for yourselves, away from this madness. I will think of you every day for the rest of my life."

"Which won't be too long," Srikar said grimly, "when my esteemed grandfather's goons get their hands on you."

"Why hasn't he done anything to me then, *hanh*?" Ammamma asked. "If he had anything in mind, don't you think he would have done it already? Don't forget, your grandmother is a dear friend."

"Ammamma," Srikar said. His voice was soft. "He'd sell his own wife if there was anything to be gained from it. You'll never be safe as long as you have something he wants."

"Which is his Goddess," I said dully.

"Lata and I will have to suffer whatever fate has written for us. You two go somewhere far, far away," Ammamma implored. "Never come back."

I shivered to think of Ammamma's fate if Srikar and I disappeared.

"There has to be another way," Srikar said, rubbing a hand across his eyes.

Ammamma put her head in her hands. "To think that a granddaughter of mine... Something like this, before marriage..." She choked up. "I thought it was youthful ranting. I thought once she got married and had a couple of children, it would all go away.

After all, which village girl do we know who has studied so much, *hanh*?" She looked sorrowful. "Or, I could come with you. And bring Lata along, though I am deeply disappointed in that girl."

This was empty talk, and we knew it. There was no way for Ammamma and Lata to get away.

I knew all along what needed to be done. I'd just been putting off the inevitable.

TWENTY-FIVE

"I am going to phone your grandfather to confirm our agreement," I said.

"Why bother?" Srikar asked.

He looked beaten, I thought with a pang.

"I think she should," Ammamma said. "If he has any spark of humanity at all..."

Poor, dear, loving, honourable Srikar. In an effort to protect me, he'd as good as severed his ties with his grandmother, the loving lady who'd raised him. Now he might have to sever ties with me, too.

Heart pounding, I huddled in the corner of the *paan* shop-cum-phone booth, and made the call to Kondal Rao. "This is Pullamma. I will be coming back to the village with my grandmother."

"Of course."

"I will be free to leave after you win the elections?"

"*Bah!* Didn't I already say that?"

"What about Lata's wedding?" Ammamma clutched my arm. "Ask him that."

Kondal Rao said in the phone, "Tell your grandmother, I will arrange the wedding at my own expense."

"Thank you, thank you," I said, feeling gratitude towards him.

"But you will have to bless the wedding as Goddess." The phone was disconnected.

I hung up the phone in shock. I had hoped to be back with Srikar right after the elections.

"He changed the plan, didn't he?" Srikar said.

"He wants me to bless Lata's wedding. He won't let me get away after the elections."

Ammamma looked at me in disbelief. "He's going back on his word?"

Srikar's smile was cynical.

After the call was made, Srikar didn't say much. What was there to say?

Kondal Rao had made arrangements for money to be made available so I could shop for the 'right' look. He wanted me decked up in expensive silk saris, but Ammamma put her foot down, insisting on starched cottons; silks were too hard to manage in the village heat. She bought me Mangalagiri saris with big borders to emphasize my natural height, a few Gadwals thrown in for variety. I stuck to leaving my hair braided loosely, but now I had a big, red *kumkum bottu* on my forehead. Seemed the Goddess-y thing to do.

Dangling gold earrings, lot of green and red glass bangles interspersed with gold ones. I was being given fancy, expensive adornments; in reality, the only thing I desired was my husband.

On my last day as an ordinary married woman in our flat in Hyderabad I practiced my stoic expression. "You can't show your true feelings," Ammamma cautioned. So I brought out a mirror and practiced till she decreed I had my impassive expression right.

Then it was time to leave. Srikar had stacked the luggage by the front gate. Ammamma cleared her throat. "I, uh, will be downstairs with the luggage."

Srikar touched her feet. She kissed him on the forehead and took leave.

I looked at my husband across the room, my throat tight with unshed tears. He leaned against the wall, arms folded. "Aren't you going to say goodbye to me?" I whispered.

He came to me then. He caught me in an enveloping hug. I could feel his shoulders shake. I held him tight, committing to memory his unique scent – Liril soap, Ponds Talcum powder, the strength of his arms.

He moved me to an arm's distance, his eyes red. "Take care of yourself." His voice was scratchy.

"I have Ammamma." I looked at his face, memorizing his features. "I will be fine. It is you I am worried about."

He blinked back tears.

I cupped his dear face. "I will come back to you, if it is the last thing I do."

I did not cry.

I entered the packed courtyard of my grandmother's house in the village, heart beating so hard I feared it would tumble out of my chest. Since I was supposed to have returned from my meditation retreat in the Himalayas, I couldn't possibly show up, husband in tow. My husband and I were in the ignominious position of being married, but unable to publicly acknowledge our relationship.

As I surveyed the surging crowds, face impassive despite a pounding heart, I thought with some bitterness that my best performance wasn't being recognized. In school play re-enactments of the *Ramayana* and the *Mahabharata*, I'd been relegated to playing a tree, or a foot soldier at best, because I was deemed lacking in acting skills.

Now, I'd be acting to save my life.

Ammamma had packed Lata off to Malli's house, wanting to keep things as uncomplicated as possible. She told me later that Lata was very angry to be missing out on the goings-on.

Kondal Rao hurried forward, head bowed in reverence. "*Ammavaru.*"

I flinched, then realized my mistake. I'd have to get used to being called Goddess.

I watched as my husband's grandfather struggled to bend his corpulent body in the general direction of my feet; I prayed to God, begging him not to strike me down for this huge transgression. Not only was I being prayed to, but it was by an elder, and not just any elder – the grandfather of my husband. The spherical little politician, panting and struggling to catch his breath, was assisted up by a henchman on either side. He hurried me to a corner where a silk cloth was draped over something. He pulled the cloth with a flourish, and looked at me expectantly.

For a moment, I froze. What would a Goddess's response be to such a lavish gift? A silver throne, no less. I frantically went over my options – a pleased expression, delighted, bored, blank, what? Finally, I settled on a serene countenance and gave a gentle nod.

That seemed to be the appropriate response because the congregation beamed.

Kondal Rao bent over at the waist – such as his girth would allow – and bade me to accept his gift. My little payment for a job well done. I'd appeared to oracle Ranga Nayakamma in a vision three days ago, warning of a five year drought if Kondal Rao's opponent were elected.

Two days later, Kondal Rao swept the elections.

I settled myself on the ornate silver throne in which were inlaid precious stones. The sides and the seat of the throne were cushioned a deep red of the softest velvet. If I hadn't been so miserable being away from Srikar, I might have felt a thrill of ownership. The only chairs I had ever sat on were rickety metal chairs with curling edges in which clothes sometimes caught and tore. And in our flat in Hyderabad, not even those.

Ammamma was also settled in an armchair, though not as fancy as mine, but more comfortable from what I could tell. The privilege of that less fancy chair was that she was free to come and go.

Ten days till Lata's wedding. Ten days before I could be back with Srikar.

I felt the beginnings of a headache. Nausea followed. I prayed I wouldn't embarrass myself by throwing up in front of a couple hundred people. People were praying to me, while my prayers went to a higher God – the irony of it didn't escape me.

"*Ammavaru*, I got your blessings," Kondal Rao said with a sniff, "and the very next day I won the election as an MLA. I waited patiently in the sidelines for seventeen years." He looked at me indignantly. "Seventeen years to become an MLA again! *Ammavaru*, you tested me for such a long time," he said, voice choking. He flicked an angry tear. "Now, with your blessings, I shall be confirmed as a Minister."

I marvelled at the acting abilities of this man; if there was something I could learn from him, it would be this.

"Anyhow," he said briskly, "past is past. You have showered your divine blessings on me. I am your number one devotee for life. The throne is only the first of my offerings."

Oh no!

Even as I was struggling to hide my dismay, a *pancha* clad priest – the thread of his sacred *jandhyam* angled across his bare chest, three streaks of grey ash applied across his forehead – hurried forward. The tall, skinny priest with a short face, long nose, and a semi-circle of white tufts on his bald head, bent at the waist, and sought my blessings.

I steeled myself not to react – that first flinch, when Kondal Rao touched my feet, had been a grave error. It was so hard to allow older people to do so – it just wasn't right. The priest had to be fifty, at the very least.

"*Ammavaru*," he said, palms of his hands joined. "Allow me to introduce myself as your most humble servant. My name is Satyanarayana, but everyone calls me Satyam."

I inclined my head again, acknowledging the greetings. After some frantic internal debate, I'd decided the less I talked, the less the chance of making a fool of myself. This came with a risk, of course – it would allow Kondal Rao to speak through Ranga Nayakamma. But what else could I do, if sagely advice wasn't tumbling out of my mouth?

Priest Satyam bowed. "With your permission, I would like to start in your service with the day's prayers."

As the priest started to apply *kumkum* to my head, I held up my hand.

Kondal Rao's face tightened. The congregation drew in a breath as one. Why was *Ammavaru* displeased?

I pointed at the pantheon of deities placed at the elaborate marble altar. Then I moved my head up and down.

Understanding, the priest turned to pray to them instead.

I released a breath, along with the rest of the people. The Gods would have never forgiven me the sacrilege of allowing myself to be prayed to in their presence.

After the *puja*, I blessed the *prasadam*.

Then Kondal Rao's henchmen took over. They organized the worshippers for *prasadam* distribution in two lines – one consisting of women and children, the other men. The devotees touched the packets to their eyes before consuming the *prasadam*.

Then audience with the Goddess – me – started.

"*Ammavaru*, please bless me with a male child. I am already cursed with four daughters."

Jhampiah, the day labourer who'd warned us away from Kondal Rao even before Malli's bride-viewing.

"My son is appearing for his tenth class exams. Please help him pass in First Class."

I looked at my primary school teacher in shock. But he was focused on my feet.

"I have bought a new tractor. Please bless it."

Lakshmi *garu*'s neighbour.

Each request tightened the pressure around my head, till it felt ready to explode. These poor, trusting souls! I hoped their faith alone would get them through – I was certainly not in a position to do anything for them. To each person, I gave something. A flower to the women, a fruit to the men. All of them touched the offering to their eyes and gratefully accepted the blessings.

By the time I went through the initial two hundred people, and the others that had lined up outside, it was close to two o'clock. The headache, which had begun at seven in the morning, was now raging. I was hungry, and tired, and getting cranky.

Kondal Rao had left, fortunately.

I indicated with a finger that the courtyard gates were to be shut.

The priest started forward, but already more people were lining up at the gate.

I was close to tears, and trying hard not to show it.

Ammamma walked across and put her hand on my shoulder. "*Ammavaru* is preparing to go into *dhyanam*. She will see other devotees only after her meditation is complete."

"What time shall we open the gates?" the priest asked.

"Six in the evening," Ammamma said, jerking her head in emphasis. "Not a minute before. After the *puja*, *Ammavaru* will give audience until eight o'clock this evening. Then again next morning from seven until eleven a.m. Same timings every day. Sundays, she will not see anyone."

The priest shut the gate. That left him and four or five other devotees in the courtyard.

"Come," Ammamma said, helping me up.

By now, my joints were so stiff, I could have sworn they creaked. My head felt heavy from the burden of my devotees' torment.

Ammamma led me to the front room.

A couple of women devotees stood by the door. They bowed in respect. "My name is Sarala," one of them said. "We want to make sure *Ammavaru* is comfortable."

"I sincerely thank you for it," Ammamma said. "But I can take care of my granddaughter. You may go back to your houses, and rest till the evening."

Sarala bowed again. "I humbly request that we be allowed to take over the functioning of the ashram."

My grandmother's house, a public ashram!

"With your permission," Sarala continued, "we will start by taking charge of the kitchen. We would like to make daily meals for *Ammavaru* and yourself, and the *prasadams* for each puja."

Wordlessly, Ammamma handed over the keys to the kitchen.

"May we bring you tea?" Sarala asked.

"Please knock once, and leave it outside," Ammamma said, thanking them. Then she locked the door to the front room. Finally, Ammamma and I had the front room and the bedroom to ourselves.

I reached for papier mâché globe Srikar had bought me, and dragged a stool.

"What are you doing?" Ammamma rushed forward.

"Putting this up." I showed her the globe.

"I can see that. But you're so tired. Why now?"

"I need this to get through the days. Srikar bought it for me."

Ammamma looked stricken.

I tied the globe to a hook on the ceiling, and hobbled to the bed, feeling as if I had aged rapidly.

Five minutes later, there was a single knock at the door.

Ammamma brought in the tray, with tea and snacks on it, but I was too exhausted to eat.

I fell face forward onto the bed and broke down.

Ammamma sat on the edge of the narrow bed, rubbing my back in circular motions.

"This is just not right, Ammamma," I said through sobs. "We are cheating decent, God-loving people. This is just not right."

"I know, Child," Ammamma said. "I know."

I swiped my face with the back of my hand and sat up. "How do we make this right?"

"Just because my hair has turned white doesn't mean I have any more wisdom than you."

"We have to do something, Ammamma. We cannot be frauds. God will punish us badly, I know he will."

"Cheating is when we knowingly do something wrong. In our case, we didn't choose to do this. In fact, we tried our best not to get in this position." Ammamma gazed at me steadily. "You know what I think? I think this is God's will. Having been placed in this position, we have to do what we are destined to do with clean, pure hearts. I am sure we will pass this test."

"But what about my husband?" I asked, throat hurting. "He doesn't deserve this."

"He is an honourable man," Ammamma agreed, eyes tearing

up. "He lent you support when everyone else was ready to let you fall by the wayside."

"What about him, Ammamma?" I asked, starting to cry again. "How does he fit in God's plans?"

"I wish I knew, Child," Ammamma said, holding me tightly, "I wish I knew."

We held on to each other and cried, because we could do nothing else.

Twenty-Six

K ondal Rao, with all the resources he had at his disposal, hadn't been able to track Venkatesh down. Ammamma, Lata and I sat in our courtyard after the gates had been locked up for the night, trying to find a way out of this nightmare.

Ammamma said, "Since we haven't been able to find any trace of Venkatesh –"

Lata cut in, "Pray, enlighten me, what new plan do you have for my life?" Bitterness gave her voice an edge.

Ammamma winced. "Kondal Rao sent word that he has found another groom for you."

"I'll be sure to fall at his feet the next time I see him."

"Please, Lata," she said wearily. "You should be grateful he even found someone to marry you, you being..." Ammamma's voice trailed away.

"Soiled goods? With some else's child? Not rich enough? Which of the three, *hanh*? Or is it all of them?"

When Ammamma didn't say anything, Lata asked, "And who is this upright citizen, might I ask?"

"Narasu."

Lata opened her mouth, then shut it.

"The school peon?" I was shocked. "My God, Ammamma! He is just an uneducated lout. Cleaning blackboards and making tea for teachers is all he is good for."

Our time in school had been spent trying to dodge his too-familiar hands and shifty eyes. Why, he had to be at least thirty years old! Was he so desperate he'd marry a fallen girl?

I put my hand on Lata's shoulder in support, but she pushed me away. Her was face white. "Ammamma, the only time he saw the inside of a class was when he came in to dust and sweep. He couldn't tell one end of a pencil from the other."

"He is 4th class fail." Ammamma's voice was diffident.

"And that makes it okay? While I've passed my 12th class with distinction?" She dared Ammamma to deny the huge difference in education.

Ammamma didn't even try. "But that other boy – Venkatesh – he wasn't educated, either."

"Yes, but he'd agreed to let me study."

I didn't want to point out the obvious – it was easy to agree to anything at all when you had no intention of seeing it through.

In the early hours of the following morning, Lata miscarried.

Ammamma rushed Lata to the hospital. From there she sent word to Sarala to shut the ashram down for ten days on account of my meditation. The two returned from the hospital on the third day.

Lakshmi *garu* came over as we were helping Lata to a cot on the veranda. "How are you?"

"Never felt better." Lata rolled over to a side, raised her knees up to her stomach, and moaned.

"Be grateful the product of your sin is now purged from your womb."

Lata buried her head in the pillow.

"Too bad you can no longer have children."

No response.

"Lata?" Lakshmi *garu* was persistent, if nothing else.

"What?"

"Aren't you going to inform your would-be husband's family that you are barren?"

Lata raised her head. "You aren't still expecting me to marry that bum?"

"That bum, as you call him, is doing you a favour. Who else would marry a fallen girl like you?"

"I'm blessed." Lata whimpered, her face dotting with sweat.

Why *had* Narasu agreed to marry Lata? He was a man; surely it couldn't be hard for him to find a bride? Whatever his reasons, we could only be grateful he'd agreed to provide Lata with the protection of a married name.

"It couldn't have been easy for Kondal Rao *garu* to find you a groom, in your condition."

"My heart breaks on his behalf."

"You can't back out now, just because... you know. He'll lose face."

"Ammamma," Lata said through gritted teeth, "just bash my head in. End my agony."

"Lakshmi," Ammamma said tiredly. "Perhaps you can come back later?"

"I was only trying to help. Didn't I lend you my son, and my tractor for two days?"

"And I'm very grateful to you for it. It's just that Lata is in so much pain."

Lakshmi *garu* sniffed, and flounced out.

"Pullamma, help me up," Lata demanded.

I settled her against the pillow.

"Now that there's no baby, there is no reason for me to get married."

Ammamma wouldn't meet Lata's eyes.

"Ammamma? You talked to Kondal Rao, didn't you?"

She nodded miserably.

"And?"

"He said he has already paid the caterer a deposit for five hundred people. Can't back out now."

"You're joking, right?" Lata was incredulous. She turned to me. "Pullamma. You're a Goddess. Can't you do something?"

"She's a Goddess, not a magician." Ammamma's shoulders slumped. "Kondal Rao said after your folly, you have no choice but to get married to whoever will have you. He said, no tricks, or we could expect serious consequences."

I was bitter. If fate had to have miscarriage in store for Lata, why couldn't it have been sooner, before Kondal Rao got wind of it? I could have been back with Srikar by now. As it were, we were forced into postponing the wedding to give Lata the time to recover.

But get married she must.

Gopal, the devotee who had been managing the collections, came to me a few days before the wedding. He fell at my feet, face streaked with tears. "*Ammavaru.* I don't know how to tell you this."

I bade him up and said, "Please, have no fear. Tell me."

"Five hundred rupees have disappeared from the collections."

I was stunned. "How could that be?"

Gopal wouldn't meet my eyes.

"You have some knowledge of this, I take it."

"How can I say such a thing in your presence?" He looked down at his hands.

"You won't be held responsible, I promise you." Even a month ago I couldn't have imagined saying something like this to a person older than me.

"Lata madam..." his voice trailed off.

God, No!

In the three weeks since I'd returned, collections had been pouring in.

As she recovered from the miscarriage, Lata watched the money pile up, as the devotees lined up. "Since you're forcing me into marriage, you might as well increase my dowry."

"No." Ammamma was firm. "This money is meant for God."

"For God, or for the Goddess's grandmother?" Lata said, her voice hard. "I can see the quality of your own life has gone up."

Ammamma struggled for control. Probably because she wasn't in a position to defend herself. The devotees had indeed spent some of that money on making improvements around the house. Our protests were ignored.

Now, as I looked at the troubled Gopal, I had no reason to doubt him. He was a hard working devotee. I sighed. "I will deal with this."

Visibly relieved, he bowed, and left.

After dinner, I broached the topic. "Lata, Gopal came to me today to discuss the finances."

Ammamma looked curious.

"For someone who had no interest in studies," Lata said, "you've been using an awful lot of big words."

"Lata, please," I said wearily, rubbing my neck.

"Did he come by to tattle about the money?" At the look on my face, she said, "Oh, he did, *hanh*?" She flicked her braid over the shoulder. "I took it. So what? It's not like you are going to miss a measly five hundred."

"Five hundred rupees!" Ammamma clutched her chest. "You stole five hundred rupees?"

"*Bah*! Not like the Goddess can't afford it."

"Lata!"

"I gave it to my future in-laws to buy a few household necessities, okay? It's not like you, or those pathetic creatures that are going to be my in-laws, are sinning directly. Besides, who is going to miss the money?"

"That's not the point. It is stealing. That, too, from God." Ammamma's face became so red, I was afraid she was going to have a heart attack.

"Oh, I need a lesson in morality now?" Lata's face was tight with fury.

Before I could stop her, Ammamma picked up the broomstick, and started to thrash Lata with it.

Lata was so shocked by this unexpected assault, she didn't move for a second. Then she started shouting. "Stop her! Stop her! She has gone mad."

But the relatives and friends helping us prepare for the wedding had left for the day.

"Ammamma, it's been only two weeks since the miscarriage," I begged.

Lata tried to dodge the broom, but Ammamma was like a raging bull. Lata tripped and fell.

"Want more money?" Ammamma said, panting, "I'll give you more money, you ungrateful wretch!"

By the time I was able to wrest the broom away, Ammamma was spent. She collapsed to the floor crying.

Lata lay on the ground, hands up to ward off the blows. Angry tears flowed down her cheeks. Her hair was in wild disarray, her lips in an ugly twist. "You... you..." She was so angry she couldn't form a coherent sentence.

I went up to her, thanking the Gods above that no one had been there to witness this madness that was tearing my family apart. I tried to help her to a chair, but she turned on me. "Didn't you and that cow-faced friend of yours always say – *help arrange a wedding, even if you have to tell a thousand lies to do so*? That was forgotten in a hurry, wasn't it?"

I never realized how much Chinni and I had wounded Lata with our teasing.

She turned on Ammamma, face venomous. "I will never forgive you for this. Never." She stormed out of the room, aiming a vicious kick at the door.

My heart thumped in tune with the vibration of the door. I sank onto the floor next to Ammamma and put my hand on her back.

She raised her head. "Where did I go wrong?" Grabbing my hands, she begged, "Tell me, Pullamma. What I did – was it so wrong? I was trying to do right by my dead daughter. I swear on that *Yedukondalavada* – may he knock me dead if I'm lying – I never desired anything for myself. All I wanted was for her daughters to settle well."

I helped Ammamma up and held her tightly. "Don't, Ammamma. You did no different than any other grandparent. You can't hold yourself responsible for other people's actions, even a granddaughter's."

Ammamma pushed herself back, panic in her eyes. "Watch out for that one, Pullamma. Don't let her get away with things just because she is your sister. You know the saying – *atta sommu, alludu daanam*?" Literally mother-in-law's property, son-in-law donates; Ammamma was referring to people who took credit for charity by donating what did not belong to them.

When I nodded, Ammamma said, "It kills me to say such a thing of my own grandchild, but she is the kind who will accept offerings in your name, and spend it without a second thought, and stab you in the back while she is at it."

TWENTY-SEVEN

From the corner of the stage, I watched my sister get married, wishing it were Chinni's wedding I were attending. But Chinni was long gone, married and settled – happily, I hoped – in Kurnool.

After that terrible fight, Lata and Ammamma hadn't exchanged a single word. It didn't help that despite her miscarriage, Lata wasn't allowed to back out of the wedding. What a terrible position for a girl to be in. Ammamma's position wasn't much better, though Lata didn't seem to realize it – after having settled this alliance with all the drama leading up to it, Kondal Rao wouldn't allow loss of face. This wedding, after all, was to be a showcase for his munificence.

Help arrange a wedding, even if you have to tell a thousand lies to do so.

I gave a short laugh. We'd certainly told a lot of lies, some of omission, others more direct, to get to where we were – Lata's wedding. My heart clutched – was my own wedding based on a thousand lies? A thousand devotees did not know I was married, a thousand people lied to. Would Srikar and I pay for it? Forcing my thoughts away from my husband, I wondered if any of the ancient sayings covered my little Goddess problem.

The ornate carving of the armchair I sat in dug into my sides through the three or four really expensive silk saris draped over the back and sides. There was a time when I would have swooned over the saris; now they only made me sweat in the back. I would have happily given up a hundred such saris to be with Srikar again.

I couldn't help but compare this fancy wedding, with its five hundred attendees, with that of my own, where the only participants had been Headmaster *garu*, the registrar, Srikar and I. Other than missing Ammamma, Chinni and my sisters, I wouldn't have had it any other way. Srikar – no, I wouldn't think about him now, or I would fall apart, devotees or not.

Lata, sitting cross-legged on the raised platform, stared glassy-eyed at the sacred fire in front, her lips a straight line. Her husband-to-be sat next to her, following the priest's directions to pour more ghee into the fire.

And so the happy couple weds.

Ammamma sat stiffly behind the couple, not looking at Lata. The groom's parents sat to a side, sneaking awed glances at me every so often. Lakshmi *garu* and Murty *garu* were officiating as parents of the bride; as a widow, Ammamma couldn't be part of anything auspicious.

Kondal Rao's henchmen walked around, occasionally bowing at me, making sure everyone knew of their boss's connection to me. My devotees sat on thick, woven cotton rugs. Only a hundred-odd guests had been invited by the bride's or the groom's side. The rest had been rounded up by Kondal Rao as a show of strength.

Each time I thought of that man, my blood pressure spiked. The sudden, and increasingly frequent, violent feelings within me ended up leaving me terrified. I lived in fear of losing control, of lashing out at whomever crossed my path, of ripping apart everything around me. The next time someone touched my feet, I feared doing them grievous harm. Sometimes my head felt ready to explode with all the anger that had no expression, all the sorrow that had no resolution. I was desperate to give this all up and hurtle down the highway to Hyderabad, to Srikar.

I watched the wedding rituals, trying to take in deep breaths without drawing attention to myself. I rubbed a hand across the back of my neck to loosen the tension. Migraine. A devotee sprang up, palms of his hands joined together. "*Ammavaru*, what is your desire?"

Was the Goddess allowed aspirin?

I thought not. I waved him away.

"*Melam*," the priest shouted. The three snoring musicians, who'd been curled up on the floor, recovering from an all-night wedding, rose up in one fluid motion and assumed their positions. Sounds of the *sannai* rent the air in under thirty seconds. The bride and groom pressed the cumin-jaggery mixture on the top of each other's heads. The priests chanted hymns at a shout, trying to make themselves heard over the loud music. The *sannai* players blew louder. Turmeric coated rice was showered on the newly-wed couple. Job done, the musicians set their *sannais* on the floor, and went back to sleep. The couple was married. The wedding was over, but the rituals would continue.

There was only so much I could take. I got up to go. My entire retinue hurried up along with me. I stifled a sigh.

"Pullamma!" Lata called across the room. "Bless us before you go."

I swallowed a surge of resentment. Like Lakshmi *garu*, Lata seemed to revel in my new role. She made sure everyone was always aware of her relationship to me. Unlike Chinni's mother, Lata liked the attention my 'powers' brought her.

I waited for the newlyweds to come up to me. I blessed them, and stalked out.

My entourage rushed to catch up.

We proceeded the one kilometre to Ammamma's in a four-Ambassador convoy. Once there, I was helped out of the car by a devotee. He held a long, ornamental umbrella high above my head to protect me from the sun as I walked across the courtyard. Another helped me onto an intricately carved bench swing, fortunately more comfortable than the chair at the wedding. She helped tuck my feet beneath me. A third devotee pushed the swing in gentle rhythm, while yet another fanned me with a palm-leaf. Power cuts were on four hours each day, so each devotee took a thirty minute shift. Kondal Rao had promised to speak to the local electrical substation to make sure I was exempt from this foolishness, but till that happened, the fanning would continue.

The devotees were alert to my smallest need. They'd have fanned me through the night, had I allowed it. Hard as I tried to appreciate their selflessness, this near-constant attention to my comforts drove me crazy. Unfortunately, the devotees took it as a personal affront if I declined their services.

But, now, too restless for politeness, I got down from the swing and walked in to the house, indicating I was to be left alone. Closing the door, I paced about, waiting for Ammamma to send Lata off to her husband's house, and return home.

Three hours later, the door rattled. With great relief I let Ammamma in.

She sank to the mat. "I'm glad the wedding's out of the way."

"Did you talk to Kondal Rao?"

"I did."

At her tone, I said sharply, "He won't let me leave?"

"He said you can leave whenever you want. According to him it's less headache for him if you go into hiding."

"So what's the problem?"

"I told him you couldn't leave openly. The devotees won't let you go." Her lips quivered.

"So?"

"He said he didn't have the time for trivial issues. Then he left."

The phone, newly installed, rang. I knew better than to answer my own phone. Yet another devotee ran up with it, the long extension cord trailing.

I reached for the phone, hand trembling. Srikar, or Kondal Rao? I waved everyone away, waiting till they closed the door behind them.

"Hello?"

"Pullamma, it is me," Srikar said.

"You can't call here!"

"Don't worry, no one's listening."

"How can you be sure?" All long distances calls were routed through the operator, a terrible gossip.

"I'm in the village," Srikar said. "Is your entourage around?"

"No." He'd come all the way to the village just to make a phone call? I looked at Srikar's mirrored globe suspended from the ceiling, wishing he were here, instead.

"The way things have been going, I wasn't sure the wedding would actually happen," Srikar said. "Now that it is out of the way..."

"Thank god, you're here. Your grandfather refused to help me get away."

Srikar was too decent a man to say *I told you so.* "For my grandfather to act honourably would have been out of character." He hesitated, then rushed into speech. "Now that Lata is married, why don't we take Ammamma and disappear? I have a job offer from a construction company in Dubai. I'll get our passports made. Let's leave all of this behind. We can make a new life there."

"How will we get away? They won't even let me leave the compound."

"We'll work out a plan."

I started to cry. "*Yemandi*, please. Do it as soon as possible. I don't know how much more of this I can take."

TWENTY-EIGHT

S rikar's escape plan gave me renewed hope. Everything became easier to bear now that there was an end in sight. I got up at 4:30 a.m., performed my prayers, practiced meditation under Ammamma's guidance, had breakfast, saw devotees, had lunch. Then Ammamma and I locked ourselves in our private sanctuary. If not for this, I might have gone mad. Ammamma sensed this and kept everyone out, no exceptions. Other than Lata, that is. Nothing could have kept her out.

I wished I could have seen Malli before we left India forever. But her in-laws were so demanding, they would never allow her to visit. In my uncharitable moments I wished Lata's in-laws were half as demanding, but they were too awed by her connection to me. Regardless, she was good training ground for me to maintain my stoic facade.

Tiring as my days were, the nights were worse. That was when I allowed myself to think of Srikar. I worried constantly that something would go wrong with the Dubai plan – maybe they would withdraw the offer, maybe they wouldn't allow his family to accompany him, maybe they would deny Ammamma the visa.

With the fears came the tears. Rigid as my self-control was in public, in private it was virtually non-existent. Many nights I whipped myself into a frenzy of panic, unable to calm myself down.

"I don't know if I have the energy to keep this up," I said to Ammamma after a particularly strenuous day. "I am so tired all the time; I can't sleep at night. I don't know how Gurus keep up with this schedule." We were in our private quarters, away from judging eyes. That was the hardest part for me, the fact that people's eyes were always trained on me. Every movement of mine, every gesture, every blink was analyzed for divine significance.

When we'd talked last, Srikar said the next time he phoned, he hoped it would be with good news. It was a week since he'd called. I collapsed on the bed. Lata was back on one of her increasingly frequent visits, and it wasn't helping. I had no idea what went on in her marriage, why she had so much time to direct my life. She didn't talk about it, and I didn't ask.

I lay back and stretched out, looking at the mirrored globe Srikar had bought me, trying to derive comfort from it. Why hadn't he called? "I am so tired. I don't know if I can get up tomorrow."

"Why don't you get someone to help?" Lata said. "At least ten of your hangers-on will jump at the chance."

"How?" Ammamma asked, addressing the wall behind Lata's head; she no longer talked directly to Lata. "Get a substitute Goddess?"

Lata ignored Ammamma and bounced onto the bed, next to me. "What's the big thing about privacy anyway? I would love to have someone wait on me hand and foot."

Ammamma pointedly turned her back on her youngest granddaughter. "Let me get you some *idlis*," she said, heading to the kitchen. "I made your favourite chutney." She returned with a plate piled with *idlis,* and bent forward to help me up.

"I'm so tired, Ammamma," I said, voice slurring. "I just want to sleep."

"I'd let you," she said, sounding apologetic, "but you are losing weight."

I reached for the *idlis.* Feeling a sudden surge of nausea, I covered my mouth with a hand, and ran to the bathroom. I retched violently till I had emptied the contents of my stomach.

Ammamma rushed in. "The strain is getting to you, Child. You need to take better care of yourself. There is sickness in the air."

I washed up, and crawled back into bed.

"You need to eat at least one *idli*, Child. It will help settle your stomach."

"I can't," I pleaded, "I can't even bear to be in the same room as food."

"How long since your period?" Ammamma suddenly asked.

"I've missed two," I said slowly.

We looked at each other in mounting horror.

"Oh, no!" Ammamma felt blindly for the chair behind her, and sank into it.

Lata sat up. "What were you thinking, Pullamma? Haven't our elders said that you should never get pregnant in *Ashadha Masam*? If the child is born deformed, you will have only yourself to blame."

Newlyweds traditionally stayed apart in *Ashadha Masam* – the inauspicious period in June-July, so a child wouldn't result. Some people believed that a child conceived in *Ashadha Masam,* and therefore due in *Chaitra Masam* – sometime in March – would be born handicapped.

Ammamma leaned over, grabbed Lata's arm and yanked hard.

"What?" Lata said. "I'm only telling the truth." For someone so against traditional wisdom, Lata was certainly spouting a lot of it lately.

"If you want to open your mouth," Ammamma said through clenched teeth, "say only good things. Remember, the *tathastu devatalu* are always around."

Tathastu devatalu. The so-be-it Gods. Elders said that these Gods made words leaving one's mouth come true.

Lata snorted.

Wordlessly Ammamma pulled Lata down from the bed, dragged her to the door, opened it and shoved her out into the courtyard. It was a measure of her outrage that she didn't bother to see if anyone was watching. Shutting the door on Lata, she sagged against it. "What have you done, Child?" she asked, face ashen.

"A baby!" I said, closing my eyes and leaning against the headboard. I felt the beginnings of a smile.

"No one knows you are married. How will you explain away a baby?"

"We have a plan," I told Ammamma. I couldn't stop smiling at the thought of the baby. "Srikar is working on it." Srikar and I had decided to hold off telling Ammamma about the Dubai plan till everything was in place, but things had changed.

"You are fools if you think you can escape Kondal Rao's clutches."

"Weren't you the one who told Srikar and me to disappear?"

"Weren't you the one who told me that he'd never let you go?"

"I can't live like this, Ammamma." I put a protective hand on my belly.

"Think," Ammamma begged, "this isn't something you'll be able to talk your way through."

"I don't talk in public."

"*Bah!* You know what I mean."

"Don't worry, Ammamma. It is early yet. Things will fall in place long before my due date." I lay back and stretched luxuriously. Now that I knew the cause of my near constant tiredness, I suddenly felt energetic.

Ammamma sank to the floor and fell against the door. "Oh *Lord of the Seven Hills!* Oh *Yedukondalavada!* Watch over these young innocents."

I got down from bed, settled on the chair and reached for the phone.

Ammamma sat up, face alarmed. "What are you doing?"

"Calling my husband."

"Are you out of your mind?" Ammamma shrieked.

"Considering this is his baby," I said, "don't you think he has the right to know?"

"What about the operator? She'll be listening to everything you say."

"Make the connection for me, Ammamma. Please?" I'd just have to be careful.

Muttering under her breath, Ammamma booked the trunk call.

The call came through ten minutes later. After Srikar and I had spoken of minor matters, I prepared to give him the news. Suddenly, I felt embarrassed. Maybe I should have asked Ammamma. "Uh." I stopped, not sure how to proceed.

"What is it?"

"You know those plans discussed in the park... in the evenings... on the swing?"

"Yes?"

"Plans have to be put off, things have changed. In a good way."

"Oh no!"

I was so shaken by his unguarded reaction that I dropped the phone. The call disconnected. Despite several tries, the operator was unable to connect me back. Not wanting to face Ammamma, I got into the bed, and turned off the light.

"Pullamma?" Ammamma whispered about twenty minutes later.

"What?" I asked, trying to sound sleepy.

"Srikar phoned Lakshmi *garu*'s house. He is on his way."

TWENTY-NINE

Iran a cloth over the newly acquired chairs and flower vase. "Move," I told Lata. "I need to dust." The ashram was shut down. No one to tell me what I could, or couldn't, do. I'd already prepared the delicacies Srikar liked. Now I was cleaning, making sure everything was perfect for my husband.

"It's only your husband that's coming, not some royalty."

Ignoring her, I dragged a chair, and started on the cobwebs.

Jerking her head at me, Lata asked Ammamma, "Doesn't she have devoted followers for this sort of thing?"

Ammamma gave a noncommittal shrug.

"Stop fidgeting, will you?" Lata said to me. "You are driving me crazy."

"When Srikar comes, you will greet him, then leave," Ammamma said.

Part of me wished I could leave, too. Srikar's abrupt response last night had been as wounding as it had been unexpected. I didn't know what to make of his reaction.

"Why can't I stay back?" Lata asked with a pout. "This is the first time I will be meeting my brother-in-law formally. I want to see his reaction, too." She said to Ammamma, "You will be there."

"I wish I could have stayed out. This is, after all, a private matter between husband and wife. But we can't afford to give people the chance to talk."

Ammamma had ordered the ashram closed to the public on the pretext that *Ammavaru* – that would be me – was going into a state of meditation. Only the priest was permitted to come in for the twice-daily prayers. Even he wasn't allowed access into my sanctuary, though.

There was a knock on the door. We stiffened. "It's only me," Lakshmi *garu* said. Ammamma opened the door. Srikar stood behind Lakshmi *garu*.

I smiled at him tremulously; how much I'd missed him.

He smiled back.

Ammamma cleared her throat.

Suddenly conscious of our audience, I jerked my attention from him. I introduced my sister to my husband.

"This is the grand passion of your life, *hanh*?" Lata looked him over. "The one that keeps you awake at nights?"

There was shocked silence. Lakshmi *garu* clapped a hand to her mouth.

"Lata!" Ammamma looked mortified.

"Not bad," Lata said. "Better than what you saddled me with."

I felt terrible embarrassment on my sister's behalf. She seemed to think being married entitled her to speak her mind.

"Leave." Ammamma grabbed Lata by the arm. "Don't come back before tomorrow."

After Ammamma had shut the door, Srikar bent to touch Ammamma's feet. Ammamma touched his head gently and said, "I wish I could give you more than blessings, Son."

"Right now that's what I need the most."

"You youngsters go and talk in the bedroom." Ammamma settled in the front room.

As we stood hesitating, Ammamma urged, "Go, Children. And shut the door."

Slightly embarrassed, I followed Srikar into the bedroom, and closed the door behind me.

As we reached for each other, I said, "I'm so glad you're here. I missed you so much."

"Me, too."

I held him, not wanting to let go. But the longer he stayed, the riskier it was. Taking a deep breath, I said, "You haven't said anything about the baby."

"I want this baby, too," Srikar said. "I can't tell you how much."

But he didn't seem nearly as excited as I was. I felt a little let down. Was he upset that we had deviated from the map of our lives – college first, then kids? Or perhaps his first reaction was an unguarded honest reaction, and he did not want kids at all? The last thought jarred me enough that I found myself unable to ask what he really felt about the baby. Some things were better left unsaid.

"Do we have a date for the trip?" I asked, conscious that Ammamma sat guard on the other side of the door. Once our decision to escape to Dubai was made, I'd lost my ability to be patient. I was getting increasingly desperate.

"They turned me down." Srikar's voice was flat.

"What?" My heart began to hit hard against my ribs. "But why?"

"My grandfather is a politician, remember?"

"What has that got to do with us leaving the country?"

"Passports are never issued without police verification. They rejected my application."

"How would your grandfather know what you're up to? He isn't keeping track of you, is he?"

"Apparently, it's not uncommon for corrupt politicians to give the police a list of names to put on a watch list. As long as you're in the country, you're okay. The moment you apply for a passport, you get on their radar."

Why was I not surprised? Politicians and the police went together like food-poisoning and stomach cramps – where one was, the other couldn't fail to follow.

"I still want the baby," I said.

As we lay on the bed together, he said, "I don't see how. How will you get away from here? Where will you have the baby? Or, if you decide to get an abortion, how will you do it? There are always too many people around you."

"Two days ago Lakshmi *garu* found a woman who makes herbal concoctions that can cause a miscarriage."

"Do you want to do it?" Srikar said. "Get an abortion, I mean?"

"No."

"I don't, either."

The fact that he also wanted this baby gave me courage. I felt strong, ready to take on the world for my child. I would protect it with everything I had. With my life, if I had to. "We'll manage."

"How?" Srikar said, despair in his voice.

"Ammamma tells me my mother didn't get very big, even in the later months. Hopefully, I won't either. Anyway, by the time the baby is ready to come, we'll be in Hyderabad."

"Don't be so sure."

"Didn't you say you'd come up with a plan?"

"What if I can't?"

"I'll be trying, too."

"What if the baby comes early? What then?"

"I'm trying not to think that far ahead." My voice caught.

"You should. We'll need a few different options on hand."

Despite what he'd said to Ammamma about me being free to leave, Srikar's grandfather had me watched now. I couldn't scrunch up my nose without it being reported back to him. Getting Srikar in without their notice had been easy, because the job of his henchmen was to prevent me from sneaking out. It hadn't occurred to them that someone might want to sneak in, though I was surprised his grandfather had overlooked that possibility.

"I have a few months, yet. Hopefully his goons will get bored and slack off. I'll bide my time. I *am* going to get away," I said. "Don't ask me how, because I don't know yet. But I promise you, I will."

THIRTY

Following Srikar's return to the city, I struggled with the need to maintain a façade of calm in public. I had the urge to burst into tears all the time – whether it was due to the pregnancy, or the thwarted escape plan to Dubai, or because I missed Srikar, I couldn't tell. But I was breaking down more and more. I spent inordinate amounts of time watching Srikar's mirrored globe twirl from the ceiling, tracking it as it cast its myriad of hexagonal reflections about the room. This tangible evidence of Srikar's existence was the only thing that gave me some measure of comfort. And the baby, of course. So far I had managed to retain control in public, but I knew Ammamma was concerned.

After gaining ascendancy to a Minister's post in the State Cabinet, Kondal Rao came to see me. At a packed *bhajan* one evening, he waddled up to my chair and bowed his head. "*Ammavaru*, a thousand *namaskarams*! May I have permission to speak in your benevolent presence?"

I nodded, almost choking with the effort.

"With your permission, I would like to build a temple big enough, and grand enough to befit you."

Rage flooded my being. He'd lied! He'd never had any intention of letting me go.

"Please accept this insignificant offering from your most humble devotee." Since he was facing me, his back to the devotees, he stared directly in to my eyes, warning me not to refuse.

Blood rushed to my face. The audacity of the infernal man! The sheer gall! He had me in his grip, slowly crushing me like he might an insect, and he wanted bloody acknowledgement? My face hurt from the effort of controlling my fury. I shut my eyes, not wanting anyone to witness my rage. When I opened them, I saw Kondal Rao's face had darkened even as he struggled to remain calm. I found myself unable to give him the acknowledgement he sought, recognizing at one level that it was dangerous to make an enemy of this man.

Later that night, after the devotees had gone home for the night, Ammamma and I sat on the swing, looking up at the night sky. A chill invaded my bones. If he went ahead with the temple, I was doomed.

"You didn't do a wise thing by crossing Kondal Rao," Ammamma said. The '*garu*' honorific for him had long been dispensed with, even by my grandmother.

"Ammamma," I exclaimed. "If he builds me that temple –"

"I know, Child. I know. But you can't afford to cross him, not in public. He is too powerful a man."

"What would you have me do?" I asked, feeling fresh outrage. "Feed his colossal ego?"

"Hate him if you will, and God knows you have enough reasons, but don't give him leeway to bury you alive."

"I don't understand."

"Having made his grand announcement, he won't be able to back out. The key is to give him just enough to keep him happy, but not enough that it harms you."

"How?"

"Let him build something, anything, just not a temple."

"Like what?"

"A small ashram, perhaps."

"How will that help?"

"In the ashram you'll have the option of starting up vocational training courses for youngsters, teaching *bhajans* to children, discussing spiritual texts with older people. That puts the donations to good use, he doesn't lose face, and you aren't bound by a temple."

"He makes me so angry, Ammamma, I can't get myself to accept anything from him. It is not like he is doing any of it out of the goodness of his heart. He just wants to make a show for his voting public. Besides, you and I both know that no matter what I do, he is never going to let me go."

"Then it is even more important that we not let him build that temple. We can always hope things will change. But, till then, it would be foolish to antagonize him further."

I recognized the wisdom in Ammamma's words, but it burned me up that the wretched man was using me to further his own interests. At the expense of my happiness, my life with my husband. "The land he wants to build the temple on is not even his, you know," I said. "He has intimidated villagers into 'donating' it."

"When someone controls the police, ordinary people end up getting crushed."

"He's leeched onto our family like a bad omen. Poor Lata, to be forced into that wedding."

Ammamma sighed. "Once she got pregnant without the benefit of a wedding, even God couldn't have saved her."

I nodded slowly. There were some things in life you couldn't expect forgiveness for.

"That man is lower than the belly of a snake," Ammamma said, "husband of my dear friend, though he is. But still, you cannot afford to refuse him publicly. Men like him don't get to where they are by taking 'no' for an answer." She had worry in her eyes. "And there is that other thing."

"Ammamma, he is such a powerful man. Do you honestly believe he won't find out I am carrying his great-grandchild?"

Ammamma looked around fearfully, though she and I were in the empty courtyard and the gate was locked. She leaned forward and whispered, "Forget this fact. Don't even *think* about it again. If Kondal Rao finds out, you won't live long enough to hold your child in your arms."

How could I forget my baby? I never referred to it again for Ammamma's sake, but plans of escape consumed almost all of my waking thoughts, and most of my sleeping ones.

Thirty-One

arly next morning Satyam, the priest – lackey of Kondal Rao – brought word from his master that the ashram was to remain closed. On account of my being in meditation. Hopefully, all this unscheduled meditation was doing me some good.

Kondal Rao stormed in moments after Satyam's departure. He tapped his foot impatiently as his sidekicks closed the gate to the courtyard, then erupted. "What game are you playing?"

"What game?" I said.

"Don't try your innocent act with me," he roared, face so red I feared it would burst.

"Pullamma," Ammamma said urgently. "Let me talk."

I shut up, but not without effort.

"Kondal Rao *garu*," Ammamma said, "you are like an elder brother to me–"

"Cut the bullshit!"

Ammamma was so shocked, she abruptly shut her mouth. It would have never occurred to her that the husband of her childhood friend would disrespect her so.

Kondal Rao stabbed a finger at me. "Tell this little granddaughter of yours never to forget her place. I made her. I can also break her. I have bought and sold hundreds like her. She should be grateful I am even ready to give her my patronage."

"Of course, of course." Ammamma's lips quivered. "She is but a child, please forgive her mistake."

Trembling with rage, I opened my mouth. Ammamma quelled me with a sharp look.

Turning to Kondal Rao, she said, "We are simple village folk. What do we know of accepting unimaginable gifts like brand new temples?"

"She dared throw my gift in my face!" He gave me a furious look. "Have you taught her nothing? Has she no gratitude?"

"Please forgive her," Ammamma begged. "She is immature, yet."

I ground my teeth down in an effort to stem my words.

Ammamma soldiered on. "Little people like us cannot think big, Kondal Rao *garu*. If you were to build Pullamma a temple, and she let you down because she didn't know how to behave, it would cause you unimaginable loss of face."

And the loss of an election, though Ammamma didn't come out and say it.

"Hmm." He appeared to be thinking.

"I have a suggestion, if I may," Ammamma said, "which is sure to enhance your prestige."

"Tell me."

"Build an ashram. Bigger than this little house, if you wish."

He snorted. "And that will help me, how?"

"If you would consider it for a moment." Ammamma took a deep breath. "If you were to build the temple, people would know, of course, that it was your generosity that built it, but it would forever be associated with Pullamma." Just in case he'd missed the point, Ammamma reiterated, "The temple might cause her stature to eclipse yours."

Kondal Rao pursed his lips. "I hadn't thought of that."

I'm sure he hadn't, the snake.

"But if the plaque on the ashram carried your name..."

Kondal Rao's beady eyes glinted. "Tell me more."

"You might consider starting a free school for underprivileged children. Yoga classes. Spiritual classes. Offer free meals. That will do a better job of reminding people of your generosity." Ammamma cleared her throat. "Pardon me for speaking so, but during election time, this would be of great use."

"How so?"

"The ashram would automatically generate jobs for maintenance, teachers, and so on. Money is not an issue, obviously, with so much pouring in. In these hard times, people who are able to find, and retain, jobs will be grateful to their benefactor, especially if he throws in a little extra here and there."

"*Hanh!*" Kondal Rao stroked his chin.

"You wouldn't want people to forget, pardon my impudence, who the real benefactor is, would you? If Pullamma sat in her temple, granting boons, she would be the one who'd stay in people's minds."

I held my breath. *Please let him think this is a good idea!*

"Your idea has some merit." He pursed his lips again. "Very

well. Go bring the almanac. We'll need an auspicious date for the new ashram's groundbreaking."

"Kondal Rao *garu*?"

"What now?"

"I would like to beg something else for your consideration."

"What is it?"

"I came to this house as a seven-year-old bride. I have seen many harvests pass here."

"Most of them bad."

"Quite true." Ammamma inclined her head in acknowledgment. "I have faced many hardships. But I would like to be carried to my funeral from this house only."

"You stay then. Your granddaughter will move to the new ashram."

"Who will manage her if I am not there?"

"Then you move to the ashram, too." And he turned to go.

All my relief began to dissolve into anger. How dare he talk to my grandmother so?

"Kondal Rao *garu*?" Ammamma said.

"*Bah*! What is it now?"

"When Pullamma's mother died, when it seemed like I might have to sell this house to support my three granddaughters and myself, I promised the Lord on the Seven Hills that if he let me keep this house, I would light a lamp for him in my altar every day for the rest of my life." She turned toward the kitchen, joined the palms of her hands and bowed. "The altar in this house."

Kondal Rao swore under his breath. Even he wasn't brazen enough to come between a woman and her promise to God. "You were the one who suggested the ashram in the first place."

"That I did. Perhaps we could convert part of the house into an ashram..."

"Then I am going to make it bigger and better."

"Not bigger," I said.

Kondal Rao looked as if he couldn't believe I'd dared to open my mouth in his august presence.

"Quiet, Pullamma!" Ammamma hissed.

"If you want me to cooperate," I said, "I will not live in a mansion."

Kondal Rao's jowls quivered.

"This foolish child doesn't know what she is saying," Ammamma said, sweat breaking out on her forehead. "What she means to say is, we won't be able to manage such a place. We are poor folk. What do we know of grand mansions?" Ammamma's hands, joined at the palms, trembled.

"You have so many devotees. Make use of them."

Ammamma bent her head. "My granddaughter isn't able to recognize your big-heartedness. What if she has a breakdown? I humbly request you to set aside one room, kitchen and bathroom in this house for us to live in privacy. The ashram can be built around it."

"Hmm." He considered me, stubby forefinger tapping his chin. "Okay, your current house shall remain the same. We'll have to upgrade it, of course – Italian marble in the courtyard, fancy fans, modern kitchen, that sort of stuff. This can be the new ashram. I will break open your wall on that side," he pointed a finger, "and build your private quarters there."

I said, "But that is Buchaiah's hous–"

"Quiet," Kondal Rao roared.

"Don't let this foolish girl ruin your plan." Ammamma's face was white.

He swerved to a henchman. "Who's this Buchaiah?"

"Old man, seventy-plus, no wife or sons."

Kondal Rao struggled for control. "Leave Buchaiah to me. Old fellow like him. How much longer will he live, anyway? I can't build you some village-type rooms. I have my prestige to consider. Enough of these discussions. I shall consult the almanac myself for an auspicious day. Then the work can begin."

"Not a word," Ammamma warned as Kondal Rao stalked out.

THIRTY-TWO

Poor Buchaiah. To be hustled out of his family home, one that had seen so many generations of his family, in so disgraceful a manner. All because he had no male heirs. His wife had died forty years ago, his daughters long married and settled in the city.

The elderly man was trundled off, no fuss no muss, to an old age home one district over. The courtyard wall to the left of the front room, which adjoined that poor man's property, was broken down to open into another, smaller, diamond-shaped courtyard. Two bedrooms, each with attached bathrooms, and a kitchen were built around a private courtyard, with a planter occupying the place of honour in the middle – the sacred *tulsi* planted in it.

Our sanctuary was truly private. It was off-limits to everyone, including the maids. Sometimes I wished it were off-limits to Lata, too. It wasn't as if I didn't understand her anger – she'd been denied her dream of being a doctor, and living a life of comfort. Instead she was married to a man she couldn't abide, while I'd ended up with the luxurious lifestyle, and the supportive husband. That I was tied down as Goddess, and away from my husband, wasn't something Lata considered a negative. Still. I wished I could feel closer to my sister, but she had a way of wearing me down.

If there was any upside to being forced to live away from my husband, it was that I was able to provide Ammamma with the comforts of life. No detail was overlooked in the building of our private quarters – from luxurious furnishings, to air conditioners, to a large television, I did not lack anything.

Ammamma no longer had tedious chores to take care of. No milking the cow, no backbreaking sewing, no endless rounds of pickle-making. The old house was upgraded, as promised by Kondal Rao. Walls were repaired, paintings put up on them, good quality curtains hung on windows. The courtyard was beautified, the uneven cobblestones replaced with expensive marble. Now it served as a central gathering place for my followers.

Ammamma and I retired to our private quarters at eight each night, when I shut the door, and the world, out. Ammamma spent an hour cooking up a meal in our fancy kitchen, then got on her hands and knees to scrub the expensive flooring. I had offered to let the maid come in when we were with the devotees, but Ammamma insisted on doing this herself. All her other chores – our breakfast and lunch included – had been taken over by the devotees anyway.

Power cuts, for us, were a thing of the past. Kondal Rao had arranged for power generators running on diesel, keeping us in light while the rest of the village batted mosquitoes in the dark. I felt terrible about this, but Lata told me to get over it. For Lata, a visit to the ashram was her only chance of getting away from the drudgery of life. I felt disloyal for the thought, but I could have done with a little less sisterhood.

"Why do you lock yourself in all the time?" Lata asked as she followed Ammamma in after a particularly gruelling session. Vineeta, my schoolmate in another life, had lost her mother last night, and I wasn't up to dealing with my twin.

"Leave her alone," Ammamma said. "She deserves some quiet."

What Ammamma didn't add was that we were worried. My pregnancy was advancing, but we weren't able to feel the baby's movement.

Ammamma said, "She has a hard life being in the public glare all the time."

"If you think this is hardship," Lata said, flouncing on my opulent bed, "you should see our house. No power six hours a day. I have to draw water from the well for cooking, cleaning, for my husband's and in-laws' baths; I get to thatch the roof, make pickles for sale, scrounge around for cow dung. My mother-in-law is such a taskmaster. Why hire a servant when there is the sister of the Goddess, right?"

"I'm sorry, Lata," I said, feeling remorse. "I've been so involved in my own problems that I haven't been able to see how you're suffering."

"Then give me a monthly stipend. Enough to upgrade my house. Some for my personal use. I am the Goddess's kin, after all."

"Lata, you know I have no money to give you."

Lata ran her eyes over the place. "You're swimming in luxury, and you have no money?"

Put that way, it did sound unbelievable. "None of that is mine,

Lata. It belongs to the devotees." Ammamma and I had never used a *paisa* for personal use, never would.

"Didn't stop you from improving your lot, did it?"

What could I say? While it was true Kondal Rao had forced me into accepting a higher standard of living so he could look good to his voters, the money *had* made my life very comfortable indeed.

"Well, are you going to give me the money or not?"

My chest hurt at the thought of denying her. I didn't want unpleasantness with my sister. "I wish I could, Lata. I really do. But I have no money of my own." Other than the money Srikar managed to send, here and there. But that was barely enough for my personal use. Ammamma had her monthly pension, at least.

"Oh, so that's going to be your line, *hanh*, while you enjoy your earthly pleasures?"

Ammamma was on the verge of an angry retort. I shook my head slightly, guilt churning in my gut. Lata had the right to be bitter. Hers was not a life of choices.

Lata stretched out on the bed and wiggled till she was settled comfortably. "How come you get such a fancy bed, while my fool of a husband and I have to make do with hard, cotton mattresses?"

"*Yedukondalavada!*" Ammamma said, appalled that Lata would disrespect her husband so.

"Take it." I wished there were some way I could help my sister, but I wouldn't touch the devotees' money. Was giving away the items they had bought for my use as bad as stealing their money? I wished I knew. All I was sure of was that a mat unrolled on the floor would suit me just fine. I would have slept on the cobbled courtyard floor if it meant I could go back to living with my husband in our small flat, with a bathroom that was shared between six other families.

"So how long are you here for?" I asked.

"Already waiting to be rid of me?"

"She never said that, Lata," Ammamma said, patience strained. I knew she was also wracked by constant guilt. Guilt that she hadn't been able to prevent the breakup of my marriage, guilt that Lata had been forced into a bad one. But she was also unable to forgive Lata her actions. It was a close contest which of Lata's two transgressions was the bigger one in her mind – getting pregnant out of wedlock, or putting me in a position where I was forced to come back to the village as Goddess. Probably getting pregnant before marriage, if I had to pick one. Lata and Ammamma were not getting along at all now; quite a change from when Lata had been the favoured one.

For her part, Lata couldn't get past her anger that Ammamma had not allowed her to pursue her dream. "How come you always take her side? Is it because of all this?" Lata asked indicating the luxury surrounding us.

Ammamma gazed at Lata steadily, till Lata dropped her eyes. Whatever her failings, Ammamma's integrity was indisputable.

"So what is happening in your in-laws' house?" I asked. This constant sniping between my grandmother and sister was taking its toll on me. Surprisingly, she chose to answer.

"They are already after me to breed an heir." Lata inspected her nails. "Do I look like a performing monkey that I can produce a baby on command?"

Ammamma turned away, an expression of distaste on her face.

THIRTY-THREE

Late one evening, Ammamma and I sat on the swing, savouring the silence of the warm night. The devotees had left for the day. The ashram was blessedly quiet, but we were worried. I was already in my seventh month, but hadn't been able to feel my baby move.

"Some women can't feel movement in their first pregnancy," Ammamma said. "Because of inexperience." But she looked anxious.

I was worried, too. I should have already been under a doctor's care. I was also beginning to show. Loosely tied saris wouldn't work much longer. We had hoped that the months of uneventful days would cause Kondal Rao's men to slack off, but the wretched men never moved from their posts outside our courtyard gate.

"Help!" A shrill cry shattered the stillness of the night.

Ammamma and I looked at each other in alarm. We ran to the gate.

I could see orange flames licking the thatched straw roof of the house across from us. The guards and the villagers were already running to it, buckets in hand. I started to go towards the fire when Ammamma suddenly veered off in another direction.

"Wait here," she called over her shoulder. In seconds she was lost in the crowds.

I ran back to the house and grabbed a bucket.

A man approached. "*Ammavaru*," he said respectfully, "please take a seat." He held a hand out for the bucket. "We will handle this."

For a moment I had forgotten myself.

The man took the bucket, escorted me back to the gate of our compound, bowed respectfully and went back. A few men had climbed the roofs of adjoining houses. A human chain was rapidly forming to the well next door; the villagers passed buckets of water from person to person. Even as people started to throw water on the flames, part of the roof gave way.

I watched, grateful that no one lived in the house.

"You have to leave," Ammamma said tersely. She had suddenly reappeared.

"What?"

"Leave. Now. This is your chance. Kondal Rao's men are occupied with the fire."

"But –"

"Pullamma," a male voice called.

I spun around so fast, I made myself dizzy.

"Srikar," Ammamma exclaimed. "What are you doing here?"

My heart fluttered. "How did you get here?"

"I paid Narasu to create a diversion," he said, eyes darting furiously. "All I told him to do was run through the streets, creating a din. Instead, your fool of a brother-in-law seems to have gotten into his head that fire would be a better distraction."

I turned to the burning house. "That's a brand new house. Poor Chandu was going to move in tomorrow."

"There's no one inside," Srikar said. "I checked." He put a hand on my shoulder. "Let's go, Pullamma. Once we get to Hyderabad, I will send Ammamma the money for damage to the house."

"And I will get it rebuilt," Ammamma said. "I promise." She caught my arm and steered me to the house. "Now get going."

I looked at Ammamma, blood surging. This was it.

"Quick," she said.

I ran back into the house, grabbed a bag and started to dump my things. Then I dragged a chair and started to reach for my precious globe.

"Have you lost your mind?" Ammamma screeched. "There is no time."

But I wouldn't leave without it. I tugged at the top of the twine. Luckily, it gave way. Ammamma brought a shawl to cover my head with. We ran out the gate, terrified we would be spotted. Fortunately, everyone's attention was on the fire.

"Let's go," Srikar said, urging me on.

At the car I paused, knowing this was it. I didn't know if I would see Ammamma again.

Ammamma gave me a quick hug and said, "Get in now."

I gave Ammamma a lingering hug. Now that I was finally leaving, I almost didn't want to.

"Hurry, Child," Ammamma said urgently.

"Come with us," I said suddenly. "There is no reason for you to stay here. It's not like either Lata or Malli are going to miss you."

"I can't, Child," Ammamma said, cupping my face. "Tomorrow Malli will have babies, then Lata. Where else will they be able to rest after their deliveries, if not in their mother's house? Who else will pamper them during recovery, *hanh*?" She swallowed. "This is my home, Child. It is right that I stay here. Now you need to go to yours."

"If I never see you again," I said, swallowing convulsively, "I –" I broke down.

Ammamma gave me a tight hug. "Yes, yes," she said, voice choked. "Now go." She pushed me into the waiting taxi.

I got in, Srikar right behind. We crouched in the backseat of the taxi as it raced into the night.

We travelled through the starlit night on the unlit highway. Half-way to Hyderabad we sat up in the backseat. I laid my head against the back. "I can't believe we got away."

Srikar's hand tightened around mine. "The trick will be staying one step ahead of my esteemed grandfather. Hopefully, you'll be safe for the next five years."

Till the next elections.

That first night back, we sat on the terrace after dark, my back resting against Srikar's chest, his hands on my belly. I manoeuvred my heavy body sideways and burrowed my face in my husband's shoulder, savouring his closeness, his smell. I rubbed my cheek against his chest. He tightened his arms around me. I closed my eyes, feeling warmth flood me.

"Uh!" I shot up, hitting my head against Srikar's chin.

"What happened?" Srikar exclaimed, rubbing his chin.

In response I took his hand and placed it on my belly. I turned to look at him. The expression on his face changed slowly from worry to awe. "The baby?"

I nodded, smile trembling on my lips.

"So we don't need to worry?"

"I hope not."

"Thank God!" Srikar pulled me close and buried his face in my neck.

"We should start packing," Srikar said, early next morning.

"What for? I just got here."

"You know why. Just because my grandfather is busy with his Cabinet post doesn't mean we're safe. Besides, you were Goddess for months this time around. There's a greater chance you'll be recognized."

"But your passport application was denied."

"I didn't say we'll leave the country, Pullamma. We'll just move to a different state."

"You know Hindi, so you'll manage. What about me? All I know is Telugu."

"And some English."

"Only enough to read, not to speak."

"Pullamma, be reasonable."

But I wasn't in the mood to be reasonable. Bad enough that I was forced to give up Ammamma. I couldn't give up this flat, where I had come to as a bride. I had friends here, I was comfortable here. Besides, Kondal Rao didn't know where we were. "Let the baby come. Then we'll rethink this. Please?"

Srikar nodded, but I could see the worry in his eyes. Why couldn't he understand that after the last few months, I needed to be in a place where I felt safe?

I settled back into my life in Madhuban Apartments. It was like I had never been away, except now Srikar forbade me to carry water up the stairs. I started the weekly visits to my lady doctor. I also settled back into friendship with Sandhya and Geeta. We'd told them I had to go away because my grandmother needed the help – Srikar thought it best if we stuck as close to the truth as possible. Geeta was curious, but after my stint as Goddess, I felt capable of handling her questions.

I'd never been happier. Thoughts of being back with my husband were what had sustained me through the months of my Goddess-hood. All I had to do was to lie low, and not threaten Kondal Rao's existence, and I'd be fine.

I didn't mind standing in line for water again, filling up buckets and pots, while Srikar carried the previous one up. I wasn't tired anymore. Over Srikar's protests, I started to cook complicated, fancy meals for my husband. It brought me great pleasure to take care of him again, despite the fact that I found it harder to move because of the baby I carried.

Our neighbours started to gravitate again to our home, for the food definitely, and for the company, I hoped. One thing did change – I found myself unable to spend endless hours in Geeta's company. I said as much when she knocked at my door. "Can you come back later?"

She looked inside. "Why? It's not like you are doing anything."

"I know. But I would like to be alone."

"What did I do?"

"It's not you, Geeta. It's me."

"You'll never believe what the people in number three did," she said, a hopeful expression on her face.

I shook my head, wishing there were some way I could do this without hurting her. She'd been a good friend. But, having been forced to listen to the worries of my devotees, problems that were best left private, I'd lost my appetite for gossip.

With a dispirited sigh, she trudged back to the apartment she shared with her in-laws. I felt terrible because I knew she had nowhere else to go. But my need to be alone was too great.

But I did look forward to Srikar's return home. After dinner we went for long walks, making plans for our future, and our baby. I felt immense pleasure that I'd reverted to being a nobody. I could talk at will, or not. I could go for walks with my husband, and no one cared. It was wonderful.

"We should talk about my grandfather, you know," Srikar said. "And leaving Hyderabad."

"Please," I begged. "Can't we talk about something pleasant?"

"Pulla, wishing him away isn't going to make him disappear. He'll still search you out the next time elections roll around. Perhaps, sooner."

"That's five years away." I forbade myself to think about Kondal Rao. My baby didn't need the stress. Most of my day was spent in daydreams about my baby, about our life together as a family. There was a part of me that warned against getting too complaisant, but I determinedly shoved it away. I'd had as much unpleasantness as I could take in a lifetime. Perhaps I was being foolish, but all I wanted to do was savour life with my husband in a familiar environment. I didn't want to deal with the newness of a different flat, different area, different people.

One evening, I had just finished cleaning the kitchen when there was a knock on the door. I sighed, hoping it wasn't Geeta again. Sandhya, at least, could take no for an answer. How could I explain to Geeta, without causing her hurt, that after my fishbowl existence in the village I savoured every moment I had to myself? Deciding to ignore the door, I wrung out the cleaning cloth, and set it to dry. Hopefully she would get tired and go away.

The doorbell rang, and the knocking resumed.

Defeated, I opened the door. It was Geeta, as expected.

"You think you've become too good for us?"

"No! It's just that –"

"It's what?" she snapped.

How could I explain? What could I say?

She gave me a vicious look and left. Closing the door, I unrolled a mat and curled up on the floor, terribly saddened by the way our friendship had ended. I wished Srikar would come back soon, but I was learning that in the construction business, working hours could be unpredictable. When they had 'pouring out the slab' scheduled, they couldn't afford to halt work until the next day. Work had to finish before the concrete set. I fell into an uneasy sleep.

I opened my eyes at a gentle knock. It was pitch dark outside. I must have slept for hours. Combing my hair with my fingers, I opened the door for Srikar.

My eyes fell on a thick, stubby neck. Blood drained out of me.

"Pack your bags," Kondal Rao said.

For a wild moment, I thought I would run away. Or, seek Geeta's help. But Kondal Rao filled the doorway.

Numbly I threw a few clothes into a bag, and grabbed a piece of paper, staring at it blindly, wishing I could convey my panic at this turn of events, my deep love for Srikar. Finally, I scribbled, 'Your grandfather is taking me away. Your devoted wife, Pullamma,' and left it on Srikar's pillow. Next to it I left the jewellery Srikar's grandmother had given me. I unhooked my mirrored globe – the one Srikar had bought for me in Laad Bazaar – from the peg on the wall.

Picking up my bag in one hand, the mirrored globe in the other, I followed Kondal Rao out into the dimly lit corridor, out of Srikar's life.

Kondal Rao stumbled against someone.

"Geeta!" I exclaimed. My heart picked up speed. Maybe she could summon help, maybe –

Kondal Rao grabbed Geeta by the neck and slammed her against the wall. He pushed harder and harder, till her head flopped like a rag doll's. Then he stopped. "If you know what's good for you," he rasped, "you haven't seen Pullamma or me. Do you understand?" He released her.

Whimpering, Geeta cowered against the wall, her breath loud in the silence of the night.

Placing his hands on either side of her, Kondal Rao leaned towards her till his forehead was almost touching hers. "Don't forget, Gee...taa," he said, stringing her name out. "The wise stay away from the two 'Ps' – police and politicians. Can you remember that?"

Geeta breathed jerkily, bobbing her head in desperate agreement.

Straightening up, Kondal Rao clamped his fingers on my arm. "Let's go."

I followed Kondal Rao, terrified. If only I had listened to Srikar, if only I had agree to move. I looked in the direction of my little house one last time. I had been so happy here. In my heart I knew I would not be back.

Thirty-Four

Two jeeps waited next to the gate. The two open-topped vehicles overflowed with thickly moustached henchmen, long slashes of vermilion on their foreheads, thick bamboo sticks in their hands. Kondal Rao sat in the front passenger seat of one jeep, hanging on to the ceiling strap, watching the entrance to our building.

I took one last look hoping someone else would show up, but the place was deserted.

One of Kondal Rao's goons escorted me to his jeep. The moment I got in, the jeeps were off like thieving rats.

I shut down mentally. We travelled for what seemed like hours, finally stopping at a roadside snack stall. Someone asked me if I wanted coffee. Too weary to decline, I nodded. I reached for the coffee, and promptly threw up.

Srikar's grandfather bit out an oath.

I got down and trudged to the bathroom. A string of curses followed me. When I climbed back into the jeep, it had been restored to its pristine condition. We left without eating. A long time later our convoy drove up to a rusted gate. A signboard flapped in the wind, the angle of it obscuring the writing. The driver of the lead jeep leaned on the horn.

A *paan* chewing security guard ambled over. On seeing its occupant, he spewed out the contents of his mouth, shot to attention and snapped a smart salute. Then he hustled to open the gate.

"This is an institution for wayward girls," Srikar's grandfather said over his shoulder.

Three aging buildings that might have once been yellow loomed over a decrepit mermaid-shaped fountain. I moved my eyes over the menacing shards of broken glass embedded in the walls running the perimeter of the campus. If that weren't deterrent enough, the top of the walls were embellished with barbed wire. Convicts in high security prisons had it easier, if Chiranjeevi's movies were anything to go by.

"They keep a tight eye on their girls," he continued, "but it is possible you will manage to escape. If you do, your baby won't live to see its first birthday." He turned and said in a conversational tone, "And if you have some foolish notion that I'll care because the baby was sired by my grandson, you have some growing up to do."

I remained in the jeep while Kondal Rao went inside.

He came back ten minutes later. Reaching into the jeep, he clamped a sweaty hand on my wrist. "You little fool," he snarled, nostrils flaring. "How many people get a shot at being a Goddess, *hanh*? How many? When I think of the power you could have had..." He shook his head in disbelief. "And you gave that up for a romp in my grandson's bed?"

I stared ahead.

"Some blubbering idiot told me that he'd seen my Goddess filling water at some municipal tap in Hyderabad. That, too, pregnant. Do you even understand the fix you put me in?"

I didn't respond.

"What are you waiting for?" he snapped.

Taking my suitcase, I got down from the jeep. I reached for my mirrored globe, but Kondal Rao was quicker.

He grabbed it and held it out of my reach, gauging my reaction.

I looked at him, face expressionless.

Either I was unsuccessful in my efforts, or Kondal Rao was more perceptive than I gave him credit for, because he casually let go. The globe shattered into a dozen little bits, its tiny mirrors glinting forlornly in the mud.

"*Tch, tch!*" he said. He climbed into the jeep, wiggling till he was comfortable. A lop-sided smile hovered on his lips.

I walked around the jagged pieces, head held high. Inside, my heart was as shattered as my globe.

A woman emerged from one of the buildings. She was dressed in a white cotton sari with a green border.

Kondal Rao spoke sharply to the driver. Tires screeched. The jeeps roared out of the gate.

The woman rapped my arm and started to walk towards the building in the centre. "Your grandfather told us about your situation. How you girls, with so many privileges in life, can get into such a situation, I don't understand. Took away his honour, didn't you, with your shameful behaviour?"

I could have set the woman straight, but what was the point? Wordlessly I followed her into the building. Inside sat an overweight woman with a look on her hairy face that suggested she and acidity were close companions. Her upper arms were trying hard to escape the confines of her blouse. Her belly had it easier – it just flopped out from the open sides of her sari. She checked me out, moving her head up and down, then gave a long suffering sigh. "Sit," she ordered.

I sat.

"I am the Warden. You will call me Manga madam. Our Home is for girls like you who have lost control of their morals. You will receive no phone calls, nor make any. You will not be allowed any outside contact till your baby is born. Only after your baby is given away for adoption into a God-fearing home will you be allowed to leave. Do you understand?"

I looked on expressionlessly.

"That's the way it's going to be, *hanh*? Have it your way, then." She hefted her considerable bulk out of the chair. As she waddled out, the chair settled back with a sigh.

Something was tossed in my lap. I looked at the drab sari, white, home-spun *khadi* with a blue border – the sort one saw in those old documentaries about Mahatma Gandhi exhorting the nation to freedom. Except there, the women were wearing the clothes to make a point.

Maybe I was, too.

The *ayah* led me to the building on the right, past the doorway to the dining hall. We walked up the stairs to a long dormitory with beds lined against both walls, a narrow walkway in between. All were occupied but one. The *ayah* threw my bag on it. "This will be yours," she said past the betel leaf in her mouth. She stomped out.

I sat on the bed.

Nine pairs of eyes turned in my direction.

A girl, tall and thin, with long braids on either sides of her shoulders, and large gold hoops in her ears, came forward. "One fumble under the sheets wasn't worth this dump, was it?"

I sank onto the bed, trying not to look at the stained mattress.

"Welcome to Fumble House." The girl with hoops seemed disappointed that I didn't respond to her provocation.

"Don't mind Nandu," another girl said. She had a gentle mound where her belly was. She settled next to me and took my hand. "She likes to act very worldly, but is actually nice once you get to know her. My name is Geeta. What is yours?" Her name caused a sharp jab in my chest.

Don't think about Geeta. Don't think about Srikar. Don't think. Not now. Not until dark.

"Pullamma," I whispered.

Geeta gave me a gentle hug. "You need anything, you come to me. You hear?"

I nodded gratefully. "I am so tired. I just want to sleep."

"Have you had anything to eat?"

"Can't."

"I have some Monaco biscuits. The salt helps me."

Too drained to refuse, I forced one into my mouth. Then I slept.

THIRTY-FIVE

In the Home for Destitute Women, our alarm each morning was a screeching *ayah*. "Get up, you lazy, immoral girls. Look at the shameless creatures, sleeping in like some rich ladies of leisure. It is almost dawn."

After bathing in freezing water, we lined up for prayers. *Please, God, don't let anyone take my baby away. My husband and my grandmother have been snatched from me. And my best friend. Let me keep my baby, at least.* My prayers didn't vary.

If you tell lies, daughters will be born to you, Lakshmi *garu* always said, proud she was the mother of sons. Did that mean Ammamma, with four daughters, was a liar? I, myself, had told enough lies to have a busload of girls. I felt sharp panic. What if I had a daughter, too?

I remembered Ammamma saying it was important for expectant mothers to eat nutritious food, but I didn't have much of a choice here. Most days breakfast was watery tea, and rubbery *upma*. Meals were as unappetising. What I did try to do was keep my tension under control. That much I could do for my baby. All the girls were expected to do chores. At the suggestion of my new friend, Geeta, I signed up for yard sweeping. It got us out of the dormitory and away, giving us the chance to talk privately.

Vocational training was from 8:00 in the morning until 11:00 – this was to prepare us for 'decent' ways of making a living once we were let loose in the world. Our options were basket weaving or sewing. I chose sewing because it seemed more respectable, somehow. I would practice my skills and make clothes for my baby before it came. Later, it would help me make a living for the two of us.

I couldn't imagine they'd actually take my baby away. After all, I was a married woman; it wasn't as if I'd shamed my family with immoral behaviour or anything. I forced myself to be positive because the alternative was too terrifying.

Geeta and I sat in the yard one evening, sewing with the other girls, when an *ayah* came up with another lady. "Pay attention. This is Dr. Janaki. She will be joining our team of doctors."

Dr. Janaki was tall and graceful, with a head full of silver hair. With half-moon glasses balanced on her beak nose, she seemed terribly scary-looking.

"She doesn't look mean or wicked," Geeta whispered. "Looks intelligent, too. Wonder what trouble she got herself in."

Dr. Janaki immediately set about making changes, the first of which were mandatory educational classes. The girls cribbed and complained about having to learn, but she paid no attention. At 12th class pass, I was the most educated of the lot, so she appointed me her assistant. I helped her prepare lessons for the girls. I would soon realize that you couldn't always judge people by their looks. Dr. Janaki was one of the warmest people I'd met. She took charge of me by monitoring what I ate, how much I exercised, what my emotional state was. On her recommendation, another of the chores I signed up for was weeding.

"Won't that hurt the baby?" I asked.

"Have you ever wondered why women labourers who work in the fields have such easy deliveries?"

I shook my head.

"Because they sit on their haunches to work. This helps stretch the muscles that are used in delivery."

"I thought pregnant women needed a lot of rest." I needed pampering and cosseting, not doctor-ing.

"You are pregnant, not sick," she said. "The more active you are, the easier your delivery will be."

I must have looked doubtful because she put a gentle hand on my head. "I've delivered more babies than I can count, Child."

So had Ammamma. Without any doctor's interference, too.

"You're just going to have to trust me," Dr. Janaki said.

I'd trusted Kondal Rao, too, the rat.

Dr. Janaki started taking me on her daily rounds. After the examination was over, we'd walk around the campus.

I pestered her about what I could expect during the course of the pregnancy, but she was very patient with me. Between the two women, Geeta and Dr. Janaki, I managed to hang on to my sanity, barely.

Nights were the worst. The darkness brought with it tears. I found that once I started, I couldn't stop; the pain was beyond anything I could have imagined. Each bout of crying only scraped the wound afresh. I was aware that I wasn't the only one who gave into tears once the lights were out. But each morning the girls were careful not to look at each other. I did not know what drove the other girls, but I lived in terror of discovery; if Srikar managed to track me down, his grandfather would kill our baby.

"You don't talk much, do you?" my new friend Geeta asked one day, eerily repeating what my Madhuban Apartments friend, Geeta, had said.

I smiled slightly.

"So how did you get pregnant?"

I felt my smile go wobbly.

"Okay, I'll tell you my story. I was raped by my cousin," Geeta said matter-of-factly. "Then he complained to his mother, my aunt, that I had provoked him into losing control. My mother didn't bother to find out the truth. When my cousin's father made the arrangements to have me sent away, she just went along with it. Anything to protect family honour, you know," she said with bitterness. "And, oh, by the way, my cousin is now married to a girl from a respectable family."

I touched her arm, hoping to convey to her my distress on her behalf.

Geeta cleared her throat. "So what is your story?"

I hesitated.

"I promise not to tell anyone."

"My husband's grandfather left me here," I said, voice thin.

Geeta looked shocked. "You are married! Did your husband harass you?"

"Oh no! He is the most wonderful husband a girl could have."

"Then what is the problem?"

The truth wasn't an option. "Dowry demands from in-laws."

Geeta nodded knowingly.

For all its restrictions, the campus of "Fumble House" had a certain rustic charm. The abundance of mango trees, guava trees, even a majestic banyan, soothed my soul, though the banyan sometimes made me feel lonely; it brought back memories of that other banyan – the one in the village square across from my grandmother's house, under which Chinni and I had spent pleasurable hours eyeing boys while pretending to be engaged in embroidering and sewing. I felt a pang at the thought of my former best friend. Wherever she was, I prayed the Lord of the Seven Hills was treating her well. As for Ammamma, I could only hope was that her long standing friendship with Kondal Rao's wife would protect her.

One corner of the Home was devoted to a chicken coop. Hens roamed the campus, squawking in search of food, sometimes pecking at unprotected toes. Next to the coop were rows of vegetables tended to by the inmates. Though the vegetables were supposed to be for use of the girls, more often than not, the best ones found their way to the Warden's table, the rest being distributed amongst the staff.

I was sitting across from the coop, watching the baby chicks chase each other, pondering the unfairness of life in general, my baby's fate in particular, when Dr. Janaki found me.

"You look troubled," she said, settling on the bench next to me.

I rubbed a hand over my stomach, trying to settle the baby's kicking. "I want to keep my baby," I burst out, startling myself. "I can't bear the thought of someone else raising my child. Isn't there some way I can keep him?" Tears started to course down. Before that wretched Kondal Rao entered my life, I had never cried; now I seemed to be making up for lost time.

Dr. Janaki sighed. "I wish I could help you. But this place runs on foreign 'donations.' Though it is illegal, they have found it quite lucrative to sell babies to foreigners through unofficial channels. Most probably someone has already been lined up for yours."

Dr. Janaki spent a lot of time with us girls, helping us exercise, listening to our problems, buying us fruits and biscuits with her own money. That such a good person as she would willingly work for monsters such as these seemed inconceivable. "Why do you work for these fiends?" I burst out.

She drew in a sharp breath. "Things aren't always what they seem. I feel in my own way I am providing emotional support to these girls, support which they'd otherwise not get."

"And this is the only way you found to do this?"

"I could walk away, get a job in a big hospital. I'm well qualified, you know. But how would it help these poor girls?"

I snorted.

She closed her eyes for a brief second. When she opened them, she seemed to have come to some kind of decision. She gently took my hand. "Pullamma, look at me."

I swiped my eyes with the back of my hand.

"I have something very important to discuss with you."

"How do I know you're not working for Kondal Rao?"

She gasped like I had stabbed her in the heart. "I would rather die than work for that despicable man."

I dropped my gaze.

"I need your trust. Will you give it to me?"

I nodded.

"Have you ever thought about continuing with your studies?"

"My hus–" I stopped. "Someone I knew used to tell me I should study further."

"I have more reasons to hate Kondal Rao than you can imagine," she said softly. "If you want to talk, I am here."

Her gentleness was my undoing. The whole story – my childhood, Chinni's distancing, the Goddess drama, Srikar – tumbled out.

Dr. Janaki put her arm around me and pulled me close, listening, sniffing, not saying anything. When I was finished, she said, "I am so sorry, Pullamma. I am so very sorry you had to go through all of this. Now wipe your tears. We have to talk." She wiped her own.

Once I had myself under control, Dr. Janaki said, "If this information gets in the wrong hands, it could be very dangerous." She looked frightened.

I nodded.

"Can I trust you?"

"I trusted you."

She took a deep breath. "I'm Srikar's mother."

"What?" I jumped to my feet, causing the chickens to squawk loudly and scatter. I looked at her in shock. "*My* Srikar?"

"Sit down," she whispered furiously. "Do you want to draw attention to us?"

I sat down, but my chest continued to thrum painfully.

"I took up this job only for your sake."

"How did you know who I was?"

Dr. Janaki kept her head bent. "Headmaster *garu* in Mallepalli. He and I were neighbours in my village. He was a few years older than I. Though he took the job in Mallepalli, he's always kept track of me because our parents were friends and neighbours. He knows how badly my father-in-law treated me, how he took my only child away. He's been like an older brother, always trying to help, always keeping me informed about the developments in my son's life."

"But when he brought Srikar to my grandmother's house, he told us that you'd abandoned Srikar when he was two, that no one knew where you where."

"To protect me. No one knows of my connection to him."

"So you found me through him?"

She nodded. "He told me about Srikar's marriage to you, about the circumstances."

"And what do you feel about that?"

"The marriage?"

I nodded.

"I'm proud of my son." Her voice caught. "I'm proud that he is a man of principles. I'm proud that my father-in-law wasn't able to corrupt him."

"And what do you think of me?" My voice was small.

"I think you're a lovely young girl. A little lacking in self-confidence, but lovely all the same. Someone I'd be proud to claim as my daughter-in-law."

"What about the colour of my skin?"

"What has that got to do with anything?" She looked puzzled.

I shook my head – had she not seen the fairness ads on television?

She said, "I've been keeping track of the two of you, thanks to Headmaster *garu*'s kindness. I had someone watching your flat in Hyderabad."

"So you knew I'd been kidnapped." I was incensed. "Why didn't you call the police?"

"With Kondal Rao's connections, you think it would have made a difference?"

My anger drained away. What she said was true. In all probability, the police would have provided Kondal Rao with an armed escort all the way here.

"When Kondal Rao dropped you off, I applied for a position in this Home."

"Why would you approach me, but not your own son? He said he's not seen you since he was a baby."

She was quiet for so long I thought she wasn't going to answer. "The last time I went to my in-laws' house was when Srikar was fourteen," she said abruptly. "I begged my mother-in-law to let me see him. She, bless the wonderful lady, called him out to the courtyard, but he refused to talk to me. He refused to even raise his head. He didn't spare me a glance. He broke my heart." Her voice was a whisper. "I never had the courage to approach him again."

"Why would he do something like that?" I couldn't understand a child not wanting his own mother. I knew how much I missed my own.

"Kondal Rao filled his ears with lies. Never let me meet my son. He thinks I abandoned him."

"Did you? Abandon him, I mean."

"No! I loved him with all my heart. It was harder to leave my son behind, than my husband."

"Then why did you?"

"Dr. Janaki!"

Dr. Janaki jerked her head up at the *ayah*'s call. "We'll talk later." She sniffed, surreptitiously wiping her eyes with the edge of her sari.

I walked along the walls of the campus, mind churning. Dr. Janaki, the mother of my husband. It was just too incredible. An educated, confident lady like Dr. Janaki was my mother-in-law? My heart tripped. Maybe she could help me keep my child. After all, the baby was her grandchild.

Over the next few days, Dr. Janaki took me for a walk under the guise of discussing lessons for the girls' education. "Sad as your story is, it's not unique. Every girl here has some variation to tell, perhaps not as dramatic, but sad nonetheless. What you do next will set you apart from the rest. I think you should continue your education."

"What about the baby?"

"I'm too new here. They don't trust me as yet. Give me time to work out a plan."

My heart lightened. They couldn't take my baby away. We wouldn't let them. "Should I study to be a secretary?"

Dr. Janaki clicked her tongue impatiently. "Don't think small, Pullamma. I think you should study medicine. I have been watching you on my rounds. I see how you help the girls with their classes. You have the aptitude, and the compassion. You'd make a wonderful doctor."

"Me, a doctor?" I laughed. "My sister's the brilliant one. She was going to be the doctor."

"Be that as it may, you underestimate yourself. You pick things up very fast." She drew me closer.

"What about my school leaving certificate?"

"The Headmaster from your village will help that."

"How about admission into college? I'll have to write entrance tests."

"Not if we go to Bangalore. The private medical college I'm talking about is run by a man who was very grateful for my treatment of his daughter. He promised me he would repay me back someday. That someday is now. He will get you a seat in the management quota. We'll make a life for ourselves, the baby, you and I." Aunty's voice was insistent, as if she were trying to convince herself as much as me. "Between the two of us, we'll manage your classes, and my practice."

"What about Srikar?"

"Do you honestly think Kondal Rao will allow you to go back to him?"

I watched the chicks chase each other.

"Pullamma?"

I shook my head, bringing my attention back to Dr. Janaki. "I don't know, but if I'm able to get back to him, I'll have no use for further education."

"Fine, then. I'll help you escape. After that seek out Srikar, by all means. But, if things don't work out, and with Kondal Rao involved, I don't see how they will, keep the education option open. Okay?"

I sighed. First son, then mother. "What about the money for college?"

"I've saved enough over the years. It would give me great pleasure to use it for you, and for my grandchild."

I blinked back tears, touched by her gesture. "How would I study without Kondal Rao finding out?" I wondered how she thought we'd get away with this.

"Since the college is in a different State, your risk of discovery will be quite low."

"I don't know what to say."

She put a hand on my arm. "Say 'yes.' Give me a chance to do something for my son, even if it is indirectly." Her voice broke. "Please?"

I nodded.

"Good." Dr. Janaki sniffed. "Now go back to your dormitory. Can't make these people suspicious."

"Would you like me to call you *Attayya* there is no one around?"

"No! Dr. Janaki is fine. We cannot risk giving our relationship away." She gave me a hug. "Now, go."

That night I curled up in bed, imagining a future with my child. He'd be handsome, with Ammamma's colouring, and Srikar's features. What if he were born as dark as me? I felt a pang of fear. No, I must be positive. God wouldn't do that to me. But still, dark or not, I'd love him with all my heart. As soon as he was born we would sneak out of the hospital, get as far away from this cursed place as we could. If it meant I'd have to sew for a living, so be it. My son was far more important to me than being a doctor. Maybe someday we'd be able to live as a family – my baby, his father and I. And Dr. Janaki. Strange to think such a nice lady could be a mother-in-law. My eyes closed.

I heard a cry. Getting up, I turned on the lights. Geeta was in labour. I hurried downstairs to the dining hall, where the security guard sat upright in an uncomfortable chair, emitting half-snorts.

"Get up, get up," I screamed. "Call the doctor."

The man awoke with a jerk. Hopefully, Dr. Janaki was on call.

I rushed back upstairs, panting and out of breath. By now the rest of the girls had crowded around Geeta. "Move back. Move back," I said, waving them away. "Give the poor thing room to breathe." The girls looked scared. I rubbed Geeta's back for almost an hour before the doctor showed up. It was not Dr. Janaki.

"Back to bed," the doctor ordered the girls crowding Geeta's bed. "The drama is over."

"Can I come with you?" I pleaded. "I won't get in your way. I'll just hold Geeta's hand."

"If I needed you to practice 'doctory,' I would have told you," the woman said, shoving me aside.

Two men came up with a stretcher.

I hurriedly gathered Geeta's things together in a small bag. I called out after her, promising to visit soon. I didn't seem to have good luck with friends named Geeta. Because, by next morning, Geeta was dead. I never did find out what happened to her baby.

THIRTY-SIX

Geeta's death had left me distraught. I wondered how a healthy young girl like her could lose her life in childbirth. When I asked Dr. Janaki, she had a fearful look on her face.

I was nearing the end of my own term. Before Geeta's death I had elaborate fantasies about how I'd take my baby, and run. We'd seek out Srikar, build a cosy life for the three of us, perhaps help Srikar and Dr. Janaki reconcile. Now I had no illusions left. This place was more heavily guarded than the Chief Minister's residence. I could see no way out. The only thing I could do was extract a promise from Dr. Janaki that she would personally deliver my baby.

One night, just as we were heading to the dining hall, the obese Warden cocked a finger at me. I went to her apprehensively. Being singled out by Manga Madam was never a good thing.

"Pack your bag, and come to my office," she said.

"Why?"

"Madam has so much status now that she can question me?"

"Should I come after dinner?"

"Did I say after dinner?"

I looked at the other girls; they were pretending to look at the walls, the ceilings, the floor. Biting my lip, I went up the stairs to pack, my heart knocking against my ribs. Dr. Janaki was away. Is that why they'd picked this time? Did they suspect something?

An *ayah* escorted me down. The Warden was already in the car. The engine was running, a door held open.

"Get in," the Warden said.

I got in. "Where are we going?"

She leaned across, and slapped me.

I clutched my bag tightly, staring sightlessly out of the window as we flew past the scenery, wishing Dr. Janaki hadn't picked this particular week to be away. Something bad was going to happen, I just knew it.

We drove up to a hospital. The Warden ordered me out.

A large orderly in shabby overalls caught my arm and said, "Come with me."

The car was already pulling away, the Warden in it. The orderly took me to a room, and said, "Wait here for the operation. You are going to have your baby today."

"But I am not due yet. I have another week. No one told me about the operation." My heart began to pound. "Phone Dr. Janaki. The Warden should have her number. She will tell you that I have no complications. She said I could wait for a normal delivery."

I could have been talking to the so-be-it Gods for all the attention the orderly paid me. He stepped out, and I heard the sound of a lock. Then it hit me. My being here today was no random occurrence. They were going to do to me whatever it was they wanted to do, while Dr. Janaki was away.

I wrapped my arms, trying not to think what would happen. I closed my eyes and started to pray: *I know I lie occasionally, but don't think I have told that many. Please, God, let my child be a boy. And let them not take him away.*

My head was spinning in circles. I tried to open my eyes, but it seemed like too much effort. I touched my belly and snatched my hand back; the area around my stomach felt like burning coal had scorched it. "My baby!" The thought suddenly slammed into me. I forced my eyes open and started to thrash about, my voice getting louder. "My baby, what did you do to my baby?"

A nurse hurried over. "You have just come out of an operation. You need to rest."

"Where is my baby?" I screamed, trying to sit up.

The woman in the bed across from me was staring.

The nurse put a hand on my shoulder, forcing me down.

"I want to see my baby," I sobbed.

Another nurse ran across the room, and jabbed a needle in my arm.

I fought against losing consciousness, but darkness enveloped me.

When I came to again, Dr. Janaki was sitting by the bed. "Are you thirsty?" she asked. Her voice was very gentle.

I nodded.

She helped me sit up.

As I took small sips of water, I noticed the bed across from me was empty. I lay back exhausted. "Do you want to sleep some more?"

"I just want my baby," I pleaded.

Dr. Janaki took my hand in hers. "Pullamma, I want you to be strong. What I have to tell you isn't good."

"Just tell me," I begged. "I can't bear it."

"You had a little girl. She was stillborn."

"That is a lie," I screamed. "I was carrying a boy. I could feel it. They must have sold him. Why else would they have operated on me?" I started to hit Dr. Janaki, the tears in my eyes blurring my vision. I tore at her hair, her face, anything I could reach. Dr. Janaki closed her eyes, tears running down her own cheeks. She did not stop me.

"Please tell me they are lying," I begged. "Please give me my baby."

"She was born dead, Pullamma."

"I don't believe it." I sat up, my jaw stubborn. "You said I'm healthy. You said there was no reason I shouldn't have a safe delivery. I think they gave my baby away."

"I saw her myself. She didn't make it."

"She can't be dead. She just can't. You're lying."

"No, Child." Dr. Janaki sounded devastated.

A cry was wrenched from me. I fell back against the bed, and broke down. I cried for what seemed like hours. Dr. Janaki held me, rubbing her hands over my back. A while later I pulled away and reached for the glass of water. "How does she look?"

I had to know.

"Pullamma, she is gone."

"Does she have Srikar's features? I need to see her."

"It will just hurt you."

I sat up, shaking. "I have to see her. I have to name her. She isn't some nameless baby, some roadside trash that I can just discard. She needs to know she was loved."

Dr. Janaki rested her head on my shoulder, her body trembling. "Are you sure?"

"Yes," I said. I was calm now. "I owe it to her. I owe it to Srikar. He doesn't even know he had, then lost, a daughter."

At a nod from Dr. Janaki, the nurse brought over a small wrapped bundle. I took it gently. Then I looked into the face of my baby. "Such long lashes," I said, running my eyes over her face. My daughter! I had never known love this powerful. "She would have been such a beautiful baby." My voice caught. "I would have loved her so much."

I said to Dr. Janaki, "You know, I promised myself that my children would have beautiful names?"

Dr. Janaki nodded, tears flowing. The nurse was crying, too.

"I am going to call my baby Vennela. She brought a ray of pure love into my life. It doesn't matter she did not live. It doesn't matter she was a girl. I am going to love her all my life. My little ray of heart-warming moonlight. Isn't that a nice name?"

"Beautiful," Dr. Janaki said, voice choking.

I looked at the nurse, still very calm. "I know you need to take her away for the last rites. But I want to hold her. Can you leave me alone for some time?"

"Fifteen minutes," the nurse said, sniffling. Dr. Janaki followed her out.

And then I was alone with my baby. Mine and Srikar's. I leaned over and rifled through my bag, laying a tiny pink frock with yellow smocking on the infant. "Now I understand where my urge to learn smocking came from. It was so I could make you pretty dresses." I held her up to my cheek. "I finally understand why your aunt Lata hated all the traditional sayings related to girls." *Tell a lie, beget a daughter.* "You are worth all the lies in the world put together, my love. Your poor unfortunate father. You came and you left. He never even knew."

I rocked my baby till the nurse came.

My infant daughter, being too young for cremation per Hindu rites, was buried. I wasn't allowed to go because I was still recovering from my caesarean; Dr. Janaki was prevented from going, too – some cock-and-bull story that hospital rules prevented doctors from attending funerals of their patients. But I got Dr. Janaki to find out the location.

Ten days after the birth and death of my baby, I stood over her grave and wept. I wept for my child, for my husband, for my dead friend Geeta, for the stripping of my illusions.

THIRTY-SEVEN

Resident girls were discharged from the Home once they'd given birth to their shameful secret. But I, being a special case, wasn't allowed to leave. Dr. Janaki urged me to use this time to prepare for college, but what was the point? With my baby gone, who would I study for?

I sat near the chicken coop. After my baby's death, I had no desire to make friends with anyone. A little distance away, a group of girls were practicing a song for some silly little function the Warden had dreamed up. The Chief Guest was some politician. Not Kondal Rao. Beyond that, I didn't care. I watched the baby chicks chase each other.

"How are you, Child?" Dr. Janaki sat next to me.

"I've been watching the baby chicks, resenting that they're chasing each other, having fun, while my baby was denied that chance."

"Oh, Pullamma!" She gave me a quick hug, then took a deep breath. "The function is tonight."

"I have no desire to go." I hoped she wasn't going to badger me to join in. I'd had enough of being positive.

"You don't understand." Her voice was heavy with suppressed excitement. "This is our chance to escape."

"Oh!" My heart started beating hard. "You want me to pack?"

"No! Don't do anything to draw attention to yourself. There isn't anything you can't leave behind, is there?"

Other than my baby? "No."

"Good. Meet me here at 7:30 p.m. When the politician's convoy arrives, the guards will hurry to help the Minister out of his car. Everyone's attention will be on them. That's when we'll sneak out. A car will be waiting outside to take us to Bangalore."

"But I don't want to go to Bangalore."

"But, Child, you have admission in a college there, and I have a job."

"I want to go to Hyderabad."

"I thought, with Vennela gone... Also, the risk..."

"Studying medicine was your idea, not mine. I want to go back to Srikar. I want to tell him about the baby we lost. I want to set up house with him again."

"What about Kondal Rao?"

"I'm not pregnant anymore. I don't have a child anymore. My mistake was that I refused to move from the flat. But this time, not only will I move – to the Himalayas, if necessary – but I'll stay at home, never venture out. If I stay hidden, there'll be no risk for Kondal Rao. Why would he care?"

Dr. Janaki looked like she didn't know what to say.

"Please Dr. Janaki. All I want is Srikar. Once I go back to him, I'll tell him what a wonderful person you are. He'll listen to me. I know he will. You'll be able to reunite with him."

The hope on Dr. Janaki's face would be comical, if it weren't so sad. "Okay then."

She left on her rounds, leaving me to worry about what could go wrong. Maybe the car wouldn't show up. Maybe we'd get caught. Maybe Dr. Janaki would be held up somewhere.

Despite all the worrying, leaving was unexpectedly easy. The politician's convoy arrived, everyone rushed to welcome them, and we strolled past the unattended gates. The car was waiting. We got in. A brief stop to say goodbye to Vennela, and we were on our way to Hyderabad.

We drove most of the night. Early next morning, we stopped at a hotel to freshen up. "Let's have breakfast before we go," Dr. Janaki said.

"If we delay, Srikar will leave for office." So, by 5:00 a.m., we were on our way to Madhuban Apartments. I tried to imagine our reunion. He'd be so happy to finally know what had happened to me. Poor Srikar. It would be so hard for him to know the baby hadn't lived. I would help him with his grief. We'd never forget Vennela, but we'd have each other. These days away from him had been miserable. I felt a spurt of anticipation that our separation was coming to an end. Another five minutes, and we'd be at Madhuban Apartments. My heart picked up speed. We'd have to look for a new place, and not only because it wasn't safe anymore. We couldn't live in such a small place because Dr. Janaki would be with us. I laughed.

"What?" Dr. Janaki said.

"I can't continue calling you Dr. Janaki, can I?"

She smiled, despite the tension on her face.

"Stop!" I said, startling the driver. We'd arrived. "Park here."

Dr. Janaki and I walked to the gate. My heart beat fast. What would people's reaction to my sudden reappearance be? What had Srikar told them? I stepped in, a smile on my face. This early in the morning, there was no one in the courtyard. Sandhya would be making her husband's lunch, Geeta getting her children ready for school. And Srikar?

"Pullamma," Dr. Janaki screamed, and slammed my face into the gate.

My chin hit the metal latch.

A knife thudded to the ground at my feet.

I jerked my head up.

A man ran up, knife in hand. Another man followed, the expression on his face fierce.

I froze.

"Run!" Dr. Janaki screamed.

I sprinted toward the car. I could hear footsteps pounding behind. I opened the car door. "Go, go, go," I shouted.

The driver jerked the ignition on.

Dr. Janaki slid in, and slammed the door shut.

The car screeched, and took off. I got on my knees and looked through the rear window. Two swarthy men shook their fists at the car, knives in hand.

I sank into the seat, heart hammering against my chest.

"What happened there?" the driver said, voice high.

"I think those men were attempting robbery," Aunty gave me a warning glance.

She and I both knew that had been an attempt on my life. Kondal Rao must have learned of my escape. It was logical that he would expect me to go to Madhuban Apartments. How could I have been so stupid? How could I have put Srikar at risk?

"Can you take us to Bangalore, like we talked before?" Dr. Janaki said to the driver, her voice tense. She gave me a questioning glance.

What could I say? My foolishness had already put Srikar in danger. How could I expose him to greater risk?

"Don't you want to go back to Madhuban Apartments when it is safe?" the driver said.

"I've changed my mind."

"Alright, then."

Thirty-Eight

I n Bangalore, we settled in a flat close to the hospital. We also settled on calling Dr. Janaki, Aunty.

"Classes are going to start soon, Pullamma," Aunty said.

"It is too public an occupation. I worry about those frenzied devotees, Aunty. If they ever track me down..."

"Pullamma, the best way to hide is in full view," she said. "After all, who in their right minds would expect a Goddess on the run to be practicing medicine? That too, in a different State?"

She bullied me till I agreed. I needed something to fill my time, so medicine it was. Studying to be a doctor was hard work, but I was determined that my baby's death would not go in vain. I would try and save as many babies as I could; maybe that would bring peace to my baby's soul. My own was beyond redemption. No one could possibly go through what I had, without having committed grievous sins in their previous lives.

I enrolled in a college. Studies came to me easily enough, perhaps because there was no Chinni to distract me. When I was reading, I wasn't thinking about Vennela or Srikar, Ammamma or Chinni. I also made the yearly pilgrimage to my daughter's grave in the cemetery beyond the Home. I took her flowers and dolls and frilly little dresses; I talked to her for hours, telling her about her father, her family and my love for her. I know this worried Janaki aunty. But the visits gave me the strength to go on.

At nights, when I was too tired to fall asleep, I would hold my baby's little pink and yellow frock close to my heart. Then I would give myself permission to grieve. For her. For her father. For me.

Maybe my baby wasn't meant to be. Like Lata had once pointed out, I had gotten pregnant in the month of June – *Ashadha Masam* – and my baby came in March. She must have been doomed from the moment she was conceived. I'd been studying medicine long enough to know this couldn't possibly be true, but what if the elders were right? What if I were responsible for the death of my own child?

It was March 13th again. I was at Vennela's grave. The years had

RASANA ATREYA

not dulled my grief. Each anniversary I felt as weighted by pain as the day I'd lost her. Janaki aunty stayed with me for a brief while, then left; she knew I needed the time alone. "You were in my life such a short time," I told my daughter. "Nine wonderful months." I studied the gulmohar tree, its flowers a bright red against the cloudless sky. How cruel that the flowers should be in full bloom, while my baby never had a chance. "Your father felt such awe when you kicked against my belly. That was the only time the three of us were together as a family." Memories of Srikar washed over me, our time together, our plans for the baby. My chest constricted with pain. "You'd have been five years old today. You'd be in school by now, talking like a parrot. My heart splintered when I had to leave your father. When you left, you shattered it." I leaned my forehead against my palm, blinking back tears, unable to continue.

Something caused me to raise my head. A couple, both of them short and skinny, stood across from me, eyeing me strangely.

"What are you doing here?" the man said.

I looked at them, not sure what he was getting at.

"You are sitting at our daughter's grave."

Had the man lost his mind? "You must be mistaken," I told him. "My daughter is buried here."

"No, she's not," the woman said. "This is our daughter." She pointed to the *gulmohar* tree. "I was leaning against that when they buried her."

I felt lightheaded. Something wasn't right. "When did your child die?" I had to force the words past the terror in my throat.

"March 13, five years ago," the couple said together.

"Are you sure?" I wiped my damp hands on my sari. I shivered despite the heat.

The woman took a step back. "Not something I'm likely to forget, is it?"

"Where was she born?"

"Government Maternity Hospital," the man said, compassion in his eyes.

I got up so suddenly, the woman gave a start. I started to run. I ran past the gates of the cemetery, past the open plot of land, through the gate of the Home for Destitute Women. The watchman's jaw went slack as I bolted past him to the building in the centre, up the stairs to the office of Manga Madam, Warden.

She looked up. "You came," she said. There was no inflection in her voice.

"What did you do with my baby?" I screamed, pouncing on her, clawing at her face.

"*Ayah! Ayah!* Get this mental woman off me," she screeched.

Two *ayahs* flew in, but not before I had drawn blood, I saw with savage satisfaction. Drops started to trickle down the Warden's face. The women pulled me off, each tightly holding onto an arm.

"My baby," I shouted, crying. "Where is my baby?"

"We were instructed by your grandfather to give him away."

"Him? Him? I had a boy and you never told me?" I lunged at the Warden, feeling a hatred so intense that if I hadn't been restrained by her flunkies, I would have strangled her. The Warden took a step back. "You crazy woman! You gave birth to a healthy boy. We just told you the dead girl was yours so you wouldn't cause trouble. Don't ask me where the child is, because I don't know."

I crumpled to the floor.

When I came to, I was in the hospital. Janaki aunty sat there, the strain on her face showing. This was getting familiar.

"Aunty, do you know what they did?" I asked. I didn't even have the strength to cry.

"Yes, Child," she said, stroking my hair, crying. "I found out."

"All these years, Aunty. I thought my baby was dead. But they gave him away."

"When they showed me the stillborn girl, I thought she was yours," she whispered. "They fooled me, too."

"I have a little boy somewhere." My voice broke. I grabbed her hands. "Please find him for me, Aunty," I begged. "Please, please. I can't bear not knowing where he is."

"Pullamma," Aunty said. "The Home maintains no paperwork. Even if it did, they're not likely to tell me." She put her head to my cheek. "He could be anywhere in the world by now." She started to tremble.

When Vennela died, I thought I'd experienced all the pain I could endure in a lifetime. How wrong I was. I felt as if my body were on fire, like hot knives stabbed my heart, like cleaning acid dripped into raw wounds, all at the same time. I started to gasp,

I clutched at my throat. The nurse flew in – to put me out of my misery, I hoped.

Early next morning, Janaki aunty helped me down the steps of the hospital, and into the waiting taxi. Our luggage was already loaded. "Let's go," she told the driver.

"I need to make a stop along the way," I said.

Janaki aunty gave me a questioning look.

"I want to say goodbye to Vennela."

Aunty seemed stunned. "But I thought... I mean..."

"I may not have given birth to her, Aunty. But I held her, I named her. Five long years, I grieved for her. She will always be the daughter I lost."

Janaki aunty seemed at a loss for words, but instructed the taxi driver anyway. At the cemetery, she held on to my arm, giving me worried looks. After visiting my daughter's grave one last time, we got on the National Highway, heading away from Vennela, towards Bangalore, towards oblivion.

Thirty-Nine

B ack in Bangalore, I couldn't settle back in my internship. The thoughts of my son consumed me. "Aunty, what if he's out on the streets, uncared for, unfed, unloved?"

"Child, don't do this to yourself. Think of him safe and happy. That's the only way you'll get through this. Till we find him."

I tried hard to remain positive. I'd imagine him in my lap, his sticky little hands holding my face, his plump little arms winding around my neck. Was he doing this to some other woman – a woman he thought of as his mother? Did she love him, appreciate him, take care of him? I'd sit on the chair in our flat, watching traffic, thinking, thinking, thinking.

"Don't ruin your future with your own hands," Aunty begged. "You've come this far. Finish your education. Start working."

"My child is out there; where, I don't know. My husband is lost to me, as well. Is there even a point to my existence?"

"Snap out of your self-pity, Pullamma." Aunty was angry. "You think I've had it easy? I have a grown son who wants nothing to do with me, a grandchild who... I..." Aunty swallowed. "You have a husband who loves you, you have some hope of finding your child. Pull yourself together so when life gives you a second chance with your family, you're ready to take it."

I squared my shoulders. "You want me to finish my education, I'll finish my education. But it has to be in Hyderabad. I will not live in Bangalore. If I cannot be with my husband, I can at least be in the same town as him."

"What about Kondal Rao?"

"To hell with Kondal Rao."

"You want to leave in the middle of your internship?"

"That's your problem. You want to me finish, you find out how to transfer me to a college in Hyderabad. Because that's where I'll be."

"Fine, we'll move. But you listen to me. Before we move, you'll get your hair cut. You'll also get the mole below your nose removed, eyebrows thinned. And change your clothing style, make it more modern. The chances of being recognized in Hyderabad are much greater."

I stared at her, trembling in shock. Cut my hair? Wear sleeveless blouses? What was Aunty saying? I came from a good family. What would people think? What would Ammamma say? What would Srikar? "But Aunty –"

"Don't 'Aunty' me." Her voice was harsh. "I'm trying to help you here."

That evening I sat in a beauty parlour awaiting my haircut. When the woman snipped the first lock, I felt a pang. How Srikar had loved my long, silky hair! My hair was styled professionally – none of that jasmine scented Parachute coconut hair oil for me. My eyebrows were shaped, one painful pluck at a time. The stylist urged me to look in the mirror, probably wanting acknowledgment of her handiwork. But I couldn't. I was embarrassed at my bold behaviour, at the attention it was sure to draw to me. How could I have agreed to such a thing?

As if that weren't bad enough, the sleeves on my blouses were snipped off. People's eyes fell on my bare arms, then skittered away, as if consciously trying not to rest their eyes there. Meanwhile I worked hard at looking directly in people's eyes, pretending I wasn't dying a little each time. The mole, which had caused me hours of agonizing, was removed.

It took me a few days before I was able to look in the mirror. I had to agree it brought out my best features, though I couldn't get over my self-consciousness.

Aunty made the arrangements for me to transfer to a different college in Hyderabad. We packed up our apartment.

Then we moved to Hyderabad.

The hospital staff in Hyderabad, where I restarted my internship, often complimented me. Assuming Aunty and I were mother and daughter, they'd tell me how pretty I was, even though I didn't have my mother's skin colour, 'you poor thing.'

But I did not feel pretty. When I looked in the mirror, I saw a pretty woman all right, but I didn't see me.

Aunty also taught me how to carry myself. Above all, she tried to teach me to value myself. She saw me use my fairness cream. "Why do you use that?" she asked.

"I... I don't know." And I really didn't. It was like eating with my right hand, or oiling my hair daily – something I had been taught early on, but never thought about.

But Aunty was having none of it. "Have self-respect, Child," she said. "You have such lovely skin. Let it be. The colour of your skin can't reflect the person you are. The skin is just external – all it does is hold your body together. It's what's inside that counts, what defines you as the person you are. Look at Kondal Rao. His skin is as white as can be. Is that colour reflected in his soul?"

I must have looked unconvinced, because Aunty continued, "Surely there are more important things in life than the colour of one's skin? You are demeaning yourself by thinking you will somehow be a better person if the tone of your skin is lightened. Besides, God chose your skin. Are you saying he doesn't know what he's doing?"

God might know, but all those television ads exhorting me to buy fairness creams to make myself 'lovely' apparently didn't. I threw away my tubes of fairness cream because it seemed to make Aunty happy. But I felt bereft without them.

Every spare moment I had, I spent walking the streets of Hyderabad, searching for my little boy.

"What are you doing to yourself?" Aunty said, despairing.

"What other options do I have?" Then it occurred to me. "Aunty, do you have any contacts in that Home?"

"What do you mean?"

"There has to be some proof of my son's existence. Some private records they won't let us see. He couldn't have disappeared without a trace."

"Ganga was an *ayah* there," Aunty said slowly. "She might be able to help."

"Can you get in touch with her?"

Aunty set things in motion.

Ganga phoned a week later. "The Warden is away for two days. Come now."

"Right now?" It was five in the morning.

"By evening. You don't know what a risk this is for me."

"I do know. I'm very grateful –"

"Just bring the money. Meet me at the tea shack behind the Home. At seven, sharp. If you're late, I'll leave."

We were at the shack by six o'clock. "What if she isn't able to bring the register?" I said.

"Money is a good motivator, Child. Don't worry, she'll be here."

I rested a cheek on the grimy chipped decolam of the table. "What if the Warden lied? What if I had a girl? For all I know, she is somewhere on the streets, abused and battered."

"You need to stop this, Pullamma. Don't let your imagination run away with you."

I paced the length of the tiny shack till I drove Aunty crazy. "Sit down," she begged.

Ganga arrived at five minutes past seven. She looked around furtively, unbuttoned her sweater and withdrew a register. I stared at the book, throat dry. If this didn't have what I needed, what would we do? I reached for it.

"The money," Ganga said.

Aunty placed two hundred rupees on the table.

Ganga grabbed the notes.

I opened the register.

"Check the day of baby's birth," Ganga said.

I turned the pages till I reached March 13. I ran my finger down the names. 'Pullamma. Baby boy. Live birth.' I closed the register with trembling hands. So I did have a son. "Where?" I cleared my throat. "Where is he?"

"How should I know?" Ganga shrugged. "Not like the Warden shares information with me. Money comes to the Home, child leaves." Her eyes narrowed. "You're going to ask for your money back? You can't, you know. I took a lot of risk for you."

I waved my hand, indicating she could keep it. She shoved the notes into a cloth drawstring purse and stuffed it in the cleavage of the blouse she wore under her sari. Then she left.

I rested my elbow on the table, leaned my head against my palm, and let the tears flow.

Over the next two years, Janaki aunty built a two-storied structure, a clinic on the ground floor, a flat above it. After I finished my internship, the two of us moved upstairs into our flat, and settled in.

Then we set up practice. I wondered what Ammamma and Chinni would think of me now. And Lata.

The day Aunty handed me my share of the income, I was a little shocked. I'd never seen this much money before. "Aunty," I said, "you've been like a mother to me."

Aunty smiled, a puzzled expression on her face.

"This is my first salary."

"Child," Aunty said, her expression clearing, "that you even considered me, means a lot." She touched my face. "But that honour belongs to your grandmother."

I hugged her, glad she understood. I sent Ammamma my entire first salary, wishing I could have given it to her in person. I started sending her a big part of my salary each month, hoping it would ease her hardship. God knew what Kondal Rao had put her through.

I had lost my parents, and Ammamma and Chinni came in to occupy that spot. I lost them, found Srikar instead. He was lost to me after giving me a baby. Janaki aunty took over the void left by the baby's absence. Without her presence in my life, I wouldn't have had the strength to go on. She'd become the mother I hadn't known I missed.

I lived in a curious limbo. Time – hours, days, months – no longer had meaning. We did the exact same thing everyday – got up, finished with the cooking and cleaning, went to the clinic. Worked from 9:00 a.m. till 1:00 p.m. Had lunch, finished paperwork, took a nap, went back to the clinic to see patients. We did this six days of the week. On the seventh day, we rested.

Most days that I saw patients passed in a haze. It was only when I saw little boys that I came alive. *Could he be my child? No, too light skinned. Perhaps he was blessed with Ammamma's colouring? How about the one I saw yesterday?*

There was no way to tell. Rare were the nights I didn't cry myself to sleep – either for my son, or for my husband. It was a completely uneventful existence, but for the constant pain.

After work, we often relaxed on the balcony. One night I sat on the swing, one leg on the ground, swinging back and forth, watching the noisy traffic honk its way past. A few intrepid pedestrians darted onto the road, risking life and limb. The flow of vehicles rearranged itself around them.

"You should get married," Aunty said.

"Aunty, I'm married to your son! Besides, are you forgetting big-amy is illegal?"

"If you think my father-in-law will ever let you go back to Srikar, you're being extremely naïve."

I breathed in the jasmine-scented air wafting over the spicy scent of *sambar*. Or was it curry? That reminded me how much Srikar had loved my *vankay* curry. Did my son like it, too? I swallowed against the pain in my throat. After work I often wandered the streets, looking at little boys, trying to determine if any of them could be mine. Where *was* he? Had he been adopted out of the country? How would I find him if he was? I'd thought about contacting the police, but the risk was too great. If Kondal Rao found out, I might not live long enough to see my son.

The street lights were long on. Time was moving on, life was moving on, and I had still no idea where my baby was. Was he happy? Was he fair? Did he have to suffer for the colour of his skin? Was he being taken care of?

"Pullamma?" Aunty said now. "What do you say?"

I wished Aunty wouldn't pressure me so.

"Get married in the temple," she said. "No need for divorce."

Registered marriages were for people like me, who were forced to elope because their families couldn't, or wouldn't, support them. Couples from respectable families got married in the temple; husbands who abandoned their wives without the hassle of divorce, remarried in the temple.

Abandoned women didn't remarry, not unmarried men anyway; it just wasn't done. Those brazen enough, 'married' already married men and set up a second house with them, and were vilified for it.

"Who'd want to marry an already married woman?"

"There are always men out there if you look hard enough."

This was assuming I was interested. "As far as I am concerned, Srikar is, and will always be, my husband. I can't imagine being married to anyone else. Besides, why are you pushing me to re-marry, anyway? Don't you want me to be married to your son?"

"Yes!" Aunty was vehement. "There's nothing more I'd like. But I'm trying to be realistic here. Srikar might have remarried, you know. I don't want you to get old and bitter, while he is happily married."

"He broke off contact with his beloved grandmother just so he could protect me from his grandfather. I know him. He won't remarry."

"Child, for you, remarriage is also a way of keeping you safe. Who'd expect a girl from a decent family to marry a second time?"

"I'd rather be controlled by Kondal Rao, than be a wife to anyone but Srikar."

Aunty sighed.

"You never did tell me why you left your husband." I'd been so lost in my misery that I'd never thought to ask.

"I didn't. My father-in-law threw me out."

As close as we were, there was a part of her she held private. I understood, because I had enough secrets of my own. This was the reason I was unable to make friends with other people my age. Their biggest problem was which movie to see, while I was driven by the need to find my child. I felt unable to relate to them. "What happened?"

"He managed a small shop in the village. He thought it would be prestigious to get a doctor wife; free medical treatment for all his relatives, and all that. Build his stock among his family and friends, you know."

"And?"

She shrugged. "It was easier in theory than in practice. You have to remember, in those days lady doctors were a rarity, and therefore awe-inspiring. I was so much more educated than he, had so much respect in the village, he couldn't handle it."

"Why did your family agree to the alliance in the first place?"

"My parents knew Srikar's grandmother. They felt a cultured family was better than an educated one."

I gave a short laugh. "You let him throw you out?"

"I fought back, refusing to leave. Call it youthful arrogance, call it too much belief in my own capabilities, but I challenged my father-in-law. He'd sucked my father dry by demanding more and more dowry, till all my father had left was his pension."

"So he made his money off your family?"

"Oh, no. He was a big landlord himself. Didn't stop him from stealing. He stole from helpless widows, weak men, anywhere he could get his hands on. I refused to leave, threatened to go public with his dowry harassment."

"And?" I asked.

"He had my brother beaten up, left him a bloodied pulp at my father's doorstep."

I drew in a sharp breath.

Aunty cleared her throat. "They warned me they let my brother live that one time. There would be no second chances. I was to get out, leave my son behind."

I shook my head, unable to believe Aunty's story. And yet, I'd seen enough of Kondal Rao's to know this wasn't implausible.

"I kept returning, unable to stay away from my son. But Kondal Rao never let me meet him. Not a single time," she said viciously. "The only time I managed to get in was when he and his henchmen were called away. You know what happened then."

I nodded.

"My parents died a month before you were dumped at the Home. My brother waited barely long enough to finish the rituals for my parents, then moved his family to Sri Lanka."

Poor Aunty! My heart ached for her.

Aunty said, "You know I was away the week they did that Caesarean on you?"

I nodded.

"I went to say my goodbyes to my brother, and also to make plans to take you and run. I don't know how they found out, but they panicked. That's why they did that emergency surgery on you. They are less afraid of God than they are of Kondal Rao." She broke down. "They got away with it, Pullamma. I let them steal your baby."

I put an arm around Aunty, letting her cry on my shoulder, my heart heavy with what ifs. What if Aunty's plan had succeeded? What if I'd been raising my son? I waited till Aunty's cries reduced to sniffles. "So what happened with your husband?"

"One day when I was at the hospital in town, he just packed up and left. He left the keys, and the explanations with the neighbours. My father-in-law threw me out soon after."

"In most cases the men throw their wives out, they don't disappear."

"Kondal Rao's family is hardly most cases." She gave a short laugh. "In any case, he returned home after his father threw me out.

"You didn't remarry, but you want me to?"

"It is precisely because I didn't, that I want it for you, Child. Safety is the big part, definitely. But it is too hard to grow old alone. I was lucky to find you. What are the chances you will find someone like you?"

"I can't imagine being married to anyone but Srikar." I looked to her. "I want to track him down, Aunty. I need his help in finding our child. Do you think his grandfather will really harm me?"

Seconds ticked by as I waited for Aunty to respond. "He had his own great-grandson given up for adoption. What kind of person do you think that makes him?"

"I want to find my husband, Aunty. I'm ready to risk harm to myself. Does that make me a fool?"

Aunty shrugged, but her face showed strain.

I'd exhausted all means of locating my son. It was time to seek my husband's help. I prayed I wasn't making a huge mistake.

FORTY

I settled into the backseat of my car, and gave the driver directions to our old apartment, mine and Srikar's. Aunty and I had decided it was unlikely Srikar still lived here. But Geeta, or someone from my past, probably did.

Back when I lived in the village, the farmers loaded up carts with produce, and let the oxen loose, free to find their way home. I felt like those oxen, now. I carried my own load – of guilt, of pain, of sorrow – as I plodded my way back to Madhuban Apartments, the place where I had set up domestic life with my husband some eight years ago. To me, Madhuban Apartments would always be home.

Forty minutes later, we pulled up at the Apartments. There was still some evidence of whitewash left on the building, but mostly it was blackened with mildew. Several shutters hung askew; a few windows were boarded up. Madhuban Apartments was now 'Mad mens', the missing letters having been helped along by enterprising kids, perhaps? I felt a pang to realize how rundown this place was – back then I had viewed it through the tint of domestic contentment.

I got down from the car. I'd not been back since the day of Kondal Rao's attempt on my life. The urge to turn back was strong, but I put one foot forward, then another till I neared the gate. I compared the squalor here to the luxury in my own life – spacious apartment, a nice car, cook, maid and driver, fancy interiors, the ability to pay for any luxury I chose. Even a municipal water tap which dispensed water at reasonable hours of the day. Yet, Madhuban Apartments was where I had been the happiest.

A few people milled about in the courtyard. Almost all had turned to look when I stepped from the car; people getting down from privately owned vehicles was not a frequent occurrence in this locality.

"Who are you looking for, Madam?" a woman asked respectfully.

Old Rukkamma! Gossipy old crone, Geeta had called her. It was obvious Rukkamma hadn't recognized me. Next to her stood another woman, baby on her hip. It couldn't be, could it? I looked closely. She *was* Sandhya! I stepped forward, a smile trembling on my lips, desperate for the chance to catch up with an old friend. She looked at me, her eyes not quite meeting mine, a puzzled frown on her face. Then she turned away. I felt a stab of disappointment.

In this part of town, a car and good quality clothing could change features; in my case I also had a makeover to assist me. My first instinct was to introduce myself. For old times' sake. Then I decided against it; it might bring up questions I wasn't willing or able to answer.

"A lady called Geeta used to live here," I said to Rukkamma. "Seven or so years ago. Two children, in-laws?"

"Talked too much? Had big dreams? That Geeta?" my former neighbour asked. At my nod, she said, "She lives not too far from here."

"If you don't mind, can you give me her address?"

The old woman gave me a curious glance before rattling off an address which was only fifteen minutes away by car.

I thanked her, and turned to go.

"She moved up in life, leaving us all behind. Too fancy for the likes of us now," the woman said. "Shifted to the other building right after that Pullamma ran off."

I froze.

Seeing she had my attention, the woman said, "There used to be a really nice, young fellow. Srikar was his name, the poor unfortunate soul." The woman looked around. Everyone was listening; I had forgotten gossip was the main pastime around here. "One day the wife, Pullamma, ran away with her lover."

There was a collective gasp. Including mine.

"That's right," the old woman said, very obviously relishing the attention.

"What are you saying?" Sandhya exclaimed. "Pullamma was from a very nice family. She would never do such a thing to her husband!"

"Did you see her leave, *hanh*, did you?"

"No, but –"

"Well, I did," the old woman said triumphantly.

Liar! Rukkamma was down with fever. I could never forget the details of that night, how could I?

Rukkamma looked at one of the men. "Pullamma and Srikar used to live in your flat." Then she turned to me. "What a woman, *hanh*? She couldn't even realize how lucky she was, being so dark and everything, still managing to snare such a fair, and decent husband."

Nothing like affluence to lighten the colour of one's skin.

I struggled for a blank face, trying not to let her words wound, still unable to accept that Srikar had thought I'd run off with someone else.

Old Rukkamma continued with no hint of self-consciousness. "On top of that she left a note for her husband saying she had fallen in love with another man. And she coolly ran off with this man."

"How do you know?" My voice was harsh. I wrapped my arms tightly around myself to prevent trembling.

"Madam," Sandhya said, looking agitated, "don't believe a word of what spews out of this old woman's mouth. Pullamma was a very sweet girl. No one knows what really happened. This old woman's gossip gets more and more vicious with each retelling."

My heart overflowed with gratitude.

Rukkamma looked at her avid audience in irritation. "Do you want the true story or not?"

"Yes, yes," a swarthy man said.

"Okay then." She shoved Sandhya aside, plonked herself on the stairs with a dramatic sigh, and continued with her version. "That Geeta told us. She personally saw everything. She was the one who found the note." The woman grinned maliciously through the gaps in her reddish brown *paan*-stained teeth. "Completely shameless, *hanh*? Holding hands, they were, as they ran down the stairs." The people looked around, at each other, jaws slack, eyes wide.

"And..." the woman said, drawing out her tale, "she was seven months pregnant!" She inspected the sea of shocked faces. "No one knew whose baby it was."

"And Srikar?" I whispered.

"Oh that poor fellow? First he refused to believe it. Then he went mad."

"Such a nice couple." Sandhya shook her head, eyes soft with compassion. "Such a terrible tragedy."

A numbness started up my arms. It spread to my body.

"Always mumbling to himself, he was," old Rukkamma said. "Such a nice fellow, too. Very respectful. Colour of barely ripened mango. Always used to carry up my bucket of water for me. Such a sorry end for him, *hanh*? To end up in a mental hospital?"

I walked up the steps to our apartment, and banged on the door till Janaki aunty opened it.

"Forgot your keys?" Her eyes were puffy from her afternoon nap. When I didn't answer, she looked at me sharply. "What's wrong?"

Brushing past her, I went to my bedroom, and collapsed on the bed.

Janaki aunty followed me in and pulled up a chair. She kept rubbing my back, asking what had happened. She put a hand under my chin and turned my face to the side. One glance and she left the room. On returning, she helped me sit up and gave me a pill to swallow.

I downed it with a glass of water. It must have been a sleeping pill, because I slept.

I don't know when I awakened, but I was groggy.

Aunty sat on a chair, neck at an awkward angle, fast asleep.

I went to the bathroom to freshen up.

When I came out, Aunty was rubbing her eyes. "What happened?"

"It's two in the morning."

"Don't worry about the time," she said. "Just tell me what's wrong."

I related all that had happened.

"My poor child," she said, as tears made their way down her cheeks.

I lay back on my bed, chest hurting badly. "I can't believe Srikar ended up in a mental hospital, Aunty." I broke down.

Aunty stopped crying. "You're not talking like a doctor. His emotional problems must have been too much for him to handle. What is wrong in getting help?" She sounded as if she were trying to convince herself, as well. "Would you blame him if he needed medication for heart problems? Blood pressure? Then why not for emotional trauma?"

But doctor or not, prejudices were hard to overcome. I tried to take a deep breath to calm myself, but it hurt. I rubbed my chest. Images of my husband restrained in a bed, undergoing shock therapy, haunted me. Did they even do that anymore? *God, no! Anything but that!*

"Aunty, all this time I thought of him as being safe someplace. Wildly successful, but missing me madly. Searching for me desperately. To think of him locked away..." My voice, or was it my heart, broke.

Aunty held me tightly. "I am going to find him, Child, if it is the last thing I do."

My husband and my son. That's all I want. Please, God. Take away my degree, my education, my money, add more darkness to my skin. Just give back my family.

Cupping my anguished face, she said, "Do you think his grandfather would have gone to so much trouble merely to let Srikar languish in a mental hospital? I'm sure he got the treatment he needed, and now is quite successful in life."

"You're talking about the man who had no problem giving his own great-grandson away."

Aunty had nothing to say to that.

Let him be happy, God. Even if it means he hates me. I just can't bear the thought of him locked up.

FORTY-ONE

A unty had been scouring the city for Srikar. She had called in every favour she could think of – and being a doctor, she was owed many – but she was unable to find any trace of him. "I just don't understand," she said. "He has disappeared."

We sat, as usual, on the balcony overlooking the road, after a long day at work. As had become our habit, we relaxed with, depending on the season, either hot tea or chilled buttermilk. Today it was tea.

"I have offered large amounts of money for information, but nothing. I got in touch with my contact at the mental hospital, but that didn't pan out either."

I leaned back against the swing, drained. Aunty wasn't able to find a grown man. What chance did I have with a young child? A child I might not even recognize. Did the people who had him treat him well? Did they take good care of him? *Please, God, let him not be out on the streets all alone, nowhere to go, no one to worry whether he's eaten...*

I took deep breaths, trying to ease the tightness in my chest, trying not to think of Srikar all drugged up, and chained to his cot. "Do you think we should contact women's organizations, or the National Human Rights Commission for help?"

"And draw attention to yourself? I don't think that's wise, Child."

I sighed. "That leaves only Geeta." I could, of course, call Ammamma. God knows, I wanted to. It wasn't inconceivable that news of Srikar had trickled back to Ammamma through Srikar's grandmother. But I was afraid to put my grandmother in danger.

"Take tomorrow morning off and look for her. I can handle the patient load."

I nodded. It was time.

The next morning, I dressed with care – a smart sari from a fashionable boutique, my hair carefully done up, a fancy purse in hand. Despite a lack of money, Geeta had an innate sense of style. I had no wish to feel inferior.

Getting into the car, I gave the driver Geeta's address. Thirty minutes later we stopped across from a six storey building. Not fancy by any means, but certainly a step-up from Madhuban Apartments.

Two boys, a little older than the age my son would be now, were playing cricket in front of the building. I walked past a small room set to one side, bathroom on the outside. Probably the watchman's quarters. I took the stairs up to the fifth floor, mildly out of breath. 503. The flat Geeta lived in.

I took a deep breath and knocked, gearing up for the confrontation.

Geeta opened the door, and the years fell away.

I was back in Madhuban Apartments, newly married and amazingly naïve, excited about my husband, my new friend Geeta, my future.

She looked at me questioningly. "Yes?"

I found myself too choked up to say anything.

All of a sudden, the expression on her face changed. Recognition seemed to have dawned, because she fell into the chair beside the door. "You came," she said, voice hoarse. Almost as if she had been expecting me. Like the Warden at the Home.

"Quite a nice place you have here." Distress caused my scalp to tighten. "Three bedroom flat, is it?"

She nodded, her skin a sickly green. "You have come to find out about that day, haven't you?"

I looked at her.

"They made me do it," she burst out. "Kondal Rao's goons threatened to chop my husband to pieces and throw him in the Godavari if we didn't cooperate." She got up and grabbed my shoulders, a wild expression on her face. "Please, you have to believe me. He said all I had to do was tell Srikar I knew nothing, had seen nothing. They paid two or three people in the building, I don't know who all, to spread rumours that you'd run away with your lover."

"But Srikar couldn't believe that!"

"He didn't. He gave up his job, roamed the streets like a mad man, searching for you. I heard he even went to Kondal Rao's office and attacked him, but of course, nothing came of it. I didn't say anything to anyone. That's all I did."

"That's all you did?" Blood rushed to my face.

Geeta started to sob. "They came right after you left. I was still slumped in the corridor from the terror, unable to move. They cleaned out your possessions, including the jewellery you'd left behind. They even took the money from under the mattress."

The money we were saving to buy Srikar a motorcycle so he could search for a better job. All these years, when I thought he was out looking for me, he'd thought I'd run away with his money, and my lover?

I worked my jaw, trying to loosen the tension. "Kondal Rao is gutter filth. But you?"

She looked at her hands, tears dripping down.

"What about the note I left for him?"

"They made me copy your handwriting. I wrote a fresh note to Srikar, pretending to be you. They made me say you were running away with your lover."

Srikar couldn't have known it wasn't my handwriting. I'd never had the occasion to write him a letter.

"I didn't hurt anyone," Geeta said, desperate for absolution.

"Of course you didn't." My jaw hurt as I found myself grinding my teeth. "All you did was destroy my marriage by implying I was an adulteress and a thief. All you did was cause me to lose my child." I paused for a breath. "You know what Srikar's grandfather did? He stole my baby, and gave him away. You did nothing more, really."

Geeta swayed, her face ashen.

"Did you know they took Srikar away in an ambulance? Worked out well for you, didn't it? You got a three bedroom flat, my husband ended up in the mental hospital?"

"No!" Geeta started to moan. "I'm not responsible for that! He didn't believe me. I think Kondal Rao bribed old Rukkamma, too. Suddenly she started getting a monthly pension."

And started spreading vicious lies. I stumbled in shock. Srikar really thought I'd been unfaithful to him? I hadn't wanted to believe old Rukkamma, but this... I leaned against the wall as blood rushed to my face, clouding my vision. I lunged at Geeta, shaking her so hard she cried out. "May you never be happy," I spat at her. "May your husband suffer, like mine did. May your children be taken away from you so you understand my pain."

"No!" Geeta ran to the *puja* room and collapsed in front of the pantheon of Gods. "*Yedukondalavada!* I didn't do this with malice in my heart. They forced me!" She got up and fell at my feet. "Forgive me, Pullamma, forgive me!" she said, continuing to moan.

I looked at the woman slumped on the floor, heart full of fury. She'd betrayed me in the worst way, this woman I'd considered a friend. I stepped around her, and slammed the door shut behind me, my rage such that I wished I really were a Goddess so I could put a curse on her.

Forty-Two

What was it about me that caused my friends to betray me so? First, my best friend, Chinni. Then, Geeta. What was it about me that caused me to lose my family – my child, my husband, my grandmother? I found time slipping away. I'd turn on the TV, then realize an hour had passed with no memory of what I'd been watching. I'd gaze out the window, nothing registered. Perhaps, one day I'd forget to breathe, too.

Work was the one thing that kept me anchored to the world. I might have given that up, too, but Aunty wouldn't let me. All of a sudden she decided she'd had enough of practicing medicine. "All these years of missing my son, I'm drained, Child. I want to spend the rest of my life in prayer and charity work. Would you mind?"

I wasn't unaware this was a ploy to keep me busy, but I owed this lady so much. I couldn't possibly refuse. I hired an administrative assistant, and two more nurses. I also hired another doctor, Dr. Govardhan, to help with the patient load. Once I brought him on board, Aunty withdrew completely from practice.

Aunty had got to know quite a few neighbours, and was beginning to spend a lot of time attending *perantams* – women-only functions either involving *pujas,* or purely social in nature. Lines were drawn in these functions, invisible, but there all the same. Married women, the fortunate ones, were at the top of the social pecking order. Unmarried girls came next, because they could still find husbands, and become part of that elite first group. The widows were the unfortunate lot, the has-beens who, while invited, weren't offered *kumkum* and turmeric – the auspicious prerogative of every married woman. Abandoned women rarely went, while divorced women were rarer than politicians with morals.

I couldn't figure out where I fit in the social hierarchy. I refused to go as an unmarried woman, and couldn't go as a married one – I didn't even know if my husband was alive, or if he was, whether he had another wife. "You know why I can't," I said.

"Child, it's not healthy to lock yourself away from people. You could go as an unmarried woman, you know."

"You know what will happen. People will rush to find me a husband." Doctor brides, in their twenties, like I was, were considered

Rasana Atreya

a catch by the middle- and upper-classes because of their potential for future earnings.

In my mind, though, I was still married to Srikar. I still wore my *pustela taadu*, the one he'd tied around my neck at our wedding in the registrar's office. This symbol of marriage remained carefully hidden underneath my clothes, through my stay in the Home, and beyond. I'd not stayed with my husband long enough for him to afford the gold chain the coins would have eventually been attached to. After Aunty and I set up practice, I bought the gold chain myself, and had the coins affixed to it.

What it came down to was that I was married, but not married. I was a mother, but not a mother. And I'd lived longer with my mother-in-law, than I had with my husband.

I put my head down on the desk, cushioning it with my arms. Yesterday, Dr. Govardhan's day off, had been very busy. Today I was feeling the after-effects.

"Why don't you go home?"

I raised my head to see the lanky form of Dr. Govardhan at the door.

"There are no patients right now. Now's your chance," he said, grinning at me. "Escape before the hordes start to queue up. Quick."

I looked at him, hesitant.

"Go, really. You deserve a break." He winked. "See a movie, smile at a handsome man, do something F-U-N. Don't show your face here for twenty-four hours. Doctor's orders."

Dr. Govardhan, with his perpetually sunny outlook on life, made me feel old, even though he was older in physical years, forty to my twenty-five.

Giving him a grateful smile, I decided to take him up on his offer. Feeling a delicious sense of irresponsibility, I decided to talk Aunty into going to a movie with me. She'd been complaining I worked too hard. I walked up the stairs trying to decide between a Telugu movie, and a Hindi one.

We rarely locked up during the day, so I pushed the door open – and gasped. I blinked, stepping into an alternate universe. Muted sounds, diminished colours. I saw tears stream down Aunty's face.

On seeing me Srikar's grandfather, Kondal Rao, abruptly released his grip on her shoulder.

Staggering to my bedroom, I drew up the bed sheet and curled up.

"Pullamma!" Aunty called, her voice sounding distant.

My head felt as if it were enveloped in cotton. I tried to ignore her, but her tone was insistent. I forced my eyes open. Aunty was looking down at me, a frightened expression on her face. She started to sob hysterically. She was scaring me. I'd never known her to lose control. I tried to say something, but my tongue seemed to have thickened; I found myself unable to formulate words. I forced myself up. The image of Srikar's grandfather formed in my head again. Pushing past Aunty, I stumbled to the kitchen for water.

Had that terrible man really been in my house?

Aunty followed me into the kitchen, her eyes red and puffy.

I leaned against the counter and drained the glass of water. I blinked, hoping it would help me focus. How had he found me? Why was I still alive? I refilled my glass, throat still parched.

Aunty twisted the loose end of her sari between her hands, looking as if expecting something. I couldn't tell what, but I knew this wasn't going to be good.

"He didn't come for you."

I stared at her blankly.

The moment stretched out.

"You want to know what Srikar's grandfather was doing here?"

I said nothing.

"He found me near Srikar's house and followed me home."

The steel tumbler slipped from my hand. I traced its path as it hit my foot, then bounced its way across the kitchen – the clanging of it the only sound in the room. It rolled till it came to rest against the cooking-gas cylinder, making one final clang before lying spent.

"Did you hear what I said?" Aunty's voice was shrill. "I said he told me to stay away from Srikar."

"We have worked, and lived together how long?" I cocked my head. "Hmm. Let me see. I moved in with you when I was seventeen. Now I am twenty-five. Eight years."

I wasn't falling apart, I thought with surprise.

Aunty had a stricken expression on her face, though.

"You know how desperately I've been searching for Srikar. And yet, you didn't feel the need to share this little nugget. Amazing."

Aunty stood unmoving, seemingly unable to respond. How I knew the feeling.

"Tell me something," I said, making myself comfortable against the counter. "Did you also forget to tell me other little things? Like, perhaps, you've reconciled with Srikar?"

Aunty blanched.

"Ah! So all this time I've been grieving, you've been meeting my husband? Is your father-in-law part of this happy little family, as well?"

"Pullamma!" Aunty's voice was hoarse. "Let me explain."

I had to get away. If I fell apart, I'd turn into Humpty Dumpty; unable to put myself together again. "Didn't I mention a movie?"

Aunty made a sound of distress.

Don't think about it, don't, don't. I struggled for a blank face. "Well, I am off to one. Got to improve my Hindi, you know. I'm getting lots of North Indian patients now."

I walked out of the flat and took an auto-rickshaw to the nearest movie hall, completely forgetting I had a car and driver waiting. The movie I wanted to see was playing, so I bought a ticket. Luckily, there was hardly anyone in the hall, probably because it was a weekday matinee show. I picked a seat in the last row, and settled in with a cup of tea and a plate of steaming hot samosas. I could see a few people ahead, but no one in the last rows.

The movie started, and the trembling started. Then the tears came.

Two and a half hours later I lurched out of the theatre, no improvement in my Hindi skills whatsoever. Outside stood Aunty, her face grey with fatigue. I found myself unable to respond to her mute appeal. Appeal for what? I didn't know, and didn't particularly care. I'd loved this woman like a mother and she'd betrayed me.

The driver held the door of the car open. I slid in. Aunty stood, hesitating. I turned away. She got in the front. Once home, I slammed my bedroom door, and crawled into bed. When I awoke, it was dawn, and my face was wet from the tears.

Aunty was asleep on the chair in my room.

I couldn't bear to look in her direction. The woman I'd trusted with my deepest secrets hadn't trusted me enough to tell me where my husband was.

I turned on the electric water heater in the bathroom, and went to the kitchen to make myself a cup of coffee. I put the cup to my lips, and felt a sharp surge of nausea. Pouring the coffee down the drain, I went to the bathroom, turned off the heater, and took a long, hot bath. When I emerged, Aunty was no longer in my bedroom. She sat huddled on the sofa in the living room, her fingers wrapped around a rimmed steel tumbler of coffee. She looked up when she saw me. The skin of her face seemed to have sagged overnight. "Do you want me to move out?"

"I don't know."

She flinched. "Can you ever forgive me?"

"I don't know that, either."

She set the steel tumbler aside and rubbed her eyelids. "If I had to do this again, maybe I'd have told you sooner. But..." Her voice trailed away.

"You might as well tell me the rest."

"I went to my father-in-law's political party office and bribed someone to give me Srikar's address. I thought I was so smart." She gave a self-deprecating laugh. "I've been going over to Srikar's house, watching from a distance. Yesterday Kondal Rao followed me home. I led them to you, Pullamma." She sounded distressed. "I'm such a fool."

Suddenly I knew with deep conviction that this woman, whom I loved like a mother, was no more a manipulator than Ammamma was. I reached for her, and hugged her tightly. She trembled with emotion. I rubbed a hand over her back, feeling rage build up at Srikar's grandfather. "I am sorry I reacted so badly yesterday. I was in shock."

She looked pathetically grateful.

"However, I am very hurt that you didn't feel you could trust me with this information."

"I'm sorry," she whispered, reminding me she wasn't the villain here. She'd suffered, too. "But after his taunts, I just couldn't tell you."

"What are you saying?" My heart thumped uncomfortably against my ribcage.

Aunty gave a short laugh. "He's known all along where your son is."

My heart picked up speed. My hands turned clammy. Wrapping my arms around myself, I began to rock. Back and forth. Back and forth.

Aunty looked at me with compassion. "He said the child is where he belongs."

I sat up with a jerk. My heart started to pound painfully. "Which is where?"

"With his father."

"With *Srikar*?"

"Yes."

I leaned back and closed my eyes. My limbs felt weighted down. "Pullamma?"

I couldn't believe this. I had been searching for my son for so long, hurting for Srikar that he didn't know the fate of his child. I stared blankly, anguish welling up within. All this while he'd been the one raising our son. Kondal Rao must have stolen my baby and left him with Srikar. Kondal Rao – well, he'd stayed true to character. But Srikar? To believe I was unfaithful, was one thing. But to deprive me of my child?

"Say something," Aunty begged.

I forced my eyes to blink. "What do you want me to say? That I miss my son desperately? You know I do." I swallowed down the bile. "For my son's sake, I'm glad he's known the love of his father. I am glad it isn't a stranger who's raising him. But for my sake –"

Aunty put her hand on mine. "You are angry."

"Wouldn't you be, if you'd spent years searching for your child, not knowing whose hands he'd fallen into?"

"What are you going to do?" Aunty asked.

"Get back my stolen child. Convince Srikar I wasn't unfaithful. See if we can build a life together." I looked at Aunty. "How long have you known Srikar's address?"

"Five months." At the look of incredulity on my face, she grabbed my hands, pleading, "I was only trying to protect you."

"From what? Happiness?" I shook her hands off. "So that's where you disappear to each morning. You've been having a gala time with your son and grandson while I spend my days worrying myself sick about their welfare."

"Pullamma –"

"Stop!"

"I didn't know he was raising your son."

"Enough of your lies," I shouted.

"He passes by on his motorcycle, and he doesn't know," Aunty whispered, head down, tears wetting the fabric of the sofa. She started to sob in my shoulder. "He doesn't know I'm his mother."

"And you couldn't tell me this."

"No," she said, sniffling.

"Why not?"

She sobbed harder.

I pushed her off my shoulder. "Aunty, I need to know. Why couldn't you tell me?"

"Because he was with his wife."

FORTY-THREE

I started at Aunty. She couldn't be serious. *Oh God, she means it!* "Aunty," I said, heart clutching, "what if he's taught my baby to hate me?" *Don't think about the wife. Focus on your child.*

Aunty hugged me. "He wouldn't do that to his own child."

"And Kondal Rao would never break up his own grandson's marriage, right?" I swallowed. "Why was Kondal Rao here today? The real reason." I'd had enough of people keeping information from me 'for my own good.'

"He did find me near Srikar's house. He came by to warn you to keep a low profile, and for me to stay away. Some journalist's been trying to dig up dirt on him. He doesn't want information about you popping up."

"What about that attempt on my life?"

"He claims it was a knee-jerk reaction. You escaped, he sent his men after you. It won't happen again."

I gave an incredulous laugh. "He said that?"

"That's what he said."

"I curse the day I met Kondal Rao." I swallowed my tears. "Aunty, please tell me where they are, I'm begging you."

"Pullamma, I don't want you rushing off –"

"Rushing? After eight years, I'm rushing?"

"Pullamma –"

"Are you going to tell me or not?"

"No."

I was shocked.

"I'm trying to protect you." Aunty was apologetic.

"I'm sick and tired of people deciding what's best for me. You won't tell me? Fine. I'll ask Kondal Rao himself."

"Pullamma!"

I grabbed my purse, and shot through the door. Bloody Kondal Rao had gone too far. I sprinted down the stairs, ignoring Aunty's pleas to come back. Hailing a passing auto-rickshaw, I jumped in, and directed him to the office of Kondal Rao's political party. I arrived at the gate the same time the bloody man's convey was pulling in. He descended from the jeep, laughing at something the man welcoming him said.

A roaring sound encompassed my head – he'd stolen my son, denied me my husband, and the monstrous man had the temerity to laugh? With a determined stride I took off towards him.

"What are you doing?" A strongman tried to block my path.

I pushed past him.

Kondal Rao raised his head at the commotion. When his eyes fell on me, his face darkened.

I lunged at him, grabbing fists-full of his *kurta*. "You stole my son," I screamed. A goon grabbed my arms and twisted them behind my back. The goon started walking me backward. "You stole my husband," I spat out. "Be a man. Face me without your goons. Tell me where they are."

Kondal Rao smoothed the front of his kurta. "Poor woman. Must have suffered some trauma. Some mental thing. Why else would she make such a spectacle of herself?"

Enraged I opened my mouth. A meaty hand clamped down on my mouth, covering my nose. I almost gagged. I struggled to breathe. The man moved his hand lower, but didn't release me.

Kondal Rao flicked a finger at his henchman. "Take the poor woman outside the compound, give her some money and release her."

Patronizing bastard! If only I could get my hands around his stubby little neck.

Kondal Rao turned his back on me, and disappeared into the building. The remaining strongmen lined up against the entryway in a show of strength.

I bit down on the hand covering my mouth.

The man uttered an oath and let go.

I ran through the gates and jumped into an auto-rickshaw parked by the side, offering to double the fare if the driver got going. He took off, tyres screeching. As he sped through the city streets, I closed my eyes, feeling a sense of desolation.

When he pulled up at my building, I shoved money in his hands and dragged myself up the stairs.

"Where were you?" Aunty said shrilly.

"Kondal Rao's office." Wearily, I sank to the floor.

"Oh no," Aunty moaned. "How could you do such a thing?"

"Don't worry, he walked away."

"It is a fool who jabs a poisonous snake with a stick." Aunty looked scared.

My stomach muscles clenched in spasms. I bent over double, gasping from the pain.

"Pullamma!"

I crumpled to the floor in a foetal ball, pain radiating in all directions. The anger was gone, leaving behind despair. Gut wrenching despair.

To imagine Srikar with another woman... holding her... touching her...

This same woman was bringing up my son, the child I'd carried within me for nine loving months. Did the two of them lie in bed together, my husband, and his wife, holding each other, discussing my son? Another spasm shot from my stomach. *Oh God, Oh God, Oh God. Spare me this suffering.* I lay on the floor writhing in agony; the pain, both physical and emotional, more than I could bear.

Aunty slid to the floor, weeping. "Please, Pullamma, talk to me. I can't bear to see you like this."

"What would you have me do?" I gasped. "Jump in joy? My beloved husband is cavorting with another woman, his *wife*," I spat out. "And they're happily raising *my* son together."

Aunty sagged against the wall. "I knew I shouldn't have told you."

"My sister, Lata, used to mock my 'perfect' love." I clenched my teeth as another spasm speared my belly. 'Chiranjeevi' she'd called Srikar after the Telugu film star my friend Chinni and I had such a crush on. "Leave me to my misery."

I lay on my side, not moving, not caring that Aunty wept.

The shadows lengthened. I watched the street lights come on. My husband and his... that... that woman... would be putting my son to bed. The window framed a sliver of the moon. Bedtime for my husband and that...

"It's been hours, Child. Let me help you to your room."

I curled into a tight ball.

A while later I sat up, disoriented, wiping drool from my cheek. Then it all came rushing back. My husband, my child and that... that...

At my sound of distress, Aunty scooted over and put her arm around me. She helped me to my feet and to bed.

"Get up, attend a prayer session, go for a walk, see patients, do something," Aunty said as she sat by my bedside. "I've been filling in for you, but Dr. Govardhan's asking if you need to consult with specialists for your health situation. How long will you keep this up?"

"Why? Who needs me?"

"Your son."

"He doesn't know I exist. He has a mother; he's happy. My husband has a wife; he's happy, too." At some level I realized I'd shut down for self-preservation. Perhaps Aunty had been right to try and spare me the pain. Because it was a pain beyond measure.

Aunty got angry. "Great plan. Just lie in bed. Be depressed. Don't fight for what's yours. Your son probably loves his stepmother anyway. Why shake things up?"

"Aunty! How can you be so cruel?"

"Someone needs to. You've been moping for three weeks. Get yourself out of that bed and think about what needs to be done."

"I don't even know his name."

"And you never will, if all you do is loll around in bed."

"No!" Suddenly I was filled with rage. They'd taken away what was mine.

"Then do something about it."

I swung my legs to the floor with grim determination. Enough was enough. They wouldn't get away with stealing my child.

Later that evening Janaki aunty and I stood by the pale yellow house at the junction of two roads.

Srikar's house.

The house was set to the back, the area in front a cemented rectangle. We walked to the house, trying to shield ourselves with the guava tree that grew to one side. A coconut tree, fruit ripe for the picking, stood on the other. An independent house in the city. Srikar seemed to have done well for himself. With a wife that wasn't

RASANA ATREYA

me. Raising *my* son. I clenched my fists, shaking with emotion. "This is nonsense," I said. "I haven't done anything wrong. Why am I hiding here like some thief? I'm going in to get my child."

"Don't be a fool." Aunty grabbed my arm. "You can't traumatize your son by springing up with no warning. As far as he is concerned, he already has a mother."

"I'm hardly liable to forget that, am I?" Blood rushed to my face. "And this 'your son' business – we should know his name!"

"We will. I just prefer to do it without hurting –" Aunty's voice caught, "our baby." She sighed. "I'm not the enemy here, you know."

I felt ashamed. She was right. I shouldn't be taking my anger out on her. It was hardly her fault that Kondal Rao was filthier than a cow's behind.

A child came into the yard. My heart picked up speed. My son? Had to be. He didn't appear young enough to be Srikar's child with his wife. He came to the edge of the hedge, chasing a butterfly, arm upraised. I watched him through the dense hedge, straining to get a clear look. He passed a few feet from me, face turned away. To be this close and not touch him, not to see his face even...

I ached that I knew nothing about my child beyond his date of birth. It galled me to think he could pass me on the street, and I wouldn't know.

Early next morning, I waited for word from Janaki aunty. She was near Srikar's house, waiting for my son to leave for school. Then we'd go in, confront Srikar and his loving wife. I'd opted to wait a distance away; another glimpse of my son, and I'd break down.

"Let's go," Aunty said, walking up. "We got lucky. His wife just left with a shopping basket."

I was relieved. Much as I hated to acknowledge this, the wife was probably an innocent bystander about to be caught in the crossfire. If Srikar and I decided to be a family again, what would his wife's status be? Venkat, back in the village, had lived in the same house with both his wives. Forget the bigamy aspect of it, I'd rather swathe myself in honey and tumble into an anthill than lower myself to that level.

Raising my hand to knock, I had a sudden attack of nerves. What if my husband didn't want me back? What if my son hated me for disrupting his world? "By going in, we'll be destroying an innocent woman's life." I wiped damp palms against my sides.

"By not going in, we'll be destroying your own," Aunty said recognizing my fear for what it was. "You'll never get to meet your son."

"And you'll never get to meet yours," I said softly.

"There is that," Aunty allowed, nodding her head at the truth of it. "This is bad business, Pullamma. There can be no winners here. Someone or the other is going to get hurt for no fault of their own."

"What if Srikar wishes we'd never found him? What if my son hates me?"

"Stop making excuses."

My eyes chanced upon an abandoned plastic tricycle. My son's! I took a deep breath. There was no going back now. "Okay. Let's do it." I knocked and waited tensely.

The door opened.

Srikar!

I swayed toward him, heart full.

"Who are you looking for?" Srikar asked, a polite smile on his face.

I felt like he'd stabbed me in the heart.

Foolish me, to believe the connection between us was so strong he'd recognize me, no matter what. I realized I was being illogical, but the hurt was too great – come nightfall, he'd get into bed with another woman. "It isn't enough that you raise my son, it isn't enough that you remarry when I'm still alive? Now you question my identity?"

"Pullamma?"

"No, your grandmother." I couldn't believe he'd not recognized me, that he'd made a life without me. I pushed past him and leaned against the wall, trembling with emotion.

"*Yedukondalavada*! It that really you?" He looked disbelieving.

"How could you have married someone else?" I said, breaking down. "How?"

"Pullamma –"

"What is it, tell me." I grabbed his shoulders, shaking him, crying, broken up that he no longer belonged to me. "Did you have so little faith in me that you married someone else?"

"It's not that..."

"Then what?" I forced myself to take deep breaths; getting hysterical wasn't going to help the situation.

"Our son needed a mother, and you were not to be found..."

My heart started to beat painfully. "How did he get to you?"

"You don't know?" He looked confused.

"For many years I didn't even know we had a son. I thought I'd given birth to a stillborn girl. That's what Kondal Rao had them tell me."

"Oh my God!"

We looked at each other a long time, this man, my husband, who was not my husband. He was the only reason I kept going when I thought I'd die from the pain. He and our child.

"How..." I swallowed past the painful constriction in my throat. "How did our baby get to you?"

"I stormed my grandfather's office, threatening to call the media and expose his misdeeds if he didn't tell me where you were. He promised to bring you to our flat that evening. Instead of you, an ambulance showed up and transported me to the mental hospital."

I closed my eyes, trying to take it all in. Opening my eyes, I said, "And this man is your grandfather?"

He shrugged.

"How did our son get to you?" I asked again.

"I was close to breakdown, getting too unpredictable for my grandfather, making a nuisance of myself by begging the staff to track you down. He came to the mental hospital one day. I'd been there many days by then, I don't know how long. He told me I had a son." He looked at me, tears flowing. "You can't imagine my joy, Pullamma. All those days of intense agony, and then to hear this –"

I smiled at him, my heart breaking for what he'd been through.

"He'd give me my child, he said, but I had to give up my search for you."

I drew in a sharp breath.

Srikar looked at me in anguish. "I fought long and hard, Pullamma. You *know* I'd never have given you up willingly." He looked at me pleadingly.

I nodded, unable to speak past the tears.

"I demanded proof that the child was mine. He laughed and said he didn't particularly care if I didn't believe him. He'd be happy to give the child away. I couldn't take that risk, Pulla –" He choked. Taking a moment to compose himself, he said, "I said it was either both of you, or nothing. He said if I didn't take his offer, he had the resources to lock me away indefinitely. He'd give the child away for adoption because he could never let you loose, it was too dangerous for him. He warned that after I took my son, if I resumed my search for you, he –" He swallowed hard. "He'd have you *and* our child killed. I made a bargain with the Devil, Pulla."

I leaned forward, my hand hovering uncertainly. I'd lost the right to touch him when he married someone else. Then I touched his cheek gently. "You did what you had to do," I said, even as my heart was breaking. "I'm glad our son had the love of one parent."

Pressing his hand against mine, he let his tears flow.

"You remarried."

He looked up sharply. "You've met her?"

I shook my head. "Why?" My voice was hoarse. "Why did you remarry?"

"It wasn't a wife I was looking for, Pullamma. I needed a mother for our son. My grandfather wouldn't allow my grandmother, or yours, to help. And I had to get to my job, in order to support our child."

I doubled over from the sharp agony.

"I'm sorry," he said hoarsely. "I'm so sorry."

I leaned forward, covering my eyes with my hand. Tears dripped. *I should have been the one taking care of our baby. I should have been the one being a wife to my husband.* "Is there a chance for us? For the three of us to be a family?" I wiped ineffectually. *God, let him say he wants me back.*

"I can't see how," he whispered. He looked devastated.

"Don't you care for me anymore?" I wasn't sure I wanted to know.

"How can you even say that? In fact –"

"What?"

He cleared his throat. "One of the big issues with my wife has been that I've not been able to get over you."

I closed my eyes. So many tears shed over my husband and child; how was it that I had so many more left?

RASANA ATREYA

"I... uh... I still love you."

My eyes shot open.

He flushed.

I felt a rush of tenderness for this man. I knew how hard it was for him to say this out loud. Ammamma always said, this I-love-you business was not worthy of our conservative culture. Of course husbands and wives loved one another. But who went about declaring such things?

"Where do we go from here?" I asked.

He looked troubled. "I remarried in good faith, Pulla. I was convinced my grandfather had you killed, despite what he told me. I could see no other way you'd let our child go."

More tears joined the ones wetting my sari. "Your grandfather kidnapped me and dumped me in a home for destitute women."

Srikar looked shocked.

"Geeta came across us as we were leaving. Your grandfather assaulted her and threatened her with dire consequences if she ever told anyone what she'd seen."

Srikar's face lost colour "Unbelievable that I'm related to that man!"

"In the Home, they did a forcible Caesarean on me to take the baby out. They took away my child, telling me I'd given birth to a stillborn girl." I broke down. "For many years I didn't even know I had a child that lived. And, from the time I found out, I've been searching for him."

Srikar pulled me into his arms, holding me as I wept.

"What now?" I said.

He sighed.

"Can the three of us ever be together?"

"I don't know how to make it up to you. I can't see how to make it work."

A tiny sound of distress escaped my lips.

"It's not what you think, Pulla."

My heart crimped at the endearment.

"I married a woman whose first husband threw her out of the house because they couldn't have children."

"You... you don't have other children?"

"No."

Thank you, God!

"How can I, in good conscience, abandon her?" His eyes begged for understanding. "What would her life be like, her status in society, after being abandoned by two husbands?"

"What about me?" I hated that this sounded like pleading.

"She took care of us when we needed her, even though she knew I'd rather be with you. I tried hard not to show my true feelings, but she knew, Pulla. She always knew. She stayed only because she had nowhere else to go. How can I throw her out now, when we don't need her anymore?" He looked troubled.

"But it wasn't my fault." Tears slowly made their way down.

He cupped my face in his hands. "I know, Pulla, I know."

I rested my head against his, letting the tears flow. "All these years," I whispered. "The only thing that sustained me was the certainty of reuniting with you. And our son."

He took my hand in his. "I'm so sorry, Pulla. Between my grandfather and I, we ruined your life."

"No." I covered his mouth with my hand. "Never compare yourself with your grandfather. That man wouldn't know integrity if it punched him in the gut."

He pulled me into his arms. Then he wept.

FORTY-FOUR

S rikar sagged against the chair, rubbing his eyes with his palms. "God, what a mess."

I inspected his face. Eight years ago Srikar had been a boyish twenty-two, scraggly beard sprouting; now I could see a stubble on his chin. He had filled out, become more muscular. His hair still fell endearingly over his forehead, though.

He was staring blankly at the jewel-studded picture of Lord Krishna across the room. I ran my eyes over the room. My son was growing up with these chairs, these walls, this daybed. I felt an irrational jealously of these objects that had seen my son, touched him, held him.

Through the window I could see Aunty leaning against the gate, watching traffic go by. Conscious of the fact she was waiting to meet her son, I gathered up my courage and put a hand on Srikar's arm.

He looked at it for a long moment before turning his gaze on me. "All these years," he said hoarsely. "What a waste."

"It is unbelievable how conniving that man is!" What a personification of evil. "I escaped from the home a few weeks after our son was born. I went to Madhuban Apartments. Two thugs were waiting to kill me."

Srikar blanched. "My... my grandfather?"

"Who else?"

He fell back against the wall.

"What is our son's name?"

"Pullaiyya."

Stick boy.

"Will you let me raise Pu... Pullaiyya?"

"That would be the right thing to do. He was, after all, stolen from you."

I had never doubted Srikar's integrity. I touched the back of his hand. "Thank you."

"But, Pullamma –" He cleared his throat. "I wish it were that simple."

"Why? He is my child. I was denied the right to raise him."

"I know that, and you know that, but..."

"But what?"

"Pullaiyya doesn't."

I drew in a sharp breath.

He pulled me into his arms again. "I want to make things right for you, I really do. What my grandfather did to you was terrible. But we have to find a way of doing this without hurting our child."

"I've waited so long for him," I sobbed into his shoulder. "Is it fair to expect me to wait longer?"

"He's a child, Pulla. He doesn't know about fairness. All he knows is that his world is safe right now."

I moved away. "And it won't be safe if I claim him." I was bitter. "Can you at least tell me what he looks like? Who he resembles? Does he have friends? Is he happy?" It galled me that I had to ask.

"He takes a little time to warm up to people he doesn't know. But once he does, he's just another little boy. If I let him, he'd play all day. He can be, in turns, happy, sulky, irritable, lovable. Gets into a lot of mischief. Doesn't much care for his studies. I wonder where he got that from?" Srikar smiled.

But I couldn't get past my anguish. I shouldn't have to find all this out second hand.

"He looks like me," Srikar said.

"Do you have a picture?"

"Hmm. Let me see. I think there is a picture of him. That's probably the latest one." Srikar got up and rummaged through a pile on the corner table. "Here it is."

I grabbed at it with eager hands. A solemn little boy in school uniform stared back. His hair was slicked back, probably for his school ID. Roundish face, big eyes. I ran a finger over the picture. I blinked back tears. "Can I keep it?"

He nodded, eyes wet.

"Is he close to Ammamma?"

Srikar had a look of regret on his face. "No, he's never been to the village. My... uh... wife didn't want to keep up that connection."

Poor Ammamma. To be denied her great-grandson!

"As soon as you talk to him –"

"You'll meet him, I promise. Now tell me what you've been up to."

"This sounds like two friends catching up, not a reunion between husband and wife." I felt bitterness well up within.

"I'm married to someone else," Srikar mumbled, not meeting my eyes.

I looked at him for a long moment, then sighed. "You remember we'd plan our future on our late night walks?"

Srikar nodded.

"I took your advice and studied."

He nodded approvingly. "It shows," he said. "You look more self-confident, more self-assured. What did you study?"

"I became a doctor."

"A doctor?" His face split into a disbelieving smile. "My Pullamma, a doctor?" He gave a delighted laugh. "I can't believe it."

I smiled back. "What do you think of my looks?"

He gave my question serious consideration. "As long as the person within hasn't changed, it really doesn't matter."

I was glad.

"It was your quiet dignity that drew me in the first place," he reminded with a faint smile.

I felt warmth spread in my chest. I felt more connected to the Pullamma of old, too. "Were you able to study?" I asked.

"I got my MBA. I run my own construction company now."

"I'm glad for you," I said quietly. My throat hurt. "To think you suffered so much because of me."

He put an arm around me and pulled me close. "It wasn't all bad, Pulla. I had our son. Without him, I don't think I would have made it."

For that at least, I was glad.

Now to administer Srikar his second shock of the day. "*Yemandi*?" It seemed wrong to be addressing him thus when he was married to another, but I didn't know how else to. "What happened to your mother?"

"Why do you want to know?" Srikar sounded suspicious. "Why now?"

"Please, can you just tell me?"

"She abandoned me when I was two years old. She was a wicked woman. I neither have the knowledge of her whereabouts, nor do I have the desire to know."

"Why was she wicked?"

"Because –" He stopped. "Why are you asking anyway?"

At the look on my face, he jumped up. "No! Don't tell me my grandfather had something to do with her disappearance, as well."

I tried to reach for his hand, but he pulled away in shock. "Where is she? How do you know about her?"

"When I thought I would lose my mind from missing you, she stepped in and took care of me and our baby-to-be. I have been living with her for eight years. I love her as much as I would my own mother."

Srikar had a wild expression in his eyes. "That lady outside?"

I nodded at him with compassion.

"You can't just walk into my life after so many years, turn it upside down, then turn around and tell me you have found my mother," he shouted. "You showing up after so many years is shock enough. You can't just spring something like this on a person." He paced faster and faster till I thought my head would spin. Abruptly he fell on the daybed.

"She has lived with the pain of losing you for more than twenty-eight years," I said softly. "Doesn't she deserve a chance?"

Srikar dropped his head into his hands.

I stood up. "I will send her in."

Outside, I took Aunty's hand and led her to the door. Then it was my turn to step out and close the door behind me.

I walked around. The yard was hard-packed mud, with lots of fruit trees bordered by bricks painted white. This was the home my husband shared with our son and another woman. I walked around the whitewashed walls, looking around at the detritus of childhood – a broken cricket bat, a couple of punctured balls. A notebook lay carelessly to the side. My son's? I picked it up and opened it. The front page had Pullaiyya scrawled all over. I flipped a page. Steeply triangled mountains through which the sun rose. The rays of the sun were rigidly placed. I smiled through my tears – an artist, my son wasn't. The stick figures were exaggerated – really long hands curving around the tiny heads. I put the book to my cheek, trying

RASANA ATREYA

to absorb the essence of my child. How could I convince Srikar to be a family with my son and me?

Aunty waved me over.

Srikar and Aunty stood with their arms around each other, their faces wearing deeply contented smiles. Aunty pulled me into a hug. She turned to Srikar, "There is probably a first for everything, but I love my daughter-in-law as much as I love my son!"

We all laughed.

Their reunion gave me deep pleasure. But it was tinged with deep sadness. My husband wasn't my own, anymore. "What about Pullaiyya? When can we meet him?"

Srikar looked uncertain. "I don't know how he will react," he finally said.

"What about your wife?" My chest hurt to say that word.

Srikar opened his mouth as if to say something, then closed it again.

"Srikar?" Aunty prompted.

"That is going to be a problem," he said heavily.

"I don't want to disrupt Pullaiyya's life," I said. "I'm sure Aunty doesn't, either. But we want him in our lives."

"Give me some time. I'll phone you. Please?"

Aunty and I nodded. It was the best we could do.

Forty-Five

J anaki aunty and I waited till we got home before we talked
about our reunion with Srikar; drivers and maids were notori-
ous spreaders of gossip.

Aunty sighed. "To think one man is responsible for ruining so
many lives."

Srikar, married. That was one possibility that hadn't occurred to
me when I set out to find him. Despite what he said, I wasn't able
to give up on the hope that the three of us would be a family someday. Especially since I knew he still cared for me.

I'd thought I would return from my reunion with Srikar feeling
happy; instead I felt more depressed than ever. My son was still out
of reach. The only good thing to come out of this was I knew my
child was healthy and well cared for.

From the look on her face I could tell Aunty wanted to add
something. "Aunty," I said softly. "I've never doubted your love for
me. If you want to say something, please don't hesitate."

She smiled gratefully. "If you are expecting your son to bond
with you instantly just because you gave birth to him..."

"I know," I said painfully. "As far as he is concerned, he already
has a mother."

Now that I knew what my son looked like, my dreams of him became more vivid. I saw myself taking care of him, cooking for him,
helping him with homework, bandaging his hurts. I wished Srikar
would phone to tell me when I could meet him. Only the fear of
traumatizing my child kept me away. Many times I was tempted
to rush to their house and grab my son. Now that I knew where he
lived, it was getting harder and harder to stay away.

Over the next few days, I went to the clinic, saw patients, did
paperwork, occasionally cooked, generally lived my life as I had
before Srikar came back into it. But in the back of my mind was
that phone call Srikar had promised me, the call telling me that I
could meet my son.

But Srikar did not call.

Instead, he appeared at my doorstep six days later. I looked up from the sofa – and there he was. Aunty gave me a hug in silent support and picked up her purse. She gave Srikar a hug, too, and let herself out of the flat. I felt a rush of affection for her.

Srikar sat on the other sofa. Back and forth, back and forth, the keys went between his hands. He wouldn't meet my eyes.

"Say something," I said, unable to stand the tension.

"I married your sister," he said abruptly.

"Malli?" I was confused. "But she's already married."

"Your other sister. Lata. We've been married almost six years." He seemed tortured.

I felt a whirring sound in my head. My husband married to my twin? *No, God, that would be too cruel!*

"Pulla?" Srikar looked anxious. His voice seemed to come from far away.

I slashed a vicious hand through the air. I'd fall apart if he showed sympathy now.

Srikar's eyes pleaded for understanding. "What I didn't mention earlier was that one of the conditions my grandfather laid down was that I'd have to marry Lata. If I wanted my son, that is."

"But why?"

"He claimed that it was to provide Lata the protection of a married name. Perhaps he did not want Lata in her grandmother's home, reminding people that the marriage my grandfather had helped arrange had failed. Whatever the reason, he would not budge on that. He said he would hand the baby over only after I married her. Say something, Pulla."

I couldn't; my throat had closed.

Srikar continued. "I was angry with my grandfather for forcing me into this sham of a marriage, Pulla, but I wanted our son too badly. How could I let him be raised by strangers?"

When I said nothing, Srikar said a little desperately, "You know when a woman with children dies, the husband often marries his wife's younger sister to ensure the children are loved."

"Not if the sister herself is married," I said bitterly. "And not if the wife isn't dead, to begin with."

He reared back as if struck. "You know this is the only thing I could have done."

"But Lata? How could you, knowing our history?"

God! Malli, Chinni – almost anyone else, I could have accepted.

"What happened to Lata's husband?" I asked dully.

"Her husband – her first husband," he corrected himself, "and his parents threw Lata out."

"Because of dowry?"

"Because she wasn't able to conceive."

I was speechless at the irony. Lata had been forced to marry *because* she got pregnant.

He said, "Lata's in-laws got their son remarried to another girl, but the second wife couldn't conceive either." He looked at me, longing in his eyes. "Pullamma, I wish –"

"Don't," I said sharply. I couldn't handle more pain today. I refused to acknowledge the wounded look in his eyes. "So what now?"

"I don't know," he said, miserable.

I was so angry at Lata's betrayal, I could have wrung her neck. It wasn't enough that she'd caused Ammamma so much trouble with the illegitimate pregnancy, it wasn't enough she'd given Kondal Rao something to manipulate me with, it wasn't enough she'd stolen money; she'd gone after my husband? The husband she knew I cared for more than anyone else?

"Lata is the only mother Pullaiyya has ever known..."

My vengeful sister, the mother of my son – that was the cruellest joke of all.

Aunty came back a long time later. I'd not moved from my position on the sofa since Srikar left.

"Did you decide on something?" she asked, a hopeful expression on her face.

Had we decided on how to untangle the mess that was our lives? Was it even possible? "He married my sister Lata."

She drew in a sharp breath. "Oh, Child."

"I asked Srikar why he named our child Pullaiyya." I rubbed a hand over my chest. I needed an antacid, maybe two.

"Lata insisted?"

"She convinced Srikar that was the only way to stop this chain of calamities."

"Srikar didn't protest?"

"I never told him how much I hated my name."

RASANA ATREYA

Aunty's lips tightened. "I know that scoundrel Kondal Rao had a hand in arranging Lata's marriage to Srikar. Don't ask me how, because I couldn't tell you. I just know he did."

"Lata always knew how much I hated my name," I whispered. She made fun of me almost as much as the other children did. To name my child that name..." My throat choked from the tears. "She married my husband, Aunty. My husband. She knew how much I cared for him; she made fun of me often enough."

Aunty pulled me into her arms.

I said between sobs, "And you know the worst thing?"

"What?"

"I'm dreading the day she finds out I became a doctor. She will never let me anywhere near my son." I had told Aunty the general story of my life, but not about Lata's involvement; I was too ashamed.

"Why?"

"Because being a doctor was all she talked about. It was her greatest desire. And she was intelligent enough to be one, too."

"But?"

"Ammamma fixed up an alliance for Lata behind her back. Lata was so angry that she slept with a boy in the village, and got pregnant by him."

"Oh God!"

"That boy ran away, so Kondal Rao arranged her marriage to someone else completely beneath her in education."

"So she got trapped into a marriage she did not want, and ended up with neither a child nor a medical degree."

"She did end up with something," I said with bitterness. "My husband and my son."

"And you ended up with everything she'd ever wanted," Aunty said. She sighed. "What a nightmare! And to think your grandmother had only your wellbeing at heart." She paused a beat before asking, "Is Srikar going to let us meet Pu – the child?"

"You can call him Pullaiyya," I said. "That is his name. About seeing him, Srikar said Lata was having a hard time with it."

"Hard time, my foot! Must be the bloody woman's way of making you pay for whatever wrongs she thinks you did her."

FORTY-SIX

"How much longer before I can see my son?" I asked Srikar on the phone.

"He's away on a school trip."

"The last time I called he was in the middle of exams. Before that it was the chicken pox. Do you ever intend to let me see him?"

"Of course, I do. It's just that –"

"What? It's been two whole months. I can't go on this way."

"I'm sorry."

"Sorry isn't working anymore. Give me a time and a date."

"I –"

"It's Lata!" I could have smacked myself for not seeing it. "She's pressuring you, isn't she?"

"It's not that."

"Tell me," I screamed. "Enough is enough."

"He doesn't want to meet you."

"What?"

"When I told him about you, he ran away from home." Srikar's voice sounded strained. "It took me two days to find him and bring him back."

"Why didn't you tell me?" I whispered.

"How could I?"

The phone clattered to the ground. My son didn't want me. My husband didn't want me. *Yedukondalavada! What kind of test is this?*

I had stopped sleeping at nights because dreams of my husband with my sister tormented me. Now, because my son didn't want me, would I have to stop sleeping during the day, too?

I ran down the stairs, got in the car and directed my driver to Srikar's house. I wasn't really sure what I was going to do once I got there, but I couldn't sit around doing nothing.

I had the driver park on a side road, and walked to the junction where the house was.

The front door opened. I held my breath as Srikar came out, followed by Lata. I was shocked at the change in my sister – her lips seemed to have a permanent twist of discontentment, frown lines crowded her forehead. Lata said something. Srikar bent down to hear better. Acid burned the back of my throat. Lata held the gate open. Srikar got on his motorbike and drove away. Lata closed the gate, went back in, only to come back five minutes later, a young boy swinging his bag next to her.

I gasped. My son. Almost unconsciously, I raised my arms to him. A passing woman gave me a strange look. A small school bus pulled up. Five minutes later, my son was gone. A pain ripped my chest, the agony so sharp I almost doubled over. I straightened up with difficulty.

This was my son. The son who didn't want me. I finally understood the pain Aunty had lived with all these years. Trembling, I started to walk away.

"Wait!"

Oh, no! Lata had recognized me. Srikar must have told her to expect the changes.

I turned around.

Lata was running to catch up with me.

I started to walk faster. Whatever it was, I did not want to hear.

"Wait, I said!"

I started to run, almost tripping on my sari. A hand clamped down on my arm. I was turned around roughly.

"What are you doing near my house?"

I shivered at the hatred in her eyes.

No, how are you, Pullamma. No, where have you been all these years, Pullamma. Just 'what are you doing near my house.'

No 'Pullamma,' either.

"What are you doing with my husband?" I asked back.

She gave my arm a vicious tug. "He is *my* husband now, and don't you forget it."

I looked at her, disbelieving that we could have been born of the same mother. Where was the special connection twins were supposed to have?

"We have been married for a long time now," she said. "Don't you poke your nose where it doesn't belong."

I'd never realized Lata's eyes could be so cold. My palms became tingly. That numbness again. I forced myself to concentrate. "We registered our marriage."

Lata froze.

I felt savage satisfaction. She hadn't known!

"Since Srikar and I are not divorced, you are the other woman. I am still his wife. Ask any lawyer. You have no standing. No rights. None at all."

"But you abandoned your marriage," Lata said, shouting. "You have no rights on him anymore."

So this is what my relationship with my sister had come to – fighting over a man on the streets of Hyderabad. People had stopped to look. A passing peanut vendor took advantage of the gathering. He parked his bicycle and started doing brisk business selling coal-roasted peanuts wrapped in newspaper cones.

"Why don't we talk inside your house?" I said, embarrassed. "People are staring."

"You will never step inside the house I share with Srikar."

"Fine, then," I said, getting angry. "I did not abandon anyone."

"You went willingly, no protest, no nothing. Just picked up your bag, and your precious globe and left. How can you complain now?"

"How do you know that?" I asked softly.

Lata must have heard the menace in my voice because she tried to backtrack. "Uh, Srikar must have heard it from someone in your old apartments."

"No one saw us leave." And the one person who had wouldn't say anything.

"Why are you fussing? The point is, you did leave."

I took a step closer to this sister of mine, this wife of my husband's.

Lata took a step back. "What are you doing?" She sounded flustered.

"I've always wondered how Srikar's grandfather found out," I said softly. "We were very careful not to take any risks. You gave us away, didn't you?"

"I don't know what you are talking about," Lata blustered. "I have no time for such nonsense." She turned to go.

This time, I grabbed her arm.

Across the road, people were watching us with interest. One man gave us an encouraging wave.

"Why Lata? What did I ever do to you?"

Her face twisted in a vicious mask. "If you had stayed, my marriage wouldn't have broken up."

The force of her hatred was almost physical. I stumbled back. "What are you talking about?"

"You could have given my in-laws enough dowry to shut them up. It was bad enough that I had to suffer a scandal before marriage. You could have spared me humiliation a second time. Had you stayed, you could have shared with me some of that luxury being a Goddess brought you. But did you think of me? Oh, no! You had to run off to your perfect love, to your perfect marriage."

I was astounded by her version.

Lata was not done. "After you left," she said, starting to shout, "my in-laws threw me out because there was no child. Their fool of a son was infertile. And, because you ran away, there was no dowry to keep them happy."

"Catering to your in-laws instead of being with my husband – that was your plan for my life?"

Lata harrumphed.

"Didn't you tell me that if I came back and helped you get married, you would find a way for me to be with Srikar?" I said, trying hard to keep my voice down. I stole a glance at the people gathered. A few bystanders had settled on the footpath. "Did you not?"

Lata had no answer to that.

"Nothing to say? You put me in a position where I was forced to come back to the village and bail you out. I got you married. You paid me back by ratting to Srikar's grandfather? And stealing my husband?"

"Don't take it personally. I was trying to escape my marriage. Any man would have done."

I leaned forward and gave her a tight slap.

She put a hand to her cheek, her mouth open in shock.

"Does Srikar know you have a special relationship with his grandfather?"

By the scared look on her face, I knew he didn't. "I didn't steal your life. You stole mine – my husband, my child, my home."

Lata crumpled on the footpath, beginning to cry in earnest. "You managed to survive," she said between sobs. "You seem to have done well in life. I have a borrowed husband, a borrowed son. What else do I have?"

I turned my face away from my sister, feeling terrible anger at her betrayal, terrible sorrow for ruined lives. Marriage to Srikar was Lata's payback for ratting on us to Kondal Rao. Who else would have married a cast off woman, a 'barren' woman? Who but an honourable man like Srikar? Lata continued to sob, holding up the edge of her sari to shield her face. The audience wasn't going anywhere.

My driver walked over, speculation in his eyes. I had no doubt I'd be the topic of the month for the drivers and the maids. "Doctor *garu*, is everything okay?"

Lata looked at the driver and then at me, as if she could not believe her ears.

Oh no!

She got up slowly, wiping her tears with the edge of her sari. "What did you say?" she asked the driver, menace in her voice.

The driver seemed confused.

"Go back to the car," I told him. "I'll be there in five minutes."

"Why did you call her Doctor *garu*?" Lata asked the driver again.

"What else will I call Madam *garu*..." The driver's voice trailed off, sensing there was more to it than a mere question. He backed away.

Pure malevolence radiated from Lata's eyes. "Oh, so Madam is a doctor now?" She tossed her head at me. "Madam has grown so much in stature that she can afford a car and a driver?"

"Lata, please," I said, trying to minimize the issue. I couldn't afford to antagonize her. Lata was the only mother my son knew. "It was just something that happened. It is not important..."

"Just happened?" Lata gave an incredulous laugh. "Not important? You knew that's all I wanted to be. You knew that." Her voice rose. "I didn't give up on my dream even after I married Srikar. I enrolled in a college. But your son was a sickly child, always needing attention. I had to give up my dream because of *your* child."

"He... he is still sick?" *No. Srikar would have told me if he were.*

"Didn't you hear what I said?" Lata screamed. "My dreams died because of your child. Now I'm too old to get admission in a college."

"But Lata," I said, close to tears. "None of this was my fault. If I had any say, I'd still be married to Srikar, raising my son with him. I never wanted luxuries, or education or anything else. All I ever wanted was the chance to be a wife and mother."

"Life's not fair, Pullamma." Lata's face was hard. "Look at me.

No education. No respect. Not even a real marriage." At the look of shock on my face, she screamed. "Like he didn't tell you? Like the two of you didn't laugh behind my back? So what if he made it a condition for our marriage, *hanh*?" She leaned forward, face a mask of fury. "What kind of man stays away from something that's so freely offered?"

I felt a fierce surge of joy flood my being. Not telling me this in order to protect Lata's privacy, that's exactly the honourable man I'd fallen in love with.

"What did I get out of this marriage, *hanh*? Not even a child of my own. My marriage is as barren as my womb. Someone else's child to tie me down. That's all I got." She leaned forward, her tone fierce. "See if I let you an inch near my son." She grabbed my arm, nails digging in. "My son, do you hear? My. Son."

FORTY-SEVEN

I shook with rage as I climbed the stairs to our flat. My own sister, my twin, had knifed me in the back. If that weren't bad enough, she was using my son to control me. I tightened my lips. I wouldn't let my child be used as a pawn. His welfare had to come first. I'd take him away. Eventually, he'd learn to love me. He had to, if we were to have a chance together.

A part of me, admittedly a very tiny part, felt sorry for her. She was in love with my husband. But there was no excuse for colluding with Kondal Rao to destroy my marriage, just so she could escape hers.

In my room I opened the cupboard and dumped out the contents of the locker. Spying the passbook to my bank account, I pounced on it. Not as much money as I'd have liked, since I was sending a large part of my salary to Ammamma each month. No matter. I could always earn more. I'd take my son and leave tonight. Srikar would have to let me – after what his grandfather did, he couldn't possibly refuse.

I rushed around the house taking only the essentials, wanting to leave before Aunty returned. It broke my heart that she couldn't come with us, but I couldn't ask her to go into hiding again. Not when she'd just been reunited with her son. As for Ammamma, I hoped Kondal Rao would recognize that I'd not been in touch with her for years. Hopefully, that would protect her.

Don't think about Aunty or Ammamma now. You don't have the time to fall apart. But I couldn't stop thinking of Srikar. Knowing the kind of man he was, how could I have ever doubted him? How would I survive the rest of my life without him? It did not bear thinking about.

At the knock on the door, I tensed. What would I tell Aunty?

I opened the door, and my eyes fell on that stubby neck.

My grandfather-in-law pushed his way past me, and parked himself on my sofa.

Maybe it was the passage of the years, maybe it was that I was older and wiser, but Kondal Rao was just another old man. Now that I had a plan for my son, he had lost his ability to frighten. I folded my arms and rested a shoulder against the door, curious to see what he would come up with.

He sat back, crossed his legs and looked at me without saying anything. An old trick, a policeman patient of mine had once assured me; an effective interrogation technique to intimidate a person into breaking the silence. I looked right back.

"Aren't you curious?" he finally asked, the cords in his stubby neck standing out. He hadn't liked to be the one giving in.

I raised my eyebrows in response.

"Getting very friendly with my grandson, Doctor *garu*."

"Is that what caused you to crawl out from that dung pile of yours?"

"Disrespecting your elders, Pullamma? *Tch. Tch.*"

I snorted.

He sighed. "Your sister. Getting too big for her boots, isn't she?" He lay back against the cushion of the sofa, folding his hands over his belly. "I'm not a monster, you know –"

"Trying to get me killed is just part of doing business?"

"*Bah*! You're going to hold that against me?"

I shook my head in incredulity.

"Give me a berth in the Chief Minister's Cabinet, and I'm a happy man. Then, you sisters can fight over my grandson, or share him, or bring in a third girl, I don't really care."

"What's the problem, then?" I said, looking him over. The old man was mellowing. "You go your way, I go mine.

"Pullamma, Pullamma. You can't be that innocent. Your little sister is turning out to be as unpredictable as a *Diwali* firecracker. Never know when she'll explode."

"What do you mean?"

"Forcing my hand, is what she's doing. Says she'll expose my connection to you, if I don't take you back to the village as my Goddess, the silly girl."

I gasped.

"Making a proper nuisance of herself, she is."

"I can't believe she said that!"

"I don't like to be manipulated, you know." He examined a finger nail. "Today she does it, tomorrow you will get bold. It's the principle of the thing."

"What do you mean?"

He put his little finger in the ear, then pulled it out to inspect it. "It means you have a journey coming up in the near future."

"I thought you didn't like to be manipulated."

"As it happens, it also serves my purpose."

I started to get angry. "The last time I went quietly because I was too young to fight back. This time you'll have to take me kicking and screaming. Don't think I'll be the same brainless Goddess as before."

He leaned forward, the black of his eyes glittery pinpoints. "You will do exactly as I say."

"Or what?"

"I tracked your father down in the Himalayas. The esteemed Sri. Simhachalam and his two whores are shacked up in a small temple town, very much enjoying earthly pleasures. When this news spreads in the village, oracle Ranga Nayakamma will tremble from the fury the Goddess plans on unleashing on an unrepentant village." His oily tone conveyed intense satisfaction. "Only thing that'll calm the Goddess down will be punishment for that sinner's kin."

"Ranga Nayakayamma is already under your control," I shouted. "Why don't you use her? Why ruin my life?"

"Blame your beloved sister for that." He sighed. "I was happy enough chugging along with the crackpot oracle. Can you believe it, two bottles of whiskey is all it took for her to set you up as my Goddess?"

Blood rushed to my face.

He cocked his head in thought. "What would be the most suitable punishment for your grandmother, and your other sister, Lalli, is it?"

"Malli!"

"Disrobe them and parade them through the streets? Hmm. Now, that's a thought."

I stared at him, appalled. He wouldn't, would he?

"No Goddess – no honour for grandmother." He grinned.

Hot tears flooded my eyes. Ammamma would commit suicide, rather than live with the dishonour. "Your wife and my grandmother are childhood friends."

He snorted, as if my outburst were unworthy of attention.

"And there is something else I can do," he purred.

"What?" I shivered in spite of myself. I had been very wrong to underestimate this man. He was no more harmless than a snake charmer's basket of cobras.

"I will personally guarantee your boy is never found." His tone was conversational, like he was discussing the latest fortunes of the Indian cricket team.

The bastard would do it, too. "Why now? There are no elections. You are secure in your post. Convince Lata to back off, and you're safe."

"Ever heard of an invention called the television, Doctor *garu*? Very useful. Tells you all kinds of things. Like the fact the Chief Minister's government is in danger of collapsing. No confidence motion. The coalition has fallen apart. New elections might be called."

"When did that happen?" God, how had I missed that?

Kondal Rao peered at his watch. "Umm... about twenty-two hours ago. Let me weather this crisis, then I'll worry about your little sister and you."

I sagged against the door. If Pullaiyya disappeared, both Srikar and Aunty would be devastated. As for Ammamma's dishonour... that did not bear thinking about.

"I was hoping age and your 'doctory' would have made you a worthier opponent." He sighed. "Such a fancy degree. Of what use? *Aiyyo!* So disappointed." He grinned, the pink of his tongue pushing against the fence-like gaps in his teeth.

I looked at him in mute appeal.

"*Cha!*" he complained. "What is this? You are taking away all my fun."

"Don't you care at all for the happiness of your grandson and great-grandson?"

"*Bah!*" Kondal Rao said with an expression of distaste. "Still the village mentality, I see. You learned nothing in the city?" He abandoned his casual pose, body stiff with tension. "Power, Pullamma. Power. One who has power, has it all. Never forget that." His eyes had a feverish glint. "Last time you publicly endorsed me, I got a berth in the Chief Minister's Cabinet. I will not allow anything to get in my way. Not you. Not your mother-in-law. Not that sister of yours." He jabbed a finger at me, lips tight. "Do. You. Understand?"

I nodded, understanding dawning. As long as one of us lived, I would never be free of this man.

He looked at me, stubby forefinger tapping his chin. I knew what was coming, of course.

"You're ready to pack, or what?"

FORTY-EIGHT

L ater that night, I stood at Ammamma's door, suddenly desperate to see her.

Kondal Rao, in a surreal rerun of my journey to the Home, had escorted me back to Ammamma's, jeep loads of henchmen and all. The sickle-and-bamboo-stick wielding henchmen had given way to gun-toting sidekicks – a sign of changing times.

Ammamma came out. She looked curiously at the group of people at her doorstep.

Eight years had passed since I left behind my beloved grandmother to try and make a life with Srikar. Ammamma's hair had more grey now, her face more wrinkles. The crumpled cotton sari tucked in at the waist was the same, the white *bottu* on her forehead, slightly off-centre, was still the same. Throat clogging with emotion, I gave her a tremulous smile.

"We are blessed," a man exclaimed. "*Ammavaru* has taken on a new avatar. She's given *darsanam* again after so many years."

The confused expression on Ammamma's face changed to shock. "Pullamma!" she squealed, dragging me into her arms. She pulled back, her eyes darting from me to the group of people behind.

Kondal Rao's lackey, to whom had I supposedly given *darsanam* by appearing to him in my Godly form, had become the celebrity of the moment. The man beamed.

"*Jai Ammavaru!*" a roar went up behind me. Long live the Goddess.

Ammamma's face paled to the colour of flattened rice.

"Can I come in, Ammamma?" I said softly. "I am very tired."

Ammamma dispatched the people at the gate saying I would give *darsanams* only after a week of meditation.

I closed the gate and hugged my grandmother tightly, my heart awash with love for her. It was good to see Ammamma again, no matter what the circumstance.

Ammamma pulled back, wiped her damp eyes with the back of

her hand and cupped my face, examining my features one by one. "You cut your hair short!" She looked dazed.

Good thing she hadn't seen me in sleeveless blouses. "Long story. Can I tell you about it later?"

"Of course, of course. Come, I'll make you coffee." She took my hand and led me towards the kitchen.

I looked around the courtyard, saddened by the air of neglect. The marble floor, even in the moonlit night, seemed grimy. The walls were patchy.

"You should have used some of the money I sent, for repairs."

Ammamma smiled noncommittally.

"You did get the money, didn't you?"

"Every month," Ammamma said.

"And yet, you never used it. Why?"

Ammamma appeared uncomfortable.

"Ammamma?"

"When a girl sends so much money every month, more than what a man in the village can hope to earn in a year..."

"You thought I'd been selling my body?"

Ammamma's reddened face gave her away.

I started to laugh. "Oh, Ammamma!" I clutched her and laughed till my sides hurt. "How could you think such a thing?" I said through gasps. "Didn't you know me better?"

"I didn't think you were the kind to abandon your child, either."

That sobered me up. "Kondal Rao stole my child, Ammamma. He kidnapped me, then gave my son to Srikar." Telling her he'd tried to have me killed would only scare her.

Ammamma's jaw dropped. "I never, ever believed that you ran away with another man." She was quite emphatic about that. "But your child was with Srikar, and you were gone."

"And yet you thought I'd prostituted myself?"

"Perhaps you were desperate." Ammamma seemed embarrassed.

"Not that desperate. Never that desperate." I gave Ammamma a hug.

"So what are you doing here?"

I would never, never tell Ammamma about Kondal Rao's threat to dishonour her. "You know Srikar married Lata?"

Ammamma looked sorrowful. "I know."

"Lata informed Kondal Rao about our whereabouts in Hyderabad because she couldn't bear to stay married to Narasu. Kondal Rao kidnapped me. Marriage to Srikar was her payment."

Ammamma's face drained of colour. "I can't believe she descended to such depths."

"Well, she did."

Ammamma gave me a lingering hug. Her voice choked. "I'm sorry you suffered so much, but it is so good to see you, Child."

I held her tightly. I'd missed her so much.

Some fifteen minutes later, we settled on a mat with coffee the way only Ammamma could make.

"Did Kondal Rao harass you a lot after I left?" I said.

"Petty things, nothing major."

"Like what?"

"Suddenly people I'd been selling pickle to for years wanted to try out someone else, their relatives in the neighbouring villages started to sew their clothes, that sort of thing."

Paapaatmuda! That sinner had struck at Ammamma's livelihood!

"I lived alone, it wasn't hard to get by." She looked at my face every few minutes, as if to reassure herself that I was really back, but carefully avoided looking at my shortened hair.

"I wished you'd used the money I sent," I said.

"I managed." She shrugged. "Enough of me. How did you end up here?"

I realized with a shock that she knew nothing of my life after I'd supposedly sent Pullaiyya back to Srikar for raising. I sat on the floor next to Ammamma, taking her through the happenings in my life. I stressed the love and support I'd received from Janaki aunty, glossing over the more painful moments.

"Would Srikar have let you take Pullaiyya away?"

"He's a good person, Ammamma. He feels obligated to Lata because she took care of Pullaiyya when he needed the help, but is appalled by what his grandfather did to me."

"Oh, Child."

I held my head in my hands and started to cry. "By now I could have been on my way with Pullaiyya, Ammamma. I could have had my son with me. Lata doesn't care for him. She's been using him to remain close to Srikar, and now to control me."

Ammamma held me as I sobbed. When I raised my head, her face was wet, too.

"All I've ever done is bring you sadness, Ammamma."

"Don't be silly, Child. You are a mother, too. Could you ever regret Pullaiyya?" She sighed. "The three important people in your life – your child, your husband, your mother-in-law, I hardly know them."

Catching up with Ammamma was bittersweet. So many changes. Lakshmi *garu* and Murty *garu* had moved to the city to be with their children. Vanita's brother, who had spent all his time playing cricket, was now a teacher in the village school. That one was a little hard to believe. And Chinni. Her family had prospered in Kurnool.

Ammamma brought me up to date on my older sister's life. Within a year of marriage, Malli was back at Ammamma's, pregnant. She was there till her delivery, and another three months before she returned home.

That first time Malli delivered two healthy girls. The in-laws claimed to be happy, but there would be more pregnancies. A male heir was not merely a matter of pride, or necessity for the continuity of his clan, he was also needed to perform rituals for the well-being of his parents and ancestors in after-life. Luckily for Malli, she was fertile. In the next six years, she would be back at Ammamma's annually, delivering another four daughters and then thankfully, three strong sons, the last two, again twins.

"When I finally had enough of this," Ammamma said, "I told Malli to discretely visit a lady doctor and get herself fixed. No need to involve men in such things, is there? It was a huge relief to both of us."

It was strange having Ammamma recite Malli's story to me; I felt like a railway passenger whizzing past the stations in my sister's life. I was sad for having missed the births and milestones of my nieces and nephews. Before I left, all our energies had been focused on trying to get Malli and Lata married off; Malli and I had not had the time to be sisters; Chinni was more a sister to me than Malli or Lata ever were.

The months Malli was home for her deliveries would have been the time to get to know her; that was when in-laws typically let go of their daughters-in-law. Strict in-laws like Malli's rarely gave permission to their daughter-in-laws to visit their mothers' houses at other times – after all, if the daughter-in-law went away, who would cater to their needs?

In the midst of Malli's pregnancies, Lata's troubles, and worries about me, Ammamma had aged quietly, but gracefully. She couldn't be much more than sixty because she'd had my mother at fifteen or so, and my mother had Lata and me when she herself was nineteen; but in village years, it was a lifetime.

I lay back exhausted, marvelling at the starlit sky. The 'luxuries' of the city had denied me life's simpler pleasures. Because of the street lights, stars weren't always visible in the city.

"How much I missed you, Child. How much I begged *Yedukondalaswami* for your return," Ammamma said. Her voice broke. "But not like this; never like this." She stroked my hair tenderly. She peered at me. "You're the same, but not the same."

I laughed. "I had to cut my hair so people would not recognize me. And I use makeup."

"Makeup, Child?" Ammamma looked appalled. As far as Ammamma was concerned, makeup wasn't something respectable women used – only women who sold their bodies, and film actors. Of course, I used it so sparingly that it was barely there, but it did make me look different.

"And the mole below the nose?"

"I got it removed."

"It made you pretty, Child. But even English medicine has its limits, *hanh*? Unable to turn you fair, it was."

I smiled, strangely comforted. Some things would never change.

"So how did you earn that money? What you sent me?"

"By selling my services," I teased.

Ammamma smacked my hand.

"I became a doctor, Ammamma."

Ammamma's eyes became round. "You had so much brains? I never knew."

Laughing, I raised myself on an elbow and gave Ammamma a hug. "You didn't want Lata to be a doctor. Too much education for a woman, you said. Now look at me."

"Now look at you." Ammamma shook her head. "Of everything I imagined you to be over the years, this wasn't it. How much I scolded that headmaster fellow for trying to make Lata one."

We laughed, but it was a laughter tinged with sadness. A big part of me hated Lata for what she'd done to me. The pain I'd had to deal with should have been too great for me to feel any sympathy for this backstabbing sister of mine. But a part of me felt sadness, too, for the loss of Lata's dreams. I could still see her, ten years old, walking about the village, chest puffed up, a plastic stethoscope around her neck, listening to the heartbeats of indulgent elders.

"And you still think it is wrong for women to want to make something of themselves?"

"Eight years away, and you have become a city girl. What happiness did your 'doctory' bring you, *hanh*? Or your Janaki aunty, for that matter?"

"But Ammamma, being a doctor did not bring on my troubles. It kept me from destitution, allowed me to lead a life of dignity. Otherwise, I would be weaving baskets at a roadside stall, barely scraping together a living."

"Like me, you mean."

I sat up. "No! That's not what I meant and you know it. What you did was very honourable and respectable within the means you had available to you. But I had the chance to do something more with my life, and I took it."

"You have changed," Ammamma said. She looked sad. "You talk complicated talk. I don't understand you anymore."

"Ammamma, I am the same person I was. It is just the exterior that has changed. I am still the Pullamma of old."

Ammamma appeared unconvinced, so I just gave her a hug. Not all things in life could fit into prescribed patterns. "I love you anyway."

"Oh you!" She pushed me away, a little flustered. "You and your citified ways." But she was smiling.

"What I don't understand is how Srikar's marriage to... came about." I know Kondal Rao had blackmailed Srikar, but how had Ammamma got involved?

"That was my fault." A teardrop made its way down her cheek.

"Don't," I said. Ammamma had shed enough tears on my behalf to last a lifetime.

She let out a heartfelt sigh. "I thought I was doing the best for your son." She gripped my shoulders. "I never believed that you had run away with another man. Not for a single minute." Her lips tightened, the wrinkles around her mouth bunching up. "When Lata came to me for shelter after her in-laws threw her out, I talked to the bank to take my house and give me money for Lata's dowry, but they refused."

Probably Kondal Rao's doing. It wasn't inconceivable that he'd also paid Lata's in-laws to throw her out.

Ammamma looked remorseful. "It's not right that a married girl continue to live in her birth home. And the infant still needed taking care of. After everything that went on with Lata, her in-laws accusing her of barrenness, then throwing her out on the streets, I felt maybe I had been too harsh with her. I tried to make up for her misfortunes by arranging her wedding to Srikar."

My husband and my sister! Though I knew it wasn't a real marriage, I still couldn't bear to think of them living together, raising my son together.

Ammamma continued, "This was also my way of making sure your son was loved. How could I trust my great-grandchild with a stranger?"

Put that way, it made sense. Not that 'sense' made it any less painful.

"And how does she repay me? By never letting me see my great-grandchild. She won't come to the village, she won't let me visit."

"Did Srikar's grandmother suggest this alliance?" I asked.

Ammamma looked startled. "How did you know?"

Another round to Kondal Rao.

FORTY-NINE

Before I knew it, I was back where I'd left off. People started to queue up before the temple bells had tolled, before the birds had roused. They waited patiently in line till I was ready to grant them audience. They came in bullock carts, on tractors, on bursting-at-the-seams State Transport buses. In cars, in three-wheel tempos, and on bicycles. They came to see for themselves the miraculous rebirth of their Goddess. A slightly different avatar, but *Ammavaru* nonetheless.

I no longer limited myself to Mangalagiri or Gadwal cottons – these were fine saris for when I turned sixty, but for now I'd wear whatever I chose. The love of my family might have forced me back here, but I was damned if I would be cowed.

Kondal Rao was not impressed with my little bursts of defiance.

Because I was more 'mod' now – with my fancy haircut and un-oiled hair, and owing to my years of seeing patients, I exuded an authority I had not previously had. I was also older and sadly wiser, and therefore able to deal with Kondal Rao a little better.

"Start oiling your hair again," he ordered. "Your hair looks like discoloured straw."

"No."

His eyes widened. "What do you mean, no?"

"Never heard that word before, Politician *garu*? It means I get to decide what to do with my hair."

His jaw dropped at my defiance, but I had to hand it to the man. Without missing a beat, he ordered, "Very well, you will grow it back. We can pretend your hair is short because you offered it to the Lord of the Seven Hills."

"You don't get it, do you?" I said, staring him in the eye. "Don't confuse my love for my family for weakness. I will not be controlled by you."

His face darkened, but I was past the point of caring. This was the man who had denied me my son and my husband.

It was a month into Goddess-hood my third time around, and I could see no way out. The expected elections hadn't been called because the Chief Minister had managed to cobble together enough support. Janaki aunty had informed Dr. Govardhan not to expect me back. She was considering selling my share of the medical practice to another doctor because Dr. Govardhan was unable to handle the patient load by himself. This scared me, because it was as good as admitting that she did not expect me to escape Kondal Rao's clutches.

The one good thing that had come out of this mess was that Aunty was now living with Srikar. After so many years of being denied her son, she deserved every bit of happiness. Being happy for her didn't stop me from missing her. And Srikar. And the son I'd never met. How I wanted to hold him in my arms. But I was in the village tending to my devotees, and Lata was in the city playing house with my family. I talked often to Aunty, and occasionally with Srikar, too. Lata was another story.

Deciding to give it another try, I called Srikar's house. Lata picked up. "Why are you harassing us like this?" she screamed.

"Just give me my son," I begged. "That's all I ask of you."

"I put in all the effort, bring him up to this age, and now you want to reap the benefits?"

"Please, Lata."

"If you go after Pullaiyya, Kondal Rao will not leave Ammamma alone. You know that. Are you willing to take that risk?"

I was speechless.

"Did you hear me?" Her voice was screechy.

"Kondal Rao couldn't care less about your petty issues. He forced me back to the village only because the government was in danger of collapsing. He's keeping me around just in case. As long as I stay, Ammamma's safe."

"He'll never let you get away." Lata sounded triumphant.

"Maybe not." I wasn't about to tell her I would never give up trying. "But I can still raise my son." I took a deep breath. "Lata, I'll give you as much money as you want."

"I thought you'd never touch the Goddess's money," Lata mocked. "Never isn't such a long time, is it, big sister?"

"I'm talking about my own earnings. The money I sent Ammamma over the years is gathering dust."

"You're talking about your doctor money."

"Yes, I –"

"No." She hung up.

I wished I knew what to do. I didn't know how to force the issue. There was no hope of Malli interceding, either. She paid a quick visit to the Goddess with her in-laws; her in-laws would not allow a personal visit.

This caused Ammamma deep pain. "My granddaughters are so different," she lamented. "Lata's tongue is like a knife, slicing its way through life. And look at Malli. Silly face. Not a proper tongue in her mouth."

As I sat on my freshly polished silver throne – courtesy Kondal Rao – a stream of people walked past, touching my feet, seeking blessings, easing themselves of their burdens. I mechanically touched each of their heads, and gave them *prasadam*. Kondal Rao had arranged for a couple of security guards, whether to keep the lines moving, or me in line, I couldn't tell.

"Pullamma."

I jerked up in shock and found myself looking into Lata's eyes. Next to her stood Srikar. Between the two, below the line of my vision, was a child. But I dared not lower my head, or my guard. I gave Srikar a quick glance, willing him to explain. With so many devotees milling about, I was not in a position to question him. I was aware they were holding up the line of devotees; no one spent more than a minute with me in order to ensure everyone got an audience.

Srikar had an expression in his eyes I could not interpret. He inclined his head slightly at the little boy by his side and nodded.

My son!

My priest, Satyam, was considering me with speculation, so I closed my eyes and desperately willed myself to drain all emotion. When I opened my eyes again, I was calm.

I let Srikar walk past, though Satyam's sharp eyes were trained on me; how could I commit the sacrilege of blessing my own husband? And then I put my hand on my child's head, touching him for the very first time. My hand trembled. I couldn't help it. I bit down hard on my lip, trying not to let my mouth quiver. I struggled not to look at my child's face; if I did, I knew I would break down, yard-full of devotees or not. I trained my glance at his ear as he stood directly in front of me, though I craved to pull him into my arms and never let go.

"Move," the security guard said, raising his stick to my son.

"No!" I said sharply.

The security guard froze. I had never spoken out loud during *darsanams*. Srikar's eyes widened in horror, but Lata's smile bordered on the malicious. Satyam, the priest, looked shocked. I gave Srikar what I hoped was a calm smile, but the speculative look had not left Satyam; whoever said women were gossipy had never had the occasion to cross paths with my priest.

Ammamma sat in her chair across the room, but I dared not glance at her, either. She had not called a halt to the proceedings, probably because we could not afford to draw attention to the incident. She did, however, get up and leave the room soon after my husband and son left.

The next few hours were excruciating. The stream of people was endless. The invisible band around my head tightened to the point I was afraid my head would burst. After the last devotee had left, I wearily found my way back to my private quarters. I waved away a few hopeful looking devotees; some days I had dinner with a select few, but today I was too agitated.

"What happened wasn't good," Ammamma said, sounding anxious. "First time back in the village in years, and see the stunt she pulls."

I collapsed on the bed. "How could he do this to me? To have me meet my son in public, that too, without warning."

Ammamma snorted. "You are a fool if you think Srikar had a say in this."

The whole village had seen Lata with Srikar and Pullaiyya, establishing them as a family. No question of me trying to lay claim to my husband and son now.

"Ammamma," I said, anxious. "Do you think people heard me when I spoke out loud during the *darsanam*?"

"Since Srikar and Lata were directly in front of you, I don't think so. It was too noisy."

"But the security guard and the priest did."

"I can talk to the guard. But the priest..." Ammamma sighed. "Just be careful of that man. Anyway, right now, Lata is the bigger worry. I don't know how something that evil could have come from the womb of a daughter of mine."

"Pullamma!" Srikar stormed in.

I sat up, heart thundering. If he was here, my son couldn't be far behind.

But it was just Srikar, dragging Lata along. He shoved her into a chair. "Pullamma, I am so sorry," he said. "If I'd known she would pull something like this, I would never have agreed to come. I came only because she said that it was time you met Pullaiyya."

"Where is my son?"

"You may have given birth to him," Lata snarled, "but he is mine."

"Lata!" Srikar shouted.

I'd never thought I would live to see Srikar lose control. His eyes were rimmed red, and the cords in his neck stood out. "You lied to me. You claimed it was time Pullaiyya got to know his mother."

"I will never let Pullamma have him," Lata said, eyes blazing. "Never."

"Lata!" Srikar said.

"When you needed me, you used me. Now, when your precious Pullamma shows up, you're ready to throw me aside. How noble!"

Srikar threw a quick look at Ammamma, face reddening. "We'll discuss this later. Let's go."

She gripped the sides of her chair. Srikar knelt by her chair and said something to her. She shook her head, her lips set in a stubborn line.

I watched them, feeling sharp envy for the intimacy their relationship allowed them.

"This is my mother's home," Lata said. "I'm sure my family is eager for my company. You go take care of our son. I'll come in a little bit."

Srikar took a deep breath. I could tell he was struggling for control. "Pullamma, I was happy when Lata said she was ready for Pullaiyya to meet you." He gave Lata an angry look. "We were going to slip into your private quarters when all of a sudden she took Pullaiyya to join the *darsanam* line, and waved me over. I couldn't avoid it without causing a scene." He was remorseful. "I wish you could have met your son in a better manner."

"I didn't even get a good look at him." I knew the yearning in my voice was giving me away. "I wish –"

"What, *hanh*?" Lata spat out, "What do you wish? To deny your son the love of his mother?"

Before I knew it, I'd reached across and given Lata a hard slap.

"How dare you!" Lata shrieked, massaging her face. She jumped to her feet, fists clenched.

"Why do you hate Pullamma so much?" Ammamma asked despairingly.

"You took my life away," she shouted, jabbing a finger at Ammamma. "You did not let me study, you made me marry when I didn't want to, that too, to a man I detested," she said, enumerating on her fingers. "Pullamma has always been the favoured one. She has the money, the degree, the child. I have nothing." Lata started to scream. "Do you hear? Nothing!"

"Tea?" a tentative voice said.

All of us whipped around. Sarala stood with a tray of tea and snacks. She looked flustered.

Ammamma flushed a deep red. "Leave it here, please." She pointed at the table.

How much had Sarala heard? I cringed at the thought of being at the centre of speculation. After she'd left the room, I said to Lata, "You have my son and my husband. Isn't that enough?"

"Save your godly wisdom for your devotees," Lata snapped. "Luckily for me, Kondal Rao is still a threat to you. Otherwise Srikar would have gone running to you, tail tucked between his legs. Don't think I don't know."

Srikar's jaw tightened.

Ammamma said to Srikar, "This is just degenerating. There are still people around. Perhaps you could come back when everyone has had the chance to calm down."

"You don't even have the guts to blame me directly," Lata spat out.

Srikar gave Lata a long look. "Perhaps you are right, Ammamma. I'll be back."

I looked as Srikar walked away. How were we ever going to resolve this situation?

"What kind of sister are you to make Pullamma pay for my mistakes?" Ammamma burst out. "You know she's suffered so much."

"Poor little doctor Goddess," Lata mocked.

FIFTY

L ata stayed for another two hours, looking straight ahead, not responding to Ammamma's offer of food or water. By the time she left, the two of us were drained.

"I don't understand Srikar," I said. "How can he be okay with Lata using our son as a pawn?"

Ammamma sighed. "That's the problem with honourable men, Child."

"What do you mean?"

"Because they adhere to a certain code of conduct, they believe everyone else does, too. He probably doesn't see Lata's behaviour for what it is." She dropped her head back. "I'm so sorry, Pullamma."

"What for?"

"I've messed up all my granddaughters' lives."

"Malli is fine."

"No thanks to me."

"You did the best you could, Ammamma. Come, now." I helped her up. "Time for bed."

She shuffled to her room. I was frightened by how old she looked.

I slumped on the swing in our private courtyard. How could things have gone so wrong?

The doorbell rang. Drowsily, I turned to the wall clock. Only 10:00 p.m. Somehow it felt a lot later. Only Kondal Rao had the bad habit of dropping in at odd hours. God! I hoped it wasn't him. I had no energy to deal with him tonight. I hurried to the gate before the doorbell woke Ammamma up. I opened the gate to the main courtyard. "Srikar!" I said, aware I'd addressed him by name, instead of the more proper *Yemandi*.

Srikar raised his eyebrows a fraction at this departure from convention. But he said nothing. I was glad. The older I got, the less conventions seemed to matter. Not that adherence to them had done me much good.

"Is it too late?" He sounded anxious.

"No, no, of course, not."

Srikar walked in, and behind him – my son!

"What – I mean how –" I stopped as Srikar mouthed 'later'. I stood in shock, hugging myself as my eyes devoured my son.

"Why don't we go in?" Srikar said.

My heart hitched. After closing the gate to the courtyard, I followed Srikar and my son in. They settled on the swing in my private courtyard.

My son! I blinked back tears and looked directly at him. Eight years I'd waited for this day. Eight lonely years.

His face was softly rounded, traces of baby fat still visible. He had Srikar's colour – thank God for that! Long eyelashes, stubborn mouth, pug nose. A lock falling endearingly over his forehead. I trembled with emotion. I had to physically restrain myself from running to him, dragging him into my arms, never letting go.

I settled on the step of the veranda, not daring to say anything. Srikar said gently to my son, "Remember, what I told you? That your mother had to leave you behind with your aunt Lata and me because she had to go away?"

Pullaiyya leaned back in the swing and looked up at the sky.

Srikar slipped an arm around him.

Pullaiyya shook it off.

"This is your mother," Srikar said.

"I already have a mother." His mouth was set in a stubborn line.

And I'd waited years to hear my son's voice.

"Don't you want to get to know her?"

"Not really."

I felt my lungs getting crushed inside my ribcage. *God, please, what did I do to deserve this?*

"You made me come here," Pullaiyya said, not looking at Srikar. "Even when I didn't want to. I am ready to sleep now."

"Can I take him to your bedroom?" Srikar asked.

I nodded, my throat full from unshed tears.

Srikar came out fifteen minutes later. "How much longer can you stay?" I needed his comforting presence tonight.

"I'm not leaving."

"What?" I sat up, heart beginning to pound.

"I have had it with Lata and her manipulation. She let it slip today that she was the one who led my grandfather to us."

"Marriage to you was her payoff."

"You don't seem surprised."

I shrugged.

"I can't believe Lata would behave in such a manner. I thought I knew her. I lived with her for six years, for God's sake!" Srikar shook his head in disbelief. "You know, when you were forced into coming back as Goddess that first time? We should have just taken Ammamma and run."

"Don't be so hard on yourself. You were trying to do right by Lata and Ammamma."

"To compound my mistakes, I married Lata."

"Why did you?"

"Not that my grandfather gave me much of a choice, but I convinced myself that it would provide a loving home for our child."

"Did it?"

Srikar shrugged, a hand covering his eyes. "It's not like she tortures him or anything..."

"But?" I asked, throat raw.

"Sometimes, ignoring a child can be as bad."

I tried to swallow against the surge of grief. My poor baby!

"You know what?" he asked.

"What?" I whispered.

"I've had it with Lata and my grandfather." He held out his arms. I walked into them, buried my face in his shoulder and broke down. Once I started to cry, I could not stop. Srikar pulled me onto the swing with him and held me.

"What happens now?"

"You, Pullaiyya and I are going to find a way of living together openly as a family. I don't know how, but we are."

"How will we get away?"

"Pullamma, I'm thirty years old. I cannot continue to live in fear of my grandfather. We'll find a way."

I smiled up at him through my tears. "That's wonderful!" But I still hurt. "Pullaiyya is not ready to accept me."

"Give him time, Pulla," Srikar said. "Till a month back he thought Lata was his mother. We can't rush him."

I nodded through my tears and held my husband, without guilt, for the first time in eight years.

"How dare you!"

I opened my eyes, a little disoriented. Lata stood at the door to the private courtyard, eyes blazing in the early dawn. I moved away from Srikar, feeling guilty. Then I sat up. I had done nothing wrong. Srikar and I must have fallen asleep on the swing, my head on his chest.

"You spent the night with my husband!" Lata screamed.

"Don't start again, Lata," Srikar said wearily. "We've already been over this."

Lata's face darkened till it was almost black. "What about me?" she screamed, the pupils of her eyes dilated. "What about the years I spent taking care of Pullaiyya and you?"

"Be honest, Lata. You never wanted me," Srikar said. "It is Pullamma's husband you wanted."

"So you're going back to her."

"Can't we keep this pleasant? For Pullaiyya's sake?"

"So you can whisper sweet nothings in the rich Goddess's ear? How sweet."

"This has nothing to do with money, and you know it."

"It has everything to do with money." Lata's face was white. "I wouldn't count on her financial support, if I were you. Doctor *garu* keeps her money very close to her chest." She trembled with rage. Suddenly, she turned and stalked out.

"Amma!"

Pullaiyya! How much had he heard?

"Take me with you." Pullaiyya started to cry. "I don't like it here."

Lata did not look back.

"Amma," Pullaiyya called out.

Lata ignored him and continued towards the gate.

"Please!" He took off after Lata.

Srikar ran after them. I followed. Lata streaked out of the gate. I followed them to the road, breathing harshly. I turned my head left, then right. She was nowhere to be seen.

"Where did she go?" Srikar asked in disbelief.

I wished I knew.

The villagers were called out to form a search party. Srikar had been on the road for hours. At my suggestion, the doctor from the nearest town was summoned; I doubted Lata would want me anywhere near her.

Ammamma often said, giving birth is not merely bringing forth a child. It is cutting out your heart and gifting it to your child. If he feels pain, your agony doubles.

My little son sat slumped in the empty courtyard by the *sampangi* tree, there since Lata had gone missing. My chest convulsed each time he looked at the gate for his mother.

Ammamma had been trying to tempt him with food all morning, with no success. "I give up," she said, choking. "What kind of a woman am I, that my great-grandson won't feel comfortable with me?" She sat down heavily. "Won't accept even water from me."

"Let me give it a try." I walked across the courtyard, hoping I sounded more confident than I felt. At least there were no devotees milling about – we'd shut the ashram down for the day.

"Pullaiyya," I said, trying to tempt him with a glass of buttermilk.

"Don't," he hissed, as he hit my hand. The buttermilk splattered on his shorts. He didn't spare it a glance. "Stay away from me. It is because of you that my mother is missing. You are the one who makes her sad, you are the one who makes her cry."

As I stood in front of him, heart ripped, he leaned back against the tree. "I already have one mother. I don't need another."

I continued to stand there, willing him to look at me.

But he turned away, mouth set in a stubborn line.

Slowly I walked back to Ammamma, feeling like an old woman. Srikar had sent for Janaki aunty. Maybe my son would react to his grandmother better.

"*Aiyya! Aiyya!*" A cowherd hurtled into the courtyard.

"What?" Ammamma screamed. "Tell me."

The cowherd bent over, trying to catch his breath.

Ammamma grabbed him by the shoulders. "Tell me. Tell me."

Dragging in a deep breath, the cowherd straightened. "I was sick this morning, so I got up very late. I was able to tend to the cows only after lunch. When I reached the –"

"I don't need the *Ramayana*," Ammamma snapped. "Just tell me if you found my granddaughter."

"She was curled up behind Devamma's cows."

"And what?" Srikar asked, out of breath himself, as he rushed into the courtyard.

Pullaiyya sat in his corner, trembling.

"Was she all right?" Ammamma asked.

"I don't know, Amma," the cowherd said apologetically. "I just ran to tell you."

Even as Ammamma was getting started on the cowherd and his clan, Srikar grabbed him by the arm and dragged him through the gate. Ten minutes later, he returned, Lata in his arms. "Doctor!" he shouted, shoving his way through the crowd gathered by the courtyard gate. "She is unconscious." He kicked the gate shut behind him.

Pullaiyya, Ammamma and I paced by the door to the front room while the doctor examined her. How I hated the waiting. How much worse for my little boy.

In another ten minutes, Janaki aunty arrived.

"Bamma!" Pullaiyya ran into her arms.

She held him tightly, her face in his hair. She straightened up and said to Pullaiyya. "Shall we go over and give Pullamma a hug?"

I was grateful for Aunty's sensitivity towards Pullaiyya. To refer to me as his mother, when Lata lay sick, wasn't what my child needed.

"I don't want to," he said.

"That's okay," she said, giving him another hug. "Is it okay if I do?"

He didn't say anything, so Aunty held out her arms to me. I hugged her, soaking in her warmth.

"Come, come," she said, wiping away my tears.

Finally, the doctor came out. Srikar followed, his lips a grim line.

"How is she?" Ammamma asked.

"What were you all thinking, *hanh*?" the doctor said. "Letting her loose on the roads? That too, such an unstable person?"

"Doctor," Srikar said pointing his eyebrows at Pullaiyya. His voice was rough.

But sensitivity didn't seem to be something the good doctor was familiar with. "The child is stupid, or what? He won't know his own mother is a mental case?"

Pullaiyya had a stricken look on his face.

Srikar grabbed the doctor by his arm. "So glad for your help. My mother has arrived, so she will take over now. She is a doctor, too." He steered the doctor to the gate.

I ached to comfort the huddled figure of my son, but his attention was riveted on his father.

Aunty knelt by him. Srikar came back in. He looked down at Pullaiyya and Aunty, his face tense. Aunty put out a hand. Pullaiyya put his small hand in hers. "Is my mother really mad?" he asked in a small voice.

My heart clutched.

"Of course not, Child."

"But the doctor said..."

"Some doctors are good at one thing, others at another. Do you think I am a good doctor?"

Pullaiyya nodded.

"Then you'll have to believe me when I say your mother is not mad."

"My friends in school call her 'crazy Aunty.' "

Srikar closed his eyes briefly. "Why didn't you tell me?" he whispered.

Pullaiyya shrugged. Ammamma's eyes were bright with tears.

Aunty cupped Pullaiyya's face. "Sometimes children say things without knowing what they are saying." Her voice was gentle. She looked up at me. "Pullamma, you are a doctor, too. Do you think Lata is mad?"

I shook my head, throat too tight to get the words out.

"See? Pullamma also says your mother isn't mad. When two good doctors tell you the same thing, you have to believe them, don't you?"

Pullaiyya nodded, but didn't seem convinced.

She drew my son to her. "You know sometimes the body gets hurt and needs treatment?"

My son nodded, face streaked with tears.

"Your mother's thoughts are hurt. She just needs some rest."

"Then she can come home with us?"

"She is sick," Aunty said gently. "Remember the time your friend Raman got pneumonia and had to be in the hospital for a few days?"

Pullaiyya nodded.

"This is no different. Your mother will need to spend some time in the hospital, too."

I thanked God for bringing Janaki aunty into our lives.

Srikar gave his mother a tremulous smile and grabbed Pullaiyya in a bear hug.

I watched them, feeling about as needed as rain in midst of the pickle-making season.

Srikar looked at me, eyes bloodshot. "You know what I have to do, don't you?"

I said nothing.

"It'll destroy Pullaiyya if we abandon Lata now."

I nodded dully.

"He says she needs us now more than ever."

I sat, unable to get the words out.

"I'm going to take her back and hire a full-time nurse." His shoulders slumped.

"How can you let Lata near Pullaiyya?" Ammamma burst out. The last few hours had added twenty years to her. "It is not healthy for a child to live with so much uncertainty. What happens the next time she decides to run away, *hanh*?"

"What choice do I have? She is the only mother he has known."

That's what it came down to always – who was there first.

FIFTY-ONE

Kondal Rao was in Hyderabad, doing what he did best – hanging onto power. Srikar, Janaki aunty and Pullaiyya were in the city as well, where Aunty spent all her time protecting my son from Lata's emotional outbursts. My childhood friend, Chinni, was in the village visiting her mother, though she had not taken the trouble to get in touch. Perhaps I wasn't worth that extra effort.

Loneliness gnawed at my soul. To be shown the promise of family life, only to have it all snatched away. Ammamma made excuses for my absence from the ashram activities, worrying about my deteriorating mental state as I spent hours in bed, grieving for my child. And my husband – each time I thought of him, my heart splintered afresh. I found it harder and harder to drag myself out of bed each morning.

One day I did not get out of bed at all. Ammamma came into my room and touched my head, checking for fever. "It is seven o'clock. You need to get up, Child," she said. "People are waiting."

I gave a short laugh. "People queue up to ask me for blessings; they don't know I'm unable solve my own problems." I broke down. "The only thing I've ever wanted was my son and my husband."

Ammamma sat on the bed and clasped my hand in hers. "I've sent for Swami Chidananda."

I'd heard about the Swami, of course, as had most of the State. The revered Guru was known for his discourses on being accepting of one's self, the meaning of life, and all the other ancient philosophical mumbo-jumbo people seemed to want. I didn't see how meeting with him could possibly unite me with my family.

"I've sent word that you will receive him after lunch."

"What's the point, Ammamma?" My voice slurred.

"Do this one thing for me, Child." She bent to kiss my forehead. "He might be able to help. Srikar holds him in very high regard, you know. Seeks advice from him all the time."

I closed my eyes.

"I will tell them to close the ashram in preparation for the Swami's visit. You rest until lunch."

I closed my eyes, about the only thing I had the energy for.

RASANA ATREYA

I forced my eyes open a while later. With some effort I got up and pushed aside the curtains; it was dark. Like the day, my life was slipping away. In the bathroom, I scrubbed at my face, trying to scour the sadness out of my soul. When I stepped out, rain was falling.

A mountain of a man in white – white *kurta* and *pancha*, white bushy eyebrows, white beard that reached his belly – arose from the chair on the veranda and reached out to cover my hands with his.

I closed my eyes, hearing the rhythmic sounds of water hitting the courtyard floor. I remained like that for many minutes, saying nothing, visualising the falling rain carrying away the torment of my soul. I opened my eyes and looked up.

"So much sadness," Swami Chidananda said. His eyes were incredibly kind.

I felt grief afresh.

"I've spent the last few hours telling *Swamulavaru* about your situation," Ammamma said, using an honorific for the Swami.

The invisible band around my head loosened; I did not have to put on an act with this gentleman. I fell at the Swami's feet. He put his hands on my shoulders and bade me to rise. "Sit, Child." He led me to the chair next to Ammamma's.

I sank into it, suddenly thinking longingly of Ammamma's two rickety chairs – back then our biggest worry had been to remember on which side of the chair our clothes caught. Or was it just nostalgia making it seem so?

"*Swamulavaru*," Ammamma told me, "has frequently counselled Lata and Srikar."

I wasn't sure where Ammamma was going with this. As far as I was concerned, I would be happy if I never heard Lata's name again.

"He is the one person Lata respects," Ammamma added.

I looked sideways at the Swami; I hadn't known.

"Child," Ammamma said, "you should feel free to tell Swami Chidananda all that ails you."

The dam within burst. "My life is a sham, *Swamulavaru*. I am a married woman, but can't acknowledge my husband, I am a mother, but can't lay claim to my child. I have to live my life as a Goddess, without the freedom any ordinary woman could expect."

"This is your penance for the sins of lives past," Ammamma said.

But I wasn't ready accept this explanation any more than I was ready to accept 'God's will'; this was a convenient way of explaining away life's little knife jabs.

"What do you want, then?" the Swami asked.

"What I want and what I can have are two different things," I said.

"I got a phone call from Srikar this afternoon," Ammamma said.

Let it not be anything bad, Oh Yedukondalavada!

"Lata is not doing well. She lies in bed all day, unable to care for Pullaiyya, unable to care for herself. If it weren't for Janaki..."

I felt tears clog my throat. *My poor child!* At what inauspicious moment had he taken birth?

"Srikar is at his wits end." Ammamma's voice wobbled. "Trying to take care of them both."

"Help me out of this vortex," I begged the Swami. "I can't do this anymore."

"How can I be of help?"

"Help me get my family back."

"Srikar might not agree to leave Lata," the Swami said.

"It's just guilt that's holding him back."

"Guilt can be a powerful motivator, Child. Don't dismiss it so lightly."

"So you're saying I have to live out my life without my husband or child, because my husband feels misplaced loyalty to another woman?"

"No, I'm saying your best option, your most realistic option, is to negotiate with Lata. Srikar might continue to live with Lata, but at least you'll have your child back."

"I can't accept that."

"You don't have that many choices, Child. I talked to Srikar before I came here. He won't leave Lata because the child won't allow it, but he is willing to let you have your son. Besides, we need Lata's cooperation, too. If it came down to you and her, who do you think the child would choose?" He let that sink in. "Lata is an angry woman. I may be able convince her to let you raise your child, saying that it is getting to be too much for her. But she'll need to feel she hasn't totally given up control. Lata's child for her *maangalyam*."

Maangalyam. Marriage-hood. The most important thing in a

woman's life. Other than her children, of course. All the *pujas*, the prayers women did, the fasts they kept, were solely to ensure the happiness of their husbands and children.

"Kondal Rao would never allow it."

"Leave him to me," the Swami said calmly.

Ammamma said, "Kondal Rao knows *Swamulavaru* has a huge following. He won't risk alienating his voter base."

"If that's the case, why can't *Swamulavaru* order Kondal Rao to leave me alone?"

"If merely telling him helped, I'd do it right away, Child. But Kondal Rao is power-obsessed. I cannot predict how he'll react. What if he did something unpredictable – like declaring you *Graam Devata*?"

"If you try to corner a rabid dog," Ammamma said, "be prepared for it to pounce on you."

"Not worth the risk," the Swami added.

So we were back to Lata's *maangalyam*. I closed my eyes, my heart aching. This had never been my plan for life. "Will Srikar agree to this?"

"He will, because he is an honourable man. He knows you were cheated of your child," the Swami said. "He put you off only because he didn't want to rock the child's world."

"Nothing's changed."

"Oh, but it has. Lata's not been well. Srikar understands it is an unhealthy environment for the child to be in. But he will not leave Lata as long as she needs him. Both for her sake and the child's."

What about me? This was no choice at all.

The Swami continued, "The first time Srikar visited me was after you came back into his life. He was heartsick at what his grandfather did to you, at what he himself did to you. We had a long talk about his son, and you two sisters. And the complicated situation he is in. You can trust him to do the right thing."

Right for whom?

"If I am able to get Lata to agree, how will you claim your son?" the Swami asked. "The world knows him as Lata's son."

"If he can't be the son of my womb, he can be the son of my soul." Not what I'd have chosen, but like the Swami said, I didn't have too many choices. Fortunately, no one would think it odd if he or any other child came to live in the ashram.

"It's not going to be easy," the Swami warned.

"I know. I will be ripping him away from the only family he's known. I will be forcing him into something he has no desire for."

"And you are prepared for that?"

I did not answer right away. I watched rain foam along the sides of the courtyard and tumble into the open gutters by the walls. Inside the gutter, the water swirled around, as much in turmoil as I was, before being swept away.

"No, *Swamulavaru*," I finally said. "I'm not prepared." How could anyone possibly prepare for something like this?

The Swami looked at me steadily, his grey eyes piercing.

I turned away, unsettled.

He leaned back, eyes closed, hands steepled on his belly. A beak-shaped nose, high cheekbones, which served to reinforce his saintly image. Stories about the elderly Guru were legendary. His followers talked about his gentleness, his love. He offered no magical solutions, but people came away with a feeling of hope.

Now that I had met him, I allowed myself to feel a sliver of hope, too.

He opened his eyes. "I will talk to Lata about letting you keep your son. I make no promises, though."

I nodded. "*Swamulavaru*?" I said, a little hesitant. I knew Ammamma wasn't going to like what was coming. "Could you give him a new name?"

"The boy?"

"Yes."

Ammamma was looking curiously at me, but I forged on. "Growing up, I hated my name. I was teased mercilessly for it. I always thought if I had children, I would give them beautiful names."

"I never knew that." Ammamma looked upset. Then something occurred to her. "Lata must have known."

I nodded.

"Yet, she still named him Pullaiyya..."

What could I say?

"I'm so sorry, Pullamma."

"I never blamed you." I put my hand on Ammamma's. "You did what you thought was best."

"But children can be very cruel," the Swami said.

I nodded. "I don't want my son going through life defending his name. It is possible, of course, that he is happy the way he is. If that is the case, we can let him be. But if he's not, I want him to have the choice."

"You can name him whatever you want, Child," Ammamma said softly.

Thank you God, for a wonderful grandmother.

"Something similar to the name you gave your daughter?"

I nodded.

Ammamma seemed confused. "But *Swamulavaru*, the girl was not Pullamma's."

"Pullamma named her, therefore she must have loved her."

I bit down on my lip, trying to contain my emotions. Though Ammamma and the Swami both knew of my past, only the Swami had been perceptive enough to divine how much Vennela meant to me. Close as I was to her, even Ammamma hadn't understood. I knew now why the Swami was so highly revered. "Her name was Vennela," I said, a catch in my voice.

"What a beautiful name," he said. "How about Ved for her brother?"

"I like it," Ammamma said.

I smiled gratefully at her.

The Swami bent forward and touched my hair in benediction. His gentleness was my undoing. I rested my forehead on the arm of his chair and broke down. I cried till I could cry no more.

"That many tears," he said, stroking my head. "You have waited a long time for this."

Janaki Aunty and I still talked, but I felt adrift, cut off from her. Kondal Rao had decreed, possibly on Lata's instigation, that I sever ties with Aunty. I had refused to bend quite that far, but now that Aunty lived with her son, I missed her advice, her love. I missed her, but was happy for Aunty and Srikar because they needed this time together. And the way things were going with Lata, I was particularly grateful Aunty was there for my son. "Other than Ammamma, I have no one I can confide in, *Swamulavaru*."

"Isn't that the case with Gurus and Goddesses, even reluctant ones? People look to us for solutions. We have to find our own answers from within."

"Can false Goddesses look to real Swamis for solutions?"

He gave a slight smile. "I know it is hard for you to leave the ashram. May I visit you once every two weeks?"

"Please don't make me feel small. I am your humble servant. This ashram is yours. Anytime you wish to come."

"Very well, then," he said, getting up to leave.

He had been well named, I thought, as I watched him leave. Chidananda. Eternal bliss. If I had been named differently, who knows how my life might have turned out?

FIFTY-TWO

Swami Chidananda kept his word. Every two weeks he came to my ashram to dispense advice, to listen, to hold my hand – whatever it was I needed that particular visit. Looking forward to these visits was what kept me going, the other, unanticipated benefit being that I now had a legitimate reason to ask that the ashram be shut down for the day. The constant din of ashram workers preparing large scale meals, the muted sounds of people in lines waiting for an audience with me, the various day-long activities – these were beginning to wear me down.

Waiting for the Swami, I settled back in one of the four armchairs we now owned. On a regular day, when I saw devotees, the courtyard was chock-full of people walking up and down and about, while I was forced to sit in a corner and be Goddess. Some nights I dreamt I'd jumped out of my silver throne, and was running around the courtyard in ever widening circles, even as the crush of devotees pressed themselves against the walls on all sides, shaking their heads in unison because their beloved Goddess had lost her mental balance.

If I were lucky I would awaken from my nightmare with my heart pounding; but most times I would get up in the morning very tired from all the exercise. Because of the constancy of my nightmares, I lived in terror of losing control; I feared giving in to a crazy impulse during an audience – or perhaps when a *bhajan* was in session – running circles around the singers, arms spread out like a plane, preparing to take off. By the end of each day, the rigid control would have given me a headache; Ammamma now had a woman come in daily to give me a massage to relieve this stress. Much as I loved Ammamma, and was happy to be with her, I desperately missed Aunty and her practical advice. I felt terrible that my stress was taking its toll on my elderly grandmother.

I forced myself to push aside thoughts of Pullaiyya and Srikar and Janaki aunty, and take advantage of the moment. My grandmother was visiting Malli. The devotees had gone home after the morning session and the ashram was blessedly peaceful. The patterned marble flooring – white, with black diamonds – sparkled clean. Our cow was long gone – it had moved on to its reward in the sky. The tamarind tree, a runt in our youth, and now full-grown thanks to the diligent attention of the ashram volunteers, had spread its branches wide against the sky. I lay back and looked up through its tiny green leaves. The sky was a blinding blue, summer having scorched its way past. I closed my eyes, feeling the breeze caress my face. A deliciously sweet smell, sugar and spice, teased my senses. Somewhere, a mother called out to her child. The blissful warmth of the winter sun made me pleasantly drowsy.

When I opened my eyes, Swami Chidananda was settled in his familiar contemplative pose, fingers steepled over the white beard flowing down his belly. I jumped out of my chair. "*Swamulavaru,* I didn't realize you –"

"Child, you were enjoying a beautiful winter morning. What is there to apologize? Sit."

I sat.

"You appear rested," he said.

I sighed. "I had a very nice nap, but..."

"Something is bothering you."

I told him about my dream, about my feeling of being trapped with no way out.

"Are you having a crisis of faith?"

"No!" I was startled. "Yes." I sat up slowly. "Maybe, I am. After all, how could God let me be a false Goddess?"

"Hmm."

"I live in fear of losing control."

"Because you must keep such rigid control over yourself?"

I nodded.

"Is there anything you can do to make you feel you have more control over your life?"

"Be a doctor?" I said, expecting him to laugh.

But he looked thoughtful. "Why not?"

"How will I do that *Swamulavaru*?"

"When they brought you back a second time, did they not say that you had appeared to one of your devotees in the form of a doctor?"

"On my insistence, yes."

"There you go. That is your solution. Start healing people's bodies instead of their souls."

"Will they accept it?"

"Sadly enough, people will believe whatever they are told to believe. You can tell them you have been called to heal. You always worry you are duping people. Isn't practicing medicine more honest than what you are forced to do now?"

It was true, what the learned Guru said. This time around, I had not conformed to people's expectation of a Goddess, so people had changed their expectations to accommodate my behaviour. If I now declared I was going to start treating their bodies as well as their souls, perhaps people would take that in their stride, too. I had sensed this change myself.

"What about Kondal Rao?"

"We'll worry about him when we have to. Till then, you do what you have to."

I got up and touched Swami Chidananda's feet in gratitude.

"May you find the peace that eludes you so."

With the Swami's blessings, Ammamma set a plan in motion to distance me from my Goddess role.

We had a *bhajan* session with only a few, key devotees. Swami Chidananda was invited. After the *bhajan* was over, and the *prasadam* distributed, he declared, "Henceforth, *Ammavaru* shall be known as Doctor *amma*." Small change in wording, huge difference in import – one meant Goddess, the other a normal lady doctor, albeit one deserving respect.

"But," Sarala, my devotee, asked, "why is this, *Swamulavaru*?"

"Because above Doctor *amma* rests a higher power."

She seemed unsure, but it was amazing how little convincing the other devotees needed, now that the Swami had spoken.

Now, if only Kondal Rao would be convinced.

FIFTY-THREE

The Swami had spoken.

The devotees accepted that my audience-giving days were in the past. The ashram activities – the *bhajans*, the group sessions on various spiritual texts – continued, but I stayed away, not wanting to confuse people. Practicing medicine was still unthinkable. How could I, as long as my home was not my own?

I also worried about Kondal Rao's lack of interference in my life; his continued absence was a phantom itch I could not scratch.

In the meantime, the Swami had not been idle. On one of his visits, he told me that Lata had agreed to let me have my son.

"But?" I asked.

"But you have to agree to stay away from her home, and her husband."

Even though this wasn't unexpected, it still pierced my heart.

"Pullaiyya won't forgive you," Ammamma said, "if you take Srikar away from Lata."

My throat jammed with tears. "And Srikar? What did he say?"

Ammamma gave a short laugh. "What can the poor man say, caught as he is between warring sisters?"

I knew Ammamma didn't mean this unkindly, but it wounded all the same.

"Srikar said he would want to come to the village every so often to meet the boy," the Swami said. "Lata wants your assurance that you will make no attempt what-so-ever to reunite with her husband."

I nodded, though I hurt. "What was my son's reaction?"

"He cried." The Swami looked at me with compassion. "But you already knew that."

❧

Srikar had arrived the previous night to drop Pullaiyya off. Now it was time for him to leave. My son clung to Srikar, his little hands gripping his father's arms. As Srikar tried to gently pry away his hands, my son broke down. "Please, Nanna, if you take me back with you, I will never take your pens without telling you. I will always wash my hands before eating. I will take good care of Amma. Please don't make me stay here."

Srikar pulled the little boy to him, close to tears himself.

I watched, heart heavy. What were we adults doing to this poor child?

"Pullamma is your mother, Child. I'm not leaving you with strangers. Don't think of this as punishment."

"Please, Nanna, please!"

Srikar knelt by Pullaiyya and put a finger under the child's chin. "I still love you. Amma still loves you. But you know Amma's not been well lately, right?"

He nodded tearfully.

"You know she needs time to get better?"

Another nod.

"So you will be a brave boy for me?"

Pullaiyya nodded again.

"Then let me go."

At the gate to the courtyard, Pullaiyya clung to Srikar's leg, crying hysterically, not letting go.

"Ammamma," I said, choking up, "what right do I have to inflict my needs on an innocent child? Maybe it is best he continue to stay with Srikar and Lata." Lata might be sick, but at least Pullaiyya wouldn't be traumatised by their separation.

"Don't you dare!" Ammamma gave me a ferocious look. "It will be hard till he settles down, but settle he will. Because you love that child."

Srikar gently untangled his leg, gave his son a final hug and walked away. I could see his shoulders shake even beyond the courtyard gate.

I phoned Janaki aunty in Hyderabad that night.

"How is he?" she asked.

"Aunty, he has been sitting in the same corner since Srikar left, refusing to move. He's gotten up only twice, both times to rush to the bathroom and back. He's had two glasses of milk, but no food."

"Poor child," Aunty said. I could tell she was crying.

"I'll send him back," I said, defeated.

"No!" Then her tone softened. "No, Child. Much as I miss him, his place is with you, his mother."

Now, I looked at the little body slouched in the corner of my bedroom. It was the following morning and he'd not moved. My heart sank. This wasn't going to be easy.

"Are you hungry?"

No response.

"Do you want to see what happens in an ashram?"

No response.

I bent forward and put a tentative hand on his.

"Don't touch me!" He pushed.

I tripped, falling against the flimsy side table. The table broke from the force of my elbow. I pulled my arm up hard. A sharp pain shot up.

He scuttled to the corner diagonally across from me.

Supporting my throbbing arm with my good one, I got on my knees and propped my good elbow on the chair to get up from the floor. Another sharp pain shot up my elbow. I moaned involuntarily.

My son didn't spare me a passing glance.

Ammamma came into the room with a plate of food. "Pullaiyya, look what I have for you. I made your favourite *payasam*. Would you like to try some?"

Pullaiyya burrowed his head into the cemented corner.

Ammamma gave a sigh. She turned to me. "*Ai-yai-yo*! What are you doing on the floor?" She slammed the bowl of *payasam* on the other side table and rushed to me.

I was woozy with pain now.

Ammamma knelt next to me and exclaimed, "Your arm is broken!" She didn't need a degree in medicine to determine this – the bone in my arm had pushed all the way through. "What happened?"

The little body across the room stiffened.

"I was careless. I slipped and fell."

My child raised his head slightly and looked at me from the corner of his eye.

My arm felt like someone had set fire to it. Ammamma opened her mouth to say something, but I gave a slight shake of the head. My son had actually turned around to look at the offending piece of bone. The pain was so fierce I wanted to claw my arm off. And yet, if this was what it took to get a positive response from my son...

Ammamma got up. "I am going to get a doctor."

"Isn't she a doctor?" Pullaiyya said, jerking his head at me, as my grandmother ran out of the room.

I almost passed out – from the pain, or from the joy of hearing my son speak, I couldn't tell; probably a little of both. I was beginning to see two of him. I blinked hard to focus. "Doctors can't treat themselves," I said, voice beginning to slur.

"Is that really the bone?"

I supported my broken arm with the good arm and raised it to him; sweat broke out over my upper lip. "Do you want to see?"

He scooted closer. "Are you going to die?"

A laugh was wrenched out of me, even as tears threatened. "I hope not. After all, I've just found you."

"Good. I don't like to be near dead people."

I leaned my head back against the wall, not bothering to hold back tears. I would happily break my arm a thousand times for the pleasure of having my son respond to me.

It would be a stretch to say that was the beginning of our mother-and-son relationship, but at least my son did not push me away when I talked to him. Since we had two-bedroom quarters, and Ammamma and I used a bedroom each, I got a small bed for Pullaiyya and set it next to mine.

He didn't talk much at nights, but during the day he followed me around, intently watching everything that went on. I no longer gave *darsanams*, but people came for blessings, nonetheless. Unable to refuse, I met a limited few in my private courtyard each day.

Pullaiyya did not interrupt, but at night he had a stream of questions. 'Why was the man upset at the birth of his second daughter? How come that little girl was born with a crumpled lip? Why did that boy's father have to die?'

But the one thing he didn't talk about was Lata. I knew he missed her. Many times I heard him weeping softly, face stuffed in his pillow. I longed to drag him into my arms, to never let go. His anguish made me feel terrible.

But Ammamma was adamant that he belonged with me. "It is

unfortunate that he is suffering because of what Lata and Kondal Rao did, but you're doing the right thing."

"But Ammamma, he's hurting."

"Through no fault of yours. If you send him away, he is never going to know you, his real mother. It's not like Lata's is in a position to take care of him anyway." And she would not reopen the subject.

Sending my son back was not a real option. Just two days ago Janaki aunty had summoned Srikar home in the middle of the day because Lata was missing. After an hour of search he found Lata wandering about the streets in her night clothes, weeping. Aunty had had to take over Srikar's household. Aunty said that days went by when Lata acted completely normal; during those days no one would believe she was having breakdowns.

Swami Chidananda was more approachable, but he refused to make my decisions for me. "I wish he would tell me what to do about my son," I complained to Ammamma.

"That is not his way. He will listen, but he wants you to arrive at the solution yourself."

"But why?"

"Because you are the one who has to live with the consequences of your actions."

But the Swami listened to me.

"Am I doing wrong, *Swamulavaru*? Denying my son his mother?"

"You're doing what you have to do. The question is, what do you feel about it?"

"It makes me more happy than I thought possible." I had to stop because suddenly my heart was full. "But I live with guilt."

"Why?"

"Each time my son cries, but refuses my comfort; each time he waits for you to share his joy with."

"What do you think is the best thing for him?"

"Lata is unable to take care of him. She doesn't really love him. Even the name she gave him was to punish me. Being with me is the best thing for him." This, I was sure of.

"There's your answer, then."

RASANA ATREYA

My breaking an arm had an unintended, though welcome, consequence.

My devotee, Sarala, was puzzled when I appeared with a cast. "What purpose does your breaking a bone serve, Doctor *amma*?"

"Nothing. I'm just an ordinary mortal, Sarala, not a Goddess." Despite the *bhajan* session, a sliver of doubt remained. "Think about it," I said. "Avatars of Gods arrive on the earth for a specific purpose. Lord Rama was born to rid the earth of an evil like Ravana. Does it make sense to say I arrived on the earth to further the political ambitions of someone like Kondal Rao?"

"Then why were you a Goddess before?"

"I wasn't. People were manipulated into thinking I was."

Sarala did not respond, but I could see it had given her something to think about. She bowed and left. I would chip away at Kondal Rao's voter base, one devotee at a time.

FIFTY-FOUR

Pullaiyya began to get more comfortable with the Swami. He often sat at the Swami's feet, resting his chin on the elderly gentleman's knee, not saying much, but listening to us talk about the various people that had come my way, or the Swami's. I wasn't much into philosophy, so we talked more about practical matters.

One day Pullaiyya said, "Something happened at school today."

"What, Child?" the Swami asked.

Pullaiyya shot a quick look at me and flushed. "Uh... nothing."

It hurt me that Pullaiyya was unable to open up to me, but knew he needed someone he could talk freely with. I started sending him to the Swami's ashram in the neighbouring village on some pretext or the other. I never asked what they talked about, and he never said, but I sensed the visits were helping.

The Swami had not let me forget about my desire to start practicing medicine again. "Why are you not doing anything about it, Pulla-mma?" he asked one day. "It's been long enough since that *bhajan*. Your arm is fully healed, too."

"I'm not ready," I said and left it at that, because Pullaiyya was listening. He knew a sanitized version of his birth, but I tried to keep away as much unpleasantness from him as possible; he had as much 'real life' as he could handle right now. Already he knew there were certain things he could not talk about in public – his mother's deteriorating mental health, his relationship to me. Besides, how could I practice out of the same ashram I'd presided in as a Goddess?

I was also nervous about Satyam, the priest. He hadn't done anything with his suspicions that I knew of, but with a person like Satyam, one could never be sure.

Then Kondal Rao stormed into the house just before dinner one night, his two gun-toting sidekicks following. In a way I was glad. Waiting for him to make an appearance was like waiting outside in an open field in a thunderstorm, metal rod in hand.

RASANA ATREYA

"Where is my great-grandson?" he shouted. Fortunately, Ammamma had already put Pullaiyya to bed.

Ammamma pointed with her eyes at the few volunteers cleaning up.

Kondal Rao subsided.

"Why don't you come tomorrow morning?" Ammamma said, palms of her hands joined together deferentially. "Swami Chidananda will be there, so the ashram will be closed. We can talk things over a cup of tea."

Kondal Rao stood there, his stubby neck tensed, a vein twitching madly. Making a conscious effort to relax, he gave a short nod and stormed back out. It was amazing how fast the portly man moved once he set his mind to it.

We finished dinner and went to our private quarters. Occasionally I had dinner with my former devotees, now that I had completely stopped giving audiences. Meeting them was a humbling experience. I had a lot to learn about faith and selflessness from them.

I called Srikar and told him about his grandfather's visit. Calling him was bitter-sweet. Bitter, because there was no hope for us. Sweet, because I yearned for the sound of his voice.

Srikar arrived at the ashram in the early hours. I hadn't been able to sleep all night, knowing I would see him again. As he sat across from me, I saw that he had hollows under his eyes, a few grey strands in his hair. Funny, I had just discovered grey in my hair, too.

Ammamma greeted him and went back to her room.

Srikar appeared exhausted. We sat apart, avoiding one another's eyes. I grieved for the awkwardness between us; he was still my husband, the man I'd hoped to share more than grey hairs with.

"How is Aunty?" I asked. A safe topic.

He smiled. "She is wonderful, isn't she?" Then he sobered. "I'm glad she was in your life, Pulla."

A little prick in my heart at the endearment.

"She must miss Pullaiyya terribly." Aunty didn't say much about this in our weekly phone calls. To spare me the guilt of separating her from her grandson, I suspected.

"She does. But she is happy he is with you."

Lata knew, and I knew, and probably Srikar knew, too, that if it were up to Aunty, Srikar, Pullaiyya and I would be a family. She'd been firm that Pullaiyya's place was with me. I loved Aunty for her loyalty to me, even over her own son. Some bonds were made, then strengthened over shared suffering – ours was one of those.

"What do we do about your grandfather?" I asked, addressing the real reason he was here.

"Let's not talk about him. He will be here soon enough." All of a sudden Srikar knelt next to my chair and put a hand on my cheek. "Remember, how we used to talk about studying further, making something of ourselves?" he asked softly.

I smiled tremulously.

"I am so happy you were able to make something of yourself, despite great sorrow." His damp eyes shone with pride. "Use that education now," he urged. "Now that you're distancing yourself from the Goddess chapter, start practicing medicine again. Do this for yourself."

I nodded.

"I wish the three of us could live together as a family," he said, lowering his head to my lap. I stroked his hair gently, trying not to let regrets overwhelm me.

He got up and stumbled back to his chair, stiff. "What a mess." He massaged his eyes with his palms.

I looked at him, pain twisting my heart. He had set out to rescue me all those many years ago, when he married me. How had it come to this?

"Anyway," he said briskly, "my grandfather is an old man now, with only pretensions to power. He can bluster all he wants, but there isn't really much he can do. There's probably no reason for us to worry."

But I worried; I would not make the mistake of underestimating Kondal Rao again.

Morning arrived, and with it, Kondal Rao.

Ammamma and the Swami were settled in chairs. I perched on the steps of the veranda, while Srikar lounged against the wall. Pullaiyya was safe at Headmaster *garu*'s house.

The gate was slammed. All of us whipped around. Kondal Rao. Furious, I opened my mouth, but Srikar beat me to it.

"What are you up to?" he demanded, his nostrils flaring.

Kondal Rao stopped midstride. "Wha...at do you mean?" The obligatory henchmen behind him froze into postures.

"Out," Srikar said to the henchmen. "This is a family meeting."

The men looked at Kondal Rao, who nodded slightly.

"And close the gate behind you," Srikar ordered as the men stomped out.

"I want my great-grandson back with his mother," Kondal Rao said.

"He *is* with his mother," Srikar and Ammamma said simultaneously.

"What do you mean?" Kondal Rao sounded incredulous. "Lata is your wife; the woman who mothered your child."

"Pullamma is still my legal wife, the mother of my child."

"Lata is distraught without her child."

Lata was playing a dangerous game, blackmailing Kondal Rao.

"Pullaiyya is not her child," Srikar said.

Kondal Rao's nostrils flared in disgust. "Don't be stupid, Srikar, wasting your time on a black twig like Pullamma, when you can bed a luscious flower like Lata."

Srikar swooped from his position, grabbed the older man by the collar and slammed him against the tree. Kondal Rao's head bounced from the impact.

Time froze. Ammamma and I froze.

With an expression of extreme disgust, Srikar let go and Kondal Rao stepped back, rubbing his neck where Srikar had grabbed him. "Why are you angry with me when I'm saying the true thing?"

"Why?" Srikar roared, blood rushing to his face. "What am I angry, you grimy-souled bastard? You lied, and you cheated, and you ruined lives, and I never said anything. You took Pullamma away from me, deprived my son of a mother, my wife the right to family life, and I never said anything. You know why, *hanh*?" He went nose-to-nose with his grandfather. "Because I wanted to prove to myself that I didn't have your blood running in my veins." Rage poured out of him. He grabbed Kondal Rao by the shirt and shook him hard.

The Swami rose and placed a gentle hand on Srikar's shoulder. Startled, Srikar jerked his head sideways, breathing heavily. He shoved Kondal Rao backward into the chair. "You deprived me of a mother, now you want to inflict the same on my son?"

"But I provided both of you with a perfectly good step-mothers, no?" Kondal Rao looked bewildered. "Lata is a good lady, your step-mother was a good lady."

Srikar shook his head in disbelief. "My step-mother was a perfectly nice lady. But she was not my mother. You were my grandfather, one of the adults who should have kept my world safe. But you damaged it beyond repair. And now you want to do that to my son?"

My eyes swam, but my heart bubbled over with joy because Srikar had stood up for me.

"It broke my heart to send Pullaiyya away," Srikar said. "But every child deserves a mother. And every mother deserves her child. All this while I thought you were merely amoral and dangerous. But you truly don't understand, do you?"

"But I gave you a pretty wife, a fair wife," Kondal Rao exclaimed.

"You talk like any fair-skinned girl would have done. The only woman I've ever wanted for my wife is Pullamma. All I wanted was the chance to raise my son with her."

I held my breath, counting out the beats in my head.

"But I don't know how to extricate myself from the mess you've made of our lives – my son's, Pullamma's, mine, even Lata's." Srikar looked sorrowful. "Not without hurting my son."

I watched Srikar, hurting for him, hurting for me.

"Fine, after the next elections are over, take Pullamma back, send Lata on her way. You want me to set her up in a mental asylum?"

Srikar looked at his grandfather bleakly. "You truly don't understand what you've destroyed, do you?"

Kondal Rao started at Srikar with a puzzled frown, shook his head, then turned to the Swami. "*Swamulavaru*?" he said, addressing the Swami in a respectful manner.

"It's time for us older people to step out of the lives of these youngsters," Swami Chidananda said gently.

Kondal Rao looked as if he would have liked to argue, but he was nobody's fool. He couldn't afford to ignore the clout the Swami wielded. He bowed and left, leaving me fretting about his next move.

It was not in Kondal Rao to give up this easily.

FIFTY-FIVE

No one seemed concerned about Kondal Rao's non-appearance during the hot summer months.

"He is too quiet," I said to Janaki aunty during our weekly phone conversation.

"Perhaps Srikar's unexpected blow-up shook him up."

I gave a short laugh. "Kondal Rao, the self-involved, amoral, conscienceless politician, worried about something as insignificant as someone's feelings?" Glad as I was to see Srikar stand up to his bully of a grandfather, nothing had changed for the two of us. He was still in Hyderabad, I was still here in the village. "He's up to something, Aunty."

"Don't invent trouble. It is more likely he is just busy managing his new portfolio in the State Government. No time to bother with you."

I certainly hoped so.

"I miss our days together," I said.

"I do too, Child. Much as I am grateful to God for giving me a second chance with my son, I miss you terribly."

Swami Chidananda, meanwhile, had not been idle. He mobilized funds and started building a complex, with rooms and a central courtyard, around the existing Durga temple. He planned to move over all *bhajans* and prayers from my ashram to the temple complex. Then I would be completely free of this onerous responsibility. Dared I think I could lead a normal life?

A commotion drew me outside. A group of children stood in a circle, chattering excitedly. Wondering what had caused it, I went closer. Two boys were engaged in a fist fight, rolling in the mud so hard that they were raising dust.

"Stop," I barked, moving to separate the boys.

One of the boys snarled and pushed me back. He saw me and froze. Pullaiyya!

Wordlessly, I pulled the boys apart. I helped the other child up

– his clothes were caked with dirt, his face grimy. He harrumphed and started to limp homeward.

I held out a hand to Pullaiyya, but he ignored me. He wiped the back of his hand across his cheek, smearing mud and blood. My heart lurched. The gash above his upper lip ran all the way across his cheek. "Go home, all of you," I said, shooing away the children. Silently, I walked Pullaiyya home.

Inside, Ammamma rushed up. "What happened?"

"He got into a fight."

"Let me help you," Ammamma said.

"No!" Pullaiyya rushed into the house, and slammed the door behind him.

He refused dinner.

Later that night, he lay in his bed next to mine. I'd turned the lights down. The All India Radio played 'dard bhare geet' in the background – melodious songs of grief and sorrow.

We often talked at night, never looking directly at each other; it seemed less threatening that way. I had come to treasure these late night confidences.

Now, I said, "Do you want to tell me what happened today?"

"Why did you have to name me Pullaiyya, Doctor *amma*?" he burst out.

My poor baby! He must have gotten into a fight over his name. For a moment I wasn't sure how to answer him; after all if it had been up to me, Pullaiyya would have been named anything but. Deciding it was best to stick as close to the truth as possible, I said, "My sister named you after me because I had to go away." I tried not to get distracted by the hurt that he wouldn't call me Amma – as far he was concerned, his mother was Lata.

"Where do such stupid names come from, anyway?"

Lata, how could you? "Even in my generation, it wasn't uncommon for babies to die at birth. Parents who'd lost one or more children resorted to such names in the hope of tricking the fates. Or, in my case, a grandmother who was trying to halt the stream of calamities."

"How did that help?"

"Well, our names – yours and mine – come from 'puli vistaraku,' which means a heap of used or dirty plates. Desperate parents threw their children on a pile of such plates to show the fates that the child was as good as dead. The hope was that once the attention of the fates was diverted, the child would live."

"Didn't the child get hurt?"

I laughed. "It's not like they threw the children on metal plates. They used woven-leaf or plantain leaf plates."

Pullaiyya pushed himself up on an elbow, looking interested despite himself. "Did they throw us on dirty plates, too?"

I laughed again. "Not you, I'm fairly sure. But Ammamma rested me on twigs, which she thought was better than throwing me on used plates, because 'Pulla' means twigs, too."

"So Pentaiah or Pentamma were thrown in garbage."

"Symbolically, yes."

"Any other funny names?"

"Daanaiyya or Daanamma come from the word 'Daanam.' Children with these names were donated to another family, then taken back."

"Would you have called me Pullaiyya, too?"

I wasn't sure what answer he sought; did he want me to say yes, so he could feel closer to me? Or no, so he could distance himself from me? I hesitated an instant, then decided to be honest. "No, I would have named you something different." Something nicer, I thought silently.

"Why?"

"Because I got teased a lot, too."

"Did Amma know about this?"

I shrugged. Not much I could say to that without hurting my child. "Other kids would collect little sticks, tie them up and wrap a ribbon around them, dressing the bundle up as a girl. They would follow me around, but pretend to be talking to the bundle. 'Pullamma, you little bag of sticks,' they'd say giggling. Or they'd call me 'Nalla Pulla.'" Little black sticks. "I hated it."

"I hate my name, too," my child said. "It is funny when you tell it as a story, but not so funny when other children tease you."

I closed my eyes, trying to stem my tears. I hadn't wanted a child of mine to go through what I had. "Swami Chidananda suggested a name for you..."

"What is it?"

"Ved."

"Ved," he said a couple times, trying it out. "*Swamulavaru* gave me that name?"

I nodded, holding myself rigid.

"Would you be upset if I asked to change my name?"

I felt tears clog the back of my throat. "Not at all," I managed to whisper.

"You can call me Ved, then," he said.

He turned on his side, examining my face in the dim light. "You think my parents will mind?"

"I don't think so." Srikar wouldn't; of that I was certain. As for Lata – who knew?

"That can be my new name when I start in my new school."

"I'll check with Srikar, then speak to Headmaster *garu* and take care of the change." A rush of love for this child engulfed me. I held out my arms, not really expecting a response.

He crawled over to my bed and got under the covers with me.

I held him tight, and wept.

FIFTY-SIX

This was the turning point in the relationship with my son I had so craved. Ved opened up to me. Progress was slower than I would have liked, but it was there. Since I no longer involved myself in ashram activities, I had a lot of time on my hands. I was reluctant to start up my medical practice for the fear it would cut into my time with Ved. I helped him with his homework, listened to his day at school, practiced singing bhajans with him. When Ammamma, Ved and I sat down for dinner at night, I came the closest I had to contentment since the time Srikar and I had set up home together.

One evening Ved seemed listless, not his usual self.

"What's wrong?"

He wouldn't meet my eye.

"Ved?"

He looked uncomfortable.

"You can tell me whatever is bothering you. I won't mind."

"You won't be angry?" he asked, raising his head.

"No, I promise."

"Can I keep a photo of my parents next to my bed?"

I drew in a sharp breath.

"Ved!" Ammamma looked agitated.

Ved's shoulders drooped.

Ammamma said, "Pullamma is your mother. You –"

God bless Ammamma for her support, but this wouldn't go away by reprimanding. "Ammamma," I said cutting her off. "Please?"

She didn't look happy about it, but didn't say more.

"Child," I said, holding out a hand. He put his hand in mine. It broke my heart that he looked so fearful. "This is your house as much as it is mine or Ammamma's. You can do whatever you want. I'll ask your father for a photo."

He smiled uncertainly.

"What, Child?"

"Can I go over to Ramu's house? For cricket."

"Of course," I said, giving him a hug. He squirmed out of my hold, and ran to the courtyard gate.

Ammamma waited till Ved shut the gate behind him. Then she

burst out. "How can you let him put Lata's photo in your house? You are letting that girl take over your life even when she's hundreds of kilometers away."

"What choice do I have? Besides, this isn't about Lata, it is about Ved. I have to do whatever it takes to make him feel secure with us. If I deny him this simple request, tomorrow he won't feel comfortable asking me something else."

Ammamma tightened her lips in disapproval.

A week later Srikar sent a framed picture of him with Lata and Ved, which Ved put on the table next to my bed. I tried not to let bitterness overwhelm me each time my eyes fell on the happy family. I had to keep reminding myself that I was doing this for the sake of my child.

The one thing he continued to do, which continued to hurt, was call me 'Doctor *amma*.' Ammamma wanted me to make him call me Amma. But I did not want to force my son into doing something he so clearly wasn't comfortable with.

"Doctor *amma*," Ved asked after homework every afternoon, "can I go out to play?" All his evenings were spent at various friends' houses, playing one game or another.

"You've been going to your friends' houses each day. Why don't you invite them over?"

He made a face, but didn't say anything.

"Ved?"

"How can I?" he burst out. "This is an ashram, not a home."

I swallowed my hurt. "Will you ask them to come if I shut down the ashram once a week?" The ashram had activities seven days a week now.

"You will send all the devotees away?"

"I'll try."

"Okay, then."

When I broached the topic of shutting down the ashram one day each week, Ammamma was taken aback. "But why?"

"We did it the first time I came back as Goddess."

"That was then. You haven't shut the ashram down on a regular basis for a while."

"I'll start now."

"Why the sudden urgency?"

"Ved can't invite his friends over to an ashram. He needs a home."

"Tongues will wag," Ammamma warned.

"About what?"

"About why this little boy is so important to you."

"Ammamma, all I do is live my life for other people. For once I'd like to do something *I* want."

"There is Satyam to consider."

That gossipy old priest. I sighed. "Ammamma, there is always someone to consider. I don't care anymore. If my son can't feel comfortable bringing friends home, what is the point?" There was so little he asked of me. How could I deny him a perfectly valid request?

Ammamma shrugged, but I could see the worry in her eyes.

I ordered the ashram shut down on Sundays.

"But why?" Satyam, the priest, asked.

"Because the volunteers need to spend time with their families." A feeble explanation, if there was one. We had so many volunteers that if each of them took three days off a week, we'd still have enough to crowd the ashram. Besides, in our rural community, there were no 'off' days. People came in whenever they could. "And I want you to take the day off, too. My grandmother will take care of the *prasadam* and prayers."

I could see the speculation in his eyes, but I couldn't get myself to care.

FIFTY-SEVEN

In my personal altar at home, the biggest picture was that of Swami Chidananda. I owed him my life and my sanity. He had commandeered an army of volunteers to move out the ashram activities to the temple complex. It had taken a whole year to get the complex ready, but it was now complete. Kondal Rao was not happy with the elderly saint's involvement, but there wasn't much he could do; Swami Chidananda had a legion of loyal devotees Kondal Rao couldn't afford to alienate. As a result of his intervention, our ashram was back to being home again.

Swami Chidananda often urged me to practice yoga to attain peace; Ved was my yoga. Allowing him to keep a photograph of his parents in our room had been a significant step in our relationship.

Loving Ved allowed me to open my heart; he could get inside of me and rip my insides to pieces, and I would let him. It took every ounce of willpower I possessed, then some, to give him the space he needed. I couldn't bear to see him walk away from me. If he was five minutes late coming back from school, I worked myself into a frenzy. Knowing that I was trying to compensate for the missed years, I tried hard not to stifle him. But Ammamma saw my struggle. And she fretted.

I also missed Aunty. And Srikar. Despite the promise to my sister to stay away from her husband in thought and deed, his absence from my life was like an untreated childhood injury on the elbow – a jab on the scab and it bled afresh.

For years I had gone without thinking of him hourly, but his son's presence in my life was the prod that reopened the wound. That particular way Ved had of saying certain words, the way he held his head, the way his hair flopped on his brow.

The nights Ved chose to sleep in Ammamma's room – he had become intensely curious about his family history – I allowed myself to cry for Srikar.

Ved had been with me five months, but he still missed Lata. The nights when he cried for her, I felt sharp jealousy. I wished I could hold him to ease his pain, rock him as I might have, had I raised him, but he held me at a distance. He'd started school. Since his name change, he seemed to get along better with the other kids. The only thing I couldn't do was break through his reserve.

I knew Srikar talked to Ved on the phone frequently; in the months Ved had been with me, Srikar had come to the village every other week, staying over at Headmaster *garu*'s. Headmaster *garu* took Ved to his father. Lata never came, not even to visit Ved.

"I've had enough of your moping," Ammamma declared one day. "I've talked to Swami Chidananda about your clinic."

"Clinic?"

"The office where doctors treat patients."

"*Bah*, Ammamma. I'm not sure I'm ready to start practicing again."

"You have nothing to occupy your mind since the ashram activities were moved out. It is not healthy. Get a bank loan. Start the clinic."

"There's also my prostitution money that you wouldn't touch."

Ammamma flushed.

Perhaps, it was time for the next phase of my life. I felt prickling of excitement. "We could use that to fund a vocational training centre for girls. Have both buildings on the same parcel of land."

Ammamma nodded, looking relieved.

"Ammamma, I'll start looking for land right away. You should plan on going to the bank sometime next week. Check how much money we have."

"I'd never trust those oily fellows with your money."

I was taken aback. "You keep that much money under the mattress?"

"I'm not a fool!"

"Then, where?"

"It's in that black pot in the kitchen attic."

"You have thousands of rupees sitting in a mud pot? In an open attic?" I was staggered. "Don't you worry?"

Ammamma straightened, dignity injured. "I put rat-traps all around it."

I gave Ammamma a hug, hiding my smile in her shoulder. When I told Lata the money I'd sent to Ammamma was gathering dust, I hadn't meant it literally.

I set up a foundation to give scholarships to deserving girls, naming it after Janaki aunty. I couldn't think of a better way of paying her back for my medical education, and for the love and support she'd given me over the years. I bought land to build the clinic and vocational training centre. Classes would be offered free of charge. I planned to offer free treatment to young girls who enrolled. Hopefully, that would be added incentive to attend the classes.

The centre progressed rapidly. Hiring teachers was easy enough. The clinic was a little less straightforward. I had to seek Swami Chidananda's help to hire a nurse. He set an auspicious date for me to start practice, and blessed the clinic as well as the training centre on the opening day.

FIFTY-EIGHT

The Swami dropped into the clinic about two weeks after its opening. "Not a very busy day," he remarked, looking around.

He was being kind. The place was deserted, except for the nurse and me.

"It's been like this since we opened," I said. "The training centre next door is doing very well. But the clinic... Considering I am the only doctor in a 50-kilometre radius, I expected some patients."

"Your Goddess aura lingers."

I sighed. "I've heard that even in emergencies, people are going all the way to the Government Hospital." The overcrowded hospital, with its perpetual staff shortage, was a two hour bus ride away.

"I'll see what I can do." He was as good as his word. Over the next few days, patients started to trickle in. Most had fearful looks on their faces, but the Swami sat in a corner, reassuring people, calming their fears.

People started to come for consultations from as far as Hyderabad. I didn't know if it was my medical skills that brought them, or my Godly reputation. I couldn't complain, though. I was busy, with no time to obsess about Srikar.

One night, as I prepared to wrap up, there was a timid knock on the door. I turned around.

Geeta stood by the door, head bent, not looking at me. "May I come in?" she said, voice barely audible.

"Yes, of course," I said, trying to hide my surprise.

She sank in a chair. Her skin seemed pale.

"Are you anaemic?"

"You, a doctor?" She shook her head in disbelief, her voice sounding hoarse from disuse. "I'm not here for treatment. I came to see you."

I waited for her to go on.

"I traced Srikar, sought his forgiveness. Then I came looking for you."

"If forgiveness is what you're after, don't bother. I stopped blaming you a long time ago."

"Really?" Finally, a spark in her face.

I thought of the last time I'd seen this woman, collapsed in a heap on the floor. I looked at her now, her sallow skin, the nervous tick in her cheek. I took her hand in mine. It was cold. "Really, Geeta. Your only fault was that you were in the wrong place at the wrong time. I should have told you this the last time I saw you. Unfortunately, I was too consumed by grief."

"You mean it, then." The taut lines of her face sagged.

I nodded, feeling sadness that the bubbly woman I'd known was reduced to this. "Yes, I do." I sat in the chair next to her. "You and I, Srikar and my son, and a whole lot of people you don't know about, were pawns in Kondal Rao's desperate quest for power. He used people, ruined lives. You need to believe me. I don't blame you one bit. Had I been in your position, I might have done the same thing. It's not your fault. I know this in my heart."

"Thank you."

"Go home. Go back to your husband and children. Forget this ugly episode. Don't look back."

She sat unmoving for a while. Then, with visible effort, she got to her feet. "May God be with you."

I watched as she stepped out of the room, feeling sorrow for a precious part of my past lost. But I didn't call her back. I didn't offer friendship. We'd both moved too far apart for that.

Let go of the anger, the Swami often counselled me. *Forgive and forget.*

I laid my head against the back of my chair, feeling peace steal over me.

Srikar phoned from Hyderabad, asking to take Ved to his great-grandmother. I was happy to agree; Ved needed to know not all relatives on his father's side were sewage sludge like Kondal Rao. Srikar started to take Ved on monthly visits. Ved returned from these trips happier; he was bonding with his great-grandmother.

Over a period of two years, I devolved from Goddess to doctor, though a little of the awe still remained in peoples' minds. With time, I hoped that would go away, too.

RASANA ATREYA

Kondal Rao had an important post in the Cabinet, so he'd left me alone. I saw him on television often, making some self-important speech or the other.

My son was thriving. He had made friends, and spent his free time playing cricket in the village square. He missed Lata less and less, for which I was profoundly grateful. Busy with patients, I had less time to fret over Ved, though he was still the top priority in my life. I made sure I spent enough time with him on a daily basis, but not enough to stifle him. I was happier too, less constrained in what I could do. One of my favourite things to do was take a walk with Ved to the Lotus pond, and sit by the water. There we talked about school, about cricket, about life in general. Everything, but Lata, that is. Ved didn't seem to want to talk about her, and I wasn't particularly anxious, either.

My medical practice picked up dramatically. I had a lot of patients and although I knew that curiosity was one reason for patients coming in from villages half a day's walk away, I felt more content than I had in a long time. I missed Srikar, but it was like a nagging toothache. Always there, in the background, but ignored for long periods of time.

One day I was seeing patients in the clinic when I heard squealing brakes. I hurried out. An older man was lifting up a child who looked like she was choking. "Food stuck in her throat," he shouted.

I ran to the girl, grabbed her from the man and turned her over, resting her belly on my upraised knee, and thumped her on her upper back with the heel of my palm, using the Heimlich manoeuvre. A piece of vegetable flew out of her mouth. She started to breathe again. A crowd of patients gathered around us.

"A miracle! You saved my grandchild's life, Doctor *amma*," the man said, struggling to hold back tears.

I touched him gently on the shoulder.

People milled about restlessly. I held up my hand. "What I did was not a miracle," I said, moving my head around the crowd to catch people's eyes. "Any doctor would have done the exact same thing." They looked at each other uncertainly.

My nurse, a plump, bustling woman named Ramani waved her arms at the crowd. "Didn't you hear what Doctor *amma* said? Move, move. The show is over. Doctor *amma* does not have all day."

I could have hugged her.

I turned and walked back into the clinic, conscious of the skittish crowds. They followed me in. The tide seemed to be turning.

Chandrasekhar, the man whose child's life I'd saved, came to see me that evening. The rugged looking man with compact build, and integrity reflected in his eyes, was accompanied by his wife, the elegant Bhavani.

"I am indebted to you," the man said. "You saved my beloved daughter's life."

"I'm glad I was able to get to her in time. But I want you to understand it was not a miracle."

"It was for us," Bhavani said with a tremulous smile. "But I know what you mean."

The tension in my scalp slackened. "How is your daughter doing?"

"She was climbing a tree when we left," the woman said, laughing.

"We moved to Mallepalli a couple of months ago," Chandrasekhar said.

I had heard, of course. The village grapevine was nothing if not efficient. "Any particular reason?"

"My grandparents are from the neighbouring village," Bhavani said. "We grew up on stories about Renuka, that woman who was stoned as a witch. Have you heard of her?"

"She was a friend of my mother's."

"Really?" Bhavani sounded shocked.

"These things happen a lot in the villages. More than you know."

"Did you believe she was a witch?"

"At the time I did," I said with regret.

"And now?"

"Do you know of my background?"

"Yes," Bhavani said. "I know they tried to make you a Goddess by claiming you'd brought a child back to life."

"To answer your question... no, I don't believe it any longer."

"Do your... uh..." Bhavani glanced at her husband, then turned back to me. "Do your healing powers come from miracles?"

I laughed. "That, and years of medical education."

"So there's no mumbo-jumbo involved?" Bhavani still looked doubtful.

RASANA ATREYA

"None at all." I was amused. "Purely medical knowledge."

The couple looked relieved.

"Well, then," Chandrasekhar said. "Perhaps, you would be willing to help."

"How?"

"I despair at the fanaticism in the villages," Bhavani said. "Ever since I heard about Renuka's death, I've been haunted by images of her. Chandrasekhar also wants to do something about the rampant superstition, lack of education for girls, the early marriages, and so on."

"So we decided," Chandrasekhar said, "that Bhavani would work with the villagers, and I would try and make a difference through politics. I intend to contest elections from here."

"You are aware of Kondal Rao, of course."

"Of course," Chandrasekhar said. "I am preparing to take him on. With the Swami's blessings."

"You're a brave man," I said. "I hope you know what you're getting into."

Chandrasekhar nodded.

"We know a little bit about his involvement in your life," Bhavani said, a look of sympathy on her face. "Just your luck to be entangled with the most corrupt politician in the history of the State."

"My platform will be anti-corruption," Chandrasekhar said. "I will accept no money or favours from anyone. I want to educate people about their rights, about voting for the person who will serve them best, not just for the person who waves around the most money."

"Don't make the mistake of underestimating Kondal Rao," I warned.

"We won't," the couple said in unison.

I looked at them in turn. Chandrasekhar exuded a calm confidence, while Bhavani looked like a woman with a mission. I allowed myself to feel a surge of hope.

Janaki aunty phoned. "How is Ved?"

"His teacher complains that he gets into all kinds of mischief. If only he'd put his brain to good use."

Aunty laughed. "Don't forget, I know all your stories from school."

I smiled. I was finally reaching a stage in life where I was fairly content.

Bhavani showed up at my house early next morning, a determined look about her. "I want your help in setting up classes for girls."

"I already run free classes in the centre next to my clinic. Why don't you join me?" I'd recently introduced free midday meals for students; anything to get the girls to class.

"You're teaching basket-weaving and child-rearing," Bhavani said. "Don't get me wrong, but I want these girls to set their sights higher."

"I would love for each of these girls to be scientists or doctors or engineers. But I don't want the elders up in arms."

"Why would they oppose free education? It's for the good of the girls."

"You think that, and I think that. But for the villagers, it is great hardship trying to marry off overly educated girls. Where would they get suitably educated grooms? City alliances require much bigger dowries."

"And you are okay with this attitude."

"I am not." How could I forget the pulverizing of Lata's dreams? "But I'd rather have the girls come and learn something, than nothing at all. If they were to stay home, all they'd do is household chores. When they are here, I also talk to them about hygiene, nutrition, risks of teen marriages and pregnancies, that sort of thing."

"But I want these girls to realize their potential."

"You certainly won't get that by pushing higher education. I am very cautious about how I impart information – anything too overt, and the next thing you know the girl is back at home, scrubbing the cow."

Bhavani's voice rose. "But they need to understand that they have to let their bodies and minds grow before they are able to take on marriage and children."

"I realize that, but you can't expect to wipe away generations of belief in a few classes. We've been imparting this information in a manner that does not threaten their parents and elders. If

Rasana Atreya

they pulled the girls out of these classes, how would it serve our purpose?"

Seeing that Bhavani was not convinced, I said, "When my twin and I were young, Headmaster *garu* came home to tell my grandmother that my sister had the intelligence and aptitude to study medicine. My grandmother panicked and pulled both of us out of school."

Bhavani was incredulous. "But you're a doctor, aren't you?"

I sighed. "Long story. I'll tell you about it someday. For now, believe me when I say you'll need to take things slowly. You've grown up in the city, so you don't know how it is in the villages. You need to be patient, Bhavani. Change will come, but in increments. If you are looking for overnight shifts, you're setting yourself up for failure."

Bhavani agreed, but reluctantly. She and I were about the same age, but she had the fire, the burning desire to change the world. I was glad for her, but sensed the need to temper her enthusiasm. We finally agreed we would do no formal sessions. Bhavani would hold cooking and pickle-making classes, while I'd continue to offer free clinics for young women one day a week.

I felt warmth wash over me. Bhavani was the first friend I'd made as an adult.

FIFTY-NINE

I settled in my armchair in the afternoons, watching my son play with his friends, unable to get over the awe that, thanks to Swami Chidananda, our house was back to being a home again.

Some days my son and his friends raced discarded cycle tyres, hitting them along the edges with sticks. Other times, they played cricket.

In one corner of the courtyard, near the old cowshed, a tractor tyre hung off the tamarind tree. Instead of the gaggle of devotees, a swarm of boys gathered, alternating swinging on the tyre, or jumping through it. I watched with pleasure as Ved argued with a friend about who had jumped higher. At eleven years of age, Ved reminded me a little of the gawky boy-man Srikar had been when I first met him.

Someone knocked.

"Ved, see who is at the gate, Child."

Ved sprinted to the gate and opened it. A plump woman with deep creases in either cheek entered through the gate. She was dressed in a rumpled cotton sari, a big red, *kumkum bottu* on her forehead. Her arms hung like short stumps from her armpits. Despite the weight on her frame, she had an impish look about her.

"Pullamma?" the woman said, a tentative smile on her face.

I waited for her to go on. Then it struck me. She had called me by name. It had been years since people outside my family had called me anything other than *Ammavaru* (thankfully not much anymore), or Doctor *amma*. I got up, heart thumping. It couldn't be, could it?

"You don't remember me?" She thumped her chest dramatically. Her chins quivered. "Me? The keeper of your secrets, the stealer of your guavas?"

"Chinni!" I squealed. Then we were in each other's arms, laughing and crying. From the corner of my eye, I saw Ved look at us in alarm. I urged him over. "Ved, this is my best friend."

"Chinni, my nephew," I said, aching that I didn't know my former best friend anymore, not enough to trust her with my deepest secrets anyway.

My friend extended a plump arm and pulled him into our hug. "Malli's son?"

"No, Lata's," I said, almost choking on it.

My son wiggled out. From a safe distance he asked, "You're the same person who hid in the mango tree under a white sheet, and made moaning noises in the middle of the night?"

Chinni laughed. "Hasn't your aunt told you the things *she* did?"

"The tree didn't break?"

"Ved!" I said, appalled, but Chinni just laughed.

Ved and his friends were watching the two of us with undisguised interest. "How come you didn't recognize your own friend?" one of them asked.

I'd last seen my friend more than a dozen years ago, when we were both sixteen. A lot had happened since. She had changed, I had changed. I was trying to think up a suitable answer, but Chinni beat me to it.

"Because where there was one of me, now there are three Chinnis." A wide grin arced across her face.

The boys tittered, some of them hooting.

"And," she said, looking at me intently, "if I hadn't been warned to expect changes, I might not have recognized you, either."

"Later," I mouthed from behind Ved. "Go and play outside, all of you," I ordered the boys. "My friend and I have a lot of catching up to do."

"Because there is so much more of her?" Ved said.

Before I could reprimand him, Chinni said, "Oh, so you are the class joker now?"

The boys laughed.

"Are you younger than my mother or older?"

"Twenty days younger," Chinni said, eyes twinkling. "What of it?"

"Since you are my younger aunt, will you make me call you Chinni *pinni*?"

The boys roared with laughter. Chinni joined in. I shooed all of them out.

"Chinni *pinni*, Chinni *pinni*," they chanted, as they marched out.

After the children left, Chinni sobered. "I wasn't a very good friend to you, was I?"

"You were young, with a life ahead of you."

"So were you, but I let you down." Chinni had tears in her eyes.

"Don't," I said softly, putting a hand on her arm. "I have enough regrets to last me a lifetime." If a tiny part of me could have believed that Renuka *pinni*, close confidant of my mother and loving friend to us, was a witch, could I blame Chinni for fearing I might be a Goddess? Over the years I had kept track of Chinni. I knew she had married a businessman and moved away to Kurnool. There, business had prospered. She had two children, a girl Ved's age, and a boy, about six years old. "I'm glad to see you," I said, my voice cracking. She gave me another hug. "What brings you here?"

"My mother is getting old, so we decided to come back to the village to settle down. My husband is setting up a hardware shop here."

"I'm glad to hear that," I said. And I was. "But your mother won't be happy that you came to meet me."

Chinni sighed. "Believe it or not, she misses you. She's bitterly ashamed of her behaviour. She talks about coming to see you, but doesn't have the courage."

"I'd love to see her again, Chinni. I've been working on letting go of my bitterness. What better way to move forward than meet your mother?" Chinni's mother was an integral part of my childhood memories; meeting her would be another step towards calming my inner turmoil.

"We were cowards, Pullamma. Maybe if we had stood up for you, we could have got the other villagers to see what was being done to you." She bent forward and clutched my hands, her belly making it difficult to lean all the way. "Forgive me." Tears pooled in the half-moons above her cheeks, then dripped to the floor.

"There is nothing to forgive," I said, turning my hand up and clasping hers. "No one wanted to risk being the first one to say I was no Goddess, just their little Pullamma. People were scared." Mainly because no one knew how the others would react. I had come to this realization soon after I married Srikar; coming to terms with it had taken a whole lot longer.

"Your forgiveness is more than I deserve," she said, voice breaking. She raised our joined hands to her forehead. "I hurt you."

"Yes," I admitted. "You were my very best friend, and I expected you to support me, no matter what." I wiped away my tears.

"Anyway. All that is best left in the past. What brings you here today?"

"Something is happening that I thought you should know. I wanted to tell you about it myself. But mostly, I just wanted an excuse to see you."

"You, of all people, never needed an excuse, Chinni."

"Still." She sighed. "This is about your priest, Satyam, is it?"

"What is he up to now?"

"Has he done something before?"

"No, but I have been expecting mischief from him. He is that kind of a man."

"He went sniffing at my mother's house."

"What for?"

"For dirt on you. He thinks since you and I haven't talked in years, my mother and I would be willing to gossip about you."

"Why?"

"He says..." She paused, before saying in a rush. "He claims you have been trying to pass off your own child as Lata's." Her cheeks burned.

"He is right," I said, looking steadily at my friend. "I am."

She inhaled sharply. "Who is the father, may I ask?"

"My husband."

She seemed truly shocked. "Who is that?"

"The man Lata's trying to pass off as *her* husband."

Chinni looked at me with disbelief, so I gave a short laugh. "Sounds like one of those never-ending TV melodramas, doesn't it?" I led her through the happenings in my life starting from when Srikar married me, to Kondal Rao's interference and murder attempt, Lata's shenanigans, and everything in between.

"Pullamma, please forgive me," she whispered. "I should have been there to help you through all of this."

"I've reached a point in my life where I am fairly content. I have my son, my medical practice."

"But not your husband." She hadn't been my best friend for nothing.

"I've come to terms with it. I'm learning to be happy with what I have."

"It's incredible that you became a doctor!" She grinned impishly. "Remember how much our Master despaired at us?"

I grinned back.

"I can't believe how Lata turned out. Wasn't she the one who was always angry at how women were treated?"

"As years go by, I feel more and more sorry for her. If she'd been allowed to study, if she'd not been forced into marrying a man so beneath her in education, who knows how she might have turned out?"

"We always thought she would be the one to blaze a trail across the world," Chinni said.

"She feels betrayed that I, the mediocre student, fulfilled her destiny."

"You can't be that mediocre if people travel hours to consult you."

"That could be my Goddess aura, too," I said. "Lata resents my degree, my fame, my money, even my looks. Everything she's done in life has been driven by that resentment."

"What a waste of a life."

We were both silent.

Then Chinni said, "How are you coping?"

"I've made my first friend after you."

"Who?"

"Bhavani. Wife of politician Chandrasekhar."

"I'm glad."

"Me, too. I wonder what Satyam plans to do with his information."

"My husband did some poking around of his own. It seems Satyam is addicted to gambling. Cock fights. He owes some very unsavoury people a lot of money."

"Kondal Rao appointed him as the priest," I said slowly. "I should have known he wouldn't have picked just anyone; he would have wanted someone he could control. Probably even got thugs to tempt Satyam with the money."

"And now Satyam might be getting ready to blackmail you with this information."

"I don't need this," I said, rubbing the back of my neck. "I wish Kondal Rao and his endless machinations would just disappear."

"What are you going to do about Satyam?"

"I wish I knew."

"Kondal Rao is a dangerous enemy," Chinni said. "Be careful."

"I will."

"I have to go now." Chinni scooted forward in her chair, balancing on an elbow to get up. "Too fat," she said, laughing. "I will talk to my husband; maybe we can come up with a plan."

"I'll talk to Srikar, see if he has suggestions."

We hugged again and Chinni left, promising to be in touch.

Before I could get around to talking to Srikar, my grandmother fell sick. "Ammamma, you really need to get yourself checked," I said.

"Just because you are a doctor, doesn't mean you see problems everywhere."

"You've been losing weight."

"Why is that such a bad thing? If you have noticed, I've been trying to cut down on food. At my age, one should be consciously working towards separating one's self from earthly desires, from lust, anger, attachment; all manner of worldly appetites."

"It is more than that, and you know it. Why have you been suffering from nausea?"

"Because my earthly body is still fighting its desire for food."

Nothing I said would move Ammamma.

Two weeks later she showed up at the clinic. "Perhaps you should do that check-up."

"Why now?"

"Well –"

"Well, what?"

"I've been coughing up blood."

My life had been a balancing act of sorts – if joy outweighed sorrow, sorrow moved in to compensate. And so it was, when my child started to bond with me, Ammamma was diagnosed with adenocarcinoma.

Fifty years Ammamma had squatted in front of a coal-fed earthen stove in a poorly ventilated kitchen. Fifty years of lovingly cooked meals, and all she had to show for it was lung cancer.

I got in touch with Dr. Govardhan, my former colleague from Hyderabad. I begged him to come to the village to monitor Ammamma's treatment. Once he got past his astonishment at my background, he proved to be a wonderful doctor and friend. He drove in once a week to check on her. I took Ammamma to the city whenever she needed to be in the hospital.

Ammamma's days consisted of bouts of chemotherapy, followed by retching and intense pain. I watched with a heavy heart as she suffered.

Chinni had become a daily visitor now. She spent an hour with Ammamma every day, and then a couple of hours with me in the clinic, helping in any way she could. My former devotee Gopal – the very person who had discovered Lata helping herself to the collections – had gotten particularly attached to Ammamma. I was grateful for his help in the clinic and around the house, because it freed up my time to concentrate on Ammamma. She had moved back to the railway compartment rooms she had come to as a bride, leaving the private quarters for the use of Ved and me.

We were losing Ammamma, and there was nothing I could do about it. I refused to involve myself medically because I didn't want to second-guess the oncologist, or Dr. Govardhan, but I knew enough to be depressed. I walked out of Ammamma's rooms into the courtyard, intending to call Ved for dinner. Ved was moving back and forth listlessly, his upper body halfway through the tyre swing. I realized with a shock that it had been a long time since I'd seen a smile on my son's face, and even longer since any of his friends had come over. How could I have become so involved in Ammamma's condition that I'd neglected my son so?

I slowly walked over and put my hand on his shoulder. He reared back as if struck. His eyes were damp. It shook me to the core; he had lost a lot of weight and I hadn't noticed. I tried to pull him into my arms, but he resisted. Trying not to let my hurt show, I unrolled a straw mat and settled on it. Ved sat down, too, but a little away.

"Amma says she cannot live without me."

I was stunned. "When did you meet Lata?"

Ved wouldn't look me in the eye.

"Ved?"

"She's been coming to meet me."

It came back to me though the fog in my mind. Srikar had mentioned that Lata and he were alternating visits to Ved. Ved was now old enough to walk to Headmaster *garu*'s house by himself, so it hadn't registered that Lata was meeting him. Taking care of

Ammamma had sucked up so much of my energy that I hadn't paid attention to anything else.

Then the import of Ved's statement struck me. "You're going away?" I whispered.

"Going back to her is the right thing to do, isn't it? After all, she was the one who fed me, bathed me, took care of me, when you were off being doctor."

Lata's words.

I was numb. Ved was only eleven years old. He did not deserve to be torn between Lata and me.

"Amma is miserable without me."

"What do you want to do?" My throat hurt, but my eyes were dry. My son had lived with me for three years, but 'Amma' was still Lata.

"I will go with her. She is so sad without me. Who else will take care of her?"

How about your father, my husband?

Why was it that my anger at Lata was mostly infused with sadness? Perhaps it was the guilt that ate at me. Guilt that, as a doctor, I was in a place in life she'd staked claim to.

My insides were being systematically shredded, but I wouldn't let my child be caught in my battles. "Child, all I've ever wanted is for you to be happy."

"Then you'll let me go."

My chest knotted, but I nodded.

"Amma also wants me to change my name back to Pullaiyya," Ved said. "After all, she chose that name with so much love."

SIXTY

"Help me up," Ammamma demanded.

I looked with sorrow at this woman who had seen me through times good and bad. Her eyes were sunken. Chemotherapy had caused her to lose most of her hair. As I put my arm around her, I felt her bones jut out. *Oh, Ammamma!*

Ammamma's eyes flashed with anger. "How can you let Lata get away with this?"

"Kondal Rao is behind it," Chinni said pacing about the room.

At this point I had no idea who was manipulating whom. Maybe Lata and Kondal Rao had thought this up together. Or, maybe not. After all, there was nothing in it for Kondal Rao.

Chinni said, "We have to do something. We should request Swami Chidananda to talk to Lata. He was able to make her see reason once, maybe he can do it again."

I shook my head, feeling darkness descend on my soul. Lata would not be convinced a second time. Ammamma didn't have too much time left, a couple months at the most. I had barely enough energy to fight one battle, let alone two.

Chinni and I were going over the accounts of my medical practice when Kondal Rao descended on us, entourage in tow.

Why does the blasted man always have to make an entrance?

"You have heard the news?" His eyes glittered bright enough to burn holes through me. His two sidekicks positioned themselves behind him, legs spread wide, arms locked behind their backs.

"What news?"

"I have a shot at being Chief Minister of the great State of Andhra Pradesh."

"Spare me your histrionics. I'm not your vote bank."

"Ooh! The little Goddess has sprouted claws."

"Having Satyam blackmail me over my son. Age getting to you, Kondal Rao *garu*, that you're unable to do your own dirty work?"

"Oh, him!" He flicked a finger, dismissing the priest.

"Pullamma," Chinni said urgently, pulling me down to her

RASANA ATREYA

height. She whispered furiously in my ear. "He is still a powerful man. Don't push him."

"You are getting extra-friendly with Chandrasekhar." He leered at me. "What a family. One sister shacks up with her brother-in-law, the other manages a little fun on the side."

"May the filth in your mouth choke the life out of you!" I quivered at the insinuation.

"*Tathastu!*" Chinni whispered.

I snorted. I'd given up on the so-be-it Gods.

"For someone who has crawled out of the gutters," Kondal Rao said, "filth is a friend, Little Goddess. You'd do well to remember that."

"Can't you do better than the villain of a B-grade film?"

"Let it go," Chinni urged, her nails digging into my arm. "He is just trying to rattle you. Don't give him the satisfaction."

I struggled for control.

"I don't care what you do in private," Kondal Rao said. "But, publicly you will support me."

"Pray, why would I do that? With Srikar and my son not accessible to me, what do I have to lose?" If hatred could kill, there wouldn't be enough of this man left to consign to flames.

"I still hold the winning hand, Goddess," he mocked. "One word from me, and Lata and your son disappear."

"He is your only heir, your only chance for salvation after you die."

"Screw my salvation," he shot back.

His eyes had a feverish glint.

"I am an old man now. I have only one chance remaining at Chief Ministership." He leaned forward, his face close to mine. "Only one chance, you understand?"

If there was a God, Chandrasekhar's feet would powder Kondal Rao's head to the finest dust in these elections.

The surrounding villages were in uproar. Chandrasekhar had converted more and more people to his side and his win seemed a given. I heard from my patients that Kondal Rao was getting more desperate by the day – he had been storming the villages trying to whip up frenzy, buying votes, offering rice at one rupee a kilo, invoking my name despite my refusal to endorse him, threatening people with dire consequences.

I had thought about publicly declaring my support for Chandrasekhar, but two things held me back. Firstly, I couldn't be completely sure Kondal Rao wouldn't do anything to my son, and secondly, Ammamma was terrified of the consequence of Kondal Rao's filth tossing.

I'd told Ammamma about Kondal Rao tracking my father down in the Himalayas. Ammamma worried that Kondal Rao was saving this information to use when it would be the most damaging. She was also convinced he was just looking for a chance to have me stoned for the supposed adultery with Chandrasekhar, the same way he'd had Renuka *pinni* stoned to death for supposedly being a witch.

Bhavani came to the clinic during the campaign, looking morose.

"What's wrong?" I asked.

"Chandrasekhar might lose. Kondal Rao has vast amounts of cash at his disposal that he is using to buy people. He has been distributing clothes and grain. A few TVs, too. Even if we had that kind of money, Chandrasekhar would never bend his principles."

"Which is how it should be."

"Sounds well and good," Bhavani said, "but it won't win him the election." She gave a dispirited sigh. "This system beats us down. How can an honest candidate ever win?"

"I can't believe you're saying this. Where is your spirit, *hanh*? Where is your fire? So many people are depending on Chandrasekhar. How can you let them down?"

She rested her head on my desk. "What can we do?"

"Contact the Election Commission. Draw their attention to Kondal Rao's underhanded practices. Talk to the TV stations. See if you can get them to investigate."

"These things take time," Bhavani said.

"This is not the early '80s, when the Government controlled the news. Talk to a private TV channel. You can't let Kondal Rao win."

Bhavani straightened her shoulders. "You're right."

"If I ask you something," Ammamma said, "will you give me an honest answer?"

"Of course." I looked down at the shell of my grandmother. Through the months of cancer, she had lost all of her comfortable weight. Now she had barely enough outer covering to hold her bones together.

I hoped she wouldn't ask to see Malli. My older sister had asked her in-laws for permission to visit, and been refused. Her father-in-law was sick, too, and Malli was needed to take care of him, in addition to running her household.

"Will I make it through the night?"

Shaken, I turned away.

"Tell me," Ammamma demanded, bony fingers biting into my hand. "Will I live to hear the temple bells toll?"

I looked down at her, tears streaming.

"None of your doctor nonsense," she warned.

"I don't know," I whispered.

"Then will you promise me something, Pullamma?"

"For you, Ammamma, anything."

"Fight for your family, Child. Don't give up."

I nodded, heart heavy.

"Now bend down and give me a hug. I am tired."

I hugged her as tightly as I dared.

She closed her eyes, and went to sleep.

SIXTY-ONE

I made an incoherent call to Janaki aunty. Then I collapsed, feeling like a helpless fish caught in the currents of a breached dam. The turbulent waters lifted me high and battered me repeatedly against the rocks; I felt bruised and broken. I sat on the floor all night, my head on the nightstand, replaying the precious years of my life with Ammamma, my wonderful grandmother.

Aunty arrived a few hours later. She sat on the floor next to me, her hand on mine, not intruding in my grief, but not leaving me alone, either.

I thought of how Ammamma had sustained me, how she had fought the villagers on my behalf, how she had urged Srikar and me to escape, even at cost to herself. How, despite great poverty, she'd not touched a paisa of the thousands of rupees I'd sent over the years because she couldn't be sure how that money was earned.

Aunty put her hand on my shoulder.

I didn't know what time it was, but the temple bells had tolled; the milkman had made his way past on his bicycle, the distinct sounds of foot pedals clanging against the aluminium milk containers balanced on either sides of his handle bar. I looked at her, eyes dry.

"Do you want me to check in on her again?"

I nodded.

Aunty was back in minutes. "She's still breathing, but very weak. I think we should take her to the city."

"I'm afraid she won't be able to take the journey."

"If she could survive the night, she deserves a chance at the hospital."

With Kondal Rao's attention on his campaign, I ordered an ambulance, rode with Ammamma to the city and admitted her in the hospital. All night I sat by her bedside, aching that she was losing the fight, willing her to open her eyes. When she finally did, it wasn't to say what I wanted to hear. Catching hold of my hand, she begged, "I don't want to die here, Child. Take me home."

"Ammamma, please." My voice broke. "I can't treat you. I'm not a cancer specialist, and I'm too close to you. You need to remain in the hospital."

"No more treatment."

"But, Ammamma –"

"No more treatment." Ammamma closed her eyes, forestalling argument.

I trudged out to the dreary waiting room, its patchy yellowed walls reminding me how depressing this place really was. I collapsed into the uncomfortable bench seat next to Janaki aunty. The smell of cheap disinfectant stung my nose.

Aunty looked at me sideways.

I sighed. "Ammamma's refusing treatment. Kondal Rao is demanding I return to the village, but Ammamma's too weak to travel back."

Aunty folded me in her arms. "You go ahead, I'll stay with your grandmother till she's strong enough to travel. Then I'll bring her back."

I hugged Aunty, grateful for her support. As I moved away, my eyes fell on Ved. I jumped to my feet.

He looked at me, as if unsure of my reaction.

I held out my arms, hating that my cheeks were streaked with tears. Why couldn't I be strong for my child?

He ran to me and buried his face in my shoulder.

I held him, trying to memorize the feel of him in my arms, storing the memory for when I was back in the village, and was missing him like mad.

He mumbled something.

"What?" I held him a little away, not sure I'd heard right.

"I want to live with you."

I dropped my arms in distress. *Yedukondalavada, I don't think I can take much more of this.*

His young face was serious. "Bamma agrees." He darted a glance at Janaki aunty for confirmation.

Aunty nodded tearfully.

"Why now?" I needed to be sure.

He looked embarrassed.

"Ved?"

"I miss you," he mumbled.

"What about your father?"

"He's agreed to my request."

I put my hands on his shoulders. "There is nothing in this world that's more important to me than you. Nothing."

"Not even Nanna?"

"Not even him. But," I said, taking a shuddering breath. "You need to be sure this is exactly what you want. If you decide to go away again, I don't think I'll survive it."

"You care for me that much?" His voice was small.

"How could you doubt that?" I choked. "I love you more than life itself."

"I want to come home," he said softly.

Ved and I returned the day before the elections, only to find Kondal Rao had struck again.

Satyam, the priest, was tied to a donkey and paraded through the village, half his head shaved off. Punishment for his 'newly discovered' sin of gambling. Publicly, there would be no connection between his unmasking and Kondal Rao. The wily politician couldn't afford the Election Commission's scrutiny this late in the game.

But we knew, of course, it was Satyam's punishment for muscling in on Kondal Rao's territory, for trying a little blackmail on the side. The priest had crossed the wrong man – Kondal Rao had appropriated the rights to all the wrongdoings in the State.

At a special *bhajan*, Kondal Rao appointed a new priest. "What is the world coming to," he roared to thunderous applause, "if you can't expect piety from a priest?"

Satyam fled the village in humiliation – he didn't even bother to collect the money the temple owed him for his services.

Kondal Rao won the election in a landslide.

Janaki aunty phoned. "How are you?"

"Terrible isn't it? About Kondal Rao?" It was intolerable that he was being considered for the Chief Minister of the state.

Aunty sighed. "And Ved, how is he?"

"Wonderful," I said, smiling and sniffling. "I can't tell you how happy it made me when he chose to come back to me."

"I'm happy, too." Aunty sniffed. "How is Ammamma's health?"

"Not too well." My voice caught. "How is Lata?" I said mainly to change the topic. I really didn't care to know.

"Surprisingly, she seems to be missing Ved a lot. She's finally on medication, is able to control her mood swings a lot better. The only problem is that she won't take her medicines consistently."

"I don't want to keep Ved away from them, you know. He can visit them as often as he wants, as long as he continues to live with me."

"You seem to be making a life without Srikar."

"Do you blame me? I've finally come to the realization he's never going to be able to leave her."

"It's not out of choice, Pullamma. He feels honour-bound to be with her as long as she is unwell."

"I don't disagree. If he were a different man, I wouldn't miss him as much. But I need to get on with my life, Aunty. I have my child. I'm as content as I can be, under the circumstances."

"You're settling for so little. What about a husband, more children? You're not even thirty!"

"I'm free to come and go as I please, free to practice medicine, free to love my child. I also have you in my life, Ammamma, Chinni, maybe a new friend, Bhavani. What more can I ask?"

"I suppose." Aunty sounded sad.

Bhavani sat on the cot in my courtyard, shoulders slumped.

Chandrasekhar looked down at his shoe, lost in thought.

When I thought of that Kondal Rao, my blood roiled; I could have happily dismembered the rotten scoundrel.

"We tried our best but still lost," Chandrasekhar said.

"Let's face it," Bhavani said. "We were routed."

"Kondal Rao is an old man," I said. "How long can he hold on to power?"

"That's not the point," Bhavani said.

Of course that was not the point. My friend had fought an honourable campaign, which he would have won, but for Kondal Rao employing blatantly unfair tactics. But how could I console my friends, when I myself felt so helpless?

"The Party elders will be coming to help Kondal Rao celebrate his massive win," Bhavani said gloomily.

Chandrasekhar looked up suddenly. "I will go, of course."

"Why?" I was startled.

"I'm not so ashamed that I am going to slink off into the night. I ran an honest campaign and I am going to make sure Kondal Rao doesn't forget it. I want to remind people that I might have lost this time, but I'm not going anywhere."

I despaired at the naïve idealism of my friend.

On her next visit, Janaki aunty said, "Your grandmother's health seems to have improved."

"She is looking better, isn't she?"

"It's more than that, Child."

"What do you mean?"

"Have you considered she might have had spontaneous remission?"

"Aunty, there's a greater chance Kondal Rao will start a charity for widows." Cure of cancer without treatment was so rare, it could almost be a myth.

"Maybe so, but I'd like to order a few tests."

"If it makes you happy." I couldn't allow myself hope, only to have it snatched away. But the thought sneaked in – what if Aunty were right? Most spontaneous remissions did occur when the patient was at peace and preparing for death, having accepted the inevitable. It was almost as if the body had given itself permission to rally its own defenses.

Aunty took Ammamma back to Hyderabad. She called me from the hospital, her voice tight with excitement. "I was right. There is no trace of the cancer."

I sank to my knees, the receiver clutched to my chest, my head resting against the wall, willing, hoping, desperately needing for this news to be true.

"Pullamma? Pullamma?" Aunty's voice through the receiver increased in pitch.

I put the receiver back to my ear and tried to clear my throat. "I'm here."

"Your grandmother wants to talk to you."

Ammamma had only one thing to say. "My body has rid itself of its cancer. What are you doing about the cancer in yours?"

My cancer was on his way to becoming the Chief Minister of Andhra Pradesh.

SIXTY-TWO

I t was four short months since Ammamma had returned from the hospital, cancer-free.

It was four long months since Kondal Rao had managed to secure a toe-hold on the steeple of his life's greatest aspiration.

Everything my grandfather-in-law had pillaged for, ravaged for, plundered for – had led him to this particular place in time – the Chief Ministership of Andhra Pradesh. His journey was at an end. For us, the hapless denizens of this state, it was just beginning.

I settled in my armchair on the veranda and closed my eyes. If I could get past Kondal Rao's triumph, perhaps there was a God after all. Ammamma sat on the cot knitting for Ved, a sweater he might need about three times in any given year because of the way seasons were in our little corner of India – pleasant, hot and very hot. Ved lay across the swing, arm pillowing his head, eyes lazily tracking the passing clouds. My son was back where he belonged, and happy with his choice. Ammamma was getting stronger by the day.

Now, if only Srikar and I would find our way back to each other.

Janaki aunty reported that Lata was still swinging between the highs and lows of her moods, though frankly, I'd never been subjected to any of her highs.

Why did my thoughts always circle back to Lata? Srikar, I could understand. But why Lata? I forced myself to think of something pleasant, not work-related, not Kondal Rao-related... How about a new recipe? Srikar would love...

Ammamma's gasp dragged me out of my reverie.

Lata stood at the gate, Srikar a few steps behind her.

I sat up, disoriented for a second. Where had they come from?

"Nanna!" Ved jumped from the swing, and raced to his father, almost knocking him over. Srikar laughed. My heart warmed at the sight of my husband and son hugging; I was resigned to spending the rest of my life watching my husband from afar.

"What are you doing here?" I asked Lata. *Please, God, don't let her disrupt Ved's life again.*

Srikar looked strangely tense. "Ved, do you want to go over to Ramu's house?" he said.

"No!" Ved folded his hands, mouth mutinous. "I'm twelve years old. I deserve to know what's going on in my family."

Srikar looked at me questioningly. I shrugged, not knowing what this was about.

Lata walked over to Ammamma, knelt by her cot and took her hand in hers. "I've come to apologize to you, Ammamma."

"Oh?" Ammamma looked dazed. Not surprising, considering these were the first civil words the two had exchanged in years.

"What's this about?" I asked.

"Lata wants to talk to you first," Srikar said.

Apprehension made my hands unpleasantly moist.

Lata turned to me. "Pullamma? As you know, my marriage is no marriage at all."

I pointed my chin at Ved, who was listening avidly.

Lata took a deep breath. "I'm really ashamed that I aligned with Kondal Rao. I've used Ved to control you in the past, so if you don't believe me, I'll understand." She squared her shoulders, as if gearing for something.

What, I wasn't able to determine.

"Will you let me raise Ved?" she said in a rush.

"Just like that?" I was astounded.

Ved looked distressed. I shook my head at him, trying to reassure him.

"Didn't you tell me you were here to reconcile with your family?" Srikar looked incredulous.

"Ved is my family, too." Lata leaned forward, as if waiting for my verdict.

Curious to see where this was going, I said, "What's in it for me?"

She cleared her throat. "*Maangalyam* is so important for every woman. I'll not fight it if Srikar and you want to be a family again."

Ved shot a look at Srikar. Srikar put an arm around him, pulling him closer.

Lata was trying to bribe me with marriage-hood? "Why now?"

"It's no secret that Srikar doesn't want to be married to me. I have no desire to marry again. I want to do something with my life. It is too late for medicine, but I can always investigate other options. I'd like Ved to be part of my life." She looked at me, beseeching. "Will you give him to me?"

"He's not a toy that we can toss back and forth, Lata. Besides, he's old enough that he be allowed a say in this." I looked at Ved, tense with fear. If he chose to go back to Lata again, I didn't know what I'd do. "Do you want to go?"

"Do you want me to?"

"No!" I was fighting for my son here. I knew now that he loved me, and I would not give him up. He streaked across the courtyard and slammed into me, hugging me fiercely. I held him tight. *Thank you, God!*

"Fine, then." Lata looked sad beyond belief. "Let's go home," she said to Srikar.

"Lata," Srikar said. His voice was gentle. "You can't go around making decisions for other people, you know. Remember what we talked about?"

"I didn't realize you were serious." Her voice was oddly small.

"You married me because you wanted to punish Pullamma, and also get away from your first husband. Now it's my turn. I want to be with Pullamma, but it's not because I want to get away from you. I want to make a family with my wife and son." He looked at me, uncertain.

Suddenly, I was angry and hurt. "Why did you wait till Lata forced the issue? Why couldn't you have been the one to take the first step? You think this is easy on me – the way you seesaw between her and me?"

"Pullamma!" Ammamma clapped her mouth. "You're questioning your husband? Isn't this what you've waited for all these years?"

Ammamma wouldn't understand. Not in a thousand years. "I waited for my husband, Ammamma. Not for leftover crumbs from Lata. Why do I always have to settle for being second, *hanh*? Have I no feelings, no pride?"

Srikar looked bewildered. "But Pullamma, I thought this was what you wanted."

"This *is* what I wanted. But I wanted it to come from you."

Srikar was silent for a long moment. "I know I've put you last, Pullamma. I've done it over and over. I know I've hurt you. But I've hurt myself, too."

Why was I fighting my husband? Just when my greatest wish was on the verge of coming true? "And that's supposed to make me feel better?"

"It is, actually." He sighed. "Look, Pullamma. I'm not reacting after Lata made her declaration. A month ago I told Lata that I was going back to my family – to Ved and to you. I sold my business, transferred the house in Lata's name, set her up with enough money that she can lead a comfortable life. Now I'm here."

"Why did you wait so long?"

"I had to make sure my grandfather was no longer a threat to you. Ask Lata, if you wish."

"I have no desire to ask her. Not now, not ever. She's been the third person in our marriage for far too long, and I've had enough."

"So you're saying you don't want me back?"

Ved made a sound of distress.

I sagged against the wall. "No, I'm not saying that," I said slowly, tears beginning to stream down. "I might be proud, but I'm not foolish." Dear God, I'd waited so long for this. Why wasn't I happier?

"Lata, perhaps you should leave." Srikar looked at me for confirmation. I nodded. "It'll be for the best if you and I have no further contact."

Lata's shoulders drooped. She trudged towards the gate. Her hand on the gate, she looked back, her eyes lingering on Srikar, then Ved. Then she was gone.

Ved broke down. Srikar took him in his arms, rocking him gently. Ammamma rose up, wiping the edges of her eyes. She put a hand on my shoulder in support. Then she hobbled to the front room of her portion of the house and closed the door behind her.

I swallowed, feeling intense sadness for a relationship ripped beyond repair. I might never forgive Lata for what she'd done, but when it came down to it, we had shared a womb.

"Who will take care of her?" Ved asked, sounding heartbroken.

"We are not banishing Lata from your life, Child," Srikar said, holding Ved's face in his hands. "You can visit her whenever you want, okay?"

Ved bit his lip, sniffling.

Srikar ran a gentle hand over our son's hair. "As long as she takes her medicines regularly, she'll be fine." He put an arm around Ved, hugging him closer. "You know that, don't you?"

Ved nodded, burying his head in Srikar's side.

"Pulla?" Srikar walked Ved over to where I stood. "Do you think we can make this work?"

I looked a long time at him and Ved.

"We owe it to our little family, don't we?"

SIXTY-THREE

Three Months Later

I opened my eyes, disoriented. Someone was banging at the door. Srikar propped himself on an elbow, rubbing sleep from his eyes. He smiled at me and dragged on a shirt. I sat up, smiling sleepily, the old familiar warmth flooding my chest.

He opened the door, and Ved fell in.

"Amma! Nanna! There's *kumkum* and a dead chicken by the gate." His face was ashen.

Sleep fled as I jumped to my feet. "What are you talking about?"

At the gate, a crowd had gathered. Most eyes were on the heap. *Kumkum* and chicken. The very items that had been left at Renuka *pinni*'s house, supposedly confirming to the villagers that she was a witch.

Ammamma collapsed against the compound wall, the edge of her sari stuffed in her mouth. "*Yedukondalavada!*" she whispered.

I looked at the rapidly expanding crowds with a pounding heart. Chinni pushed her way through, badly out of breath. Srikar held Ved tightly to his side as he scanned the crowds. Chinni's mother came up and stood a little apart. I gave her a distracted smile, but she wouldn't meet my eyes. A muttering swept through the crowd.

Kondal Rao was advancing, palms joined together, multiple flower garlands swinging from his neck, looking very much like an ox decked up for a festival. Only missing were his horns. He stopped every few steps, talking to people, kissing babies, blessing youngsters.

What was this man up to now?

A couple of his goons, big streaks of red tilakams on their foreheads, followed. I could hear Ammamma chanting furiously, prayer beads in hand.

"He got what he wanted," Srikar said angrily. "What is this drama about?"

"The Party Chief might be forced to replace Kondal Rao as the Chief Minister," Chinni whispered.

"Why on earth?" I was shocked.

"A tape of him has surfaced. He was caught promising favours in return for money to fund his election campaign. It's causing great embarrassment to the party."

Bad luck for Kondal Rao. As far as political parties were concerned, getting caught on tape was the only sin; demanding favours was business as usual.

"Arrogant bastard," Srikar said. "Coming here without police protection. What's he trying to prove? That he doesn't need the security because this is his home constituency?"

"But why would he be here?" My heart began to thud. I shrank against the compound wall thinking again of Renuka *pinni*. He wouldn't, would he?

"Pullamma. Srikar." Ammamma began to tremble. "He's brewing up trouble, I know he is. Go in, all of you. Right now." She tried to drag me in.

A man stepped closer to the *kumkum* and chicken, then another man, then another, till we were forced against the wall.

"Pullamma!" Ammamma started to sob in terror. "He's probably cooked up an affair between Chandrasekhar and you. He'll incite the mob, have you stoned. Come inside, I beg you, come inside." She pushed Ved back towards the gate and hurried him in. The gate clanged shut. "Come in Pullamma, Srikar," Ammamma begged from behind the gate. "The gate isn't locked."

The roiling cauldron of humanity closed in, trapping us against the wall. I breathed in short jerky breaths, trying desperately to clamp down on mounting hysteria. Faces blurred together, melding into accusatory eyes. I hugged myself, trembling violently. This couldn't be happening. Not now, not after all that Srikar, Ved and I had been through.

"Aaa... aaa... aaa... aaa!"

The crowds parted. I watched in shock as they flowed around Lata, enveloping her as well. Where had she come from? There was excited chatter; the crowds parted again, this time to reveal an advancing Kondal Rao. Lata moved closer to me, casting frenzied looks at Kondal Rao. I lunged for her arm.

"What are you doing here?" I shouted in panic. What had she cooked up with that vile man?

She elbowed me aside, raised her arms, grabbed the pins and rubber band from her hair, and threw them on the ground.

"Lata!" Chinni clapped a hand to her mouth.

Kondal Rao was moving closer by the minute.

Lata planted her legs far apart, thrust her head forward, hair spilling over, and started to move her head in a fast circular motion. "Aaa... aaa... aaa... aaa!" Her hips swayed in an almost indecent manner.

Kondal Rao dropped his folded hands and stared at Lata. "What's wrong with her?"

What! He didn't know either?

Srikar's eyes were frozen wide.

"Aaa... aaa... aaa... aaa!" Lata's voice was eerily high. She began to move faster and faster. Spittle flew from her mouth. Faster and faster she went, hair covering her face. "Kon...dal... Rao... you have angered the Goddess."

Sweat began to pour down Kondal Rao's face. "She is a liar," he shouted. "Just pretending to be an oracle." He whirled around. "Jaggaiah? Yaddaiah? Where are those bloody fellows when I need them?"

A couple of henchmen bounded up, one of them waving his rifle wildly. He looked nervously at the skittish crowds.

"Kondal Ra...a...a...o...o...o," Lata said in a high pitched voice. "The Goddess speaks through me. You have sinned. You pretended Pullamma was a Goddess. You destroyed her life. You lied, you cheated for the sake of elections. Stoning is too good for you. Hell is too good for you."

"But... but..."

What was Lata doing?

The crowd fixed their gaze on Kondal Rao.

Kondal Rao took a step back. "She's mad. Don't believe her." His voice wobbled.

"Hai...aah," Lata threw out. "Doubting the Goddess herself, he is." She pointed an accusing finger at Kondal Rao, moving faster and faster.

The crowd stared at her, then Kondal Rao, in horrified fascination.

"The sinner has to be punished," Lata moaned at high pitch. "Has to be held accountable for his sins. His lies brought on last year's drought."

"I'm the weather or what?" Kondal Rao shouted, terror causing his jowls to quake. "How can I cause drought or floods, you stupid woman?"

"Aw-wa! Calling the Goddess stupid, he is." Lata swayed. "He has tricked the fates long enough. The Goddess demands retribution. Aaa... aaa... aaa... aaa!"

Crack!

Kondal Rao put a hand to his forehead. It came away bloody. He stared at it in disbelief.

He took one step back.

The crowd took one step forward.

He took another step back.

The crowd spread out, encircling him.

He pushed past, and sprinted to me. He fell at my feet, and looked up. "Protect me, Pullamma, protect me, I beg of you." He was sobbing.

I was close to fainting.

A man stepped forward and grabbed Kondal Rao by the collar.

"No...o...o...o. Help me. Someone help me."

The gun-toting henchman fired in the air. The mob froze. A man leapt on the gunman. A wild shot struck the banyan. The gun fell on the ground. The gunman tried to fire another shot, but the gun jammed. Hurling it on the ground, he took to his heels. The other henchman followed, chest heaving. That left Kondal Rao alone – and unprotected.

"This is wrong," I pleaded. "Don't harm him. Hand him over to the police. Let the courts punish him."

Most people separated themselves from the mob, edging the sides of the road. The rest eyed Kondal Rao in tense expectation.

My blood chilled. Srikar was frozen in horror.

The mob took a step forward.

Kondal Rao stumbled to his feet, swerved on his heel and took off at a run.

"There goes the sinner," the mob roared.

They took off after him.

I stared till the mob grew smaller and smaller. Then they were gone.

I fell against the wall, shuddering violently. The remaining spectators were still as trees on a breezeless day. Not an eyelid moved. When the dust settled, the silence was eerie.

Lata had stopped her swaying. She was breathing heavily, drenched in sweat.

"What about her?" Someone pointed at me. "The *kumkum* was at her gate. She's a witch."

There was murmuring in the crowds. Tense expectation again.

"Fools!" Chinni roared. "All of you are fools. Can't even see how Kondal Rao manipulated you." She grabbed my arm. "This is Pullamma, our Pullamma, the same girl who grew up with us, played at our doorsteps, ate food in our houses."

Chinni's mother stepped forward, dabbing her forehead with her sari. "Kondal Rao bribed Ranga Nayakkamma to pretend Pullamma was a Goddess. Even today he was behind the planting of the dead chicken and *kumkum*. I know, because I saw his henchman, the one without the gun, do it."

The crowd gasped as one.

"But why?" another man shouted.

Chinni's mother said, "Kondal Rao was on the verge of losing his Chief Minister's post. He planted the *kumkum* and the dead chicken at Pullamma's doorstep to divert attention from his scandal." She looked at the crowd. "Leave this poor girl alone. She has suffered enough."

There seemed to be no more questions. I looked at Srikar.

Suddenly, he seemed to reach a decision. He took my arm and pulled me forward. "I am Srikar, grandson of Kondal Rao." His face was grey.

The crowd gasped.

He slowly moved his eyes around the crowd, meeting eyes with as many people as he could. Then he put his arm around me. "Pullamma is my wife. Ved is our son."

Another shocked gasp went around. People covered their mouths in disbelief.

"How come you didn't acknowledge her for so long, *hanh*?" a belligerent man shouted. "What kind of man leaves his wife to live with the sister?"

"The kind of man who loves his wife enough to protect her from his unspeakably evil grandfather."

We had been trying to combat gossip, well aware that people thought I was living with my sister's husband, but in the villages, trust didn't come easy.

"So you say!" A woman taunted.

"If you had doubts about Pullamma's character, why didn't you come forward?" Srikar shouted back. My grandfath-"

A police convoy was pulling up.

We stood in a frozen tableau. I against the wall, Srikar standing protectively in front of me, Lata in the middle of the road.

Eyeing the police, the crowds began to disperse. Chinni's mother touched my arm in mute apology. I nodded, and she left with Chinni.

"Come," Srikar said, taking my arm. He looked drained. We stepped through the doorway of the compound gate. My twin threw herself against the doorway.

"Can I have Ved?" Lata said, breathing harshly. "I came because I knew Kondal Rao would be here. I helped you out, didn't I?"

Srikar turned around to face her. "Yes, you did," he said quietly, "and I'll never forget it. However, from now on it would be for the best if you stayed away from my family and me." Gently, he closed the gate on her.

Inside, he put one arm around a terrified Ammamma and Ved, the other around me.

I closed my eyes against his shoulder, trying to blot the horror out of my mind, and replace it with the warmth of his strong arm around my shoulders.

I was truly home.

EPILOGUE

Chandrasekhar is now the elected MLA from our district.
Srikar, Ved and I have set up home in the private quarters of my former ashram. Srikar bought our portion of the house from the daughters of Buchaiah, that poor old man who was shunted out from his own house by Kondal Rao, and who later died in an old age home.

Srikar's grandmother and Janaki aunty moved in with Ammamma. Srikar laughingly complains that as the only males in our household, Ved and he are vastly outnumbered.

Lata is busy setting up a computer training centre for girls; she always was ahead of the times. In an effort to make up to her, Ammamma raised money for the computer centre by mortgaging her house. She asked my permission to add my 'doctor money' to it, what was left after the construction of the clinic anyway. I readily agreed. In the grand scheme of things, money sits the lowest on the rungs of my life's ladder.

Lata phones to talk to Ammamma, and to Ved. We've told Ved he is free to visit her, but he isn't ready. Someday, perhaps.

My Goddess aura has dissipated, thankfully. But life isn't a fairy tale which ends in 'happily ever after' just because the last line of the story is written. Hurts have to heal, resentments have to fade, trusts have to mend.

But I see hope for us.

We adopted a baby girl – Ved, Srikar and I, who we named in honour of my other daughter. The lives of us all revolve around the terribly spoilt Vennela.

For this daughter, too, I'd tell a thousand lies.

About The Author

Rasana Atreya, the author of *Tell A Thousand Lies*, left a comfortable job in IT because she thought roughing it out as a penniless writer was romantic. She's a blogger, and the mother of two grade schoolers who want her next book to be PG, so she's working on *Tell A Lie, Beget A Daughter*. The one after, *The Temple Is Not My Father*, will definitely be PG-16.

If you want to find her on the Internet, you don't have to look too hard.

Rasana@RasanaAtreya.com

Amazon US	http://ow.ly/9A83N
Amazon UK	http://ow.ly/9AJit
Website	http://rasanaatreya.com
Book Trailer	http://youtu.be/DMuo8cwoB1g
Blog for Writers	http://rasanaatreya.wordpress.com
Twitter	https://twitter.com/#!/rasana_atreya
LinkedIn	http://in.linkedin.com/in/rasanaatreya
Goodreads	http://goodreads.com/Rasana_Atreya
Facebook	https://www.facebook.com/RasanaAtreyaAuthor

8300011R00198

Printed in Great Britain
by Amazon.co.uk, Ltd.,
Marston Gate.